PRAISE FOR

THE LA

"This is a plot worthy of Daphne du Maurier . . . a compelling tale of innocence lost."

—*Houston Chronicle*

"Sissel's writing is strong and the characters and their motivations clearly drawn."

—Bev Vincent, author of *The Road to the Dark Tower* and *The Stephen King Illustrated Companion*

"A taut psychological-suspense thriller, exciting and quite dark with no light in sight, adding an almost gothic feel."

—*Midwest Book Review*

"Sissel's first novel is a worthy achievement . . . along the lines of Iris Johansen. Frightening . . . poignant. Sissel's strength lies in her multidimensional characters . . . that make the reader react—with fear, with relief, with anger, with tenderness."

—*Book Browser Review*

"*The Last Innocent Hour* will ensnare you in a web of family secrets and suspense, with powerful, crisp writing and characters so real you'll think you've met them."

—Colleen Thompson, bestselling author of *The Salt Maiden* and *Phantom of the French Quarter*

THE NINTH STEP

"Barbara Taylor Sissel crafts a sure-handed, beautiful garden of a novel on ground tilled by Jodi Picoult and Anita Shreve . . . Sissel's vibrant voice, rich characters, and deft plotting draw the reader in and keep pages turning to the gripping, unexpected end."
—Joni Rodgers, *NYT* bestselling author of *Crazy for Trying*, *Sugarland*, and memoir *Bald in the Land of Big Hair*

EVIDENCE OF LIFE

"The . . . pace of Sissel's novel allows readers to savor the language and the well-drawn characters . . . Enjoyable and insightful."
—*RT Book Reviews*, four stars

"A chilling mystery with a haunting resolution you won't see coming."
—Sophie Littlefield, bestselling author of *Garden of Stones*

SAFE KEEPING

"Past secrets contribute to present-day angst in this solid suspense novel, and the even pacing keeps the reader's interest until the captivating conclusion."
—*Publishers Weekly*

"Impressive writing and affecting subject matter."
—*Kirkus Reviews*

"A gripping read . . . perfect for a book club."
—*Library Journal*

"A book you need to set aside time for because you will not be able to break away."

—*Suspense Magazine*

FAULTLINES

"An in-depth portrayal of how one moment—and one mystery—can crack a family open. These compelling characters will stay with you long after the final reveal. Sissel's fans will not be disappointed."

—Catherine McKenzie, bestselling author of *Hidden* and *Fractured*

"This is that rare sort of book that grabs you from the very first line and refuses to let go. Beautifully written, intricately plotted, and perfectly executed, *Faultlines* is an intimate look at the unraveling of a family after a tragic accident. Sissel weaves a clever web of emotional fallout as she alternates seamlessly between two story lines that converge in a devastating way. An atmospheric, emotional, suspenseful journey that will stay with you for a long time after you've finished the last page."

—Kristin Harmel, international bestselling author of
The Sweetness of Forgetting

"Barbara Taylor Sissel brilliantly weaves a compelling, suspenseful, and emotional family drama . . . As the parent of a teenager, I immediately connected with the story and the characters and was hooked from page one. Ms. Sissel is a masterful storyteller when it comes to suspense and an exceptional writer. It's a definite page-turner!"

—Kerry Lonsdale, bestselling author of *Everything We Keep*

"A gripping tale of secrets and obsessions in which nothing is quite as it seems. After tragedy and accusations of blame rip a family apart, Barbara Taylor Sissel masterfully unravels the shocking truth."

—Barbara Claypole White, bestselling author of *The Perfect Son*

"I was completely sucked into *Faultlines*. Told with great skill and compassion, *Faultlines* had me feeling for so many of its flawed but very human characters, each of them struggling toward the grace that can only come of forgiveness. My favorite of Sissel's many fine books, *Faultlines* kept me reading long past midnight . . . and the powerful yet hopeful resolution will stay with me for a long time."

—Colleen Thompson, author of *The Off Season* and *Fatal Error*

THE TRUTH WE BURY

"Once again, Barbara Taylor Sissel has kept me up into the wee hours of the night with an unputdownable masterpiece that explores family, love, and the ramifications of the decisions we make. The perfect blend of mystery, danger, and the type of secrets people kill for, *The Truth We Bury* will keep you reading furiously until you reach the perfectly executed end."

—Kristin Harmel, international bestselling author of *The Sweetness of Forgetting* and *When We Meet Again*

"What would you do if your grown child were implicated in a brutal murder? . . . As family secrets, lies, and betrayals are revealed, the characters also find the strength to take ownership of their own mistakes. A gripping book club read!"

—Barbara Claypole White, bestselling author of *Echoes of Family*

"Engrossing murder mystery . . . Sissel's characters are all too real, their harrowing devotion and blind love for their children not far from what every parent feels. As their choices play out and the consequences and truth unspool, you will be riveted until the very last page."

—Emily Carpenter, author of *The Weight of Lies* and *Burying the Honeysuckle Girls*

"Barbara Taylor Sissel ratchets up the suspense . . . Rich with beautiful prose, compelling characters, and questions about the imperfect nature of family relationships, this is one of those books that will stay with me for a very long time."

—Colleen Thompson, author of *The Off Season*

"Beautifully written . . . the perfect emotional storm of family secrets, regret, and revenge. *The Truth We Bury* will keep you guessing until the final shocking reveal, all while making you wonder which of your own little buried truths could come back to haunt you."

—Jenna Patrick, author of *The Rules of Half*

"Compulsively readable and gorgeously written, Barbara Taylor Sissel's *The Truth We Bury* had me enthralled from the first page to its stunning conclusion. Readers will love the blend of suspense, mystery, and family drama, and book clubs will find much to discuss. This is a novel you won't want to miss."

—Karen McQuestion, bestselling author of *The Long Way Home* and *Hello Love*

"Part riveting mystery, part moral dilemma, *The Truth We Bury* is a beautifully written exploration of the depths of a mother's love."

—Robyn Harding, author of *The Party*

WHAT LIES BELOW

"Infused with heart-stopping suspense, emotional resonance, and startling imagery, *What Lies Below* swept me along a river of urgency and dread. Barbara Taylor Sissel effortlessly weaves together prescience, regret, grief, love, and revenge—all wrapped in the mystery of a young girl's abduction. Beneath the breathless immediacy of the story lie deeper questions: How do we forgive ourselves—and others—for remembered transgressions, and can we ever break free of the past?"

—A. J. Banner, #1 Amazon and *USA Today* bestselling author of *The Good Neighbor* and *The Twilight Wife*

"Barbara Taylor Sissel's *What Lies Below* is suspense at its finest—heartrending, compelling, and beautifully written. If you're looking for your next up-all-night read, look no further."

—Jessica Strawser, author of *Almost Missed You* and *Not That I Could Tell*

"*What Lies Below* is a fast-paced thriller with a touch of the paranormal and a broken, brave heroine who stole my heart. Struggling with sobriety, grief, and dark premonitions, Gilly seeks anonymity, but as she becomes entangled in a child abduction, lines blur between dreams and reality, secrets and memories, truth and lies. The result is a wild ride with an adrenaline-pumping plot twist. I could not put this book down!"

—Barbara Claypole White, bestselling author of *The Perfect Son* and *The Promise Between Us*

"Take a deep breath and hold on! *What Lies Below* takes the reader from the opening paragraph to the last satisfying page at breakneck speed. With jaw-dropping reveals and unexpected twists, I found myself rapidly turning the pages, as desperate to learn the outcome as were Sissel's characters. A fast-paced thriller—Sissel's stories just keep getting better and better."

—Kerry Lonsdale, Amazon Charts and *Wall Street Journal* bestselling author

"A beautifully written story that kept me on the edge of my seat, *What Lies Below* explores the boundaries of grief, guilt, and forgiveness, along with its dark flip side, revenge."

—Colleen Thompson, author of *The Off Season*

"In *What Lies Below*, a little girl goes missing, but it's the story—and the impending emotional unraveling—of the woman who's having dreams about the kidnapping that is the beating heart of this compelling mystery. Readers will revel in the small-town Texas setting and root for Sissel's damaged yet sympathetic characters as they race to learn how the puzzle pieces fit together in the most satisfying way."

—Emily Carpenter, author of *Every Single Secret*

"I cannot emphasize this enough: you must read *What Lies Below*. Barbara Taylor Sissel manages to combine an unreliable narrator, twisting plot, and well-imagined characters to create a world where nothing is as it seems and secrets abound. I had intended to savor the novel's lovely prose but wound up devouring the book in a day. Simply fantastic."

—Karen McQuestion, bestselling author of *Hello Love*

"In this story about a deeply broken woman forced to employ her psychic ability—a dark gift directly connected to the tragedy that destroyed her own life three years previously—in order to try to save an abducted child, Sissel creates a heart-wrenching page-turner full of unexpected revelations. Clear time from your schedule—you won't want to put this one down."

—Kerry Anne King, bestselling author of *Closer Home*

TELL
NO
ONE

TELL NO ONE

BARBARA TAYLOR SISSEL

Text copyright © 2019 by Barbara Taylor Sissel
All rights reserved.

No part of this book may be reproduced, or stored in a retrieval system, or transmitted in any form or by any means, electronic, mechanical, photocopying, recording, or otherwise, without express written permission of the publisher.

Published by Lake Union Publishing, Seattle
www.apub.com

Amazon, the Amazon logo, and Lake Union Publishing are trademarks of Amazon.com, Inc., or its affiliates.

ISBN-13: 9781542040457
ISBN-10: 1542040450

Cover design by Faceout Studio, Lindy Martin

Printed in the United States of America

Again, for the guys in my life and my two greatest teachers, Michael and David

1

Caroline—Sunday, January 7

It was seeing the house that unhinged her. After all these years she hadn't expected it would look so familiar, so endearing. Memories came, images, sights, the sound of old laughter unspooling across the surface of her mind, cinematic, painful in their beauty. She could nearly see her dad, football tucked under his arm, dodging and feinting a path toward the designated goal—the old thick-trunked Douglas fir was still there at the right edge of the broad expanse of lawn, brown now in the dead of winter.

On the flight up from Houston she had imagined a thousand scenarios, planned any number of speeches she might make. But now she doubted the wisdom of the impulse that had brought her. She ought to have called ahead, given some warning.

It's a fool's errand, Caroline, her mother's voice whispered through her brain.

She rang the doorbell, and her heart seized in unexpected delight when the opening notes of the Tillman State University fight song pealed and faded. If her dad were here, if she were still the little girl she'd been when they'd last come, he'd grin and tell her to do it again. And again. He'd be laughing when Coach Kelly opened the door. Coach had always acted as if he were annoyed, but then he'd lean out the door and push the button himself. He'd always had such mischief in his eyes.

She stiffened at the sound of steps approaching from the inside, becoming acutely aware of her mouth, dry as a bone, her heart fluttering, the smallest of bird wings. The door opened; a white-haired man peered out. His gaze, magnified by the lenses of his glasses, was cloudy, unsure.

She had thought herself prepared for the change in Coach Kelly that would be inevitable after more than thirty years. But this . . . no . . . he would be in his seventies now, but he looked much older and so frail, when in her memory he was huge, such a presence, a bear in her mind like her dad. It was everything she could do not to react; it took all she had to make herself smile. "Hi," she said, and it was such a perky syllable. "You probably don't remember me, but my dad and I used to come visit you a lot during football season back in the 1980s. He was Garrett Hoffman, went by Hoff? I'm—"

"Caroline? Is it really you?"

"Yes." She felt relieved and gratified that he seemed to remember her, but when he turned from her, calling out, "Jace, she's here," she was a bit dismayed. She hadn't counted on anyone else being here, certainly not Coach Kelly's son, whom she hadn't seen since they were kids.

"Caroline," Jace greeted her smoothly, coming alongside his father. They were both tall, well-built men. Coach Kelly was gaunt now, but Caroline could still see something of the cute guy in Jace's grown-up self. He still had a puckish look, with his upturned nose and pointed jaw. He was taller than she remembered and wider through the shoulders, but still muscled, although age was softening him. He was like his dad, and her own: built to play football.

Coach Kelly widened the door. "My goodness, I didn't believe Jace when he said you were on your way here."

"How did you know?" she asked Jace.

"Alexa, the trainer you spoke to at Tillman State, called me."

"Really?" Alexa hadn't been at all forthcoming when she had spoken to the trainer a half hour ago in the athletic office at Tillman State University, yet she'd called Jace to alert him to Caroline's presence? A thread of apprehension tightened along her spine. No wonder he'd beaten her here—it was sheer luck that Caroline had ultimately found the Kelly house. She'd known the neighborhood and the street, but not even providing those details had inspired the trainer to give Caroline the exact address. She'd said school policy prevented her from giving out personal information.

"Come on in here, young lady." Coach Kelly beckoned her in. "Let me get a look at you."

Caroline stepped inside the wide, paneled entry hall, reveling in the details of the surroundings that only moments before had been figments in her mind. There was the painting, an original Leroy Neiman, hanging over the marble-topped table on her left; the same narrow persian runner in shades of blue, red, and yellow was under her feet. Even the smell of wood burning, the fainter underscore of gas heat, was evocative of the past.

"Let me take your coat," Coach Kelly said.

She slipped her arms out of her black wool blazer, feeling half in a daze.

He hung it inside the closet. He took her purse and laid it on the seat of the prettily carved french chair beside the entry table, and as he straightened, he said it again, that he couldn't believe it. "Little Caroline Hoffman all grown up and come to visit again after all these years."

"It's Corbett, Caroline Corbett, now." She tugged unnecessarily on the cuffs of her long-sleeved sweater.

"Well, of course. You're married, a long time by now, I imagine. Do you have children?"

She started to answer. "A daughter, Nina—"

"Come into the library where it's warm. I've got a fire going in there." He led the way down the hall.

Caroline followed him, and Jace fell in behind her. "Why are you here?" he asked her, and while his tone wasn't quite hostile, neither was it welcoming. But possibly he was annoyed, rightfully so, that she hadn't called first. He went on. "I'm guessing this isn't a social visit—"

"I'm sorry." She shot Jace a glance over her shoulder. "It was rude of me not to let you know I was coming—"

"Don't think twice about it," the coach said. "We're glad to see you, aren't we, Jace?" He stood back, allowing her to enter the library first, and once she was inside the cozy, book-lined room, she was immediately transported to the past. She could see her dad sitting in the old winged armchair, one of two pulled near the fireplace. She could hear his laughter, the resonant timbre of his voice . . . the memory of him was alive now, here in this room, unsettling and hurtful. It made her ache.

She shouldn't have waited so long to look for him.

What if he'd died? That very real possibility was the one that most worried and frightened her. But if he hadn't, if he was living, how would her father greet her? With warmth like Coach Kelly? Or was he still angry with her, as she had been all those years ago with him? Would she have to endure his rejection once more? Her heart fisted at the thought. It made her want to run for the door, forgetting the critical circumstances that had brought her. Turning to the fire, she stretched her hands toward it. She had always thought there would be time to put things right. She knew now that wasn't true.

"When Jace told me you were coming, I got out an album of photos—"

"I doubt she came to look at old pictures," Jace said.

Caroline shot a questioning glance at him.

"I'm concerned he'll wear himself out," Jace said, but Caroline sensed there was more to it, that he wanted her gone. Tension coiled heavily in her stomach.

"I'm not a child, Jace." Coach Kelly picked up a leather-bound book that was probably close to three inches thick. "There are all kinds of pictures in here of you and your dad and Jace from when you were kids."

Caroline hadn't expected this, that they would sit down and visit, and from the tight look on Jace's face, neither had he. But possibly he was only concerned for his dad. Coach Kelly did look almost feverish now with anticipation and a longing she recognized. Her mother could get the same expression. Out of the blue she might say: *Do you remember when we . . . ?* She had recently confessed that as she got older, she experienced the odd moment when the past seemed more alive to her than the present. Sometimes, when her mom related some memory, Caroline detected notes of remorse in her tone, but she never pressed her to explain. The past was bad country, a half-submerged battleground. Even Caroline didn't know where all the land mines were buried.

"Pull that chair over," Coach Kelly instructed.

She did as he asked, dragging the wing chair nearest to her closer to its mate, thinking he was probably lonely. Last she knew, he'd been a widower, having lost his wife to cancer when Jace was seven. Caroline had shared that with Jace—the loss of a parent at a young age. Not in the same way. Neither of Caroline's parents had died, but when she was five, they had divorced. Her dad's absence from her day-to-day life had felt irrevocable. Her mom had retreated then, too, into a cave of grief. In the aftermath Caroline had left bowls of cereal beside her mom's bed. She'd learned not to ask when her daddy was coming home. Her saving grace then had been the weekends she'd spent with her dad at his sister's, her beloved aunt Lanie's house. By Sunday, though, dread at having to return home to her mom would set in. Squatted on the porch steps after her dad had dropped her off, watching him drive away, she'd whisper, *Come back, come back, come back,* as if his return—her family's restoration to their once-upon-a-time life—were a matter of asking, or begging, or any words at all.

Coach Kelly turned the pages of the album, pointing out photos of various players he'd coached through the years. "I still hear from some of them," he said. "You remember this guy, don't you? Brick Coleman?"

"Sure do," Caroline said. Brick was one of her dad's most successful recruiting stories, one of the handful of his discoveries who'd gone on to play pro.

"Dad's been ill." Jace circled to the window and came back. "He tires easily—"

"Oh, I'm sorry to hear that—" Caroline began.

"I'm fine." Coach Kelly shot Jace a hard glance. "I had a stroke a while back, and now Jace has turned into Old Mother Hubbard." He shifted the photo album on his knees. "Brick lives here in town, did you know? His uncle does too. The three of us still get together from time to time. They're on TSU's board of trustees."

The coach went on. And on. Caroline uncrossed and recrossed her knees, barely able to pay attention. *Do you know where my dad is? Have you seen him? Where can I find him?* The various ways to pose the question she'd come here to ask rattled through her brain, an endless cycle.

Coach Kelly turned another page. "Ah, look at this one," he said, tapping a photo that had been taken in the yard outside his front door. "Do you remember the year your dad brought you to homecoming? That mum, just look at the size."

"Do you ever hear from him? My dad?" She couldn't hold her query inside a moment longer. "Do you know where he is?"

Coach Kelly looked at her, startled.

Jace straightened. "Why are you asking?"

"We—we lost touch some years ago." Caroline couldn't bring herself to admit how many—twenty-eight and counting. "I need to find him. My aunt Lanie—my dad's sister—did you ever meet her?"

"No. I heard Hoff speak of her," Coach Kelly said.

"*You* talked about her," Jace said, and the light in his eyes was kinder, more reminiscent of the boy she remembered. "You always said she was like a second mother to you."

"Yes." The word was all Caroline could manage. The truth was that for a time, Lanie had been her only mother. "She's not well," Caroline continued when she regained her composure. "In fact she's dying. She hasn't much time left—a matter of three months at most, and that's optimistic—and she . . . she wants to see him."

The Kellys, father and son, murmured condolences for which Caroline thanked them. "It's why I've come. Lanie wants to see her brother again—Hoff, my dad—before she's . . . gone. They had a falling-out, and it's been a long time since she's heard from him."

"Well, I'm not sure how you think I can help," Coach Kelly began.

"We can't." Jace was emphatic.

She felt the fine hairs rise on the back of her neck. He knew—something. She would bet money on it.

"He had that accident," the coach said, and in contrast to Jace, his demeanor was relaxed, without a hint of stress. "You remember. When was it?" He took off his glasses, squinting into the near distance. "1987, '88? We were on the field, third quarter. It was a bowl game, the Heartland Bowl, I recall. We were down by seven."

"It was Tuesday, December twenty-seventh, 1988." Caroline murmured the date, one she would never forget.

"It was a terrible thing," Coach Kelly said. "The refs stopped the game. I had no idea the person in the stands who'd fallen was Hoff until the ambulance came. I called your mother—"

"Yes, she told me." *Your father has suffered a traumatic brain injury.* Caroline could still recall her mother's exact words. Even now, the sound of them in her mind hurt. But in the quest to find her father, begun only days ago, this was only the latest memory to cause her pain. She wasn't sure she had the stomach for it, ripping open all the old wounds.

"I'm really sorry about your aunt." Jace stood up. "But Dad hasn't heard from Hoff in years, and this is wearing him out."

"We did the best we could." Coach Kelly spoke as if Jace hadn't. "We helped him once he was in rehab and when he got out, but he left Omaha shortly after that. Like I said before, I haven't heard anything from him in years."

"Yes, all right." Caroline spoke quickly, not allowing Jace to interrupt. "But going through my mother's things the other day, I found an old letter he wrote to her, dated in August or April of 1989. Only the *A* is visible for the month. It's postmarked Wichita, Kansas—"

"I don't see what that has to do with Dad." Jace talked over Caroline.

"He mentioned you." Caroline addressed the coach. "He said he was in some kind of trouble with you. I've got the letter with me." She stood up, intending to get it from her purse. "He wrote that he was scared," she added, coming around the back of her chair.

"I don't think Dad needs to see it." Jace stood up too. "I'll walk out with you, get your coat. Dad, you should go lie down."

"It's fine, son. I'd like to see the letter."

"It'll only take a moment," Caroline said to Jace.

"No, he's had enough. He's tired, and you need to go."

"Perhaps I can come back, then. Tomorrow? When he's rested—"

"There's no point, Caro. He—we don't know where Hoff is."

Caroline kept Jace's gaze. He was clearly exasperated, but there was something more working in his eyes, something edgier.

"I'm fine, son," Coach Kelly said. "I want to visit with her, catch up. It'll be like old times." He looked at Caroline. "I could make hot chocolate. You like it with extra marshmallows, don't you?" He seemed pleased with himself that he'd remembered.

Caroline was touched.

Jace was irked. "No, Dad. Caroline, it's been nice seeing you, but Dad really needs to rest now."

"I said I'm fine." A remnant of the Big Dog's sideline bark sharpened Coach Kelly's voice. He got to his feet, but drawing himself upright, he staggered a bit.

Instantly Jace was there, hand under his dad's elbow, steadying him, his knowing glare fixed on Caroline.

"I can see myself out." It was the polite thing to do, Caroline thought. To persist would only anger Jace further and make her appear uncaring of his father's health. But how could she just meekly go when she knew—knew in her bones—the Kellys, especially Jace, weren't being honest with her when they claimed not to know anything about her dad? Leaving Jace to resettle Coach Kelly into the chair, she walked reluctantly out of the room.

Jace followed her. "You see how weak he is. All I need now is for him to fall, break a hip."

They reached the front door.

"I need my jacket," Caroline answered, brain ticking. She was going to lose it, what could be her final chance to find out what the Kellys knew, if she didn't speak, somehow force the issue. Rude or not, she had to do it for Lanie.

Jace got her coat from the closet and handed it to her.

"I'm sorry if I upset him." She slipped her arms into the sleeves and picked up her purse from the bench. "I wouldn't push like this ordinarily, but my aunt has so little time left. All she wants is to see her brother—"

"I told you—"

"I think you and your dad know more than you've said." Caroline spoke before she could think, and while she was glad for whatever the impulse was that had moved her to say what was in her mind, her assurance was a fraud. Inside she was quaking, appalled.

"Why would we keep information about him from you?"

"I don't know. I just feel—"

"Are you calling us liars now?"

"No, I—" she began, unnerved by his accusation.

"Is that why you came? I don't care for myself, you know, but Jesus, to have you come here after what?—some thirty years?—and try to pry information out of an old, sick man—"

"No, that's not—"

"—and when he can't give it to you, you call him a liar? What kind of person does that?"

"My aunt is dying. Seeing her brother will bring her peace. I want to—I have to bring him to her. Do you understand? If you know something about where I can find him, you need to tell me, right now." Anger steadied her voice, kept the tears that burned her eyes from falling.

Jace opened the front door. "Just go," he said. "Don't come back. Don't try and contact my dad. If you do—"

"If I do, what?"

"I don't know, Caroline. Okay?"

He looked rattled and mad, but he was shook up, too—as if he were scared, Caroline thought, which made no sense.

He shoved a hand across his head. "If you're smart, you'll take my advice and get the hell out of Omaha."

"Why? Tell me." She was begging him now.

He didn't respond. He stepped around her, widening the door, leaving her no choice but to cross the threshold, and once she was outside, he closed it.

Standing alone on the porch, she heard the click of the dead bolt as it shot across.

• • •

As she left the Kellys, her mind wasn't on her driving but on them. Or more specifically Jace and what he was hiding. Because there was something. She'd felt it. She'd felt his panic too. Unless she was adding drama that wasn't there, which, given the state of her nerves, was a possibility. She remembered an afternoon when they were kids—Jace must have been fourteen or so. She'd been eleven, she guessed. He'd taken her fishing, spent hours showing her the ins and outs of baiting her hook, casting her line. There hadn't been a glimmer of that boy's patience in the man she'd seen today. She remembered having a crush on him—

She looked around, registering her surroundings. The light had been going when she'd left the Kellys, and now it was full dark. She had no conception of how much time had passed, and even less of a sense of her location—on some highway feeder road, navigating an army of construction signs and equipment. When it dead-ended, she was forced to make a right turn into a subdivision that was also under construction. The beams from her headlights picked at the wooden bones of the half-built houses, a geometric lace of scaffolding. A dirty rime of snow hugged the freshly formed curbs; ice patched the newly laid pavement. A sudden flash in her side-view mirror pulled her gaze, making her blink. Someone was behind her now. Looking back at the rearview, she could see nothing of the driver. He was close, though.

Too close.

Was he lost like her? What were the odds?

She made a quick left down another winding empty street, slowing midblock, still watching in her rearview. Nothing. No sign of the other driver. She felt a cooling flush of relief. But now something—a sound? Her intuition? She'd never know—made her look up. There it was, the other car, approaching the intersection. No headlights now. Only a predatory outline was visible in the mix of ambient city light and the muted light from the full January moon. The car—an SUV, one of the bigger ones, Caroline thought—made the turn and rolled silently toward her, picking up speed. The headlights cut on, blinding her.

This was no coincidence.

Heart slamming her chest wall, she floored the accelerator. The sound of the engine of her smaller rental sedan roared in her ears. An orange-and-white barricade marking the end of the pavement jumped out at her from the farthest reach of her headlights. A sign, lettered in red and hanging from the crossbar, stood out: **WARNING!** It seemed to shout the word. Jerking her gaze, she spotted a street to her right, and wrenching the wheel, she made the turn. Her pursuer followed her, keeping pace. Not backing off or slowing down. It was insane. She was dreaming, lost in some horrible nightmare. When she felt it, the tap of his bumper, as light as a friendly kiss, she didn't believe it. Stepping harder on the gas was reflex. Every instinct screamed she couldn't go faster; she would lose control. Her pulse hammered in her ears. Another street to her left loomed from the darkness. She yanked the steering wheel, making the turn, thanking God when the tires held.

But whoever was behind her wasn't done. The second impact was harder, and this time the tires didn't hold. They skated. Sideways.

Ice. She'd hit black ice.

Don't brake, shouted a voice in her brain. But it was useless. The car was out of control, sliding across the road. A sound tore the air, some god-awful grinding noise. Now a scream. Hers? She was thrown back. Forward. A kind of shudder went through her, or possibly it was the car that shook, and then all movement stopped.

Darkness encroached, crumbling the edges of her consciousness. She couldn't raise her head, not when she heard the crack of her car door or even when she felt the man grip her shoulder.

He said her name: "Caroline."

2

Harris—Monday, January 8

He loves the way the dream starts. He's a kid again, twelve, the same age as his youngest son, and he's got about as much on his mind as Connor does now, which is pretty much nothing. It's a good day. Harris can feel how good it is in the loose way he holds himself with no sense of fear. He doesn't know the meaning of fear, not real fear, anyway. Not yet. He's at the Wyatt High School Warriors' football field. It's a Saturday afternoon in September. It hasn't rained in weeks, and the air is thick with the smell of heat and dust. It's the fourth quarter, twenty-six seconds on the clock. His seventh-grade team is down by six points. As the quarterback he's got the ball, and he's scrambling back and away from the opposing team's defenders. He knows his only chance—the team's only chance—to win this game is if he can get off a pass, and he's looking downfield toward the end zone, hunting a likely target. He finds his mark, but the receiver is so far away.

Too far.

A sensation that he's looking through the wrong end of a telescope overcomes him. He's got no choice, though. He's out of options, out of time. He wiggles the ball in his right hand, stretching his fingers across the laces, feeling the grainy leather curve settle just so against his palm. And he knows, somehow he knows, that when the ball lifts off his hand, it'll be the Hail Mary, the miracle pass that'll win the game. In his dream he's unmolested, alone, when he tips back his head to watch as the ball spirals high, a dark and mysterious missile, following the arc of a bright-blue sky. There is a moment of awed silence, and then he hears the crowd cheer. He feels his teammates rush him. They roughly embrace him; they pummel his back. He feels himself boosted onto their shoulders, and he's swept up in the feeling of elation, borne aloft, a conquering hero.

But the sensation doesn't last.

It never lasts.

The scene becomes warped. He's on the ground in the end zone now, brought down by someone who has barreled into him from behind. A rope lassos his neck. His hands are tied, and he's dragged the length of the football field. Harris somehow finds the strength to raise his head, and as if the man, his attacker, senses he's being looked at, he stops and turns, giving Harris the full view of his face. It is a monster's face, twisted by hate, with reddened eyes as round and hard as marbles. His lips are pulled into a snarl. Now a curtain of blood descends over the face, drenching the monster, puddling at his feet. So much blood. Jesus. *Run!* a voice shouts in his brain . . .

"Harris? Harris."

Another voice, soft but firm, pulls him from the edge of a cliff, an abyss—some terrible, cold, dark place.

"Harris, wake up."

He fights to obey, kicking, flailing.

"Harris! Wake up!" The voice repeats the order.

Harris recognizes Holly's voice, sharp with annoyance. His wife has less and less patience for him nowadays, or for the nightmare that has lately and with increasing regularity plagued her sleep as well as his own. It's childish in its imagery. She doesn't understand why a man is having a boy's bad dream, the same one over and over. He has admitted to having had it as a kid a few times. He's gone so far as to say it's related to his father, but he refuses to participate with her in speculation as to its meaning. It irks her, his silence on the subject. He's closing her out. That's her perennial complaint about him. His refusal to talk. It's deliberate, she says. Willful. But when it comes to the nightmare, or certain aspects of his past, it isn't that he doesn't want to tell, to confide in her.

It's that he can't.

3

Caroline—Monday, January 8

Cold. It was so cold. She wanted to curl up, tried rolling onto her side, but she couldn't move. Tethered somehow. Pain throbbed at her temples. Now the smell assaulted her, antiseptic, harsh, a more acrid underscore of panic. Her own? Was she dreaming?

"Hey, it's all right." A voice, soft, reassuring. "Be still now. You're okay, or you will be."

Caroline cracked open her eyes to light that was blessedly dim. Above her a woman's figure took shape. "Where am I?" It was hard forming the words, pushing them through her dry lips. The pain grew, crashing around her skull, banging against its bony walls.

"Hospital, Our Lady of Grace in Omaha? You were in an accident a while ago. Do you remember?" The nurse held Caroline's wrist, studying her face, waiting for it, the dawn of Caroline's comprehension.

It came incrementally, a series of quick flashes. She was driving. Lost. Unfinished houses loomed like skeletons. Except for the heavy equipment parked alongside the curbs, the street was dark and empty.

She recognized nothing. Headlights appeared behind her, coming closer. Closer still. Blinding her. Scaring her. She sped up, slowed when she briefly swerved. Ice. She hit a patch of black ice. What was the fool behind her doing, riding her bumper? There was no other traffic. *Go around*, she shouted as if the driver might hear. *Dumbass!*

"He hit me," she said to the nurse now. "The car—I lost control on the ice, went into a ditch, I think. Cold. I'm so cold."

"I'll get another blanket."

No, don't leave me alone. In Caroline's mind, the words were a whimper, a plea that surprised and confused her. Her heart pounded. The driver had waited there, at the accident scene. She'd felt his hand clamp her shoulder. Who knew what he might have done next? But as soon as he'd heard the siren, he'd fled.

But before that, he'd said her name.

Who in this town knew her name? Or even knew she was here? Only Jace and Coach Kelly. Alexa, the trainer whom Caroline had spoken to at Tillman State University. But it had been no woman driver in that SUV. Neither had it been an old man, which left Jace. *Get the hell out of Omaha . . .* his warning scrolled through her mind.

What if he was here?

He'd want to stop her, silence her, before she could name him, accuse him.

She lifted her head, wanting to sit up, get away. The pain and a wave of nausea took her breath, and she fell back. Black dots ate at her peripheral vision. Tears scored the backs of her eyelids. She felt helpless, and it irked her.

"Here you go." The nurse was back. Caroline felt the warm weight of the blanket she'd brought settle over her, and now a small whimper of relief escaped her. "Oh, sweetie, I know." The nurse dabbed Caroline's damp cheeks with a tissue. "Just rest now."

The nurse's voice was soothing, and Caroline held on to it, letting the pain go, letting darkness overcome her.

When she woke again, though she had no concept of how much time had passed, her mind felt clearer. Still, she was cautious opening her eyes, anticipating the pain, shrinking from it, and it was there, but tolerable. She shifted her head on the flat pillow, running her gaze over the plain walls and institutional furnishings of the hospital room. The other bed, nearest the door, was empty. A machine sounded from the head of her bed. Linked to one hand, it monitored her vitals, a slow, even beeping that increased as her brain recalled the sensation of utter panic when she'd lost control of the rental car. Caroline brought herself upright now, slowly, raising the back of the bed. She tentatively felt her face, ran her hands down her thighs, shifted her legs.

She looked up when the nurse, a woman, appeared.

"Good morning," she said. "I'm Charlotte. We met a few hours ago, but you got a good knock on the head, so you might not remember."

"I do, but not clearly."

"Well, you're looking much better than you did when the paramedics brought you in. How are you feeling?"

"Pretty good, I think. I have a bit of a headache."

"The result of the concussion, although it's not serious, which is a good thing. I can get you a couple of Tylenol." Charlotte took hold of Caroline's wrist. "Otherwise you're in good shape. The doctor will be in soon, and your husband is on his way."

"Rob? How did he find out?" Caroline shifted her glance, setting off a small crescendo of pain in her skull, but she wanted her purse; her phone was inside it. She wanted to stop him.

"I think your mother told him?" The nurse let go of Caroline's wrist. "He was pretty surprised you were here. He thought you were with her in Texas. Houston, I believe."

"I was. My mother's moving into a retirement community. I've been helping her pack up her house. I'm in Omaha?" Caroline interrupted herself. Even as the nurse answered affirmatively, the details began to reassemble in Caroline's mind. She recalled her flight yesterday afternoon, renting a car at the airport and checking into the Marriott near there. She'd gone to the campus, the athletic office, spoken to Alexa, a trainer—

"You're at Our Lady of Grace," the nurse continued. "You were brought in by ambulance around eleven last night."

"I'm at Our Lady of Grace?"

"Yes," the nurse answered.

"My dad was a patient here in the eighties, after he fell at the football stadium over at Tillman State."

"The college."

"Yes. It was winter, like now. The stadium steps were icy, and he slipped. He broke his leg and fractured his skull. The head injury was serious." *He was in such a bad way, could barely feed himself, tie his shoes. It embarrassed him.* Coach Kelly's voice spoke in her mind . . . "I wonder, since I'm here, if there would be a way to look at my dad's medical records."

"He was here in the eighties? I don't think—"

"He was admitted on December twenty-seventh, 1988. His name is Garrett Hoffman, but everyone calls him Hoff."

"I'm really sorry, hon, but I don't think the hospital keeps records longer than ten years. Even if we do, I believe you'll need your dad's signature on a power of attorney, but maybe he's done that?"

"No." Caroline dropped her eyes. Of course there would be procedures, some legal instrument required, if she wanted to see her dad's medical records. "Could you get my phone, please? It's in my purse. I want to call my husband, tell him he doesn't need to come."

"Oh, I'm sure he's on his way by now. Melanie—the nurse who was with you in the ER?—she found his business card in your purse and called him right away."

Of course, Caroline thought. What wife didn't carry her husband's business cards wherever she went? But she didn't feel like Rob's wife any more than she felt like the equal partner he would, even now, claim she was in their business. There might be paperwork indicating she was co-owner of New Wheaton Transit, but paper was all it amounted to.

"Your husband said you live in Des Moines?"

"Yes," Caroline answered.

"Well, that's not too far. A couple of hours, right? You'll feel better once he gets here."

No, Caroline thought. Rob was the last person she wanted to see. "Was the man—the other driver—injured? Is he here?"

"Other driver?" Charlotte looked blank.

"Yes. He rear-ended me. Twice. That's what caused me to lose control."

"There wasn't another driver; no other car was at the accident scene, at least according to what I heard. The policeman who came to the scene said it looked like you hit a patch of ice—"

"There was a car behind me. It caused me to go off the road. I hit my head. I think I passed out." Caroline remembered the sharp pain that had seemed to cleave her skull at the moment of impact. "He was there," she insisted to Charlotte.

"That's the thing about your type of head injury. Things get mixed up. You might not remember certain details, or you add in details that never happened."

"But I can see him; I can feel his hand on my shoulder. He said my name."

"I know. It can all seem very real, but it isn't. All that confusion—it'll clear up, you'll see."

Was it possible? Had she made up the whole scenario?

"It was after dark," Charlotte said. "You were near the TSU campus, in a new subdivision that's going up. No one's living out there yet. Do you remember the location?" Her gaze was intent.

"I do," Caroline said.

"Good," Charlotte said. "That's good."

"I visited a friend, an old friend of my dad's. I was hoping he could—" Her memory of leaving the Kellys broke into her mind, bringing it all back—her disappointment and frustration. To have come all this way for nothing. It wasn't right. She had to talk to Jace and his dad again. She had to make them understand Lanie had no time left for their games.

"Did you get lost leaving your friend's house?"

Caroline looked at Charlotte. "I think I exited the freeway too soon on my way to my hotel." She'd never know exactly. Foolishly, she hadn't been paying attention. "There was road construction. It was confusing. I kept making turns, trying to get back to the interstate."

"Well, luckily there was a security guard on patrol. People are always trying to steal building materials, you know. He heard it when your car went into the ditch and got to you right away. Maybe that's who you remember seeing. Or the policeman who came," the nurse added.

"Maybe," Caroline said, because she could no longer be sure. The man she remembered, though—if he'd been there at all, she'd swear he'd been in street clothes, not a uniform.

Charlotte gave Caroline's arm a final pat. "They'll be around with the breakfast trays, and I'll come back and check on you in a bit. Okay? Try and rest."

Caroline agreed that she would and then asked Charlotte for her cell phone, but after pulling up her aunt's name from her list of contacts once the nurse was gone, she hesitated. What would she say to Lanie? *I'm in the hospital because Jace Kelly ran me off the road? I think he and his dad are hiding something?* She couldn't confirm that was even true, and such speculation would only worry Lanie sick—sicker. For widely different reasons, she hadn't been any happier about Caroline making this trip than her mom was.

Fool's errand. That was what her mother labeled Caroline's mission to find her dad. But her mother resented that Caroline would do this, drop everything for Lanie. It was nothing new. The history between them, her aunt Lanie and her parents, was troubled. To escape it, Caroline had left Texas and gone off to college in Iowa, and except for the occasional obligatory visit, she hadn't been back home much—not until Lanie's first cancer diagnosis four years ago. Caroline had come back then, staying for weeks at a time, to care for her aunt, to see Lanie through the worst of her treatment.

Now the cancer was back with a vengeance. Caroline had been so oblivious, arriving at her mom's house the week following Christmas, wrapped up in her own little dramas, her aging mother, her troubled marriage, and an unwelcome preoccupation with the memory of a boy from high school she'd once loved, whom she'd rejected . . . as if any of that was significant. Hearing of Lanie's impending death just days ago had trumped all of it. Caroline had felt as if someone had vacuumed the air from her lungs.

They'd been in Lanie's kitchen, having hot tea and slices of her homemade lemon cake, when she'd announced that she was dying, that it was only a matter of weeks, a few months at the most. Caroline couldn't have felt more leveled if someone had come from behind and clubbed her over the head with a shovel. She cried and felt horrible when Lanie comforted her. After Caroline calmed down, she was surprised when Lanie brought up her brother, Hoff, expressing a strong desire to see him again.

Other than in passing, they hadn't spoken of him in years, almost as if at some point after he'd vanished they'd agreed to let him go, that even memories of him revitalized through their words were too painful. When Caroline gently asked the reason for Lanie's wish, she said she needed to make amends. *We had a falling-out, you see.* Caroline didn't see and hadn't asked. It didn't matter. Finding her dad, bringing him to Lanie—granting her last wish—that was all that mattered now.

She set her phone on the table beside her bed and tried sitting up, shifting herself carefully, but it was no use. She could tolerate the pain, but she was unprepared for the nausea and lay back. She didn't want to be sick all over the place. That was her last thought, the one she took with her when she tumbled into a fitful sleep.

When she wakened, the room was brighter, and Rob was sitting in a chair beside her bed.

"Hey, sleepyhead." He bent toward her.

She closed her eyes. The edges of her mind were still fuzzy, malleable enough that for a handful of moments she felt herself transported back to the early days in their marriage when she'd waken to find Rob propped on one elbow, smiling down at her. *Hey, sleepyhead,* he'd say, or, *Mornin', beautiful.* The rush of her longing for those days, the man she'd thought Rob was, warred with her regret over the loss of both. They weren't that couple anymore, if they ever had been.

He straightened, folding the newspaper he'd been reading, setting it on the floor.

Caroline stared at the ceiling, spine rigid, mouth dry as sticks. She worked her tongue over her lips.

"They've brought lunch. There's orange juice." Rob held out a carton with the drinking straw already inserted.

Ignoring him, she fumbled with the bed control, getting herself upright. She waited for the pain, and it was there, but not as sharp. The nausea, too, had retreated.

"How are you feeling?" Rob asked.

"Better," she said. "Ready to get out of here."

"The nurse—Charlotte?—said you're good to go as soon as the doctor signs your discharge. From the way she talked, I don't think they'd have admitted you if you'd had someone to look after you, but with the concussion they couldn't send you back to a hotel alone."

Caroline caught Rob's look, the one that asked, *What is going on?* His inevitable inquiry came next.

"What're you doing here? After the hospital called me, I talked to your mom—"

"You called Mom? Oh, Rob, I wish you hadn't." Her mother was already annoyed enough at her for having made the trip. Only God knew what she'd make of this, Caroline in a hospital, raving about a man having forced her off the road. *It's a fool's errand, Caroline.*

Rob was on the defense. "I get woken up in the middle of the night by some nurse telling me my wife's been in an accident, that she has a concussion, that she's in a hospital in Omaha, Nebraska, when I thought she was in Houston, Texas—"

"All right, all right." Caroline raised and lowered her hands, the movement making her head throb. She closed her eyes.

"What's going on, Caro?" he asked, less hostile now. "Maggie said you came here to see some coach about your father? You're on a mission to find him—"

"Did she tell you about Lanie, that her cancer is back?"

"Yes. I'm so sorry. I know how close you two are."

"It's spread everywhere, Rob. It's in her lymph glands, her bones. Her doctor said the chemo might give her a little more time, a couple of months at most."

Rob's eyes widened. "Are you serious? Wasn't she fine when you saw her in October?"

"Yes. They didn't find it until her checkup right after Thanksgiving. She didn't tell me until the other day because she didn't want to ruin our Christmas holiday with Nina."

Rob shifted his glance, possibly at the irony in Caroline's tone. The holidays had been little more than a show they'd put on for their daughter, and although no one had acknowledged it, Caroline felt Nina must have sensed the tension between her parents. She'd always harbored a kind of regret mixed with sadness that Nina was an only child. It could be so lonely, and when things at home went wrong, it was that much darker and scarier, having no one to hold hands with, no one to whisper to in the night. At least Caroline had had Lanie to talk to. But Nina had no one, no aunt or sibling to share the burden. Unless she talked to Jessica, her college roommate. They seemed close. Caroline had been relieved when Nina flew to Vail for New Year's to join Jessica and her family for a week of skiing before heading back to Denver University, where the girls were both sophomores.

"Have you talked to her? Nina? Since you've been gone?" Rob sounded nervous.

"About Aunt Lanie?"

"Well, that or, you know—the business, the jam we're in."

"*We* aren't in a jam, Rob. You are."

He opened his mouth, probably to argue. Caroline cut him off. "I haven't spoken to her. She's having fun, I hope, and I don't want to ruin that. I don't know how to tell her anyway. What should I say? *Your dad's a crook?*"

"All right, all right." Rob was impatient. "This isn't the time or place—"

"You brought it up. Nina will have to know sooner or later."

"Not if I can fix it."

"What? By telling more lies, doing some more cheating? Have you called an attorney yet?" She knew by his expression he hadn't, and she sighed in disgust.

"I've put out some feelers. It can't be just any lawyer, Caro—"

"Having this accident, Rob—doesn't it show you how quickly it can happen? We've been lucky one of our drivers hasn't had one. What if they were to file for workers' comp? They're going to know you faked the numbers—" Her head throbbed suddenly, and she clapped her hands to it.

"You're not home—" Rob got up, pulling off his leather jacket, flinging it over the back of the chair.

"What has my being at home got to do with it? You had ample time while I was there and did nothing. You've broken every promise—"

"I know I screwed up, Caro. Please calm down. If you'd just bear with me—"

"It's more than the business now, Rob. It's us, too, our marriage."

"What's wrong with our marriage?"

Caroline averted her eyes. "You're right; this isn't the time."

"You aren't thinking about divorcing me, are you? Because I'm going to fix this. I swear."

Caroline looked back at him. Neither of them had said the word, not since all this mess started, but she couldn't deny she had thought about it. While the idea alarmed her, on some level it also relieved her that he and not she had been the one to bring it up.

"You've always said you wouldn't do it to Nina, what your folks did to you." Rob sat down.

"I was five. Nina's almost twenty. Even if I were to fall into a depression the way my mom did, it wouldn't have the effect on Nina that it did on me. It's a good thing, too, because there's going to be no"— Caroline's voice stumbled, and she took a moment—"no Auntie Lanie to pick up the pieces for Nina."

Half rising, Rob made as if to comfort her. Caroline shook her head, warding him off, and he sat down, looking hurt. She twisted her wedding band around her finger. He shifted his feet. Outside the room, in the corridor, voices echoed. Someone shouted for ice water. A doctor was summoned over the PA. But that noise was tolerable. It was the silence inside the room that was difficult. Caroline felt battered by it.

Rob broke it. "Your mom's really worried about you, Caro. She told me about the letter you found from your dad, that it's given you this idea you can find him. She wanted to know if I thought it wasn't crazy."

"I'm not crazy, Rob. Certainly not for wanting to fulfill a last wish for someone in my life who has meant the world to me, who's been there for me when my parents couldn't be or refused to be or whatever it was they were."

"I get it, but Maggie's afraid you're wasting your time."

"No, she's upset because I'm doing something for Lanie. You know how she is."

"I know you've said she's jealous."

Caroline shrugged. That wasn't it, not exactly. Her mother resented Lanie to this day for doing the very thing she'd asked Lanie to do, which was to care for Caroline. Nurture her, feed her, braid her hair. Hold her and comfort her when she cried for her daddy and her home with two parents that had once held all the love in the world. How did you explain where that had gone to a five-year-old child? What were the words you said to reassure a little girl it wasn't her fault for forgetting to recap the toothpaste or refusing to eat her broccoli? Even Caroline's aunt Lanie hadn't known those words. But she had known how to pull Caroline into her lap and rock her, read to her, sing to her when Caroline's mother could not. And even as her mother had relied on Lanie to provide this very support, she'd harbored a long-standing grudge against Lanie for having done it so beautifully and with such grace.

Caroline glanced at Rob. "I can't not look for my dad just to reassure my mother."

"Okay, but you're usually not so impulsive. I think that's what caught Maggie off guard. The letter you found is so old."

"It's the only clue I have, and it's not as if there's a lot of time."

"Have you tried the internet?"

"You know I have, and I've never found anything." Caroline was referring to a handful of attempts she'd made in the past, searching any number of the people-locater sites for her dad's name. The last time had been when Nina was a high school freshman, working on her family tree for a class assignment. She and Caroline had hunted online together. Before then Caroline's searches had been sporadic, riddled with uncertainty and apprehension, and as the years passed, it had become easier to ignore her dad's absence and the mystery it posed. If she found him, she'd have to deal with the reality of their estrangement, which had begun the year he'd remarried when she was twelve. Caroline had been furious with him, refusing to speak to him, leaving the room when he tried to visit her. She'd believed then that love was finite and that he'd chosen to lavish all he had on that boy, Harris, who belonged to his second wife. It wasn't until she had Nina that Caroline realized love was expansive, inclusive—forever. But by then her dad's trail had gone cold.

Rob bent his elbows onto his knees. His gaze was somber. "You know it's possible he's died."

"Yes, of course I know that, Rob," she said impatiently. "But regardless, Lanie needs to know. I need to know—so I'm doing this. I'm going to find out as best I can as much as I can."

"The coach you saw—Kelly—did he know anything?"

"If he did, I didn't get a chance to find out."

Rob frowned.

"His son came. It was late. Coach Kelly isn't well. I really don't think he had any information anyway." Caroline hesitated, but no, she wasn't going into it: that Jace had been hostile, even threatening, that she suspected he may have run her off the road. She couldn't trust that Rob wouldn't repeat her suspicions to her mother, causing more needless upset. More than that, she didn't trust her recollection. Maybe Charlotte was right, and her head injury had caused her to conjure the threat. It made sense, she thought, given her state of mind leaving the Kellys. Her brain had been churning.

"So how did you end up driving into a ditch?"

"I'm not sure I did drive into it. Someone was behind me . . . the road was icy. I lost control."

"Someone hit you? On purpose?" Rob stared at her.

"I'm going to get dressed." Caroline tossed aside the bed covers, swung her feet to the floor, closing her eyes against the sensation when her head went swimmy.

"Whoa." Rob reached out a hand to steady her.

She ignored it. "I'm fine," she said. She found her clothes in the bathroom, the charcoal wool slacks, tailored white shirt, and dark blazer she'd worn on the plane yesterday, and put them on. She finger combed her dark, chin-length hair, tucking it behind her ears, and wished for a toothbrush. Settled for rinsing her mouth instead.

"I know you have a lot on your mind, Caro." Rob spoke from the doorway. In the mirror, his image looked abashed and yet somehow defensive. "But this stuff with the business, if you could hold off telling Nina, give me more time—"

"I've given you time, Rob. I haven't said a word to anyone since I found out in October, more than two months ago, out of respect for you and our marriage. I wanted so much to believe you when you said you'd do the right thing, but you haven't, and you don't show any sign that you will." She kept her eyes on his mirrored reflection. "You seem to think if you wait long enough, I'll forget."

"No, that's not—"

"You've done it before, Rob."

His brow furrowed.

"In college, our junior year? When you reported your bike and television, and I don't know what else, were stolen? You filed that bogus claim with the insurance company. How much did you get? Five hundred? A thousand?"

"My God, Caro, I can't believe you're raking that up. That was before we—before we were married. We weren't even going out then, were we?"

They had dated off and on through college. At that particular time they'd been mostly off. But Caroline didn't know why it mattered and ignored his question. "You said it wasn't how you handled things. You promised me you would never do it again. We talked about it, how much we both hated cheaters and liars."

"I was busted, desperate. My folks had lost their farm, if you recall. They weren't able to give me anything. There was rent due, bills to pay. I couldn't ask them. You know all this."

"I trusted you, Rob . . ." She had believed him when intuition had warned her she shouldn't. Some sixth sense had advised they didn't navigate the world with the same moral compass, but then she'd fool-ishly gotten pregnant. It had happened after they graduated from Drake University in Des Moines, where they'd both attended college.

She'd been working for Rob at New Wheaton Transit, helping him with the start-up. She'd handled marketing and scheduling. Rob had handled everything else. It had been fun being part of his new venture, but it had also involved spending a lot of time together, working late and on weekends. Sometimes the personal and professional lines had gotten tangled, and they'd reverted to their old college-romance days, sharing meals, pitchers of beer, and, on occasion, a bed. The sex was convenient, stress relieving, easy. Too easy. When Caroline had found out she was pregnant, she'd actually been planning to move back to Houston, at least for a while. Rob had already proposed marriage sev-eral times. He said he loved her. He thought it would be a good move for them. But she hadn't been sure. She'd wanted time apart, breathing space to think—but then the prospect of a baby changed everything.

Although abortion was an available option, she'd never considered it. She'd wanted marriage and the stability of a two-parent family. She'd wanted a family unbroken by divorce. She'd wanted her child to have a full-time father. Rob was a good man, devoted to her and over the moon about the baby. Caroline had been determined to make a loving home with him where doubt couldn't enter. And she'd done that.

Until now.

"If you tell—"

Caroline met Rob's eyes in the mirror. "If I tell, we could both end up in prison. I looked it up. Lying to the IRS, lying to our insurance company, our employees—it's fraud. You've made me an accessory, Rob, for who knows how many years you've been running this scam, when you knew the risk, that we could get arrested. When were you going to tell me? When I was handcuffed? Shoved into a cop car?"

"I'll find the nurse, see if you can leave now."

"I'm not going home with you." Caroline kept his reflected gaze.

"You're not serious." His look assessed her, questioned her—pleaded with her.

"I am," she said.

. . .

Rob had gone, reluctantly, and Caroline was waiting to be discharged when a policeman tapped lightly on the open door. He introduced himself as Officer Levosky. "I answered the security guard's call for assistance last night."

"I remember," she said. "You waited with me until the ambulance came." It was the sound of his voice she recalled, the way he'd talked to her, keeping her calm until the paramedics took over. "I'm glad you were there."

"Part of the job," he said. He pulled a small notebook from his coat pocket. "You were pretty shook up, though. You kept saying it wasn't an accident. I was hoping maybe this morning you'd be able to tell me what you meant by that."

Caroline saw the headlights again in her mind's eye, closing in on her. "There was a car behind me; the driver had to see me, but he kept coming as if he meant to hit me. As if that was his intention."

"Did you get a look at him? Could you describe him?"

She shook her head. "I'm pretty sure it was a man, but beyond that . . ." She trailed off.

"Well, I had a look at your rental car earlier, and while there's some damage to the back bumper, it isn't specific enough to say with certainty when it happened or how. Do you know what kind of car was behind you?"

"It was an SUV, a big one, dark colored."

"But you don't know a make, model, or license plate." He wasn't really asking. He could see by the look on her face she had no such information. He stowed his notepad.

Caroline touched her temples. "Maybe I imagined it? The nurse said because of my head injury, I could have—it just seemed very real, you know?"

"Well, I've heard a good knock on the head will have that effect." Levosky gave her his card and said if she thought of anything else or had any questions, she could call the number on the front.

She thanked him, and looking at the card after he left, she thought all she had were questions, but there wasn't a single one that Officer Levosky could answer.

4

Harris—Monday, January 8

Harris swipes a hand across the bathroom mirror, clearing it of the fog Holly's shower has made. He strokes the razor down one cheek, avoiding his own gaze. He doesn't like the look of himself these days, like a mangy dog. Holly emerges from her closet fully dressed for her day in western boots and skinny jeans topped by a cream-colored cashmere sweater. The upscale cowgirl look is one clients on the hunt for property in the Texas Hill Country seem to appreciate, one Holly wears to perfection. She's fastening the clasp on the turquoise bracelet Harris gave her for Christmas around her wrist, and when she meets his gaze, it's by accident. They glance away from each other quickly.

They're like strangers now. The thought burns across Harris's brain. It's not the first time he's had it. He rinses his razor, apologizes. "I'm sorry for waking you."

She sighs.

An apology only works the first twelve dozen times you've screwed up, Harris has found. Shedding the towel around his waist, he ducks into his closet.

"I don't think I can take it much longer." Holly is standing out of his view beyond his closet door. "I'm not an idiot, Harris."

No, he thinks. His wife is one of the smartest, kindest, and most beautiful people he knows.

"Something's wrong. Something is obviously troubling you again, but you won't talk, and I'm tired of begging. It's not good for the boys." Kyle is seventeen, Connor twelve. Their sons are Holly's heart, but they aren't less than that to Harris. "You think they don't know, don't see . . ." She pauses, and then it's almost as if she's speaking to herself: "I don't know why I'm wasting my breath. You don't hear me."

Harris steps into jeans, puts on a T-shirt, and pulls a V-necked sweater over it. "I do hear you." After walking out of the closet, Nikes in hand, he sits on the bench adjacent to the Jacuzzi tub to put them on. "But I've told you, the stress—the situation with one of the football players at school—"

"One more thing you won't tell me about—"

"Can't," Harris interrupts. "Can't tell you about. The boy's got a right to privacy."

"You aren't his lawyer, Harris, or his shrink. You're his coach. You don't have a legal obligation—"

"If it comes out the wrong way, it'll kill his scholarship chances. It could ruin his life. It might anyway. Is that what you want?" Holly wasn't entirely correct, saying he was the kid's coach. He wasn't, not directly. The kid in question played football, rather than baseball with Harris, but *played* was too simple. He *was* the Wyatt Warrior football team, its star player. He could probably paper his bedroom wall with recruiting letters from every top program in the country—Penn State, Alabama, Oklahoma, you name it.

"You don't trust me, Harris. You never have, and I'm beginning to think you never will."

"That isn't true."

"Oh, really? Nearly from the day we were married, you've suffered from anxiety and bouts of depression. You've been having the same nightmare for years—but you won't talk about it—"

"It's not related to anything—"

"That's bullshit, and you and I both know it. There are the outright panic attacks too—"

"I haven't had one of those since—"

"I know you're back to taking something again. Drugs—Oxy or God knows what. I'm scared for you—for us—the boys."

His heart stalls. "It's—I'm not—"

Holly flattens her palm, traffic cop style. "Don't bother."

Swallowing the rest of his denial, Harris turns from her and the accusation and hurt in her eyes, and when he says, "About that kid," he knows immediately it's a mistake and clamps his mouth around the rest. It would be suicide, using the story to distract Holly. Turning back to her, he spreads his hands. "You're better off not knowing the trouble he's in, trust me. I'm trying to protect you and the boys. I've told you that."

If anything, Harris is understating the situation. What the kid is doing is big time. When he's caught—and it's only a matter of time until that happens—the charges won't be dismissed with a slap on the wrist. Harris doesn't think even the kid's rich daddy can pay his way out of it. But the kid isn't the only one who'll go down. Harris is on the same sinking ship. Collateral damage. A casualty of the domino effect. Whether he likes it or not, the kid has got him on his knees.

"This is a small town," Holly says. "Kyle and Connor could be friends with this boy you're so worried about. Are they? Do we know him?"

"I've got to go. I'm late for a meeting." It's a lie, but Harris wants out; he needs air.

"Sure. Go." Holly swipes the air in front of her face as if to erase him from her vision. "It's what you do best."

He leaves the bathroom, Holly in his wake. Her anger is palpable, and she has a right to it. He deserves it and everything else she feels toward him. Although the idea of divorce sickens him, he's thought of filing for her sake. Would it be less hurtful for her and the boys if he left—as in for good? Harris has asked himself this a hundred times, but no answer is forthcoming.

Kyle is at the sink, water running, and Connor is at the table slurping up the last of the milk from his cereal bowl when Harris comes into the kitchen.

He looks up. "Hey, Dad, can you take me to school? Kyle's picking up Sam, and he says there's not enough room for my fat ass—"

"Language." Holly shifts around Harris, heading for the coffee she put on to brew before getting into the shower.

"Kyle said it. I don't talk like that." The injury in Connor's tone is put on. He's happy by nature, the family comedian.

Harris envies that. As far back as he can remember, he's never been much on conversation, which drives Holly nuts. But by now his reticent nature is ingrained, a habit.

"I'm not fat," Connor says. He isn't. "And anyway, I don't want to go with him and Sam. All they do is play kissy-face all over each other. It's gross."

Like Harris, both Connor and Kyle are tall, well-built boys. Broad shouldered, long legged, with big hands and feet. Naturally strong and athletic like their dad. Kyle is dark haired, gray eyed, and quiet like Harris. Connor is a bit huskier, with Holly's sandy hair and her green eyes, wide, warm smile, and dimples. Harris is inordinately proud of his sons and his wife. Sometimes, like now, in the most ordinary moment, he'll be swept with a wave of love for them so strong it closes his throat. He thinks it's because, growing up, he didn't have much family. It was mostly him and his mom, trying to stay safe. He'd been determined that his wife and kids would have a better life; he'd be a better husband, a better dad. But lately the man he wants to be seems like some fake guy, no more than a front he puts on, while the guy he really is lurks in the shadows of his brain, yapping at him, goading him. It's getting harder to control that guy. Hard enough that if it weren't for his family, he wouldn't even try. But for them above all, he's got to hang on, keep his grip.

"Will you take me, Dad? I already missed the bus."

Harris glances at Connor. "Can't today, buddy. I'm already late." He gets his jacket from the mudroom and shrugs into it. He gives up trying to zip it. His hands are shaking too badly. Avoiding Holly's stare, he addresses Kyle. "Getting your brother where he needs to go is your job, ace. You get paid to do it."

"I got another job, washing dishes and busing tables at Cricket's," Kyle answers.

"Since when? And since when do you make a decision like this without talking it over with us?" Holly's incensed. She glares at Harris. "Are you okay with it?"

Kyle speaks before Harris can. "I'm only working Fridays, twelve to three, and Saturdays seven to three. It's not that much."

"Fridays?" Holly's frowning.

"Early release for seniors, remember? Sam got a job there too."

Holly pops a slice of wheat bread into the toaster. "Sam's working there? Is that a good idea? The two of you spending so much time together?" Holly clearly thinks it isn't.

"We'll be work-ing?" Kyle's emphasis halves the word into two. He looks at Connor. "C'mon, squirt, if you're coming." Evidently he's changed his mind.

Picking his fights, Harris guesses.

"I think we need a family night." Holly is determined. "How about Friday? We'll get a pizza delivered and play Risk like we used to. Or go out for dinner and then go bowling or roller-skating." Her glance dances from Kyle to Connor to Harris.

His heart hurts for her, the animated longing exposed in her expression, her tone of voice, for the days that used to be when the boys were younger. But family nights have been over for a while. Kyle and even Connor are too old to be interested in spending time hanging out with their parents, especially in public.

It's no surprise when Kyle declines. "Wildcats have a basketball game Friday night," he says, and Holly deflates. Family night can't compete. His girlfriend, Samantha, is a cheerleader, and these days Kyle goes where Sam goes. "We'll probably go out after. There's a dance at the rec center."

"I don't want to argue . . ." Holly picks up a towel, folding it.

But . . .

The word is a shout in Harris's mind. He knows what Holly's going to say and that there's no way it won't piss Kyle off, and he wishes he could stop her. He imagines walking over to her, taking her in his arms, and kissing her, deeply, so deeply she would lose her breath, lose her reason. He used to have that effect on her. They used to make each other weak in the knees. She once recognized and appreciated his signals, too, but this time she ignores it when Harris catches her eye and gives his head a slight shake, trying to warn her not to say it, that Kyle and Sam are spending too much time together.

Predictably, when she goes ahead, telling Kyle, "I think you and Sam might be seeing a bit too much of each other," Kyle's fist thumps the kitchen counter.

"We work. We go to school. She's got cheerleading practice. I have ball practice. We hardly see each other."

Holly looks to Harris, an appeal for his support. He weighs in reluctantly, knowing Kyle couldn't care less what he says. "Your mom and I are just concerned you'll get sidetracked. You can't slack off just because you've got interest from a couple of college football programs, you know. If you want a scholarship, now's the time you've got to work your ass off harder than ever."

"Now Dad said it. *Aaasss.*" Connor rolls his eyes.

"I'm working out, hitting the weight room every day after school. I'm in there as much if not more than Gee."

"Gee? You guys aren't hanging out together again, are you?" Harris regrets his obvious consternation, but he's helpless against it.

"You keep asking me that. What's your deal with him, anyway?" Kyle is nonplussed.

"Nothing. It's—"

"Weird," Kyle finishes.

"It's 'cause Gee's a smart-*ass*," Connor says, mischief lighting his gaze.

"Connor," Holly warns.

"It's what Dad says." Connor's defensive. "Gee's stuck on himself, thinks he's a hero."

"He pretty much is, on the football field, anyway," Kyle adds.

"There's no *I* in team. That's what my coach says." Connor drops this pearl of wisdom as if no one's ever heard it before. "When the Warriors win, Gee tries to play it off like it was a team effort, but then he only talks about himself, how *he* got three hundred yards passing, how *he* did this and that."

"Maybe he is on an ego trip, but he gets it done. He shows up, and he works hard. We made it to state the last four years because of him. That's why I don't get it, Dad." Harris feels Kyle's glance again, and it's unnerving. "What's your problem with him?"

"I didn't think either one of us had much use for him since the fight."

"That's ancient history. Aren't you the one who says we shouldn't hold a grudge?"

Before Harris can answer, Connor drops his spoon into his cereal bowl, setting off a clatter. "You guys never *won* state, though," he points out.

"Yeah, well"—Kyle's attention, thankfully, is drawn from Harris to his little brother—"like *my* coach says, winning isn't everything. Anyway, with me and Gee both graduating this year, it's going to gut the team. Bet they don't go anywhere next year."

"Who's bragging now?" Connor says, disgusted.

"I've got to go." Harris grabs his to-go mug, fills it with coffee, spilling some. Skimming Holly's cheek with his lips, he ducks out the back door.

5

C aroline took a taxi to the rental-car company, where she sat for an hour answering questions and filling out paperwork related to the accident. She was nearly faint with gratitude when they agreed to lease her a second vehicle. Exhaustion fell over her as she drove back to the Marriott, and while she was longing for a shower and a nap, there wasn't time for anything but the shower. She needed to go back to TSU. Doing research while waiting to be discharged from the hospital, she'd found out Jace had been head coach of the Tillman Tigers since his dad had retired. If she could find him in his office, she would try reasoning with him again, even though the idea of confronting him half panicked her. Where else could she go? Whom else could she speak to?

She didn't expect to find the man himself sitting in the hotel lobby. But there he was, reading a newspaper. She spotted him as soon as she came through the entrance door. A frisson of unease slipped up her spine. But at the same time she felt a flare of hope that Jace had had a change of heart and was going to tell her what he knew about her dad after all.

She said his name. "Jace?"

He looked up. "Caroline. God, I'm glad to see you . . ." Folding the paper, he got to his feet. "I heard about your accident," he said, coming toward her. "Are you all right? They said at the hospital you'd been discharged. I was hoping I'd find you here so we could talk."

"Who told you? Alexa?"

"No, no. Dad said someone—a nurse—found his contact info in your purse and called him. She said you'd hit a patch of ice, lost control."

She kept his glance, not responding. The lobby was deserted. She was aware of the midafternoon quiet. Even the desk clerk had disappeared. The door to the hotel office behind the desk was open, though, and voices and occasional laughter were audible. Possibly talking here was a better option than at his office. At least here if she screamed, someone would hear.

"Look, I know you were upset, leaving my dad's house yesterday. I was rude—"

"Yes. Why is that, Jace?"

Something like annoyance tightened his mouth. His glance shot to the door.

Caroline thought he would leave and she would lose her chance to hear what he'd come to tell her if she didn't soften her approach a bit. She shifted her purse on her shoulder. "Maybe we should sit down."

At his nod, she led the way to a seating area, a sofa and two chairs arranged around a low table. Her cell phone rang as she sat down in one of the club chairs, and when she pulled it from her purse, she saw it was her mother—her fifth call. There were missed calls from Rob too. Caroline silenced her phone and, returning it to her purse, looked at Jace, sitting opposite her on the sofa's edge.

"Maybe we could start over," he said.

"All right," she agreed, and she felt the tension loosen a bit from her shoulders.

"I was surprised yesterday to hear you were on campus, that you'd come into town to see my dad. I wondered why you didn't just call."

"I was afraid—a voice on the phone—it's impersonal. He might not have remembered."

"Yeah, it's been a while," Jace said. "I think I was fourteen or fifteen the last time I saw you."

She wondered if he remembered the occasion, that they'd gone fishing and he'd taught her to bait her hook.

He caught her glance. "I'm really sorry about last night. I—I know I overreacted, but it's just—Dad's in his seventies now. A year ago he had a stroke that affected his memory, both short and long term. You can't trust what he says—"

"My dad's in his seventies, too, but unlike you, I don't know where my father is."

"Neither do we, Caroline, and that's the truth. Dad hasn't heard from Hoff in years. After you left last night—"

Caroline made a face.

Jace looked away a moment, seeming chastised. "After your visit," he began again, "we tried to figure out when we last saw him, and we decided it was when he came to watch me play at OSU, a pre-season game my sophomore year, in the fall of 1989. Like in September, maybe?"

"A year after his accident."

"Almost. It's like Dad said: he wasn't the man we remembered."

"In what way, exactly?" Caroline both did and did not want to know.

"He was stressed out, wound pretty tight. At his hotel he lit into the desk clerk because the maid hadn't emptied the wastebasket in his room. We went out to eat, and your dad couldn't sit still long enough to get his meal. He went outside to smoke—"

"Smoke? He never smoked. He hated the smell."

"He was smoking like a fiend."

Caroline felt at a loss. It didn't match anything she knew about her father. The man she remembered had smelled of laundry starch and Old Spice.

"I think he was on some pretty heavy meds, too, for the pain. He had headaches. He said the pain was like nothing he'd ever felt, not even when he tore his ACL." That injury had sidelined her dad's budding pro career. He'd been drafted by the Houston Oilers right out of high school in 1969. Around the same time Caroline's mom had discovered she was pregnant. The couple had eloped. According to Lanie, Hoff had been ecstatic about the baby, riding high. He and Caroline's mom had adored each other; they'd felt they had the world by the tail. Caroline loved the story—the beginning of it, anyway.

She said, "Dad's doctors—they must have done tests—"

"You know how Hoff is. Just like my dad. They aren't going to go through any of that. Suck it up. Walk it off. Ignore it. That's how guys like them deal with their shit."

Tears welled in Caroline's eyes, and she willed them away. "I need to find him."

"I don't know where he is. Neither does my dad. Look," Jace went on when she didn't respond, "I know you don't want my advice, but you should go home, let it go."

Caroline held his gaze, a kind of pressure building behind her eyes, something willful and stubborn. "You're right. I don't want your advice. I want to know where my dad is, and I still feel as if you're holding out on me."

Jace started to rise. "I'm not going to sit here and let you call me a liar again."

"Did you follow me last night from your dad's house and run me off the road?" Caroline hadn't known she would ask. Alarm at her temerity shot up her spine, but she watched him freeze, watched his eyes widen with disbelief that could have been genuine.

He drew himself up to full height, his stare fixed on her. "You're seriously asking me that? Are you crazy?"

Caroline kept her seat and her equanimity despite the beating sense of her panic at having accused him of something that might well be nothing more than a fancy induced by the knock she'd received on her head. "You were very angry last night for no reason that I can see. I wasn't hurting your dad."

"I told you—"

"He's ill, I know. But as I said last night, so is my aunt. She's dying, very soon now, and she wants nothing more than to see her brother." Caroline forced the words past the hard knot of tears in her throat. "Finding him is what I can do, the only thing I can do for her now."

If Jace was affected, it was only for a moment. "It may be the wrong time and wrong place, and maybe it won't make a damn to you, but Dad's a candidate for induction into the coaching Hall of Fame next year."

"So?"

"So I want him to live to receive the honor, Caro. He deserves it. He's the winningest coach in Tillman history. Did you know that? Coach of the year four times out of his fifteen-year tenure. He led the Tigers to five division championships. He's universally loved by all his former players. They email him, call him up on the phone. Some say he changed their lives. The man is a force for good, a fucking legend in this city." Jace's voice rose. "I won't let you badger him, break him down, and take that from him."

Caroline's offense took precedence over her apprehension. "That is the last thing—"

"I can't let you see him again."

Caroline's own voice rose. "If you hadn't been so rude, I might have found out what I wanted to know from him last night."

"Everything all right out here, folks?"

Startled, Caroline switched her glance to the hotel reception desk and the clerk behind it, who was regarding her, brows raised. "It's fine," she said, taking a breath.

Jace wiped his hands down his face. Calming himself, Caroline thought, or erasing her from his vision.

"All right, then," the clerk said. But he remained at the desk, ready to intervene should they come to blows.

"Look," Jace said in a low voice, "it's pointless, talking to Dad. That's what I'm trying to get you to understand. You're only going to upset—"

"You're the one who's upset, Jace. Why is that? I'll ask you again—what do you know about my dad that you aren't telling me?" There was something. Caroline could feel it. He was too wound up, too invested in convincing her he and his dad knew nothing.

He sat down, and he was slow making eye contact, slower still to answer. "There's a woman . . ."

"A girlfriend? Dad has a girlfriend?" When Jace seemed to hesitate, Caroline said, "It's all right; you can tell me. I know he's not the faithful type. Is she here?"

"Not here. In Kansas. Wichita."

"Wichita." She breathed the word. "Where the letter came from. My God." It couldn't be a coincidence. What were the odds? The sense that she was finally getting somewhere lifted her heart. "How do you know about her?"

"Does it really matter? She went to Tillman, graduated from there sometime in the eighties. Pop and your dad—they kind of looked out for her. I think she worked for my dad for a while in the athletic department. She was a secretary or something."

Caroline saw it in her mind's eye, the envelope addressed in a decidedly feminine hand. Why hadn't her father addressed it himself? Caroline had wondered since finding the letter.

"Her name's Tricia DeWitt. Last I heard—and it's been a while, five or six years at least—she had opened a flower shop in Wichita. Bloom, I think it's called. Maybe she knows where Hoff is. I'm not telling you to go there, okay? I'm not saying she knows anything." Jace got up, and Caroline thought he would leave, but he stayed where he was, looking down at her. "Do you remember when we were kids, you and your dad were here for a Wildcat homecoming game, late seventies, early eighties, maybe. You must have been nine or so. I was twelve. We found the little kitten in the road?"

"Someone had run over it." Caroline was surprised and touched that Jace remembered, and surprised, too, at how the memory still had the power to close her throat.

"First thing you wanted to do was pick it up. I tried to stop you." He studied her face. "I grabbed your arm, said we'd go home, get our dads, but you got away from me."

She waited, wondering at his point.

"You remember what happened when you stuck out your hand to the kitten?"

Caroline saw it again in her mind's eye. The toy-size bundle of fluff had been lying so still. Blood had formed a halo around its tiny head, come in a stream from its nose. She'd reached for it instinctively, wanting to rescue it—heal it. She'd cried out, shocked, when it had bitten her, sinking its teeth deep into the web of flesh between her thumb and forefinger. The kitten had died by the time Jace got help, but she'd endured treatment for infection and possible rabies, not to mention an endless round of lectures from her dad about touching injured animals, stray animals—any animals she wasn't familiar with. She turned her right hand over now, putting her left fingertip over the only scar that was left, a white line no longer than a hyphen at the base of her thumb. "I still can't believe that tiny little thing bit me."

"Yeah. It sucks, but that's life. Shit happens, and sometimes the wrong people get hurt."

"What do you mean by the 'wrong people,' Jace?" She felt it again, the heated flare of suspicion that he was withholding something from her—still.

"Like I said before, Caroline, my best advice? Go home. And I offer that as a friend, an old friend," he added.

"Old friends tell each other the truth."

A moment passed when Caroline thought he might reconsider, but meeting her gaze again, his eyes were hard. "Don't stir the pot, that's all I'm saying—because you might not like what floats to the top."

•   •   •

Jace's parting words echoed and died in Caroline's mind as she watched him cross the parking lot. He got into an ordinary sedan, a cream-colored, newish-looking, regular car. Not the big black SUV she thought she'd seen following her last night. Jace's outrage at her accusation—maybe he was entitled to it.

Still, it rankled.

She crossed the lobby, and while she waited for the elevator, she turned on her phone. It rang immediately. Her mom, calling again.

"I'm fine," she said by way of greeting.

"Oh, Caro, I'm so glad to hear your voice. I've been worried sick."

"I'm okay." Caroline stepped inside the elevator.

"Rob said you have a concussion."

"It's minor. Nothing to worry about."

"You hit ice, he said. It's a terrible time of year to travel up there. I wish you hadn't gone."

"I know, Mom, but it's all right, really. Can you hold on a minute? I've got to get out my key card." Caroline searched her purse, found the card, and let herself into the room. Sitting on the bed, she toed off her flats, smoothed the striped bedspread with the flat of her hand, thinking of a hot shower, slipping beneath cool, clean sheets.

"You're staying the night there in Omaha." Disapproval nagged her mother's voice.

"I'm really too tired to do anything else."

"You don't think you'd be better off at home?"

"No, Mom, I don't."

"Honey, I know there's something going on between you and Rob. Don't say it's nothing."

Caroline imagined it, telling her mom about the completed forms she'd found open on Rob's laptop last October, the ones he'd filled out for workers' comp insurance and their last year's tax return. She could explain how at first they had seemed perfectly in order, that it was only on close and then closer inspection that she'd realized all the numbers were wrong, that Rob had falsified the information both to their insurance company and to the IRS. What would her mother say? She believed like Caroline once had that Rob was a good man.

"You aren't going to tell me what this is about, are you?"

Caroline wanted to. She could use her mother's advice. *What is my obligation?* That was the question that haunted her, the one that was chewing her up on the inside. *Do I go to the authorities?* Could she? That was an even bigger question. Her research had scared her to death. Rob seemed not to register the seriousness of his crimes. She wondered if he even thought of it as crime. Maybe he'd doctored the documents for so long the lies felt normal, like business as usual. He didn't seem to grasp, either, that he wasn't the only one at risk, that she could land in a prison cell too. But even if she escaped prosecution and he didn't—if it was her word that sent him to jail, would she sleep nights? While it was true she didn't feel the love for him that she once had, out of regard for their history, the vows they'd made to be there for one another, didn't she owe him her loyalty?

Or did she?

Her feelings, her sense of their situation, were so chaotic, skittering as they did from one side of the issue to the other. She'd chased them around in her brain so long she'd lost sight of what the right thing was. As horrible as it seemed, she was almost grateful to be sidetracked by her search for her dad.

"Caroline?"

"I won't tell you it's nothing—"

"Rob seemed to think you'd already confided in me. That weekend in October when you were here."

That weekend. When she'd run into Steve Wayman and made a complete fool of herself. It had been just days after she'd discovered Rob's dishonesty. They'd argued in circles, and to escape, Caroline had done the clichéd thing. She'd packed a bag, come home to her mother.

She'd actually forgotten that the reunion a few of her former high school classmates had organized around their old alma mater's homecoming football game was that weekend. She'd been in a taxi on her way to her mother's house from the airport when an old girlfriend had called to remind her of the event. Caroline couldn't have agreed any faster to attend the festivities. She barely greeted her mother before she left her standing, mouth agape, on the front porch. Sitting in the bleachers later among her long-ago friends, she yelled for the Riley High School Colts as if she were still their head cheerleader—until she looked behind her and spotted Steve two rows up.

Their eyes collided, but only for a moment. She faced front, feeling her heart flutter, her stomach knotting with some mix of anticipation and dread. Steve was the road not taken, the boy she'd left without seeming reason or warning, and there he was, right behind her. The last time she'd spoken to him, more than twenty years ago, she'd broken his heart. He hadn't understood why, but neither had she.

The rest of the football game on that October night passed in a haze. She was conscious only of his presence and her fretting over it. Neither one sought out the other when the fourth quarter ended, and she felt deflated. She almost didn't go when a gang of her former classmates invited her to join them for drinks at a little bar off Montrose.

The place was packed, but she picked Steve out as if he were the only one in the crowd. He indicated there was an empty chair beside his at the table where he was sitting, and she sat down, heart tapping.

They made small talk, and while his manner toward her was relaxed and friendly, she was agitated by voices in her head volleying questions: Was he going to bring up the past? Should she? Would he welcome it? Did she look old to him? Did her exhaustion, worry, and unhappiness show on her face?

He looked mostly the same. Maybe the blue of his eyes was more faded. Maybe there were more fine lines fanning the corners of his eyes, but his dark hair was still thick, albeit cut military short, and his smile was still adorable, one sided and full of mischief.

The voice in her brain kept up its nerve-racking dialogue.

She had a vodka tonic to calm herself, and then another vodka tonic—what became too many vodka tonics—while he nursed a beer, maybe two, and instead of the past, she told him about New Wheaton Transit, the successful transportation company she and her husband co-owned. Her name was all over the documents, she said to Steve, including the records her husband had falsified. Her personal information was there for anyone to find like fingerprints on a murder weapon, like DNA at a crime scene.

Later she wouldn't remember at what point during her rambling monologue Steve told her he was with law enforcement. Caroline almost choked. Last she'd heard he'd wanted to be a veterinarian. His chosen occupation did explain the haircut, though. Those were her thoughts while Steve patted her back. He told her not to worry. He was a *Texas* lawman, a sheriff's deputy in Madrone County in the Hill Country. He lived and worked in Greeley, the county seat. He had no jurisdiction in Iowa and no particular inclination to inform anyone there of her husband's possible wrongdoing. At least she thought that was what he said. Words to that effect.

The memory of that night still mortified her. Steve had felt obligated to drive her home; he'd walked her to her mother's door and handed Caroline his business card after scribbling his personal mobile number on the back of it. *Call me if I can ever be of help*, he'd said. She still had his card, she realized, in her purse.

"I don't think Rob believed me when I told him I had no idea what the trouble was between you," her mother said now.

Caroline didn't answer.

"I gather you saw Ryan Kelly."

"Rob told you."

"You do realize he's not a friend—not to you, maybe not even to Hoff."

"You mean Coach Kelly isn't *your* friend." Caroline was glad enough to be sidetracked from a discussion about Rob.

"He was always loud and full of himself, a showboater."

"He remembered how much I liked hot cocoa," Caroline said.

"How sweet." Her mother's tone was ice.

"I saw Jace."

"Ryan's son? Last time I saw him, he was still sucking his thumb, and you were in diapers."

"He mentioned Coach Kelly may make it into the Hall of Fame."

Caroline's mother hooted. "Hall of Shame is more like it."

"Dad always talked about how much his players loved him."

"They did. He was a great motivator. I admired him once myself." She paused. "He's one of those men who can't hold his liquor."

"Dad has—he had a girlfriend in Wichita."

"Who told you that? Ryan?"

"Jace."

Her mother made no comment.

"Her name's Tricia—Tricia DeWitt—she must have addressed the envelope for whatever reason. Jace said I should talk to her if I want to know where Dad is."

"So Hoff cheated on his second wife too. And you think he's worth finding."

Caroline looked at the ceiling. As far as she knew, the circumstances under which her dad had left his four-year marriage to Julia in 1989 were a mystery. "I'm going to Wichita to talk to the woman, or Dad himself, if he's there. I want to bring him to Aunt Lanie, Mom. I'm doing this for her."

"Well, I hope that's true, but I have a hunch you're also looking for some kind of apology from him for remarrying and abandoning you, or possibly you think you'll renew your relationship with him. It makes me afraid for you, Caro. I don't want him to hurt you again."

Caroline said it would be fine, and she was glad when her mother let it go.

Her mother's misgiving was still echoing through her mind, though, when she finished taking her shower. She understood why her mom was so bitter against her dad, more now in the wake of her discovery of Rob's corrupt behavior. He had cheated, too; not in the same way, but it was a betrayal of trust all the same. The difference when it came to her dad was in their relationship. Caroline shared his blood, his DNA. She had her dad's eyes, the same dimple in her left cheek, his wavy auburn hair, long limbs, and loose, easy stride.

She picked at the pasta salad she'd ordered from room service, but she'd lost her appetite. She turned on the television and almost at once turned it off.

She'd planned to stay the night in Omaha, but hours later, when it became apparent she wouldn't sleep, she flung aside the bedcovers and got up. It took only moments to dress, repack her belongings, and check out of the hotel.

She was waiting for her car engine to warm up when she opened her wallet and retrieved Steve Wayman's business card. *Madrone County Sheriff's Department*, it read below his name. She'd kept it deliberately, a sort of guilty keepsake. Running her fingertip over the raised lettering enlivened a mélange of memories: the two of them in a gondola, dangling from the top of a Ferris wheel at a county fair, walking hand in hand in Hermann Park, where they'd ridden the little train along with a dozen or more preschoolers. That day they'd planned their family of three children. At his folks' house on Lake Livingston in Steve's canoe. Steve had been trying to teach her to paddle, *not row*, he'd corrected her. *You don't row a canoe*, he'd insisted. She'd stood up, meaning to give him a playful punch or kiss him, or who knew? The canoe had flipped, and into the water they'd gone. They'd been laughing. Slippery as fish. She could almost taste the lake water on his lips.

Caroline rested her head against the seat back. They'd known each other all through high school, even dated occasionally, but that summer, after their graduation, they'd fallen in love. She might question now whether it was real. What had they known of love at eighteen? But through the years he'd never left her mind, not entirely. Her sense of him, of what they'd shared—that it had been special—filled her with a kind of bittersweet nostalgia.

She wondered if Steve even remembered. He'd given no indication, at least that she could recall, at their unfortunate meeting last fall. She felt guilty for the persistence of her memories of him—of them—since then. She worried she was like her dad—faithless. She was still married, after all, even if her connection to Rob no longer felt secure.

She turned over Steve's card, where he'd written his cell number. She'd hurt him, badly, when at the end of that long-ago summer, she'd fled to college in Iowa without explanation. But she hadn't understood it herself then. It had taken a few months' worth of sessions with a therapist after she was married to Rob to uncover the presence of the anxiety—a kind of posttraumatic stress reaction—that had haunted her since her parents' breakup. She now knew that after their high school graduation, when Steve had asked her to move in with him and attend the University of Houston, his proposal had set off a wild, irrational, and panic-stricken fear of commitment. It was as if her feelings for Steve had been too huge, too lovely—

Too good to be true.

That was how her mother had always described the bond between her and Caroline's dad when they'd fallen in love at eighteen and married right out of high school. *And just look what happened to them.* Caroline's brain had kept pointing her back to it, the divorce, her mother's terrible grief, the long, dark days of her depression. At first she'd been able to dismiss her misgiving. She'd clung to the rationale that she and Steve were different. But her consternation had grown to eventually consume every shred of logic that they weren't her parents. Back during her junior year of high school, when a cousin of her mother's who lived in Des Moines had invited Caroline to visit Drake University there, she and her mom had made the trip. Caroline had liked the school, but Drake had never been an option until she'd needed a place, preferably a place far away from Houston and Steve, to run to.

It had been a horrible wrench, one from which she had thought she might never recover. She knew Steve had suffered, too, and she couldn't blame him now if he harbored vestiges of old anger toward her. If he avoided talking of the past. She wasn't going to push it.

But he had offered his help. He'd given her this card.

Taking her cell phone from her purse, she started to punch in his number; then, remembering that even in Texas it was still an ungodly hour, she stopped herself. What would she say, in any case? *Hello, this is Caroline, Caroline Corbett, the drunk woman you drove home from the bar in Houston last fall? I know you don't deal with business fraud, but I was hoping you could help me find my missing father?*

But her rehearsal was moot at this point, wasn't it? Caroline shoved her phone back into her purse and fastened her seat belt. If her dad was in Wichita living with Tricia DeWitt, she wouldn't need to contact Steve and further humiliate herself, would she?

6

He leaves the house for work without speaking, without giving Holly so much as a peck on the cheek. The boys were quiet this morning too. Harris is pretty sure they're aware of the increasing dissension between their parents. The arguing he and Holly try to contain behind their closed bedroom door is seeping out. It's loose in the air, coloring their words, the looks they avoid, the ways they don't touch, and it's getting worse. Last night, citing her refusal to spend another hour or a single minute in the same bed with him while he thrashed at the mercy of some dream monster he wouldn't name, she took her pillow downstairs to the office they shared, where they kept a pullout sofa for guests.

Alone on his back in their bedroom, he watched the moon shadows tremble over the walls and ceiling, thinking he should be the one to leave their bed. His mind was at war. The good guy said he should go to Holly, talk to her, but the other guy didn't like it. The stuff she wanted him to spill his guts about—namely his childhood—was ancient history and had no bearing on his life now. She knew everything about him that was important. *Who cares about before?* the other guy, the smart-ass, wanted to know. *Where's she want you to start, anyway? Back when you were in diapers?*

He gets into his truck now, slamming the door, and backs it out of the driveway too fast. His to-go cup tips out of the holder, hitting the floor. "Goddammit!" He pulls to the curb to retrieve it, then sits, motor idling, staring out his windshield.

Here's what he remembers from his earliest days. The main thing: his parents fighting and his mom crying—a lot. He remembers yelling, dishes breaking, the punch of fists, hiding under his bed. He remembers leaving Oklahoma, where they'd lived until he was six, in the middle of the night. His mom wakened him and carried him in his pajamas to a car. Someone—a woman he didn't recognize—was driving. His mom got into the front seat, still holding him in her lap. He remembers her tears seeping through his sleep-mussed hair to his scalp. He remembers cycles of waking and drowsing, punctuated by the sound of low conversation between his mother and the woman. He remembers the lulling hum of the tires rolling over miles of interstate and the occasional flare of oncoming headlights swamping the car's interior. At dawn, he sat up and saw the sign that read **WELCOME TO TEXAS**. His mom had bedded him down in the back seat by then, and turning to him, she'd said, "We're going to be safe here, honey. I promise."

Harris doesn't talk about it. He never has. Out of concern for his mom. Why upset her? Why bring her down rehearsing all that crap they went through? Holly thinks he's holding on to the pain of some unknown—to her, anyway—childhood trauma. She says it's eating a hole inside him. He picks up his to-go mug, but he can barely hang on to it, he's so shaky. He wants to think it's lack of sleep, too much emotion, but he knows better. Knows he's got to get something to level himself out.

He can't go to school shaking like this, feeling sicker than a dog. He tries to think where he can go to get some relief. Who can he hit up? Not Gee again, he tells himself. By God, he can't give that punk the satisfaction. Harris stares through the windshield. But who's he kidding? Gee knows where Harris is at, knows his *need*—that it's crossed a line, crashed through entire highways of lines. He wipes his hands down his face. How has it come to this? But he knows, and while his excuse, *old back injury*, is legitimate, it only covers the first serious tumble down the rabbit hole some eight years ago, when he had surgery to repair a disk he'd herniated in college. Since then he's had two more painful surgeries. Never mind the physical therapy that hurts like hell. He needed something to take the edge off. No doctor argued that. But he wanted the stuff—needed it—longer than what his doctor thought was reasonable. In June, the last time Harris saw his doctor, Ben Cooper, he suggested Harris might have an issue, which is total bullshit. He's always been able to stop when he wants. He can go weeks, sometimes as long as a couple of months, without the meds.

It's only in recent months that it's started to get out of hand. It's the stress, the sense that he's got to go, run, hide somewhere. Then there are the nights when he sweats and shakes and can't sleep, and when he does, he has the nightmare. When he described what was happening— everything except the nightmare, which he didn't like talking about—to Cooper, the doc said he couldn't help; the symptoms had nothing to do with Harris's back. Cooper said it sounded more like Harris was suffering from anxiety. A shrink Holly found and insisted Harris see diagnosed posttraumatic stress and put him on Zoloft. What had caused the PTSD, the psychiatrist couldn't say. He recommended Harris see him once a week; they'd delve into it. Harris didn't last through the second session. He bolted in the midst of it without explanation or a backward glance, took off like the hounds of hell were after him. He wondered what in God's name he'd been thinking, going to see a shrink in the first place. There wasn't a way to tell it. There weren't words. He knew that.

He'd known since he was a kid that he'd carry it until he was dead. He never saw the psychiatrist again. He told Holly it cost too much. The Zoloft went too. After it caused him to lose his sex drive, he flushed it down the toilet and called Zeke.

Dr. Zeke Roman was the Aggies' team doctor when Harris played baseball at Texas A&M back in the nineties. He's retired now and lives alone on the northern outskirts of town, on the highway toward Greeley, where he still sees a handful of patients. He knows Harris's history. He was at the ballpark when Harris, barely twenty at the time, sustained the initial injury to his back, sliding into home plate. Zeke has been writing Harris scripts for pain meds ever since or handing him samples of whatever he's got on hand, Oxy, fentanyl, Percocet, Dilaudid, as long as Harris doesn't ask for the favor too often. The old man doesn't like seeing Harris in pain.

Now there's a sharp rap on the passenger window of his truck. Harris's jaw clenches when he sees it's Gee and the smirk on his face. The kid, whose full name is Gander Lee Drake, points to the lock, wanting in. Shifting his gaze, Harris imagines keying the ignition, speeding away, leaving Gee in the street. *If only.* He releases the lock. Gee opens the door, plunks himself down.

"What're you doing here, Coach? You're late for school."

Harris doesn't answer.

"You look strung out. Maybe you need a little something to get you through the day?" Gee holds up a small plastic bag, jostling it.

From the corner of his eye, which is all the attention he wants to give it, Harris can see the pills. Yellow tabs, look like Oxy. A sound rises from his gut, a groan, maybe a whimper. He bites his teeth together, catching it in his throat. The fury and disgust and the bitter tang of self-loathing that come are enough to choke him. He swallows. He's not this person, goddammit. He's a coach, the head baseball coach at the high school. He's the fucking Wyatt Warriors' athletic director, for God's sake. He's got a name, a reputation, in this town. He's a husband with a wonderful wife and two fantastic sons. And Gee's a kid, one who's going off the rails. Harris has known this for a few years now; in the past he's tried to help Gee. But somewhere along the line, the ground between them shifted, and now Harris is here, risking everything and everyone he loves. Why? What the hell is wrong with him? Why can't he stop, quit this thing?

He turns to Gee. "How much?" he says, reaching for the baggie.

Gee pulls it away. "Didn't say I was selling."

"Why are you here, then?" Harris wants to punch the kid. He wants to grab the dope, shove Gee out of his truck, and take off.

"You seriously don't know?"

Harris takes a closer look at Gee and sees something hectic working in his eyes, like he's hyped, agitated, or excited. Hard to say. The kid is unpredictable. But not from dope. Gee swears he doesn't take the drugs he sells. If asked, he'll say he's too smart to start. Harris used to think that way too.

"Dad and I had visitors this morning," Gee says. "Seven o'clock we got cops knocking on the front door. A Madrone County sheriff's deputy from Greeley named Steve Wayman and this other cop from here in Wyatt, Sergeant Carter, Ken Carter."

Harris has never heard of Wayman, but he knows Ken. Not well. They went through school together here in Wyatt. Ken is a couple of years younger.

"I guess you know why they were there," Gee says.

"Not to arrest you, obviously, since you're here."

"They asked me what I knew about the bunch of robberies that went on last fall." Gee's look is knowing, cocky.

Harris doesn't respond.

"They said they're talking to all the kids in school, the seniors, anyway. It's like they know—something." He waits.

Harris has got nothing for him.

Gee says, "So did they come and see you?" Harris feels his gaze but doesn't meet it. "You tell them what you saw last Thanksgiving?"

"I told you I wouldn't."

"You're in it as deep as me—you know that, right?"

Harris loosens his gaze, remembering that day. He wants to blame it on Holly, all those women she'd invited over to share the Thanksgiving meal—his mom and three of Holly's Realtor friends, two who were divorcées and one who was a widow—to keep them from being alone. If it hadn't been for them, Harris might never have left the house. But once bottles of wine were opened and the women started drinking, the female chatter went on nonstop. Everyone, including Connor and Kyle, surprisingly, was joking around, shrieking laughter like a bunch of stoned hyenas—it got to Harris. He felt on edge, wanted to punch something. He left the house, figuring a ride around town and a couple of Oxys might settle his nerves. Oxys he'd bought from Gee.

Gee, of all people, Kyle's former buddy and current teammate, a kid Harris has known since elementary school, is his supplier. Harris coached Gee in Little League, and until the fight between Kyle and Gee broke their friendship, Harris was a mentor to him. He tried to be a steadying influence on Gee. Now he's buying his dope off the kid.

It's so wrong, what he's doing. The risk—to him, to his family, even to Gee—is always on Harris's mind. It was what he was thinking about last Thanksgiving Day while he was driving aimlessly, waiting for the Oxy to kick in. The decision to pull over on the sparsely trafficked two-lane blacktop outside town wasn't conscious. Harris didn't know then that the house halfway up the hill from where he sat in his truck belonged to a family named Guthrie, but he damn sure recognized Gee's pickup when it appeared from the opposite direction and veered off the road into a jumble of shrubbery-choked juniper.

At first Harris, feeling fairly mellow by then, didn't think too much of it, not until Gee and his partner, a dude in his thirties who Harris learned later was Gee's cousin, disappeared into the thicket. He watched them threading their way through the trees, thinking it wasn't the route expected guests would take to the house, not when there was a perfectly good driveway and a sidewalk leading from there to a wide front deck. Harris kept watching, waiting to see them go up to the front door. Instead they disappeared around back. Ten minutes passed before they reappeared, this time busting the front door wide open, coming out at full speed, fueled by adrenaline. Gee was carrying a canvas gym bag. The other guy had a handled shopping bag, sides bulging. Harris straightened up in his seat, eyes wide. He knew about the robberies occurring around town on a regular basis. Everybody in town did.

When classes resumed on Monday, the news was all over school about how the Guthrie family had been away for the holiday and come home to discover they'd been burglarized. The thieves had taken jewelry and small electronics. They'd even taken a penny bank that contained the life savings of the Guthries' seven-year-old son. The police captain, Clint Mackie, appeared on local television on Friday night, cautioning those who lived in more rural areas, where the robberies were occurring, to be vigilant. He asked for help to identify and stop the thieves.

After a near-sleepless night, Harris picked up his phone to call Mackie on Saturday morning, but then he figured he should give Gee a chance to explain, to turn himself in. They met later at a deserted strip shopping center on the outskirts of town. Gee brought dope. Harris told him the meeting wasn't about that. He didn't say it to Gee, but he swore to himself he was done, that he was going to help Gee, turn himself and the kid around.

"I saw you coming out of the Guthries' house Thanksgiving Day." Harris said it right off, the minute Gee got into his truck.

Gee didn't blink. "What were you doing there?"

"Doesn't matter," Harris said.

"Yeah, see, it kinda does," Gee said. "If you, like, went to the cops or something stupid like that. Did you?"

"Not yet. But listen, there's still time to stop this, Gee. You can do the right thing, right now, and maybe you can still salvage your future. I know your family will help. Your folks have got the kind of money it'll take to keep this thing quiet, make restitution some way that doesn't involve jail. You could still sign a scholarship to play football, kid. But it's got to stop now, dealing drugs, robbing houses—" Harris broke off at the look he was getting from Gee, like he'd sprouted horns, a second head. When Gee laughed, the sound was dissonant, brassy. Dismissive.

Then quickly gone.

Gee's expression flattened. "You are kidding, right? You do know what happens if you go to the cops, that it's your ass too."

Harris didn't answer.

"C'mon, bro, you think I won't take you down with me? Why? Because you're the coach? You're the man, the hero, the guy all us kids look up to? You're nothing but a doper. Just another fucking way for me to make money."

"You don't mean that, Gee." Harris wanted so badly to believe it, that he could fix it, fix them both. "You've got it all, the smarts, the physical ability. You could make millions playing pro ball, and you could get drafted that quick." Harris snapped his fingers. "Don't throw it all away doing this kind of penny-ante shit."

Gee laughed again, and the sound was somehow both hard and easy.

"C'mon, kid." Harris was begging now. "Let's make a deal. I'll lay off the dope, and you lay off breaking in to people's houses."

Gee couldn't give a damn what Harris was saying. It was all over his face. Harris had seen the same smirk plenty of times when he was on his soapbox, going on about something in the locker room. But this was more and went deeper than that. It was in the very atmosphere between them that Harris had no authority here. There was no coach/player hierarchy in place. Gee was all done with that. He knew it, and Harris knew it. And the knowing for Harris was like ice in his gut. When he'd come out to meet Gee, he'd had so much hope. He'd wanted to be to Gee what his dad had been to him. Not his real dad but his stepdad, Hoff. Harris guessed it was thinking of Hoff and everything Hoff had meant to him that made him go on and try again to reach Gee. "You're smarter than this, kid. You've got to know it's only a matter of time until you get caught. Give me your word the Guthries' was the last one, the last break-in."

Gee grinned. "Sure, Coach, whatever you want."

"You swear?"

"Cross my heart and hope to die."

Driving away that afternoon, Harris knew it was a joke. But when the weeks passed, when even the Christmas holidays came and went with no news of another robbery, he began to hope that maybe Gee's promise was for real.

He turns to Gee now. "You think the cops are onto you?"

"That's what I'm trying to figure out. I've kept my promise, right? You haven't heard about another break-in. So why were the cops at my house? Why today?"

"You think I know? I don't."

"If you didn't sic them on me, who did?"

"Your cousin?"

"Darren'll never talk. If they put a gun to his head, he'd take the bullet before he'd give them my name. He owes me," Gee says. "Big-time."

Gee doesn't provide details, which is fine with Harris. He knows too much about Gee's dark side already. He thinks of Gee's future, laid out in front of him like a yellow brick road. That was how Harris's stepdad, Garrett Hoffman, put it when he talked about Harris's future. Harris wanted to grow up and become the kind of man Hoff was, a father, a mentor, a role model for young men. He doesn't want to think about what Hoff would say if he could see Harris now. He looks at Gee. "You know how bad you're jeopardizing your future?"

"You've said, like, a hundred times. Like you're one to talk," Gee adds.

Harris talks over him. "Breaking in to houses, selling dope. For God's sake, Gee—"

"Can the lecture, okay? All I want to know is what you're gonna say if the cops ask you questions."

Harris pinches the bridge of his nose. His turn is coming. The Wyatt police aren't about to drop the investigation. Harris has seen the local cop, Ken Carter, around campus, talking to students and teachers. He's heard both the principal and the vice-principal have been interviewed. He's scared he'll spill it, everything he knows. It's the right thing, what he should do. He's an idiot to buy Gee's promise. It's only a matter of time until the kid robs some other family, and he needs to be stopped. Gee needs help. Normal kids don't burglarize houses for the rush it gives them. Normal kids, those with the kinds of advantages Gee has, don't commit crimes, period. But to Harris's knowledge most people have never seen Gee's dark side; they don't know it even exists.

Gee tosses the baggie at Harris. "Oxy's on me this time, a little incentive."

Harris looks at it, where it's landed on the seat next to his thigh.

Gee gets out of the truck, pokes his head back in. "You talk, your life'll go bad real quick, man. That's my hot tip for the day." Retreating, he slams the door.

Bad doesn't begin to describe it, Harris thinks, watching Gee walk away.

7

It wasn't until after she'd arrived in Wichita and checked into her hotel room that she looked at her phone messages. There were only two. One from Lanie said she was thinking of her. The other was from Nina. She'd talked to Dad, she said. "I'm worried. Please call."

Caroline sat on the bed's edge, cradling the phone in her hands, torn between wanting and dreading the conversation with her daughter. How much had Rob told Nina? He wouldn't have said a word about the business. If Nina was worried, it was because he'd told her about Caroline's car accident. Maybe, like Caroline's mother, he'd have said she was off on a fool's errand looking for her dad when it happened.

Where's your daddy? Nina had been five or six years old the first time she'd asked Caroline. She'd had a sleepover with Cherie, her best friend at the time. Cherie's mother's father had died a few weeks before, and Cherie had evidently chattered half the night to Nina about the funeral. People had kissed him, Nina had reported Cherie telling her. On the lips, she'd said, adding, *Ewww.* She and Caroline had been in the kitchen, shelling snow peas from the garden, and Caroline, looking down at her small daughter kneeling on a stool, had mirrored Nina's distaste. They'd already had many talks about respecting one's own and other people's space and what was proper and improper touching. Caroline wasn't sure on which side of that line kissing a dead person fell. She'd been trying to decide when Nina had asked if Caroline's daddy was dead like Cherie's mother's daddy. Nina had known about death by then, having already buried two goldfish, a parakeet, and their Yorkie, McTavish, in the backyard.

Caroline hadn't known how to answer, how much to tell Nina about her dad and his disappearance from her life. How much could a child Nina's age understand? She'd finally said—more mumbled—something about her dad traveling a lot and not having time to visit. When she'd said maybe one day he would come and meet Nina, she'd wanted to know if he would bring her a present, which made her sound greedy. But she wasn't. Far from it. In November, the year she was twelve, Nina had asked her parents for the money they were planning to spend on her Christmas gifts. She'd wanted to shop for a family, two parents with six children, she'd heard about at school that had recently lost everything in a fire. The husband had been laid off from his job. They'd had no insurance, no relatives. They'd lived under a highway overpass for two weeks until someone who had rental property had given them a temporary home. Rob and Caroline had driven Nina there on Christmas Eve with the gifts she'd chosen. Everyone, including Rob, had teared up at the gesture. It made Nina sound like an angel, but she wasn't that either.

She'd made her share of mistakes. There had been a pregnancy scare when she was a high school junior. She'd confessed the news to Caroline. They'd gone together to the drugstore for the test. Caroline had waited anxiously on the other side of the bathroom door for the result, and when Nina had joyfully shouted it was negative, she'd nearly dropped to the floor in her relief.

Nina had asked Caroline not to tell Rob, and Caroline had gone along with her request. Rob could be judgmental, unforgiving about certain things, which in light of what she now knew of his business practices would seem incongruous, even laughable, if it weren't so . . . twisted. The word floated to the surface of her brain, dragging a plethora of mixed emotions, all clanging together, tin cans tied to the bumper of a bridal couple's getaway car. She didn't like having to think of Rob in such terms—that rather than being honorable, he was basically dishonest. It was disconcerting, anger making, even shameful on some level. Mostly, though, it was painful—

The phone in her hands rang, and she flinched. Nina's name flashed in the ID window. Caroline swallowed, steadying herself. Sounding cheerful, she said, "Hi, honey."

"Mom, why didn't you call me?"

"I was just going to—"

"Dad said you were in a wreck? You have a concussion? You wouldn't go home with him?" Nina paused in the flurry of her speech as if she needed a moment to assemble the rest of it. "He said you're looking for your dad . . ."

"I am. Yes, I'm in Wichita. I just got here."

"Something's wrong, isn't it? Between you and Dad, I mean. I can feel it, like, ever since I was home over Thanksgiving. Christmas, you guys were like strangers."

Caroline's stomach knotted. She sat on the edge of the bed.

"Mommy?"

Mommy. When had Nina last called her that? Caroline closed her eyes.

"It's—" *All right.* Caroline could have—very likely she *should* have said it, should have offered Nina comfort. Instead, at the last moment, she said, "It's complicated."

"Please don't say I'm too young—"

"Trust me, this time you really are too young. Even I'm too young." Caroline's laugh was as brittle as it was brief. "What I mean is that I would spare you if I could."

"Now you're scaring me."

"I so do not want to do this over the phone."

"Dad asked me if I could come home for a few days."

A beat.

"Mom? Should I?"

"How is the skiing?" Caroline changed the subject, wanting whatever few ordinary moments she could grab before having the discussion that was inevitable.

"Jessica sprained her ankle yesterday."

"Oh no. Is it bad?"

"Not too. But we're heading back to campus anyway. I can as easily go home, though, if you need me to." Nina paused a few seconds, and then, impatient now, she said, "Mom, just tell me."

Caroline blinked at the ceiling. *I don't know how!* The fury that overtook her was swift, jolting. This was on Rob; he was the one who should be explaining to their daughter what he'd done. She wouldn't spare him, Caroline decided, and possibly it was spiteful, even childish, but she had given him the benefit of every doubt. She had waited weeks now for him to handle the situation, and he'd done exactly nothing. She had warned him; hadn't she said Nina would have to know? "This is going to be hard for you to hear, Nins."

"Is Daddy having an affair? Are you?"

Caroline might have laughed. But when there was trouble in a marriage, wasn't that where most people's minds went? "No. Although it might be preferable," she added gently. "Hard to say."

A beat, while Caroline assembled the words, the will to say them. "Your dad has been lying about the payroll, underreporting the number of our employees to the insurance company to save on workers' comp. He's also faked the tax returns for . . . I don't know how many years." She managed to keep her voice calm, but having to tell Nina these things about Rob sickened her. It was as if she were tattling to her daughter about her husband. But Rob was also Nina's father, and although Nina was more her mama's girl than her daddy's, it still felt horrible taking down his image in Nina's eyes.

Long moments passed, and Caroline could only imagine Nina's puzzlement that would ultimately give way to colder waves of shock and disbelief. "I wish you didn't have to know this, Nins," she said finally, when she could no longer bear the awful silence.

"It doesn't even sound like Dad."

"I don't want to believe it of him either." *He's done it before . . .* Caroline debated: Should she tell Nina about the incident in college? Should she say she suspected there were other infractions, older than the current bad business? If she did, she would have to confess to marrying Rob despite her misgivings. Nina knew her parents had married in the wake of discovering Caroline was pregnant, but she knew nothing of Caroline's prior ambivalence, the doubt she'd hidden even from herself.

"What does it mean? He'll have to pay a fine or—"

"I don't really know, honey." She would spare Nina the details of her research that suggested imprisonment was a possibility. Truthfully, she had no idea what would happen. It depended on Rob. But it occurred to Caroline now that possibly she should consult a lawyer herself to find out her liability as Rob's wife and business partner. She closed her eyes. She had never in the nineteen years of their marriage conceived of a situation where she would be forced to act in her own best interests without regard for how Rob would be affected. But he'd had none for her when he'd put her in this position, no matter how much he might hotly protest, avow, and declare that he loved her and would never hurt her. How could he say that? His words . . . his actions . . . they were impossible to reconcile.

"He's such a straight arrow, always ranting about the fake news and crooked politicians. 'Never lie, Nina. Tell the truth no matter how hard it is, Nina.'" Her voice as she parroted advice Rob had given her from the time she was small was sharply sarcastic.

Caroline felt Nina's pain all the more acutely for having suffered through a similar rude awakening to her own father's disregard. "I would give anything if you didn't have to know this," she said, pushing the words through the narrowing channel of her throat.

"Oh, Mom, I know. I'm sorry for you too," Nina said. "How did you find out? Did he tell you?"

"Not willingly," Caroline said.

One weekend morning last October she'd accidentally bumped Rob's laptop, which had been open on the kitchen counter. Righting it as the screen saver cleared had given her a view of the renewal form for the workers' compensation coverage. Some odd intuition had prompted her to scan the document, and she'd noted Rob had registered the number of their employees at fifteen when the actual number was thirty-eight. No biggie, she'd thought. *Typo*, her brain had told her. But reading further, she'd found other "typos," chief among them the reduced amount of their payroll. She remembered thinking when she saw it that she could only wish it were as low as the figure Rob had entered. Still, she might have let it go if Rob hadn't walked in and caught her. It was the look on his face and the way he'd barked at her that had alarmed her. She'd stood her ground, though, and with hands shaking had turned the laptop toward him and asked him to explain. The lies were there in black and white; still she'd clung to the hope that he would make them into truths. The fact that he could not, even after days and weeks of heated arguing and lengthy, strained discussion, had ultimately shattered her faith. There was little chance now they would ever recover their past life, the quiet tempo of those ordinary days before she'd unwittingly upset Rob's laptop and brought down their world.

He wasn't the only one who was being forced by circumstance to be honest, though. As a kind of backhanded bonus, Caroline, too, had been handed an opportunity to confront what had become a lingering unhappiness, one she'd assumed was tied to Nina's departure for college. Now she realized the distance between her and Rob had been widening for some time prior to that, possibly years. They'd become almost awkward with each other. Oddly, she'd found she didn't want to undress in front of him. He slept with his back to her. Sex wasn't more than an obligatory ritual.

"He said it was a mistake," Caroline told Nina now.

"How is faking numbers a mistake?" Nina's tone suggested her question was rhetorical. "But Mom, didn't you sign the tax returns?"

Nina wasn't interrogating her. She didn't intend for her questioning to inflict pain, but Caroline felt it nonetheless. "I didn't look at them. I just assumed—" How was it possible that she hadn't known? That was what Nina was asking. That was the million-dollar question. As a partner Caroline was privy—if she wanted to be—to all the company's records. But the truth was she hadn't cared enough in recent years to pay attention. She'd taken for granted that Rob was doing his part of the job of running their business. It had never occurred to her to check the tax returns or insurance forms. She had her own duties and responsibilities. "I should have been more diligent, obviously—" That was hindsight talking.

"Does anyone—like, I don't know—the cops, the feds—do they know?"

"Not yet."

"What are you going to do? If you report Dad, won't you be in trouble too?"

"I don't know what to do. I keep waiting for your dad to take action, hire an attorney, something." A threat of tears burned Caroline's eyes, and she pinched the space between them. "I don't think I could live with myself if I caused him to be arrested."

"It's awful, Mom. You're under so much pressure. Dad told me your aunt Lanie is sick, that her cancer is back. I'm so sorry. I know how close you are."

"Yes. Thank you." Nina didn't share Caroline's bond with Lanie. They'd lived too far apart, visited back and forth too seldom. Caroline regretted it, that she hadn't made more of an effort to bring them together more frequently.

"So now you're trying to find your dad to bring him to Lanie?"

"It's what I'm hoping to do. He might be here in Wichita." Caroline went on, telling Nina how she'd come across the letter with the reference to trouble her dad might have been in with Coach Kelly. "I wouldn't have known where to start without that letter, and even though he wasn't any help, I did get the name of a possible girlfriend of Dad's who lives here."

"From Coach Kelly?"

"Yes." Caroline wasn't going to mention Jace and her misgivings about him that persisted. She couldn't rid her mind of the sense that he, and possibly his dad, too, was hiding something from her. More than that, her impression that someone had followed her from the Kellys' house and subsequently run her off the road hadn't faded. Rather it had strengthened. Her damaged brain hadn't conjured the weight of a hand on her shoulder or the sound of a voice speaking her name, and who else could they belong to but Jace Kelly? She'd gone over the incident any number of times during the drive from Omaha, and it had occurred to her that he'd never actually denied doing it. No. Instead he'd gone on the offense, attacked her for calling him a liar. It was the same tactic he'd pulled the night before, putting her outside the door and closing it in her face. His final words surfaced in her mind: *Don't stir the pot, that's all I'm saying . . .* They had the sound of a warning.

But to say them—to say any of this—to Nina would only frighten her.

"What about your dad's second wife? Julia, right?" Nina sounded as if she was thinking aloud. "I know you didn't like her—"

"Oh, it wasn't that I didn't like her. I didn't even know her." Caroline had filled Nina in on her history, minimizing the drama of her parents' divorce, her mother's mood swings. She'd spoken of Lanie's home as her safe haven. "Dad and I spent so much time together; I was so used to having him to myself. Sometimes he'd come to Aunt Lanie's and stay for a week or more. After he married, though, he had his other family. I was so angry at him for that, and jealous of Julia's son, Harris. Whenever I think about them now, I'm ashamed of myself, you know? I can't imagine what they must think of me."

"He left Julia, too, though, didn't he?"

"That's what she told Lanie."

"I guess she doesn't know where he went?"

"She said she didn't."

"I don't know, Mom. The kind of man your dad is—the way he's hurt people—it makes me wonder why you care about him. Why do you and Lanie even want to see him?"

Caroline sat abruptly on the bed's edge, brought down by Nina's disgust. "People make mistakes," she said carefully.

"Maybe my dad'll run away like your dad did."

"Oh, Nina, no." Caroline caught the edge of defiance in her daughter's voice and knew it for what it was, an attempt to cover her fear. "I know you're disappointed in him, and you have every right to be—" She paused, picking at the bedspread. "My dad wasn't there when I graduated high school or college. He didn't walk me down the aisle at my wedding. He never held you as a baby. He doesn't even know you exist."

"I get what you're saying—" She stopped. "I'm scared for you and Dad. I don't want to have to break my parents out of jail." Nina's laugh was shaky.

"Oh, Nins, try not to worry, okay? We'll be fine." Her promises sounded false even to her own ears, but they were all she had to offer.

• • •

Bloom, Tricia DeWitt's shop, was in an older section of Wichita, a small storefront sandwiched between a dry cleaner's and a health food store. Caroline parked in front, letting the engine idle, reluctant to leave the car. She hadn't slept well, and she felt shaky, a combination of nerves and the cold. It was twenty-eight degrees outside. Gray and dismal, the same as Omaha without the dirty rime of snow.

What if she won't talk to you? Nina's question from yesterday whispered through Caroline's mind.

A bell over the door rang when she entered the shop, a little breathless, heart pounding.

"Be there in a sec," a woman called out.

Her voice was low pitched and husky, reminding Caroline of smoky bars, not florist shops. "No rush," she called back. She wandered over to a small antique wooden-wheeled wagon that held pots of pink and red blooming cyclamens. Nearby, a refrigerated cabinet held an assortment of cut fresh flowers: cabbage roses, long-stemmed roses, assorted mop-head hydrangeas, daffodils, and irises. The sight had Caroline longing for spring.

"How may I help you?"

Caroline was bent over, face buried in a nosegay of lilies of the valley she'd spied in a small cobalt-blue vase on the counter, when the woman addressed her. She straightened so quickly her head swam a bit. "These smell divine."

The woman smiled. "I know. Those little beauties are a favorite of mine."

She was tall but curvy. Her blonde hair was caught in a messy chignon, tendrils falling loosely around her face. The effect was somehow seductive. She was older than Caroline but not by much. Fifties, maybe, but trying not to look it. Caroline's thoughts ran together in her mind. Was she her father's type? Was her dad in the back, behind the curtain, where this woman had come from? Was she even Tricia DeWitt?

"Can I help?" The woman was frowning slightly.

"I don't know. I'm looking for Tricia DeWitt?" *My dad's girlfriend . . .*

"I'm Tricia," the woman said. She approached the counter opposite Caroline and balanced her hands on its glass edge.

Caroline saw it then, the wide band of gold on Tricia's third finger, left hand. Were they married, her dad and this woman?

"Trish?" A man's voice, the slam of a door, broke Caroline's reverie. She stiffened.

"Yeah, Ben. Out here," Tricia called. "UPS guy," she explained to Caroline.

He appeared, nodded at Caroline, and thrust a tablet at Tricia, which she signed.

Caroline barely registered their conversation, and then Ben was gone.

"Are you looking for work?" Tricia asked when he'd left. "You seem—ah, maybe I shouldn't say it, but you seem nervous."

"I'm looking for my dad. Garrett Hoffman?"

The thrum of silence followed Caroline's query, potent, heated, while Tricia's eyes widened. Her hand rose to her throat. "Oh my God, you're Hoff's daughter. You're Caro."

"Yes," Caroline answered.

A second silence sounded, a long hollow note.

"You look like him," Tricia said finally. "Same dimple." She tapped her left cheek. "Same chin, forehead, eyes, hair. My God." She repeated it. Prayer or lament, who knew?

"Is he here?" Caroline gripped the counter's edge.

"Here? Heavens no. Why would you think he was—"

"Jace. Jace Kelly. There was a letter, too, that Dad wrote to my mom." Caroline pulled it from her purse, setting it on the counter faceup. "Is this your handwriting?"

Tricia looked at it. "Yes."

Caroline's pulse ticked with cautious elation. "It was mailed from here in 1989, April or August. Were you—was my dad—you were together, right? You were—*involved* with him. Are you still?"

"Mom?" a voice—another male voice—called out. What Caroline assumed must be the back door slammed.

Tricia held up a finger. "Out here," she called. Looking at Caroline, she said, "My son. He works for me after school when he doesn't have football practice."

A young man, high school age, appeared in the doorway. "You got anything to eat?"

"This is my son, Baker," Tricia said, addressing Caroline. "Baker, this is Caroline Hoffman. She's—" A beat. "She's the daughter of an old friend of mine. I'd like to take her for coffee, if you don't mind watching the shop for a bit."

"Sure, Mom. No prob. I get paid by the hour regardless." He grinned, and while he didn't have the Hoffman dimple, his hair was dark and rumpled, and he was tall and broad through the chest like Caroline's dad. Baker was built like an athlete, like a football player. Caroline felt light headed.

"You have time for coffee?" Tricia's look left no room for Caroline to decline, not that she would have. She tucked the letter back into her purse.

Tricia got her coat, and they walked to the end of the strip center and around the corner to Starbucks. Other than a brief mention of the cold, they didn't speak until they were seated with their caffè mochas at a table in the corner. Other customers, a mix of men and women, were bent over laptops or phones. A sudden burst of laughter erupted from a table in the opposite corner, where three women were sitting, surrounded by a plethora of shopping bags, possibly having taken advantage of the after-holiday sales. Caroline envied them, although she was no shopper. She wished her mind were so frivolously occupied.

"I couldn't have this conversation in the shop where Baker could hear," Tricia said. "He knows about Hoff, knows Hoff was part of my life—"

"Is Baker Hoff's son?" It seemed to her that her breath paused while she waited for Tricia's answer.

"I know that's what you think. I saw how you looked at him. But Baker's only seventeen. Hoff had been gone a good while from my life by the time he was born."

Caroline didn't know whether to feel relieved.

"I don't understand why you're here. What did Jace tell you? I haven't been in touch with him or his dad or Hoff for years."

"When was the last time you saw my dad?"

"In 1989, that summer. I addressed and mailed his letter in August of that year. I was here in Wichita by then, and he came to stay with me. He wanted to . . . continue our relationship—" Tricia turned her cup in a circle. "I wanted a man who would marry me, have children and make a home with me." She looked up at Caroline. "That isn't your dad. Despite his promises, I don't think he knows the meaning of the word *commitment*."

"You sent him away?"

"Yes."

"This was after his accident when he fell at the stadium?"

"Yes."

"And you haven't heard from him? Not in all this time?" Caroline kept Tricia's gaze.

"No."

Caroline shifted her eyes.

"You really don't know where he is?"

Caroline couldn't trust her voice and shook her head. She hadn't realized how deeply she'd counted on finding her dad here.

"He loved you so much. He talked about you all the time."

Caroline looked at Tricia, wanting to but unsure whether to believe her.

"I went shopping with him once for your birthday present. He thought a Cabbage Patch doll would be perfect, but I talked him into getting you a Swatch instead. I think you were fourteen that year. Too old for dolls."

"Thirteen," Caroline corrected. "I still have it." The McSwatch with its green and yellow jelly bands and red rubber face guard had been the exact one she'd wanted. Caroline had been over the moon, showing it off to her friends. Had she known his girlfriend had picked out the watch for her, though, she'd have gagged. It was unlikely she'd ever have worn it.

"I don't think you were getting along too well with your dad at the time."

Caroline sipped her coffee.

"He was married again by then to Julia. She had a son. Harris was his name, if I remember right. He was younger than you, but you were jealous of him."

Harris had been eight when her dad remarried. Caroline, at twelve, had felt superior. And bitter—against a boy she'd never met, had adamantly refused to meet. *HarrisHarrisHarris*, she'd yelled at her father during one of his visits. *He's all you ever talk about, all you care about.* Harris had played football, and even as young as he was, from everything Caroline had heard her dad say about him, he'd been showing the kind of athleticism dads dreamed about. It was only natural he'd toss Caroline to the curb. As a girl, *she* couldn't play football competitively. *She* would never land a scholarship to play or get scouted by the pros.

"Your dad was always trying to figure out ways to make you understand he wasn't choosing Harris over you," Tricia said. "He hated it that you were so unhappy."

"You knew he was married, and yet you were—sleeping with him, out shopping for my birthday present with him." Caroline would be damned before she would let this woman see how badly the knife of her jealousy over Harris had cut her.

"It wasn't—"

"When did you meet? How long did it last?"

"I was nineteen."

"What year?"

"I don't know, 1984—'85. It was a mistake."

"He's twenty years older than you, old enough to be *your* dad."

"Twenty-two years older."

Caroline hooted. She thought of Nina, that Tricia had been near Nina's age when she'd met Hoff. The mama bear in her would kill any fortysomething man who went after her daughter. What had her dad been thinking?

"Some men aren't cut out for monogamy."

"Please don't make excuses for him."

"If it helps, I know it broke his heart that you were so angry at him."

Caroline's throat closed. It didn't help. "Where is he, if his heart was so broken?" She flicked a glance at Tricia.

"He was different after his head injury. You know how serious it was—that he nearly died? He was ten days or more in the ICU. Six weeks in rehab after that. Big Dog—Coach Kelly and I took turns staying with him. I brought him home to my apartment when he was discharged. He fell in December, so it would have been around the first of March when they let him go. He couldn't do much for himself at first. We had to help him dress, tie his shoes, feed himself."

"Where was his wife? Where was Julia?" Caroline didn't want to think of herself, where she was, how she—Hoff's own daughter—had stayed away out of resentment and selfishness.

"I think Julia wanted to come. Hoff's sister, Lanie, wanted to come, too, but he was against it. I got the feeling there wasn't much money for traveling, but honestly, I think it was more pride than anything. He didn't want them—or you—seeing him so helpless."

"He didn't mind if you saw him that way?"

Tricia looked off, and when she brought her gaze back, her expression was a puzzle, conflicted in ways Caroline couldn't define. "Your dad and I—" she began, but then she bent her weight on her elbows, pushed her cup of coffee away. She glanced sidelong at Caroline. "Why should I talk to you? I don't know you, don't owe you—anything."

"No," Caroline said, "but you knew my dad. On an intimate level. And I'm trying to find him. Not just for me. Lanie is sick. Cancer. She's got weeks, maybe a few months at most. She wants to see her brother."

"Oh, I'm so sorry to hear that. Hoff used to talk about her. He loved her, thought the world of her."

"Really? Like he loved me? He's got a funny way of showing it."

"I know how it must seem, what his actions suggest, but I believe his love and concern for you, for Lanie, even for me—it's genuine and real, wherever he is."

The door opened, and a man held it for the elderly woman who was with him. Cold wreathed around Caroline's ankles, poked frigid fingers down the collar of her shirt. She was so tired of being cold, so sick of winter. What was she doing here anyway?

"Danny, my husband, Baker's father, and Baker—they don't know anything about my life back in Omaha. Not the entire story, anyway."

Caroline met Tricia's gaze.

"I've told them Hoff was my mentor."

"Your mentor." Caroline couldn't keep the irony from her tone.

Tricia slapped the table. "You know, you need to get over it. I'm not saying your childhood was perfect, but I do know it was a lot more stable than mine. Your folks might have been divorced, but they saw to it you had a roof over your head, food on the table, clothes—your own, not someone else's—on your back, and that's a hell of a lot more than my parents did for me."

"If you're going to make excuses for yourself and my cheating dad—"

"Have you never had the wish to reinvent yourself? To step away from the person you've been, the mistakes you've made, and become someone else entirely?"

Caroline might have answered yes, given her current situation with Rob, but Tricia didn't allow time for a response.

"Your dad helped me do that. He helped me see I was worth something, that I was more than some throwaway foster kid nobody wanted. He and Big Dog—Coach Kelly—both of them helped me get into college and stay there. They made me see I could have a different future. If I'm a success now—and I am—as a business owner, a *female* business owner, I have them to thank."

Caroline averted her glance, but Tricia's ferocity, the emotion blazing in her eyes, her voice, was resonant. *So what?* It was her thirteen-year-old self asking. *You got my daddy, and I got a Swatch.*

"I don't much care for your attitude, Caroline, but I'm going to tell you what I know about your dad anyway because I'm concerned."

"Concerned?"

"I don't believe Hoff would have let all this time go by without a word to you or his sister even if he wanted to disappear."

"But why would he?"

Tricia huffed a sigh. "When I met Hoff, I was working at a club in Omaha, the Blue Pearl. He and Big Dog hung out there. My boss, the club owner, J-Ray, was a buddy of theirs; he was also a bookie. There were a bunch of guys who came in regularly. They'd order pitchers of beer, get their bets down, watch the games on the big screen. Watch the girls dance. It was like a big frat party in there sometimes."

"Dad gambled?" Caroline had never heard it before.

"Not big, but yeah. Like all the guys, he came for the girls too."

"You were one of the girls—a dancer." Caroline understood suddenly. The smoky pitch of Tricia's voice, her appearance—the shade of her hair that was a little too platinum, the blue of her eye shadow that was a little too blue. Under her coat, the plunging neckline of her sweater bared more cleavage than seemed practical in such cold weather. She might have reinvented herself, Caroline thought, but she hadn't left her past behind entirely.

"I only worked there to get tuition for college. I didn't know a better way. It was for damn sure some dead-end minimum wage job wasn't going to get me there."

Caroline thought of Nina. When she was born, Rob had insisted on starting a college fund for her. Nina would never have to work to pay for her degree. Neither had Caroline. The money had been there. Could she have—would she have—worked her way through? Had she cared that much?

"Maybe you'd rather not hear what I have to say." Tricia started to get up.

"No, please. I'm sorry. You were saying how my dad came to the club—"

Huffing a sigh, Tricia sat back down. "Yeah. He and the coaching staff would bring in players, too—potential players."

"Recruits, in other words."

"Yes. Usually high school boys who were underage. Hoff and Coach Kelly and some of the other bigwigs, Tillman Tiger alums, the boosters, brought these young guys there and saw to it they had a good time. I don't know much about the recruiting process, but I don't think that's supposed to be part of it."

"You're sure." Caroline wasn't. She wanted this woman to be wrong. She wanted not to listen. Her heartbeat was rough in her chest; she felt light headed and wanted to leave, but that wasn't an option.

"Do you know who Brick Coleman is?"

"Dad recruited him."

"He was all-state, all-conference every year he was at Tillman. He put that school on the map and went on to play pro for the Bears."

Caroline nodded. She knew all of this.

"Did you ever wonder why Brick chose Tillman when he had his pick of Division One schools?"

"His uncle was an alum. He probably influenced Brick."

"Maybe that was part of it, sure, but the truth is Brick was paid."

"Paid? Are you saying they gave him money?"

"And bought him a car and set him up in a condo. The uncle, Farley Dade—we called him Uncle Big Bucks—hung out at the club too. He was a big-time booster, one of several with deep pockets. He gave a ton of cash to Tillman."

"That can't be right. Dad wouldn't—"

"Hoff wasn't the only one involved, and Brick wasn't the only player who got paid to play."

"No way." Caroline felt emphatic, even righteous, in her denial. She began naming the reasons why it wasn't possible: it was illegal; Tillman would never have taken such a risk; the NCAA wouldn't have allowed it.

"I believe the NCAA opened an investigation—" Tricia began.

"Where's the proof? Do you have any?" Caroline was angry now. Her dad might be a philanderer, and he might have abandoned her, but this—gaming the system to lure the best players—was a line he would never cross.

"You can believe me or not."

"I know my dad. But you knew him too. You slept with him, right?"

Tricia reached for her purse. "I knew this was a mistake."

Caroline touched her arm. "I just can't believe my dad would be involved in some recruiting scam. He's—at least when I was growing up, he was always saying that an athletic scholarship wasn't a gift. It had to be earned through hard work—"

"—dedication, and discipline."

Caroline's dad's pitch. "Did Dad tell you himself that he did this?"

"Not directly. But there was a lot of talk at the club back then. Enough that there had to be something to it. When I asked, Hoff warned me not to get nosy. Obviously something's happened if your dad hasn't contacted you in all this time," Tricia added after a pause.

Caroline pushed her hair behind her ears. Inside, she was fuming. *Liar!* The word was parked on her tongue. *You don't know what you're talking about.* She could have said that too. If—if she hadn't felt in her bones, in the cooler rivers of her blood, that what Tricia was telling her was the truth.

"Look, there was a guy back then who came into the Pearl who said he was a reporter. He sure acted like one; either that or he was a cop. He was always asking questions, sniffing for information. If he's still around, he might know more—more than I do, anyway. He might have your precious proof—but if you ever say I gave you his name, or that we spoke today, or ever, I'll call you a liar."

"Really? Your anonymity is that critical after all these years?"

"I'm not kidding. I don't like it that Jace knows where I am."

"All right." Caroline went along as if she accepted that anyone— any legal authority—would care about thirty-year-old recruiting violations. For all she knew, Tricia was into drama, and the entire story was an invention.

"His name was Kip Penny. He came into the Pearl a lot, asking questions, like I said. He'd order a beer and never drink it, but he tipped like crazy. He hung around with your dad, and the others, Brick and his uncle. They were suspicious of him; they were convinced Kip was from the NCAA or an undercover cop. Turned out he was a reporter, but I didn't find that out until later."

"Were you and Brick close?" Something in Tricia's demeanor when Tricia said his name made Caroline ask.

She colored slightly, and that was answer enough, but she denied it at first, saying "No." Then, backtracking, she said, "Yes, but it was a long time ago."

They'd been lovers. Caroline was certain of it. She guessed Brick would have been near Tricia in age, nearer than Caroline's dad. She'd probably had them both on the string. But Tricia's morals weren't the point. "Did Brick tell you Dad paid him to go to Tillman?"

"Find Kip. That's all I can say." Tricia started to rise but sat down again before Caroline could object to her leaving. "There is one other thing I can tell you. Kip came to my apartment that summer, in 1989, while your dad was staying with me. They went outside on the patio and talked for a long time. I don't know what was said, but Hoff was upset afterward."

"Did he say why?"

"Not really. I got the impression it had to do with a story Kip wanted your dad's help with, an investigative piece Kip was working on. I figured it was related to the shenanigans at Tillman. Your dad left a day or two after that meeting. I assumed he went back to Wyatt, back to Julia and Harris."

"If he did, he didn't stay long," Caroline said.

"How do you know?"

"He left here the same month you posted the letter, right? August of 1989?"

"So?"

"I'm pretty sure that's the last time Lanie talked to him too. She didn't get worried, though, until after the holidays. He always called at Thanksgiving and Christmas, but not that year. Lanie finally called Julia, but she said Dad had left her. She didn't know who for or where he went. Lanie accepted it because he has a history of just taking off—"

"Well, since he'd just left me, he'd have had to find somebody else pretty damn quick. Did anyone call the police?"

"Lanie did, around the same time she called Julia, sometime in early 1990, I guess, but when she spoke to them, they dismissed her concern because of how much Dad traveled." *And his reputation for being a womanizer.* Caroline kept that bit to herself. "Lanie doesn't think they even filled out any paperwork."

"Now all these years have gone by." Tricia sounded aghast. "Have *you* spoken to the police?"

Caroline shook her head.

"My God, you're his daughter. Why are you talking to me and not to them?"

8

Harris—Wednesday, January 10

Harris's mom has worked as a guidance counselor at Wyatt High since Harris was in third grade. Before that she taught algebra. The kids love her. The times he caught her in deep conversation, maybe with her hand on some kid's shoulder, looking at them as if they were the focus of her world, it made him so jealous. He got over it, though. Anyone can see she's got a gift, the way she relates to the students. Harris has tried to emulate her. He once thought he was doing a pretty good job of it, too, but that was before Gee and the dope.

He's the damn dope.

And he's made one hell of a mess.

Harris swallows the last two of the Oxy he got off Gee on Tuesday morning, dry, and gets out of his truck. He's arrived at school early, got some half-baked plan to see his mom even though he realizes where they work is not the best place for it. *It* being whatever he plans to do. Does he mean to confess? Tell her that Gee supplies him with drugs and robs houses in his spare time?

He knows what she'll say. After she has a nervous breakdown, she'll tell him to go to the cops. She'll tell Harris to get his ass into a rehab program. That is, if he doesn't end up getting arrested along with Gee. Harris knows enough about the law that he figures he's an accessory. He's witnessed a crime and has knowledge of other crimes that he hasn't reported. That's all it takes, he thinks.

He crosses the deserted atrium and turns down the corridor that leads to his mom's office. He knows she's here. He parked next to her car. The hood was cold under his hand. He just hopes she's alone. His footsteps are muffled for the most part by the rubber soles of his Nikes, which is good, because in the moment he spots the cops—Clint Mackie and Ken Carter—he's able to backpedal and get himself out of the hallway unseen by them. At least they don't acknowledge it if they notice him.

Six long, fast strides get him across the atrium. He's out the door and down the steps when a kid, John Hooper, calls out, "Hey, Coach."

"Hey, Hoop," he calls back.

He exchanges greetings with other students, a few teachers, but on the fly, desperate to get away. He wonders how far would be far enough. The athletic building that houses his office and several others as well as the weight room is on the other side of the employee parking lot adjacent to the baseball diamond and the football field. The fields are used for practice now, but when Harris was a student back in the eighties, the Warriors hosted games on these fields. Now they have a new sports complex off campus, a bigger, more modern facility five miles north of town. Local folks will say Harris is responsible in part for the upgrade. Under his guidance, both the football and baseball teams have kept up an impressive win/loss record.

The baseball team has made it to the playoffs twelve seasons out of his now sixteen-season tenure. They've brought the state championship home four of those years. The football team has done nearly as well, competing for the state championship four times and winning it twice. The players make their grades, too, for the most part.

He passes the entry door of the athletic building and walks out onto the deserted football field, stops on the fifty-yard line. He played his first real game of football here. He was six, in a peewee league, a quarterback even then. His coach and other men who knew this kind of thing said he had talent, an innate sense of the game. They talked about the size of his hands and feet and what was likely to happen once he grew into them.

But it was Hoff who showed Harris what it was going to take. They worked out here on this field, or rather Harris worked out, according to the routine Hoff designed for him. Hoff timed Harris's wind sprints, barked at him when he slacked off running the bleachers. He caught Harris's endless passes. When Harris turned ten, Hoff started him on free weights. Harris's mom thought he was too young, but Hoff showed her research that said the idea that weight training adversely affected growth was a myth, that in fact it promoted strength that in turn might prevent injury later on. Hoff believed a kid couldn't be too strong, mentally or physically. Harris hammered his mom until she gave in and agreed to the weight training. He and Hoff did it together, and that pleased her. Even though Hoff was on the road a lot as a college recruiter, when he was home, they were a family.

Hoff was Harris's dad.

Harris misses him. He misses him like hell to this day. He'd never have ended up coaching baseball if Hoff were here. He'd never have left the game of football. He'd have gone pro. He'd have made Hoff proud. But once Hoff was gone, the game lost its meaning. Harris quit the team; he quit the sport cold turkey.

He tips his head back now, eyes on fire, blinks at the sky, unseeing. It's useless thinking about the past, what could have been.

• • •

The knock on his office door makes him jump. He says, "Come in," but his impulse is to dive under his desk. Ken Carter enters first, followed by Clint Mackie. Harris has been expecting them ever since seeing them in the corridor earlier. He stands as the uniformed men enter. They shake hands across Harris's paper-strewn desk.

Clint says, "I hope we aren't interrupting anything."

Ken says, "It's been a while."

Harris says no in answer to Clint's question, and he nods at Ken. He isn't sure what Carter means. Been a while since what? They don't run in the same circles. Harris invites the men to sit down and sits himself, randomly shifting piles of paper. He's sweating and shaky despite having taken the Oxy. He hasn't done a damn thing, he tells himself. Not that they know about, anyway. *You say anything, you'll go down too.* Gee's warning drifts through his mind. He was gloating when he said it, had that manic look in his eyes. Harris wonders if he's the only one who's noticed that there's something off with Gee, something wound too tight in the kid. Harris has considered talking to Gee's cousin to see if he can get a handle on the situation. But Harris has no idea where the cousin lives, and for all he knows the cousin is as messed up as Gee. He could be an even bigger punk.

Clint is talking Warrior football. "What are the chances for the team next year, do you think?" he wants to know. "With Gee and your son leaving."

Harris wonders if he'll even be here next season. He shoves a hand over his head, leans back, loose and easy, as if the answer to that million-dollar question is all that he and the two law officers have got on their minds. "I can't lie," he says. "It's going to leave a hole." Harris goes on talking about the possibilities. "We've got Bo Nichols," he says. "He's a junior this year. He subbed in for Gee a few times and did a good job. He looks good in practice too."

A beat.

"We're working with him."

Another beat.

"We'll see." Harris is compelled by the silence, the men's bland stares, to keep talking. He feels like he looks as guilty as he is. He opens his desk drawer, closes it.

"You've heard about the home invasions," Clint begins.

"Yeah. A lot of people are nervous," Harris says.

"Eight houses have been robbed so far," Ken says.

"But not since Thanksgiving, right?" Harris asks, and he's relieved when Mackie confirms the fact.

The captain goes on. "We're not pulling the plug on the investigation, though, not by any means. We're working a number of leads."

There is a sound of feet shuffling and leather creaking when Clint shifts a bit in his chair. "We think there are two or three people involved. We're not ruling out that it could be kids. So far, they haven't gone into a house when anyone is home, which suggests they've been watching their targets, learning the homeowners' habits."

"They don't use force either," Ken says. "No broken windows or kicked-in doors. At least one of them is good at picking locks."

"Huh." Harris unfolds his arms across the top of his desk. He could say who it is—should say who it is right now. His jaw feels screwed shut. His blood hammers his temples.

"Doesn't take much," Ken goes on. "You could use a paper clip, if you can believe that. I watched a YouTube video, showed the step-by-step. There's any number of videos and instructions online that show how to break in to just about anything. It's amazing." He shakes his head. "You just need the right set of tools."

Clint looks at Ken. "You can get those online too. Amazon probably sells them."

The cops laugh.

Harris says, "Do you have any idea who it is? Which kids? They from around here?"

Clint looks at Harris. "We're hoping somebody here on campus can help us with that. We're pretty sure they're local, probably students here, yeah. They know the area, know when folks are going to be away. They go in when the house is empty, come out with all kinds of stuff. Small, mostly, easy to handle."

"They took a doll from one house," Ken says. "I still can't figure it out, what they're going to do with it."

"It was an antique," Clint explains as if Harris has asked or even cares. "Had a porcelain head. Made in Germany. Cricket says they're valuable to collectors."

Cricket is Clint's wife. She runs the café by the same name on the town square, where Kyle has just gotten a job. It's open for breakfast and lunch only. Like all the rest of the school personnel, Harris often eats a meal there. Everybody in town dines there at one time or another.

Ken's hooting, saying he has trouble imagining a kid would know anything about an antique doll.

Harris knows Gee's cousin took the doll for his five-year-old daughter. The cousin stole a pair of diamond stud earrings from the same house for the kid's mother. Gee said the cousin was from his dad's side of the family. The poor relations, Gee calls them. *Mom's people are the ones with all the money*, Gee has told Harris. He was named after them, Gee said, the Gander family. Regardless of how they came by their fortune, the family is one of the richest in the county. Gee's dad runs an oil company and an investment firm. They've got an eleven-hundred-acre ranch, the Double G, outside town that's been in Gee's mother's family for generations. Drakes have got more money than God. That's what folks in town say.

"We've been talking to the students and some of the teachers," Clint says. "We spoke with your mom earlier. We're hoping someone will talk to her. All the kids seem to," he adds.

Harris runs a fingertip along the edge of his desk blotter.

"What about you?" the police captain asks. "Any of your players talking in the locker room? Maybe you, or one of the other coaches, have heard something?"

"I'll ask around," Harris says. "If they had heard anything, though, I'm sure they'd have called you guys."

Clint nods. The men get up. If they noticed Harris didn't include himself with those who would report knowledge of criminal activity, they give no sign.

The morning passes. Harris tries to concentrate on work, but it's impossible. He paces behind his desk, weighing his options, knowing there's only one that's right, that if he had any guts at all, he'd come clean, tell what he knows, take whatever punishment is coming, and get it over with. What's stopping him—what he tells himself is stopping him—is that he knows Holly and his kids will be in for it, too, the backlash that will result once the news is out that he's been covering for Gee, the local football legend, hometown hero, robber, and drug pusher rolled into one.

Harris's drug pusher.

Dope is for dopes.

That's what Harris preaches to Connor and Kyle. He doesn't want to see the looks on their faces if they learn the truth. His throat is tight when his cell phone rings. He picks it up, studies the caller ID window. *Mom.* He answers, needing to hear the reassurance of her voice. Somehow he manages to sound normal.

"The police were here earlier," she says.

"Yeah. They came to my office too."

"Do you know who's behind the break-ins?"

"No. Why would you think—"

"This morning, before classes started, I was outside my office, talking to Clint and Ken. I saw you. You came into the corridor, and then suddenly you were gone, as if you didn't want them seeing you."

"Oh yeah. I remembered I was supposed to meet with Tim first thing." Tim Connolly is the assistant baseball coach.

His mom's silence is considering. She's not buying it. She knows him, knows his heart and mind as well as her own, and he knows every permutation of her thoughts and emotions too. They have the kind of bond that only shared adversity creates. Except for the horrible Oklahoma years and the brief time when Hoff joined their family, Harris and his mom have only ever had each other. Harris has felt at times as if they are knit from the same cloth. He has felt stifled by their closeness, and he's resented it. And during the troubled times in his life, he has relied on his mother's love, her fierce loyalty to him, as if it were his only refuge.

"Harris," she says, "what is going on with you? Don't say nothing."

"Nothing." He says it anyway. "Mom, I'm sorry, but I was just on my way to lunch—"

"Holly's worried. She says you're taking something for your back again."

"She talked to you?" That surprises Harris. Holly and his mother are cordial but nothing more. It has to do with their kids, Harris thinks. Holly perennially will complain that Harris's mom makes her feel as if her mothering skills are inadequate. Harris doesn't disagree that his mom can be a bit opinionated when it comes to the kids. But he's not getting in the middle of it. His mom is a worrier, that's all.

"You told Holly you saw Dr. Cooper as recently as two weeks ago."

"I don't really have time for this conversation right now, Mom." Harris is tight jawed. He's got no intention of ever going back to Cooper.

"She called his office, Harris. You haven't been there since last June. If you're on pain meds, you aren't getting them from him."

A beat.

"Are you taking medication? Oxy or something worse?" Doubt, possibly even the taint of disgust, crimps his mother's voice.

Harris rubs his eyes.

"Is Zeke giving it to you?"

"He's a doctor."

"He's retired. It's not the same. He's not performing an examination, taking x-rays. He doesn't know your situation."

"He was there when it happened."

"A sports injury from years ago isn't pertinent to your situation now, Harris."

"Let it go, Mom, okay?" he asks.

"You can't keep taking narcotics. Holly thinks—we both think—you're relying too much on them."

"I know what I'm doing."

"They're dangerous, especially when taken long term. I'm—Holly and I are both worried for you."

He doesn't answer. He's out of excuses, tired of coming to his own defense, tired of his lies.

"Holly mentioned something else, Harris."

"Since when do y'all talk so much?"

"I guess she's talking to me because she's not getting anywhere with you."

"Christ," he mutters.

"She said you're stressed about a student, a football player, that you mentioned a scholarship is at risk. That sounds to me as if this young man is into something very serious—like the recent rash of robberies."

Harris doesn't deny it.

"Is there a connection? If you know the player who's involved, Harris, scholarship or not, you're duty bound to report it to the authorities."

Harris stares at nothing.

His mother waits. For confirmation. Reassurance.

"Do you ever think about him?" he says finally.

The silence following his query rings with his mother's astonishment.

Her response, when it comes, is cautious. "Do you mean Hoff?"

"Yeah. I still think about him. I still wish he was here."

"Oh, Harris, he's been gone from our lives a long time now."

• • •

He sits at his desk, a folder containing team stats open in front of him, but his mind is on Holly. He can't stop thinking about it, that she spoke to his mother about him. It pisses him off; it scares him. He thinks of calling her, of saying, *Talk to me, not my mother.* But he knows she'll say she's tried talking to him.

He glances at his watch. Baseball practice starts in half an hour. But his nerves are shot. He can't face it. Can't do anyone any good, the shape he's in. He calls Tim, asks if Tim will cover for him, and he's brutally aware even before Tim reminds him that it's the fourth time since school resumed after the Christmas break that he's had to take over practice. Tim reminds Harris they have a preseason game coming up. "Next Friday," he says, as if Harris doesn't know the schedule. "We need to settle on a starting lineup," Tim says. "What's going on with you, anyway? Is it your back again? You need to get that shit straightened out. Did you make an appointment with the chiropractor I told you about?"

"I'm going to," Harris says, and the lie is like dirt in his mouth. Tim seems to know it too.

He says, "You need to get off the meds, man, that's all I'm saying," and he hangs up.

Harris pulls his cell off his ear and stares at it. Fucking Tim! What does he know? What is he suggesting? *You need to get off the meds.* Does he think Harris is addicted? Does everyone? Grabbing his jacket, Harris leaves the building. He's not an addict. He can kick the dope anytime he likes, and he likes right now. He doesn't know why in the hell he or anybody's made such a big deal out of it. Slamming his truck door, he keys the ignition, trying not to think of the other times he's tried to quit.

This time is different. He's just got to do it, man up and gut it out. He doesn't need a damn pill to get through his day.

That's over.

Everything is over. He's done lying, done covering for Gee.

He's going to the cops, and whatever happens, happens. If he lands in jail, c'est la vie. He deserves it.

It's the thought of Holly and the boys and his mother, the sense of their shock and disgust, that makes him light headed. He pulls to the curb a few blocks from the school, and getting out his cell, he punches in his wife's number. He can't blindside her; the least he can do is give her some warning, but she doesn't answer, and his resolution slides. He's afraid to leave her a message, scared his voice will break. He stares out the windshield. Neither Kyle nor Connor will be home until later. Kyle's in the weight room at the high school, and Connor's at baseball practice at the junior high. They won't be home until after five. He tosses his phone into the passenger seat. Holly must be with a client. There isn't any knowing when she'll be home. She doesn't keep him advised of her schedule anymore.

He thinks fleetingly of Zeke, that if he were to go see the old man, Zeke would write him a script. He might even have a few of the fentanyl patches on hand, save Harris a trip to the pharmacy, where he risks running into someone he knows. Catching himself, Harris pinches the bridge of his nose. *Dumbass. You're quitting, remember?*

After a bit, he shifts the truck into drive. Turning down his street, his gut clenches on seeing Holly's Navigator in the driveway. He parks, picks up his cell, and exits his truck, steeling himself, knowing he's got to confess, lay it out, all that he's involved in. He'll leave afterward if that's what she wants. That's the thought in his brain when he goes into the house.

He calls her name from the mudroom. "Holly?"

No answer, but he can hear footsteps overhead in Kyle's room. Harris goes to the foot of the stairs. "Kyle?"

"Harris? I'm up here."

Hearing Holly's voice, he takes the stairs two at a time. He pauses on the threshold of Kyle's room, looking in at her.

She's got an armful of dirty clothes, and when she sees him, she drops them on the floor. "I don't know why I'm picking up after him. He's seventeen years old, for heaven's sake." She gestures, the broad arc of her arm encompassing the mess that Harris has likened to the city dump. The family joke is that Kyle's room could qualify as a Superfund site. They'll say there are probably clues to who knows how many unsolved crimes in the rat's nest of his belongings.

"He'll be moving out soon," Harris says.

"Not soon enough," Holly mutters.

"Does he know you're in here?" He'd be mad as hell, Harris thinks.

"He asked me to come in here. He forgot his wallet this morning—again. He's at the gas station—the Exxon on 1630? He's on fumes, but he's got no money with him. What are you doing here, anyway? Don't you have practice?"

"I asked Tim to handle it. I was hoping we could talk."

"Now?"

Harris could have laughed at her look of incredulity. The history written into her expression . . . he wants to talk now? When every other time she's asked, begged, to have a conversation, he's stonewalled her?

"I wish you'd called me."

"I did. You didn't answer."

"I must have been on the phone with Kyle. Now I'm late. I've got a client waiting to look at eight hundred acres near Burnet. Can you take Kyle his wallet?"

"Sure. Where is it?"

"He said he left it either on his bed or on the top of his dresser. I looked both places and didn't find it." Holly crosses the room, and before she can get by him, Harris reaches for her. He wants to delay her, if only for a moment. He has in mind to tuck the loose tendrils of her hair behind her ear. He wants to cup her cheek, to hold her gaze, to brush the soft curve of her lower lip with his thumb. He wants to kiss her. But she only wants to go, to put distance between them. He steps aside.

"I don't know how long I'll be," she says, heading down the stairs. "I'll call you."

He listens to her footsteps as they fade, crossing the living room, the kitchen, the mudroom. He hears the back door close. She's done with him already, he thinks, regardless of what he says or how he excuses or explains himself, how much he might beg for her mercy. It's possible she's involved with someone else by now.

Some guy who talks to her.

His phone dings, signaling a text, and he pulls it out of his pocket. Mom says ur bringing my wallet? Kyle has typed.

Harris texts back: Looking for it now.

He toes piles of stuff on the floor, moves through them to the bed. The tangle of bedclothes has been shoved to the bed's foot, probably by Holly. There's nothing resembling a wallet in the mess on top of Kyle's dresser either. Opening one of the two narrower top drawers, he tentatively probes the contents with his fingertip. He doesn't like going through Kyle's things. It feels invasive, as if he's snooping. He's on the point of shutting the drawer, thinking he'll go to the station and pay for Kyle's gas and Kyle can pay him back, when he sees the ring.

At first he can't accept that it's there. It's only when he picks it up and feels its weight in the center of his palm that he knows for sure what ring it is and to whom it belongs. And the knowing sinks his belly and weakens his knees. His phone dings again.

You find it?

Harris stares at Kyle's text, heart pounding. He stabs the phone's face. No. Wait there. I'm coming.

Like I could go anywhere? Kyle texts back. He's added a laughing emoji.

Harris's jaw clenches at the sight of it.

After pulling into the gas station twenty minutes later, he parks behind Kyle's Jeep. He can't get out of the truck; he feels nailed to the seat. Regret mixed with disgust is a bitter taste in his mouth. Given his track record, who is he to accuse Kyle of anything? So what if the kid took the ring? Let someone else—someone with integrity, a leg to stand on—call him on it.

Kyle walks toward him from the gas station storefront. His face is in shadow, but Harris admires the broad, confident set of his shoulders, the careless grace of his walk. He doesn't look as if he's got a single troubling thought in his head. But Kyle has never been that kind of kid. He's never been the sort to mouth off, challenge authority, break rules. There've been a few exceptions, but without them, he might have come off as too good, the kind of good that makes you wonder if it's real. He has Holly's integrity, her character.

Harris isn't fit to wipe the spit off his shoe, much less confront him about the theft of Zeke's ring. But Kyle doesn't know of Harris's unfitness, and even though Harris does know, and it sickens him, he's still got to act like a dad. He gets out of his truck.

"Hey, Dad. Thanks for coming—"

"Yeah, listen, we need to talk. Follow me home?"

"I can't. I'm going over to Sam's to study. Chem test tomorrow."

"No. You're coming home—" Harris's phone goes off, and he jerks it from his pocket. Looking at Kyle, he says, "Hold on. It's your mom."

"Dad, I need to go. Can you just give me—?"

"Holly, I'm here at the gas station—"

"Harris?" Her voice is high; his stomach knots. "The hospital called. Connor's coach has brought him into the emergency room. Evidently he's broken his finger."

"God, are you serious? What hospital?"

"Wyatt General. Can you go? I'm halfway to my appointment. It would take me more than a half hour to get back there."

"Yes, sure. Is he all right, other than the finger, I mean?"

"I think so. Mad, the nurse said. He's afraid he's out for the season."

"Poor kid. Okay. I'm on my way."

"Call me when you've talked to the doctor, will you?"

Harris says he will, and ending the call, he pockets his phone.

"What's up?" Kyle asks.

"You got lucky. That's what's up." Harris pulls out his wallet, and extracting some bills, he shoves them into Kyle's hand.

"God, what is wrong with you, Dad? You're so weird lately."

"Your brother's at Wyatt General. He broke his finger, and I've got to check on him, but we aren't done, you and me. You understand? We're going to have a chat as soon as possible."

"Yeah. Okay, Dad. Whatever."

Harris climbs into his truck, and looking out his windshield, when he sees Kyle staring at him, challenge hot in his eyes, a feeling he can't name crawls through his gut, something coldly prescient and eerie, like footsteps over a grave.

9

Caroline—Thursday, January 11

Caroline and her mother were in the breakfast room, dawdling over coffee and slices of apple strudel her mom had bought from Neilson's while Caroline was still sleeping. The neighborhood bakery was an institution. As a little girl, Caroline had walked there with her dad to buy strudel, or some other breakfast treat, almost every Saturday morning he'd been in town. Mrs. Neilson had always given her a dough-nut hole. *A bite of sweetness for the sweet*, she would say. Caroline asked if her mother remembered the ritual.

"I do," she answered. "Mrs. Neilson had a soft spot for you. She had five sons and told me once she missed having a little girl."

"Is she still working there? She and her husband must be in their eighties."

"Their sons do most of the work now, but the old folks still go in every day." A silence lingered. Her mother broke it. "I know your mem-ories of your dad are different from mine, kinder for the most part . . ."

"But?" Caroline met her mom's glance.

"You have a life, Caroline, a business and a husband who needs you. Whatever has happened with you and Rob—I know it's none of my business—"

"No, Mom, it isn't."

Her mother averted her gaze.

"It's hard to talk about." Getting up, Caroline stacked the dishes, took them to the sink, and rinsed them. *Hard* didn't begin to describe it, she thought, and if she could think of any way to avoid it, she would. But there wasn't. "Rob has been lying about our taxes and the workers' comp, and I don't know what else."

Her mom came to the counter and opened the dishwasher. Caroline handed her a plate.

Settling it into the rack, she said, "He told me."

Caroline stared at her mom. "When?"

"While you were going from Omaha to Wichita, chasing after your dad." Her mother straightened. "You might as well be chasing a ghost, Caroline."

She didn't know which issue to address first: that her mother knew of Rob's fraud and was apparently intent on defending him, or that her mother thought her dad was a ghost. Annoyed, she shut off the water, harder than was necessary. "Are you saying Dad's dead?" she asked, picking up a towel.

"No. I don't mean ghost in that sense, although we both know it's possible."

"You mean because he doesn't want to be found. What if you're wrong?" Caroline folded the towel, keeping her eye on it. *He could be dead.* Her brain lingered on the idea. It wasn't as if it was new. Anything was possible. But until now she hadn't dwelled on where he was or what might have happened to him. He'd been gone so many years from her life, by his own choice, or so she'd believed. That she'd caused their estrangement by refusing to accept his second family was an old and worn source of guilt and shame. She'd never known how to work it out, how to fix it—what she would have done even if she had managed to find him. What would she have said?

Didn't he bear some responsibility? Having her own daughter, Caroline knew she'd never have walked out on Nina, or if she had, she would have ultimately circled back. She'd have given Nina a chance, a hundred chances. Caroline's dad had given her none.

But this now—her mission to find him—wasn't about her; it was about Lanie, for Lanie.

"I think Dad was in some kind of trouble, that he might still be, and that's why he disappeared. Tricia wondered why I was talking to her and not the police."

"What in the world can the police do after thirty years?"

"Did you ever hear that Dad might have taken money for recruiting Brick Coleman, that he—or the boosters, his uncle, somebody—paid Brick to play for Tillman State?" Caroline had told her mom some of what she'd learned about her dad in the last couple of days during their phone calls and when she'd arrived home last night, but she hadn't mentioned the recruiting issue. She'd been uncertain whether it was wise; her mother had enough to feel bitter about when it came to her dad. But her mom surprised her.

Slamming the dishwasher door, she defended him. "Not your dad. He might not be the most honorable man when it comes to his wedding vows, but he would never compromise his professional relationships. Who told you that?"

Caroline set down the towel, heartened to hear her mother's defense, which matched her own sense of the situation. But maybe they were both naive.

"Let me guess. Tricia." Her mother's disgust was palpable. "I guess she's also the one who gave you the reporter's name."

Not only his name but a possible location. Tricia had told Caroline she'd heard Kip was living in Miami and working for the *Miami Herald*. Caroline had been on the phone, speaking to a woman in personnel there, when her mother had gotten back from Neilson's. The woman had indicated she didn't know of a reporter named Kip Penny. On a whim, Caroline had asked if the woman would take down her contact information. *In case*, she'd said. Of course, once she'd been forced to explain what she was doing, her mom had declared it was crazy.

"I don't know how you can trust a thing that woman's told you," she said.

"You don't know the sort of woman Tricia is," Caroline answered, her tone every bit as clipped.

"I know she didn't think twice about sleeping with someone else's husband."

Caroline turned to the countertop. "If I could talk to Kip—"

"Another ghost."

"Probably," Caroline said. It was easier than arguing.

She spent the remainder of the morning going through the rest of the boxes stored in the linen closet, but she found no further correspondence from her father or about him. After lunch while her mother was napping, she did another internet search of Kip's name, and she was surprised when she came across an entry noting an article from a few years ago that he'd written about a local Texas athlete, a high school football star who'd been recruited to play for the Denver Broncos. The city of Conroe was practically in the neighborhood, a thirty-minute drive north of Houston. Compared to the *Miami Herald*, the *Conroe Courier* seemed like small potatoes. Still, what were the odds that there were two reporters named Kip Penny?

Picking up her phone, Caroline punched in the number for the newspaper, fingers mentally crossed, but like the woman at the *Herald*, the woman in personnel at the *Courier* had never heard of Kip either.

"His name isn't in the directory, but neither is mine. I'm new," she explained. "He could be too."

"I could leave my contact information," Caroline said. "Maybe you could ask around? Someone who's been there awhile might know him.

They could pass my name and number on to him." It was ridiculous, a total long shot, imagining she'd get a call back from Kip Penny.

Pocketing her phone, she went back to the linen closet to finish packing the contents, but she couldn't focus. Getting out her phone again, she dialed her aunt Lanie's number. "Do you feel up to having company?"

"Yes, if it's you coming to see me," Lanie said. "When did you get back?"

"Last night," Caroline answered, and she went on breezily, as if her aunt sounded healthy and strong, like her old joyful self. But she didn't. Her voice was thin and reedy, as if the horrid cancer weren't satisfied consuming only Lanie's cells, her bones and muscles and tissue. It would consume her voice too. In the end it would devour even her will to live. "Do you need me to pick up anything? Like Blue Bell chocolate chip cookie dough ice cream, maybe?" It had always been their shared favorite. "We could have it for lunch."

Lanie laughed. "I would love it. Haven't had any in ages."

Caroline left a note for her mom. *Having lunch with Lanie. Don't worry about dinner. I'll pick up something. If Lanie's up for it, maybe I'll bring her home with me.* Caroline didn't know how that would go over. But, she thought, of all times, now was when old hatchets should be buried.

Martha answered the door. "She's waiting for you on the sunporch."

"I brought ice cream." Caroline held up the sack.

"Well, maybe that'll tempt her. It's for darn sure I'm not having much luck." Martha jabbed stray gray hairs into the bun atop her head. She was older, probably in her seventies, like Lanie. The women had known each other before Lanie's cancer, having met at the library several years ago, where Lanie had been a librarian. Martha was a regular patron. She and Lanie had the same taste for mysteries, quirky literary fiction, biographies, and physics. They were both widowed and lived alone. When Martha, who was a retired RN, had found out Lanie was ill, that she was in fact terminal, she'd called Lanie and offered her assistance. Lanie had resisted at first. She wasn't accustomed to accepting help from others. She called her cancer "that bastard." In low moments she would say it had robbed her of everything, including her independence.

"The chemo still ruining her appetite?" Caroline set down the grocery sack and shrugged out of her jacket.

"She's stopped the chemo."

Caroline looked at Martha, startled. "She only started treatments in December, I thought."

"It makes her so sick she can't face it. She said it affected her the same way four years ago."

"I remember," Caroline said. She'd come down whenever she could to help with Lanie's care and had experienced Lanie's reaction to the chemo firsthand several times. It had never failed that after a treatment, driving home, they'd have to stop three times for Lanie to be sick on the side of the road. Her precious aunt, who had always been strong and vibrant, had been so humiliated, despite Caroline's reassurances.

"She says it's not how long she lives now but how well," Martha said. "It happens with most folks in the late stages. The side effects aren't worth whatever number of weeks or days they might get from taking it. What difference can it make if you're too sick to do much other than pray to die?"

Caroline willed away the tears that threatened. Lanie didn't want or need her grief.

"Lanie told me you're looking for her brother."

"Yes, but I haven't had much luck so far." She kept Martha's gaze.

How long? How much more time does Lanie have now that she's stopped the chemo? The question hung in the air between them.

"Well, if you can find him at all, the sooner the better. Want me to dish that up for you?" Martha nodded at the ice cream.

"No," Caroline said. "You go. Get out of here and do something fun, something to relax. I'll stay. I was thinking of taking Lanie to Mom's for dinner, if she's up for it."

Martha looked doubtful, and while she did leave, Caroline thought she wouldn't stay gone long. She went out to the sunporch, where Lanie was reclined on a pink-flowered chaise longue, a ruffled throw over her knees. Catching sight of Caroline, she smiled. "There you are, my darling girl."

Caroline's heart shifted hard in her chest. It had only been a matter of days since she'd last seen Lanie, but she looked so much more diminished. Her cheek, when Caroline bent to kiss her, was dry, her flesh like tissue paper. Caroline stifled an urge to lift her aunt into her arms and cradle her like a child. *Don't go.* The plea rose in her mind.

Straightening, Caroline kept Lanie's hand and her gaze. "You stopped the chemo."

"Yes. Don't lecture, okay? I can't stand the thought of living out my last days feeling as sick as a horse."

Last days . . . Caroline's mind flinched from the words. "Are you comfortable now?" she asked, and it was an act of will that her voice didn't break. "What about pain?"

"I'm fine, honey. Did you bring our ice cream?" Her eyes twinkled, full of the mischief Caroline always remembered.

She laughed. "Yes, coming right up." She was back within minutes, and handing Lanie her dish, she grinned. "Do you remember Dad's thirty-ninth birthday, when you made him wear that dress?"

"The baggy, old-lady dress we found at Goodwill."

"And the big white beads."

"We made him put them on before we'd let him eat his cake—"

"While that Jerry Lee Lewis song was playing, 'Thirty-Nine and Holding.'" Caroline and Lanie were both struggling to contain themselves now.

"He did a reverse strip."

"He was pretty good," Caroline said.

"Yes, he was," Lanie said, sobering. She set down her bowl.

"I've made you sad," Caroline said, annoyed at herself.

"No. I'm worried about you, that you've taken on the search for your dad on my behalf when you've got your own issues with Rob and your company."

Caroline shifted her gaze.

"Remember when you were a little girl, I would ask you what was wrong, and you'd say, 'Nothing'?"

Caroline smiled. "You'd say, 'All right, then, I have all the time in the world. I'll wait until you're ready to tell me.'"

"I don't have all the time in the world anymore, my darling."

No, don't say that. You can beat this. I'll help you . . . Even as the implorations rattled through her mind, she was frightened and grieved by their uselessness. The salt of her tears burned her eyes, but Lanie didn't need her fear or her sorrow. "Rob confided in Mom."

"Really? I didn't know they were close that way."

"They aren't. I think he's desperate. I'm not answering his calls. It's making him crazy, but I don't know what to say to him." Caroline picked at her thumbnail. "I had to tell Nina what he's done."

"Oh no. Oh, honey, that must have been hard. How did she take it?"

"She's angry at him, but he's her dad, so . . . you know. She's scared of what could happen."

"Well, I am too."

"It's possible nothing will—unless I blow the whistle."

"Will you?"

"Ah." The sound, a near groan, was carved from Caroline's frustration. "I wish I knew what was right. There are the employees to think about, their families, all the consequences to them if we lose the company, go bankrupt, go out of business—go to jail."

"There's your marriage," Lanie said gently.

"That too," Caroline admitted. "I could say, 'What marriage?'" she added after a pause.

It wasn't Lanie's way to question, and she didn't, and Caroline didn't know whether to go on, to burden her aunt with her confusion about Rob, the turmoil of her feelings. "I don't know if I can stay with him," she said finally. "It's not just the stuff with New Wheaton."

"What do you mean, honey?"

"I don't know exactly. It's as if having it out in the open is forcing me to confront issues I've been avoiding." Caroline looked at her aunt. "I keep thinking if I'd been more aware, if Rob and I had been in better communication, this couldn't have happened. But somewhere along the line we lost touch with each other—if we ever were really in touch."

"You were so young and unsure of your feelings for him when you married. It worried me."

"I know. I think about that now. I could have come home, had Nina here. Between us—you, me, and Mom—we would have made a family for her. But I couldn't see it then. I feel like all these years I've been blind, taken the easy way, ignored all the signs. Now I don't have that luxury. I have to do something."

"You're strong, honey, and so is Nina, and while I hate that you're going through this, you know sometimes it's the hardest things we face in our lives that lead us to our greatest joys."

"Oh, Auntie Lanie—" Caroline stopped, not trusting her voice. Who would remind her about the joy when her aunt was gone? If she asked, Lanie would say she had only to look inside her own heart or outside at the flowers and trees and birds. She had only to listen for it in the wind.

"Have you thought of speaking to a lawyer yourself?" Lanie asked. "I think you need to talk to someone who can sort out what's best for you."

She was considering doing that, Caroline answered, and after a moment she said, "Nina thinks we'd be better off if Rob disappeared."

"Well, that's no solution, is it?"

"That's what I told her." She met Lanie's glance, and Caroline knew they were both thinking of her dad.

"I can't imagine there is anything much worse than not knowing what's become of someone you love."

"Well, we should talk about that," Caroline said, and immediately, Lanie straightened as if energized by Caroline's suggestion, the tenor of her voice.

"You spoke to Coach Kelly," she said.

"I did," Caroline said, and she went on, recounting the details of her conversations with Coach Kelly, Jace, and Tricia.

"Hoff wouldn't have gone along with bribing those boys," Lanie said when Caroline finished. "He was so upset with SMU in 1986 when he heard how they'd paid players. Remember how he'd shout at the television every time he saw anyone from the athletic department being interviewed on the news?"

"Not really. We weren't seeing that much of each other by then." Still, Caroline was gratified hearing Lanie's defense of her dad, that there was actual evidence backing her conviction that he couldn't have been involved with such a scam. "Tricia talked about it—even Coach Kelly and Jace said how much Dad changed after he fell. I feel so bad now that I didn't go to see him."

"He didn't want us there, Caro. He outright forbade me to come. Your mom and I talked about you going, but we both thought it would be too much for you to deal with by yourself even if Hoff had been open to the idea, which he wasn't. He was unreasonable. I've never understood his reaction, and once he finally came back to Texas, he wouldn't hear a word about it."

"I never saw him once after he came back. I feel horrible about it now, but at the time I was still busy holding on to my grudge."

"You were terribly upset when he remarried, and when you got older, you were angry for how awful he was to your mom."

"I was such a daddy's girl—I didn't want to see how badly he betrayed her. I remember blaming her for their breakup, even myself, never him—"

"When you came to me asking for the truth—oh, you must have been fifteen, sixteen—I wanted to lie and say your dad wasn't the cheat your mother had told you he was. We argued about it, Hoff and I, for all the good it did."

Caroline sighed and traced her eyebrows with her fingertips. "I keep thinking how much my situation with Rob is the same. He's just cheated in a different way. I feel blindsided, like Mom must have felt." A beat. "If a stranger had cheated either of us in a similar manner, we'd call the police."

"It's different, though, when it's family. Harder to know what the right thing is."

"It hurts more. You don't expect this kind of treatment from someone who's supposed to love you."

"No," Lanie agreed.

"Sometimes I think it would be so much easier if I could just forget I have a dad, but the truth is I want to find him as much as you do. I want to make my peace too." The realization struck Caroline as she spoke, that it wasn't only for Lanie's sake that she wished to find her father. She had her own demons that needed to be laid to rest.

"I've always wished I could have done more to help you back then. When you chose to go to college in Iowa over staying close by, here in Texas, it broke my heart. I imagined you wanted to put space between you and your mom, but you know, no matter what, she loved you."

"Mom was only part of it." *Steve was the rest—most of it.* Caroline uncrossed and recrossed her ankles. She wouldn't say it. The thought of him, her desire to talk about him, wasn't only shameful; it was pointless. "Mom and I had our rough spots. I understood her by then, but it was still hard dealing with her depression and her moodiness. I don't think going away was necessarily the right thing, though. All I did was worry."

"She's much better now in the last several years."

"Yes. Things are better between us." Their relationship wasn't perfect; it wasn't nearly as warm and close as Caroline's relationship with Lanie, but she had accepted that it was likely as close as it would ever be.

A small silence lingered.

Lanie broke it. "I've always thought there was a bit more to it—your choosing to go to college in Iowa." Her look was canny, assessing. It was the sort of look that made Caroline feel her aunt could see way too much of her soul.

"I don't know what you mean," she said, although she knew perfectly well.

"There was a boy you were serious about the summer after you graduated high school. I imagined you would change your mind and stay—for him if for no one else. I've always wondered what happened between you."

"Steve Wayman." Caroline gave his name mechanically, closing her mind against the pleasure it gave her.

"You ran into him, didn't you, last fall when you came down?" Caroline glanced at her aunt, and Lanie looked back, unblinking, purposeful. "You mentioned him."

"I did? Really?" Caroline didn't remember talking about Steve to Lanie, but then she remembered so little of that night. Actually that entire visit was a blur, her very own *Lost Weekend*. "What did I say?"

"You talked about how nice he still is." The mischievous light was back in Lanie's eyes. "You might have also said his belly is still flat and that he's still good looking too. That was about it, but then it was the morning after. You were a bit—you know." She twirled her finger beside her ear.

As delighted as she was that Lanie felt well enough to tease her, Caroline rued the reason for it. "Did I tell you he's a sheriff in Madrone County? I almost called him from Omaha. I thought maybe he could help us. I know when you filed Dad's missing person report in 1990, the police didn't do anything."

"They likely tossed the paperwork before I cleared the exit door," Lanie said dryly.

"Maybe knowing a cop would make a difference—although after the way I behaved, I'm not sure I have the nerve to make the call." The irony wasn't lost on her that she'd had plenty of nerve last fall, blurting out her personal business to him as if they weren't virtual strangers. She imagined in seeing her home he'd been fulfilling his obligation both as a lawman and as a gentleman. There was no telling what he really thought of her.

"You have so much on your plate right now, Caro." Her aunt spoke gently. "You don't need this too. I think I should contact the private investigator I hired back when Hoff first went missing and let you finish up helping your mom move so you can go home—"

"No!" Caroline straightened. "I want to find Dad as much as you do. The way things were left between us—"

"Oh, honey, I know. I can't think Hoff would have wanted this. He was devoted to you children, both you and Harris. He wanted you to be friends. I know you may not want to hear it, but the fact that he loved that boy doesn't diminish his love for you."

"I was jealous. It was stupid. I can't believe I felt that way. You know how much it's always bothered me that Mom acts jealous of how close you and I are. It's not as if love is finite."

Lanie twitched a corner of the throw. "The trouble between Hoff and me—" She hesitated. "We had an argument—did I ever tell you?"

"Yes, but not why."

"He called one day in August of 1989. This would have been after he got out of rehab and came back from Wichita. He wanted me to bring you to Wyatt without telling you we were going. He thought if he could get you there, you'd see Harris the way he did. You'd become friends. When I refused, he hung up on me."

"Really. I didn't know . . . that's . . ." Caroline paused, feeling swamped anew with regret. Why had she been so stubborn? How might it have eased everyone's life if she'd only given the Fentons a chance?

"That was the last time we spoke," Lanie said. "Sometimes I wish I'd done what he asked, but back then I felt strongly that forcing you would have been a mistake. I didn't think too much of it when I didn't hear from him after that. I assumed he was still angry at me, and honestly, I was like you by then—I just didn't care. I thought he'd get back in touch whenever he got over it."

"Well, maybe he never did. It makes me feel terrible now—"

"No, honey. There's no blame in any of this. I did what I could to track him down. I called Julia sometime in January when I didn't hear from him over the holidays. She said your dad had left her and Harris, had just packed his stuff and gone sometime before Thanksgiving. She didn't mention Tricia by name, but she did say she thought he had a girlfriend and that he'd probably gone to live with her. I could tell she was upset, that talking about it was painful. I was so angry at Hoff. Ah—" Lanie stopped. "I know this is hard for you, hearing this about your dad."

"It's no easier for you. No matter how we wish he was different—" It was futile, as useless as trying to cure Lanie of her cancer, Caroline thought.

"To a certain degree he's created this situation. If we don't know where he is and can't find him—well, I let it go, you know, after I spoke to Julia. I was disgusted. The years went by—I love Hoff, but sometimes he makes it difficult . . ." Lanie looked away, her mouth crimped, her jaw trembling a bit.

Caroline's own throat narrowed. She patted her aunt's hand.

"Julia said what a good man he was."

"After the way he left her? That's surprising."

"But he is a good man in so many ways. It's his single flaw, his Achilles' heel, his inability to be faithful."

"Where did Dad and Julia meet anyway?" Caroline asked. If she had ever known, she didn't remember, and suddenly she was hungry for details.

"At the high school in Wyatt, during football season. Julia was a guidance counselor. Maybe she still is."

"Dad was there, recruiting?"

"Uh-huh. He didn't usually travel to the smaller schools, but one of the players—a running back, maybe? I don't remember, but the boy was breaking records at the time."

"Did you go to the wedding?"

"No. He didn't tell me about it. It happened very quickly after they met, and she was a good deal younger. He probably thought I'd disapprove."

"Would you have?"

"We lost our parents so young, Hoff and I." Lanie went on as if she hadn't heard Caroline. "We raised each other. It was hard for me to stop. Even though I'm younger, Hoff always said I was a mother hen, cluck, cluck, cluck."

Caroline laughed outright, and when Lanie joined her, it was as if a light had come on in a room full of darkness. But they sobered quickly.

"I would so love to see him once more"—Lanie's voice tremored again—"to put matters between us to rest."

Caroline took her aunt's hand, and the fragility of it, the sense that the very flesh was melting from her aunt's bones, cracked her heart in half.

"When Julia and I spoke all those years ago, she said if she heard from Hoff again, she'd let me know."

Caroline met Lanie's gaze. "Have you thought of calling her?"

"Yes, but what if all I accomplish is to reopen an old wound?"

"No," Caroline said, suppressing an inward shudder. "That wouldn't be right. I don't want to do that either."

Lanie didn't come back to Caroline's mother's house for dinner. In part it was the ongoing tension between the women, although Caroline knew they would make the effort to be congenial on her behalf. Still, Lanie was too worn out. Caroline felt terrible that she was to blame, but Martha had reassured her that any visit from Caroline was food for Lanie's soul. *She loves you like her own*, Martha had said.

Caroline and her mom were cleaning up the kitchen after dinner—Caroline had brought home pulled-pork sandwiches—when her mom asked about Lanie. "How is she?"

She was wiping the counter near the sink, her back to Caroline, but she didn't pause. Her inquiry seemed almost offhand, as if she didn't really care.

Caroline was incensed. "She's dying, Mom. How do you think?"

Her mother went still, and while the look she shot Caroline was pained, it was also sharp with warning. *You're pushing it.* That's what she'd have said if Caroline were still a child. It irked her. "You always make me feel as if I have to choose between you," Caroline said.

"You always make *me* feel as if you prefer her company to mine."

"No—"

"It's easy to be the good witch in the fairy tale when you don't have the day-to-day responsibility of raising the princess on your own."

"Aunt Lanie spent as much time raising me as you did, when you couldn't get out of bed. When you couldn't so much as find the energy to feed yourself, much less me."

Her mother's shoulders slumped.

"Oh, Mom, I'm sorry." Caroline was; she had no wish to enliven the old pain between them.

"Do you know how much regret I have for those years?" Her mother raised her eyes, filmed now with tears. "It was so difficult for me after your dad left. It was as if all the light in the world went out. I look back now and wonder why I gave him so much power to hurt me like that."

"But he did hurt you, Mom, in the worst way."

She wiped the air with her hands, a dismissive gesture. "I sent you to Lanie—who was only too willing to take over my role—because I knew I was in no shape to be the mother you needed. You left me food, do you remember? You were like a little elf with your bread crumbs, trying to entice the troll out of the cave. It was appalling to me, and it shook me, but not hard enough."

"I was scared for you."

"Of course you were. I could see that, but all I could do at the time was get you away as much as possible. Lanie didn't mind. She loved you as much as Hoff and I did."

"I think you suffered from depression, Mom. I don't mean the garden-variety 'I've got the blues' depression. I mean the clinical kind. They didn't have the treatment for it then that they do now."

Her mother sniffed, wiped her face. "I remember when it lifted, or started to, the day you got your first period. Do you remember that? You were eleven, going on twelve. Everything then was drama. You cried when you saw the blood in your panties because you didn't know—no one had told you to expect it. I was horrified—"

"At Lanie?"

"No. Myself. I don't know why it was that particular neglect of you on my part that made such an impression on me, but I do remember the realization of your ignorance of the mechanics of your own body—how it took my breath."

"You gave me a tampon and coached me through the bathroom door on how to insert it." Caroline was smiling.

Her mom smiled, too, and quickly sobered. She came to Caroline, and cupping her cheeks, she searched Caroline's eyes. "I can't imagine what it was like . . . I know you felt Hoff and I both abandoned you. Lanie made a difference then." Lowering her hands, she went on before Caroline could speak. "I'm grateful to her. If I'm angry at anyone, it's myself. I take it out on her. She doesn't deserve it."

"I've never thought of you as the bad witch, Mom." Caroline was amazed by her mother's candor; she felt drawn to it.

"Well, you have thought of me—rightfully—as neglectful, and perhaps not as rightfully, judgmental, controlling, and rigid."

Caroline held her mother's gaze. "I have admired you too. For how you brought yourself out of the cave. You got a great job at the bank. You were a single mom, raising me without any support from Dad, at least not after he dropped out of sight."

"As parents we've been hard on you, Caro, and I'm so sorry."

"I love you both, Mom. Even Dad. He'll always be my dad. But he betrayed you, betrayed us both. I didn't get it when I was a kid, but I do now." Caroline shifted her gaze. "I realize he wasn't always a good person." She said what she was thinking.

Putting her hands on Caroline's upper arms, her mother rubbed them briskly, twice, before pulling Caroline into her embrace. "We'll work it out, Caro. Okay? I'm here, right here for you," she whispered, and her breath stirred the fine hair at Caroline's temple.

• • •

She was upstairs reading in her old childhood bed when her phone rang. She didn't recognize the number and ordinarily would have let the call go, but for some reason she answered it.

"Caroline Corbett?" a man's voice asked.

"Yes?" Caroline straightened, shifting the book from her lap, turning it facedown on the bed. "Who is this?"

"Kip Penny. I got a message that you're looking for me."

"Yes." Heart pounding, Caroline swung her feet to the floor.

"You're Hoff's daughter?" Obvious curiosity tinged Kip's voice.

"Yes. You must wonder why I've called. I . . . Dad and I lost touch . . . many years ago." It killed her confessing this, the source of so much private pain, to this stranger. "This is going to sound crazy—it's been so many years—but I was hoping we could talk about the investigative piece you and my dad were working on back then that involved Tillman State—their athletic department, specifically the football team."

"Where did you hear about that?"

"Tricia DeWitt. She said if I wanted to find Dad, I should talk to you."

He laughed. "Tricia DeWitt. You talk about a blast from the past."

"You remember her?"

"Oh yeah. No way could I ever forget her or the story. It was a doozy, pretty juicy stuff. But I can tell you one thing: Ms. DeWitt wasn't privy to everything that was going on."

"She alluded to my dad being involved in recruiting violations."

"Yes, well, I got to know your dad. We were pretty close friends, and I can tell you it went a little deeper than a few simple violations."

"What do you mean?" Caroline couldn't help it when her voice rose.

"Maybe we should talk in person," Kip said. "You're in Houston?"

"Yes," Caroline said. Had she mentioned that to whomever she'd spoken to at the *Herald*? The *Courier*? Was that how he knew? Her pulse tapped lightly in her ears.

"I'm in Texas right now too. On the coast. Port Aransas. My parents' place. Clearing it out. My mom died recently, and my sister and I moved Dad into assisted living. He's pretty bad off with Alzheimer's."

"I'm sorry," Caroline said. She might have mentioned she was moving her mother, too, though the circumstances weren't so dire, but she wasn't going to sidetrack the reporter with talk of their aging parents.

"It's a bastard," Kip said. "The disease, not my dad."

"I'm—I'm trying to locate my dad, Mr. Penny. I was really hoping you would know where he is."

"I don't," he said. "I'm sorry. I haven't spoken to him in years."

Caroline felt the drag of disappointment in spite of herself. "Well, can you say—I know it was a long time ago, but do you mind if I ask when the last time was that you saw or heard from him? Tricia mentioned you came to her apartment in 1989 when Dad was there—"

"I did meet him there. It might have been—it probably was the last time we got together," Kip answered. "He was pretty stressed, too, as I recall. It was the summer after the accident, the fall he took in the winter of '88? I'm sure you know—"

"He left without a word to anyone, Mr. Penny. He dropped completely from sight after he left Omaha, sometime near the end of 1989, as near as I can tell. I haven't heard anything from him, not in twenty-eight years."

"Huh. Well—that's—I don't know—the story we were putting together, it's pretty complicated—"

"You said we could talk in person." Caroline gripped the mattress edge. "Is that possible?"

"I'm free Saturday morning if that works for you."

"Yes, absolutely. There's a bakery here in the neighborhood, Neilson's. Good coffee and danish. Is ten o'clock a good time?" When the reporter agreed that it was, she gave him Neilson's address.

10

H is tread is heavy on the stairs, his heart even heavier in his chest. He stops on the landing and fishes Zeke's World Series ring out of his pocket. Since finding it in Kyle's dresser drawer on Wednesday, he can't think about anything else. He's barely slept. His mind wants an explanation different from the most obvious one: that Kyle is responsible for putting it there. Harris knows his son, knows Kyle is not a thief. But teenagers are notorious for being secretive. Or possibly Kyle, like Harris, is leading some other life he and Holly know nothing about. Harris closes the ring in his fist, loosening his gaze, staring at nothing. Another alternative, one that sickens him, jitters in a corner of his mind.

That Gee is somehow involved.

Gee and Kyle were friends once, if you could call it that. It was some kind of growing-up-male mishmash of brotherly love spiked with the antagonism that exists between rivals. Kyle instigated the fight that ended the friendship. It happened a few years ago when he discovered Gee had stolen his baseball bat. Harris knows about the incident because he happened to be in the dugout at the Little League ballpark when Gee and Kyle, who were behind the dugout, got into it. The bat had been Kyle's favorite, an aluminum Easton bat he'd named Lucky. It had gone missing from his canvas duffel after a game the previous week. Kyle saw it again when Gee brought it back to the park in his own duffel. He'd retaped the grip and marked it with his initials, but Kyle knew his own bat when he saw it, and he demanded Gee return it.

Kyle called Gee a dirty thief.

Harris opens his hand, studying the ring, Gee's response echoing in his mind.

Prove it! he taunted. *What're you gonna do, sissy? Why don't you run home to your mama, sissy? Your* pussy *mama . . .*

Bringing Kyle's mom into it, labeling her with that profanity, set Kyle off. It brought Harris out of the dugout and around it in time to see Kyle take a swing at Gee, landing a glancing blow on Gee's jaw. While the boys are near the same height and weight now, over six feet and near two hundred pounds apiece, Gee was taller and heavier than Kyle back then. Gee beat Kyle to the ground in the minutes it took Harris to put a stop to the fight. He was breathing hard, enraged on Kyle's behalf, but in the aftermath, he knew better than to wade in, knew it could damage Kyle's pride if he were to so much as offer comfort. Thankfully, Kyle's injuries weren't serious, a busted lip, a swollen black eye, and when he asked Harris to stay out of it, Harris reluctantly agreed.

But a day or so later Darren Drake, Gee's dad, waylaid Harris in the high school parking lot, claiming Kyle had provoked the fight and bruised Gee's ribs when all Gee had been trying to do was return Kyle's bat, which he'd picked up by mistake. *My son doesn't lie,* Darren said. *My son doesn't steal.* When he demanded payment for Gee's medical expenses, along with an apology from Kyle, Harris laughed in his face. *You're damn lucky I didn't call the law on your kid,* he said. Harris was royally pissed, but still, before he stomped off, he suggested Darren pull his head out. *Your kid's got issues*, he said. *You might want to look into getting him some help before they get too big to handle.* It didn't go over well. Harris has never spoken to Darren again. Neither have the boys been friends, so far as Harris knows—unless something has changed.

Like maybe the guys are buddies again and keeping it on the down low, knowing their respective parents wouldn't approve. That would be bad, but the even worse possibility—the cliff edge Harris's mind wants to step off—is that Kyle might be doing the robberies with Gee. They could both have gone into Zeke's house and taken the ring.

Or Gee went there, solo, got the ring, and planted it in Kyle's room. As some kind of warning or threat or who in the hell knows? Since Wednesday, the scenarios have looped endlessly through Harris's mind, scaring the hell out of him. He wants to get to the bottom of it, but he's had to wait for the opportunity to be alone in the house with Kyle. Finally, today Holly's gone to the grocery store for something she needs to cook dinner. Cilantro, Harris thinks. She's a stickler when it comes to preparing meals. The ingredients have to be fresh, farm-to-table fresh. Connor's gone with her. He'll beg for some damn thing, gummy bears or iced Pop-Tarts—something sugary. He's still such a kid.

Outside Kyle's door, Harris shifts his weight from one foot to the other. The ring is a hot coal, burning his hand. His blood pounds roughshod in his ears. He knocks on Kyle's door. It's a rule in their house.

"Yeah, come in."

"It's Dad," Harris says, opening the door.

Kyle looks at Harris from where he's sitting with his phone on the side of his bed—if there is a bed underneath the mountain of crap surrounding him. It's the usual sight, so ordinary and normal—all the litter and garbage everywhere, and Kyle's face is so open, and when he says, "What's up?" he sounds so relaxed—Harris can only stare at him as his heart is seized in a fist of love mixed with panic so strong it loosens his knees. He has to take a quick step to disguise his weakness.

"Jeez, Dad, watch it. Those are my good jeans you're standing on."

Harris bends down, picks them up, tosses them at Kyle. "Why the hell can't you ever clean up in here?" Annoyance burns through the softer fog of his love and concern.

"If you came in here to lecture about how I keep my room—"

"No. I came in here to ask what you know about this." Harris opens his hand.

Kyle's glance dips. "What is it?"

"Zeke Roman's ring, the one he got when the Dodgers won the World Series in 1963. You remember. I told you the story. How Zeke came from nothing, how he worked his ass off on the baseball field, earned a scholarship, got drafted by the Dodgers—"

"Yeah, Dad, I know all that. He went to med school, became a doctor. He's your hero—I get it. But the only time I ever saw that ring was when Dr. Zeke showed it to me and Connor when we were at his house. Did he give it to you or something?" Kyle stands, reaching for it.

Harris pulls back his hand. "No. I found it in your dresser drawer."

"You were snooping in my drawers?" Offense rings in Kyle's tone.

"Looking for your wallet. Remember? You were out of gas?"

"All right. But the ring—no way was it in my drawer. Which one?"

Was it worry Harris heard in Kyle's voice? "Top, right hand. If you didn't take it and put it there, who did?"

"I don't know, except it wasn't me."

"I want to believe you, son, but you've got to admit this looks pretty bad."

"Why would I rob that old man? I don't even know where he lives." Kyle seems truly perplexed.

"You've been there." Harris is pushing, harder than he needs to, probably, but he's got to. There's too much at stake.

"Not in a long time. It's not like I remember the way. I can't believe you'd think I could do this, Dad."

There is what sounds like real pain in Kyle's voice, his expression, and Harris's heart falters. But he knows how easy it is to play someone, to act the part of the good guy. "Yeah, well, it's not like it would be the first time. You stole a Hershey bar when you were five and a *Playboy* magazine when you were twelve." Harris cites the second thing—that he knows about—that Kyle stole. He and Gee took it from Gee's dad's collection. That was before they had the fight that broke their friendship.

"Are you serious? So because I took a candy bar and a damn magazine when I was a little kid, now I'm stealing jewelry? Jesus, Dad. Next thing you know you'll be accusing me of all the other robberies around town. Maybe you should call the cops. Maybe I've got all the loot from those houses stashed in here." Kyle is red faced, pissed as hell.

Harris keeps his gaze. "I can't help you, can't protect you, if you don't tell me the truth."

"I am telling you the truth. I don't *know* how Dr. Zeke's ring got in my dresser drawer." Kyle shoves a hand over his head. "If you found it on Wednesday, why are you just now asking me about it?"

"I don't want to involve your mom. She's got enough on her plate, dealing with Connor and his busted finger."

It took a while to get Connor settled down on Wednesday night. He was upset, worried his finger was going to cause him to miss the whole season. Harris sat with him longer than usual, trying to reassure him they'd work it out. When he finally joined Holly, she was in bed, book open on her upraised knees, reading. Harris had hidden Zeke's ring by then under his socks in his dresser drawer. He wanted badly to tell her about it, along with everything else—Gee, the robberies, the dope. He dawdled in the bathroom a long time, rehearsing how he'd confess that when he couldn't get the meds he needed from Zeke, he bought them from Gee. But then the realization hit him—how Holly would know then that she was right in her suspicion. He was back taking dope. Not only that, but he was buying it off a high school student. That would be the part that would break her heart. Worse, it would break their marriage. He knew he couldn't do it, and leaving the bathroom, he crawled into bed beside her without a word, and he lay there with his back to her and his spine rigid, miserable in his self-disgust.

Now, looking at Kyle, he says it again. "Your mother has enough on her plate."

"Well, I don't know a damn thing about that ring or how it got here. You of all people ought to know I don't have any use for the kind of lowlife that'll do that shit." Kyle's referring to the fight he had with Gee over the stolen bat.

"All right, then." Harris turns away, turns back. "What about Gee?"

Kyle's brows shoot up. "What about him?"

"I'm just wondering—are you guys friends again? You hanging out?" *Do you know, for instance, that in addition to throwing for more than two thousand yards as the king of high school quarterbacks in the state of Texas his senior season, Gee is also dealing drugs and doing home invasions with his cousin? Are you by any chance part of his crew?* Harris wishes he could ask, that he could go that far, but that ground is pocked with land mines, and Harris isn't prepared to handle the fallout.

"Hell no—"

"So Gee hasn't been here, inside the house, I mean." Harris keeps his tone casual.

"No. I see him at school, on the field. We don't hang out." Kyle's at his desk now, flipping through papers like he's bored, or possibly he can't look Harris in the eye.

Watching him, Harris can't be sure he's not being fed some kind of bullshit, and his heart aches with his uncertainty and his love for his son. He would do anything, sacrifice anything, to keep Kyle safe. But without knowing the truth, he's helpless. "You're not covering for someone else, another one of your buddies, are you?"

Kyle's head jerks up; he looks at Harris. "No, Dad. What is your deal? Why are you on my ass?"

"Why aren't you more interested in how Zeke's damn ring got into your drawer? Have any of your friends been up here? Has Gee? What about at school? You hearing any rumors about the robberies around town?" Harris is thinking out loud, talking fast. He wasn't lying the other day when he told the cops, Mackie and Carter, he hasn't heard a peep about the break-ins. He feels like he would have, should have, heard some whisper about them—maybe not firsthand, but the news would have gotten back to him. A lot of shit gets said in a locker room. The guys talk a lot of smack, horsing around.

"I told you, Gee and I don't hang out—" Kyle breaks off, angry again. He seems totally at sea, and Harris wants to drop it; he wants to let it go in the worst way, but that other alternative—that scenario where it's Gee who took the ring and planted it in Kyle's drawer—is roaring in his head. And what if Gee didn't *plant* the ring? What if, instead, he *gave* it to Kyle for safekeeping?

Harris's heart is grinding like a piston. His mind is a hash of conjecture and suspicion. Maybe he's paranoid, out in left field, except he knows—knows there's something going down here. And either Kyle's part of it, or he's not. Harris hopes like hell it's the latter, but if Kyle is in it, then Harris has got to get him out. He's got to do whatever it takes to protect his son. He tucks Zeke's ring into his pocket, thinking how sometimes the medicine you have to spoon-feed your kid doesn't taste good, doesn't sit well, and they fight it. They get mad as hell at you for forcing it. He thinks how sometimes you have to let your kid hate you. Finding Kyle's gaze, he says, "I don't want your mother knowing about any of this. Not until I get to the bottom of it, and I will. You know I will."

"I'm not lying."

"Then you've got nothing to worry about, right?"

Kyle glares but says nothing.

Turning, Harris picks his way toward Kyle's bedroom door.

"It really sucks that you don't believe me."

Kyle's voice stabs Harris between his shoulder blades, circles around to his heart. He pauses.

"You know what, Dad? I don't give a shit what you think. Even if I did steal that ring, I'm not as bad, not as big a liar, as you."

Harris wheels, facing his son, who is almost a man, who could probably take him down if they were to go head-to-head. "What the hell does that mean?"

"You're back doping yourself. I heard Mom talking to Gramma about it. You're taking Oxy again or some other damn drug. They want to believe it's for your back, but that's bullshit, isn't it?" Kyle takes a step; his eyes are hot with accusation. But there's a kind of pleading in them, too, for Harris to step up, be the man, the dad, Kyle wants and needs. Harris can't stand seeing it and jerks his gaze away.

Kyle takes another step. "I bet you can't go a day, can't go a fucking hour, without it, can you? Huh, Dad? C'mon, why don't you man up and admit it? You're an addict. I love you, Dad, but I hate you, too, for what you're doing to yourself, and me, and Mom and Connor." He takes a third step, and now his voice is harsh, broken. "What're you going to do? Keep taking the shit till you're dead like Tom Petty?"

Harris recoils, as if rather than bitter accusation and terrible pain, Kyle has hurled boiling water at him. Denial is thick on his tongue, but he can't open his mouth. His chin drops. He's aware of Kyle's breath heaving hotly around the room, and he wants to go to him, to gather his boy into his arms. *I'm sorry*, he wants to say. *You deserve better than me.* The words, and something that he imagines are tears, are clogged in his throat. It feels as if an eternity has passed when he leaves Kyle's room, leaves his son standing alone, without support, stripped of hope, of any reason to believe. It's the easy way, Harris thinks, the coward's way, and he can't remember a time when the world has felt so dark or cold.

• • •

Harris never thought he would marry, never figured he'd have kids. Even in his teens he somehow knew he was no kind of role model. His mom blames herself, the lack of a long-term father figure. Maybe if he'd had siblings, she said, a more ordinary family life. But it wasn't any of that, not really. The truth is Harris was scared growing up. He's still scared. More scared now than he's ever been.

He can't wait for Holly to come home from the grocery store, can't keep his goddamn promise to quit the dope either. He can't stop seeing the anguish and fury in Kyle's eyes, and he's got to stop seeing it. He's got to think how Zeke's ring came to be in Kyle's drawer. If it was Gee who planted it—but Harris can't go down that road. It can't be Gee.

In the kitchen, he tears a sheet off her memo pad and scrawls a note. *Something's come up. Don't hold dinner. Don't wait up.* He hesitates a moment, then adds, *I love you.* Has he written that to her before, since the early days of their relationship? He doesn't think so. He can't imagine what she'll think of it.

In his truck, leaving the neighborhood, he doesn't know where to go. He wants to hook up with Gee, get something to smooth himself out. He needs to talk to Gee anyway. He needs to look Gee in the face and ask him about Zeke's goddamn ring. But he can't just drive up to the kid's house and bang on the door. He's the Wyatt High School athletic director, the fucking head baseball coach. Guys in his position don't do dope, much less have a student athlete for a supplier. They don't turn their backs on a kid's criminal activity. Harris pounds the steering wheel with the heel of his hand. Tears blur his vision. He jerks the truck to the curb. Jesus, Jesus, how did he get himself into this mess? Kyle knows. Kyle thinks he's an addict.

Kyle is scared.

Harris saw the fear in him, and his confusion, swimming behind the anger in his eyes. Harris never wanted his sons to be scared; he never meant to be the source of their fear.

Straightening, Harris wipes his face, pulls his phone out of his jacket pocket and calls Zeke, leaving a message after the answering machine picks up. "It's Harris," he says. "I'm heading your way. Be there in twenty." He figures Zeke is home, probably nodding off in front of the TV. If he isn't, Harris will wait. He pockets his phone, feels Zeke's championship ring underneath it. He wants to be rid of the damn thing.

It's six thirty, nearly dark, when he pulls away from the curb. Around him rectangles of light shine from the houses that line either side of the street. A vision builds behind his eyes of families gathering around dinner tables. He hears their idle chatter, the ease of their laughter, but he's on the outside. He's always felt on the outside of such visions.

· · ·

He can hear the blare of Zeke's TV as he comes up the front walk. The curtains over the living room window are open, and he can see Zeke is stretched out in his recliner. A glass, holding what's left of Zeke's ritual predinner cocktail—precisely two fingers of Jack Daniel's—is on a side table near his elbow. Zeke only allows himself one such drink unless he has company. *You drink alone, you're in trouble,* he says.

Zeke has all kinds of little sayings and mantras that he claims keep his attitude positive and upbeat. If it were anyone else spouting all those clichés, Harris would be annoyed. But there's something about Zeke, a rightness, a kind of constancy—Harris doesn't know how to describe it, really. As much as he once felt mentored by the guy, he now feels protective of him. From the day they met at the A&M field house, when Harris was a scared freshman, Zeke has kept Harris steady. Zeke is the only other person aside from Holly and Harris's mom who knows about Hoff, how up until Hoff dropped out of his life, Harris's ambition, his dream, was to play football. When Harris confided in Zeke, when he showed Zeke some of his old game film, Zeke was dumbfounded at Harris's skill; he pressed Harris to try out for the A&M football team as a walk-on. He pushed Harris hard enough on the issue that Harris blew up, telling him to back the hell off. The pain on Zeke's face almost undid him. But talking about it was the only thing that would make it right, and it was the one thing Harris couldn't do.

Now he rings Zeke's doorbell, and he watches Zeke come to himself, slowly get to his feet, make his way to the door. His service to his country as a marine is still evident in his bearing, and when he opens the door, the sight of Harris brings a sparkle of delight to his eyes. A perennial bachelor, Zeke has often claimed Harris is the son he never had. Harris follows Zeke into the kitchen. He's polished off the last of the Jack Daniel's, he says, but maybe he could interest Harris in a beer? Harris's grin of consent is more grimace. There's no sign the old guy is disturbed, which is a relief. He'd be ranting if he'd missed the ring. No doubt he'd have called the cops. It's what Harris should have done long ago.

Sitting at the table, they talk for a few minutes about the upcoming Super Bowl. Harris turns his bottle of beer—Stella Artois this time; Zeke is a self-proclaimed connoisseur of fine beer—in his hands. He's shaky, nervous as hell, pissed—he can't sort out the hot sea of his emotions, except his head feels like it might explode. Picking up the bottle, he takes a healthy swallow, coughs, wipes his mouth.

Zeke eyes him, squinting. "Shouldn't you be home eating dinner? Something tells me this isn't a social call."

Harris digs the ring out of his jeans pocket and sets it on the table between them.

"What the hell?" Zeke glances at Harris. "Is that mine?"

"Yeah."

"What are you doing with it?"

"I found it," Harris says. "In Kyle's dresser drawer."

Zeke sits back.

"He swears he didn't take it."

"Well, when would he have? Kyle hasn't been out here since"—he thinks a moment—"junior high, maybe? You don't bring the kids anymore."

It's the hint of disappointment in Zeke's tone that lets Harris know Zeke has noticed Harris's lapse. But the last time he brought the boys, they complained of boredom. Harris hasn't argued for bringing them again. In fact he's been glad for their disinterest. It's risky having them with him when he comes to pick up meds or a script from Zeke. Until earlier today Harris felt pretty confident no one knew what he was taking, how much, or when. But as usual he was fooling himself. Kyle—Kyle of all people knows, and he's scared the way any good, decent kid would be.

Harris was so damn wrong to think even for an instant that Kyle was involved with robbing anybody of anything. He wouldn't provide a hiding place, either, wouldn't be anybody's fall guy—Gee's least of all.

But Harris can't think about Kyle now—of his goodness and decency, or that Kyle called him an addict. It will crack him open, take him down, and he can't afford that. Kyle is all that matters, that he stays safe. Harris doesn't care what it takes. As bad a father as he is, as poor a role model as he's turned out to be, he's determined to protect his son. He knows, knows in his bones, if he finds out Gee planted the ring—and there's no doubt now in Harris's mind that someone did—he'll take Gee apart. Kid or not, Harris will crush Gee with his bare hands.

Zeke catches Harris's gaze. "How does he explain it, the ring being in his drawer?"

"He says someone must have put it there."

"What? Like they're framing him? Who would do that? Why?"

"I'm pretty sure Gee Drake is behind it." Anger crawls through Harris's brain, darts a hot tongue behind his eyes, but he's got to be careful, be cool. He wants Zeke's take on the situation, wants his help to think it through, maybe figure a way out. He doesn't want Zeke riled.

"You're serious." Zeke leans back, shock riding his gaze.

"You've heard about the break-ins all over town."

"You're saying Gee's robbing houses?"

"Him and his cousin. I think they took your ring deliberately to set Kyle up."

"Why? What the hell is this story you're telling me? It makes no damn sense."

"Yeah, probably I'm being paranoid. I shouldn't have come. I don't know what the hell I was thinking." Harris starts to rise.

"No. Jesus. Just sit down and tell me. Gee's got a beef with Kyle, is that it?"

Harris doesn't answer. He takes a swallow of beer, buying time. Why did he think laying it out for Zeke was a good idea? Once the old man knows, he'll be implicated, unless they call the cops, right now, tonight. But Harris can't keep it inside; he's too damn scared for Kyle. He looks at Zeke. Who else has he got?

"Maybe the cousin is the mastermind," Harris says, though he doesn't really believe this. He's witnessed Gee's behavior long term—in the locker room, on the playing field. His responses to horseplay, to team play, are too intense, too over the top. Harris has seen Gee slam his locker door after a bruising loss. No big deal when it's once, maybe twice or five times, but Gee—back when Gee was a freshman, Harris counted the number of slams and reached twenty-five. There's something brittle in Gee, a watchfulness, a kind of hostility. The kid hides it well. Gee plays it as if he's just one of the guys. He can dish out the insults and horse around like the rest of his teammates, but he doesn't like getting crowded. Doesn't like to be handled. He'll start to lose it. A curtain of rage lowers over his expression. Often, he'll push back, too hard, too much like he means it to hurt. Harris has seen it happen.

Gee's good, though, about catching himself. Someone gets onto him, Gee turns on the charm. He'll grin, waggle his hands. *Just joking. Just playing with you. Just having a little fun. Lighten up, why don't you?*

Harris is fairly certain he's in the minority with his observations. His mother dismissed his concern over Gee when Harris brought it up a couple of years ago. Harris glances at Zeke now. "What I hear, the cousin's older, thirtysomething, got a five-year-old daughter—a lot of responsibility, but not much else. He's Gee's mama's poor relation."

"What you hear from who?" Zeke asks.

"Gee." Harris is regretting it more now, that he came here, that he's spilling his guts.

"So Gee, who by the way is from one of the wealthiest families in this county, is robbing houses with his dirt-poor cousin, and then what? He comes to you and confesses? Is that how you know this? What are you, his priest? I didn't think his folks were Catholic."

"I saw him and his cousin on Thanksgiving Day when they went into and then came out of the Guthries' house, carrying a bunch of crap."

"You called the police."

"Obviously not, or Gee'd be in jail." Harris shifts his feet. He can't meet the old man's eyes, but he feels the heat in his gaze.

Zeke leans forward. "I'm confused," he says. "You witnessed a robbery, saw the thieves leaving the house, and you didn't call the cops?"

"Think about it, Zeke. Gee's a local hero, a football legend. He's got recruiters chasing him from every powerhouse college team you can name. If he's arrested, he'll lose all that. The town'll lose all that." Harris peddles the lie he's fed himself, shoving it past the brutal knowing in his gut that it isn't the town's collective ass he's interested in saving but his own.

"So he's better off getting away with it? Stealing other people's shit? Like my ring? They came into my house—what else did the bastards take—?" Zeke breaks off, gets up fast enough that his chair shoots across the floor.

"Take it easy, man." Harris gets to his feet too. He steadies the chair, lays a placating hand on the old man's arm. He thinks how the situation just keeps getting worse. "I shouldn't have come," he says again. "Shouldn't involve you—"

"I've got to check out my house." Zeke brushes past Harris. "See what else is missing."

Harris follows in his wake, blood hammering in his ears. "We can't involve the police. Not until we know more." But the cops are exactly who should be—who would be involved if Harris were any kind of man, any kind of dad at all. The sense of this, the enormity of his failure, is suspended in his mind, an anvil, waiting for the right moment to drop.

Zeke is opening and closing bureau drawers. He checks closets, the shelves in a medicine cabinet. Coming back across his bedroom floor, he meets Harris's glance. "I want to search the rest of the house alone. Wait in the kitchen."

Harris agrees, but it rankles, getting dismissed like he's some guy off the street who can't be trusted. He wonders what Zeke doesn't want him to see. His drug stash, probably. If there is a stash. Harris has never known. Zeke has given Harris samples of different drugs, mainly pain meds, from time to time. He has said he gets them from a couple of pharmaceutical reps he knows. It makes sense that if Gee and the cousin found drugs when they were here, they'd have taken them. Harris sits down. His gut is fisted in ice.

Zeke reappears, looking sour. Sitting heavily across from Harris, he regards him from under the white-eyebrowed ledge of his brow, and when Harris asks whether anything else is missing, he shakes his head. "Not that I can tell."

Harris pinches the bridge of his nose. He asks for another beer when what he wants is something much stronger, but he can't think how to ask for that.

Zeke sets a bottle in front of him, resumes sitting across from Harris.

"Look, if you're sure Gee's behind this and the rest of the robberies, if he's trying to frame Kyle, you've got to go to the cops." Zeke drinks his beer. "Gee's daddy'll save him, if it's consequences you're worried about. You can bet Darren Drake's got some high-dollar team of lawyers on permanent retainer who'll get Gee out of it—O. J. style. I doubt it'll be more than a speed bump on the road of Gee's life. The little shit," he mutters.

"You going to report it?" Harris nods at the ring where it sits in the center of the table.

"I didn't even know it was gone. Might never have. Maybe that's what the assholes were counting on."

"You ever worry the cops might find out about the drugs?"

The old man's eyes widen. "What're you getting at?"

Harris looks away, the bitterness of his shame riming his mouth. But he's desperate. He doesn't want Zeke calling the cops, and maybe he'll think twice if he's hiding dope here.

"Are you talking about the meds I keep here? I'm a doctor. It's what doctors do. We dispense medication."

"You're retired."

"I don't have a formal practice, no, but I've kept up my license to practice medicine in this state. I've got a license from the DEA to dispense drugs, and you know it."

"There's a lot at stake, Zeke." The old man is nervous. Despite Zeke's denial, Harris can see it. Zeke won't want the cops on his property, nosing around in his business. Maybe he doesn't have the proper licensing after all. Maybe he's a liar too. But Harris is immediately horrified. Has it come to this—that he would want to bring Zeke down to his level? Zeke would never sink so low.

Zeke finds Harris's eyes. "What am I going to say to the cops? I don't know anything other than that you brought me the ring. I'll let you handle it, okay? However you see fit."

"I appreciate that, Zeke. I really do." Relief makes his eyes water.

They drink their beers. A siren sounds in the distance. The big clock on the wall ticks away the time. Harris eyes the door, thinking of Holly and the boys at home. *There's not a house out there I can't get into.* How many times has Harris heard Gee say it? The punk has pushed the limit now, coming into Zeke's and then Harris's houses. Next thing he knows, Gee'll tip the cops anonymously. Harris imagines it—law enforcement showing up at his door, flashing a warrant to search the premises. Holly and the boys will be scared out of their minds. Harris can't let it happen. That's his first thought. Then, quickly, it occurs to him he's no longer got the ring. It's back where it belongs. There's nothing left at Harris's house for the police to find unless—

Unless Gee planted other stolen items in Kyle's room. For all Harris knows, Gee could have stashed the goods he's purloined throughout the entire house. Kyle could still be implicated; the robberies could still come back on him—on Harris's whole family. His breath shallows. It's everything he can do to stick in his chair. *Jesus Christ!* The exclamation bolts into his mouth. He tightens his teeth against it, fists his hands to keep from banging them on the table. Even so, Zeke must sense something. He's giving Harris the eye. "What?" The word is a challenge.

"Nothin'. You look like you're gonna puke is all."

"Nah." Harris runs a palm over his head, front to back. "Back's bothering me. Just sick of fighting the goddamn muscle spasms, you know?"

"You take anything? Didn't I give you a script for Oxy last week?"

"Yeah, but it's preseason. I'm out on the ball field with the guys every day. It's hard on an old man." Harris isn't lying. Coaching is getting tougher on him every season, mentally and physically. He thinks about how long he's been punishing his body—since the first year he signed up to play football, when he was six. Almost forty years ago. Some mornings nowadays he wakes up so stiff and sore he wonders how he can get out of bed.

Zeke says, "I've got a couple of fentanyl patches."

Harris could cry, he's so grateful.

"But listen here, you can't rely on this stuff too much." Zeke says this as he leaves the kitchen.

It's not the first time he's admonished Harris.

"I know you're against it," Zeke says on his return. He puts the fentanyl on the table in front of Harris, puts his hand on Harris's shoulder. "But what can it hurt, giving biofeedback a shot? Yoga and meditation too. That shit is not for sissies." Zeke sits down. "When it comes to chronic pain, you got to find some alternative to the drugs, man. I've told you—"

"Yeah. Okay. I know you're right." Harris isn't lying when he agrees with Zeke. Holly and his mom have told him the same thing. But he's tried it—the yoga, meditation, biofeedback—and none of it has worked for him. It's not just his body that turns on him; it's his mind too. It won't shut up. The tangle of his thoughts, his emotions, goes a mile a minute, wrapping him in knots. Sometimes he feels like he's walking on the crumbling edge of the deepest abyss. He can hear the loosened gravel falling, falling. There's another sound he hears, too, sometimes—a howl, long and low and hopeless. He could swear he feels the vibration in his chest. It's the sound a man might make when he's trapped, like Harris is, in a hell of his own making.

"I don't like seeing you in pain, son."

Harris looks at Zeke, and the love in Zeke's eyes causes his throat to narrow. He thinks how he's using Zeke, a man who has through the years shown him nothing but kindness.

"I meant it when I said I wouldn't report the ring was missing, if that's what's bugging you," Zeke says. "But I'm trusting you to handle the situation the right way and put a stop to it, no matter who's involved."

Harris nods and gets to his feet roughly before he can break down. He picks up the fentanyl patches. "I've got to go," he says. "Holly'll be worried." But Harris knows it's more likely she'll be pissed as hell.

Coming home from Zeke's, Harris pulls into the driveway and shuts off the engine. It ticks as it cools. He's feeling more relaxed now that the fentanyl is kicking in. Still, he's reluctant to leave the relative safety of his truck. He imagines Holly waiting for him in the kitchen, surrounded by the remains of the dinner he's missed. She'll demand an explanation, and he's fresh out, drawing a blank. Somehow he's got to find a way to search the house without her or the boys catching on. Maybe after they all go to bed? Worst case, the cops have already been here. The question then would be moot, wouldn't it? He's got no idea what to hope for. Pulling the keys from the ignition, he gets out of his truck, crosses the drive, enters through the back door, and stops in the mudroom to listen.

The sounds he expects to hear—water running, dishes and silver clanging, his family's voices, the television—are absent. His heart pauses. The kitchen, when he passes through it, is immaculate. There is not so much as a whiff left from whatever it is Holly made for dinner. Harris's pulse taps in his ears. Her name is in his throat, but he doesn't call out for her, or for Kyle or Connor. He walks through the downstairs. The great room is deserted, the fire in the grate burning low. The study, too, where the boys often do their homework, is empty. They must be upstairs in their rooms, he thinks, or else they aren't home, which would be odd on a school night. As he enters the little hall that doglegs between the study and the bedroom he shares with Holly, his blood is cool in his veins. She's there, seated on the side of the bed, elbows cupped in her hands. She looks up when he pauses in the doorway. The only light comes from the lamp near a chaise longue in the adjacent alcove. He can't make out her expression, but he doesn't really need to see it. The very air is electric, alive with tension.

"I'm sorry," he begins.

"Don't," she says in a tone that suggests she's finished with Harris's apologies.

"A guy called, a friend from A&M—" Harris launches into the only story he can think of that might fly, one that Holly can't check out. She interrupts, cutting him off. From the look she gives him, Harris knows she wasn't going to buy it anyway.

"Kyle's in his room; he won't come out," she says. "He's furious about something. When I asked, he told me if I wanted to know what it was about, I should ask you." .

Harris holds Holly's gaze.

Time passes. A beat, two—six. The silence is armed, a minefield.

"Harris? Tell me what's going on. Right now. I'm sick to death of this—"

"This?" he says, stepping farther into the room. He's angry, too, popping off, and it's wrong, the wrong thing to be doing. But he doesn't stop. No. Like an idiot he says, "This what? I'm sick to death, too, of your accusations—"

"I want you to go."

"Go?" Harris stares at his wife.

"You can't be here if you're on drugs. No, don't deny it." Her voice rises, cutting off his protest. "You're back using Oxy, or whatever your drug of choice is these days."

"What makes you think—?" He's hunting for a way to play it off.

But she won't give him a chance, and when she says, "Oh, Harris, please," her disgust etches every syllable. "I'm not stupid. The fact that you think I am makes me madder than anything. You're on something now. I can look at you and tell. It's killing me, killing us, our family. Evidently you're not doing your job either—"

"My job? What the hell do you know about my job?" Harris is back to righteous anger, as if that'll work.

"I ran into Tim's wife at the grocery store." Holly leaves the bed, disappears into Harris's closet. "Cheryl told me Tim had to run practice again today; it's the fifth time in two weeks."

Harris's gut knots. He stares at her, almost stupid in his shock, when she reappears with a stack of his clothes, his boxer shorts, Harris thinks. She flings them on the bed. "So where do you go, Harris? Hmm? Where are you when you're supposed to be running ball practice? Hooking up with some dope pusher?"

"Aw, jeez, no. C'mon, Holly—" Begging now. He feels like he's drowning, going down for the third time, the tenth time. There is no more time.

Unmoved by his plea, she retreats into his closet, brings out another armful of clothing, jeans, T-shirts, polos, slacks, all jumbled together, and dumps them on the bed.

Harris goes to her. "Stop." He takes her arm.

She jerks it away. "You stop."

"Maybe I haven't been entirely honest." Can he tell her? His heart is beating like a jackhammer; the sound booms in his ears.

She laughs at what he says from deep inside his closet, and the sound is brittle. It is a sound like shattering glass. She reappears, and this time she has a canvas athletic bag with a Texas A&M logo on it in her hand. Setting it on the bed, she unzips it, begins cramming his clothes into it.

"Can't we talk reasonably about this?" Harris, pulse thrumming, moves alongside her.

"I've given you chance after chance," she says. "I'm done now. I don't know who you are anymore. You aren't the man I married. Or maybe you are, and I was just blind before." She looks at him, and his heart stalls, seeing the pain he has caused her. "I told your mother today that for all I know you've taken drugs from the day we met and every day since."

"You know the shape my back is in. You were there for the surgeries." Harris holds Holly's gaze. He's begging, something he rarely does, but he sees it's cutting no ice with her. He can't blame her. She has a right to her anger at him, a right to hate him.

"It's not just the drugs, Harris." Holly zips the bag. "It's the way you hide things, the way you treat me as if I'm on a need-to-know basis,

142

like an acquaintance and not your wife. You have nightmares and panic attacks you won't discuss. You have a kid at school who's in trouble bad enough I can see it's chewing you up from the inside. But you refuse to talk about any of it." She jerks up the tote and thrusts it at Harris. "Now Kyle is doing the same thing, giving me the silent treatment. I don't want him involved in your secrets."

"He's not—" Harris breaks off before he can finish. Before he can lie to her again. Of course Kyle's involved. He knows about the ring, and for some reason Harris can't fathom, Kyle is going along with Harris's wish that Holly not be involved.

"I don't want to hurt you, but you aren't a good father or a good husband right now." Holly is quieter, and somehow the effect makes her seem even more impassioned and sincere. The sense of this gets into Harris. It's like the slimmest of blades, piercing his heart. "We need time apart," she says. "My wish, my hope in doing this—"

"But what is this? What are we doing? Do you want a divorce?" The idea he has had—that divorcing her is the best thing he could do for her—and the actuality, that they might literally split their lives, go their separate ways, leaves him panicked. He will not survive, he thinks.

"I want us to live apart for a while. As little as I like the idea, I hope it will scare you enough that you'll reconsider counseling, or the other ways out there to handle your pain."

"They don't work." He is grim. He wants to say it, that she's killing him.

"Well, neither is this. We—we aren't working, Harris, and we never will unless you find a better way, another way. You have to, or else I'll be forced to make the separation more permanent."

"What will you tell Kyle and Connor?" he asks, going to the bedroom doorway, pausing there.

"The truth," Holly says. "They know anyway—about the drugs. They aren't stupid either."

11

Caroline—Saturday, January 13

Neilson's was packed on Saturday morning. Caroline had known it would be, but she hadn't known where else to suggest she and Kip meet. Searching the chattering crowd, she saw him almost immediately, or rather she saw the red Astros ball cap he'd said he'd be wearing. It was pushed back on his head, giving him a boyish appearance, although he must be in his sixties. She caught his glance and gave a low wave, moving to join him. He half stood, grinning, open faced, genial. They exchanged greetings and made small talk about Kip's drive up from Port Aransas, the weather. It was a beautiful blue-skied morning, sunny and fifty-two degrees, according to what Caroline had heard earlier on the morning news.

"It feels downright balmy after Omaha," she said.

"I hear you," Kip said. "I couldn't hack the winters up there anymore. That's why I moved to Florida."

A waitress came, someone Caroline didn't know, and she was glad not to have to introduce Kip, to answer questions about herself or her mother.

Kip ordered coffee and a kolache.

Caroline said, "Just coffee for me, please."

The waitress left, and they watched her for a moment before facing each other.

"So," Kip said, "you're looking for your dad."

"Yes," Caroline answered. "We weren't on the best of terms. He remarried, and I wasn't—I didn't take the news very well."

"I recall him saying you were having a rough time with it."

"Really?"

"Yeah. You know, I went to Omaha to get a story, but your dad and I ended up being friends. He's never been too far out of my mind."

"Are you saying my dad confided in you?"

"We hit it off. I've always thought he was one of the better friends I've ever had. I've missed him."

Caroline toyed with her napkin.

"I still think about that business up there, the story, you know? It's like the fish that got away." Kip's grin was brief. "I took a lot of notes back then, and last night after we talked, I sat up reading them. You know his second wife, Julia, had a kid, Harris. I always thought he was a big part of Hoff's wish that y'all would work it out, that the four of you would be a family."

"Did you ever meet them? Julia and Harris?"

"Yeah. I spent a weekend in Wyatt once. Hoff bragged on Harris's skill on the football field so much I went down to catch one of his games. Harris was maybe ten at the time. The kid was an athlete for sure, big for his age, but watching him move, you would have thought he was a ballerina, he was so graceful, quick and agile. His hands and feet were huge. I told Hoff once Harris grew into those, he was going to make one hell of a quarterback."

Caroline shifted her glance, and her silence was overtaken by the buzz of breakfast conversation and the sharper clatter of dishes and cutlery. It amazed and irked her that she could still feel it, the sharp pinch of jealousy toward that boy. Of course, Harris was no longer a boy.

"I followed his career for several years even after I lost touch with Hoff. High school and college athletics—it's like its own small town. You get to know the players, the ones who show up regularly in the sports pages. Harris quit football. Did you know? Switched to baseball in junior high."

"That's hard to believe. Dad was always going on about what a natural he was."

"Yeah, well, what I read at the time, he was good at baseball too. Got a full ride to Texas A&M. Pitched and played first base four years for the Aggies, although he was sidelined by a back injury a lot of the time in his senior year. I imagine he would have tried out for the big leagues if it wasn't for that."

The waitress returned with their order.

"You never met him or his mom?" Kip asked when the waitress had gone.

"No." Caroline didn't elaborate.

Kip took a bite of his kolache and groaned in delight. "I might have to take a few of these back to Florida."

Caroline sipped her coffee. "You said you were working on a story when you were in Omaha. Was Dad involved in something there that was illegal?"

Kip sat back. "Do you know anything about the SMU recruiting scandal that blew up back in the eighties?"

"A little." After Lanie's recent mention of it and her description of how her dad had reacted to it, Caroline had looked it up online. "They were paying players, recruits, to come to school there. According to what I read, even the governor at the time, Bill Clements, was involved, wasn't he?"

"Yeah. He was on the board, just one of several bigwigs, SMU boosters and alumni, who were in the know, so to speak. They had athletes set up in their own apartments, sent money to their families. Even after SMU got sanctioned, they kept it up, paying recruits under the table. When the whole thing blew up, it cost SMU their entire 1987 season."

"I don't like believing my dad was involved in anything like that." Caroline remembered what her mother had said, that her dad might not have been the most honorable man when it came to his wedding vows, but he'd never compromise his professional relationships. As angry and as hurt as she'd been by her father's actions, Caroline agreed with her mom. She'd seen her dad in action, talking to the recruits. He'd loved those guys, wanted the best for them. But she'd been a kid herself when she'd traveled with him. Maybe she was only remembering what she wanted to.

Kip fiddled with his coffee mug. "Do you know how the business at SMU came to light?"

Caroline shook her head. She hadn't gotten that far in her research.

"The producer at a local Dallas TV station got a tip from a former SMU athletic-department employee. The producer decided to investigate. One thing led to another, and—well, you know the rest. My point is while SMU had been under investigation before, had even been penalized for violations prior to that time, it was this tipster who basically led to SMU's plug getting pulled, if you know what I mean."

"I'm not sure I do."

"The circumstances at Tillman were similar in those years. At the time that your dad was actively recruiting for Ryan Kelly, Tillman, like SMU, was a small school with an enrollment that barely qualified them as Division One. It was hard for them to compete with the big boys."

"So they paid players like Brick Coleman. Tricia said—I didn't want to believe her."

"Yeah, Brick—he was something. From his high school sophomore year—hell, maybe even from junior high—the recruiters were all over him like ducks on a june bug."

"It just doesn't seem like my dad, though. He was always so—when it came to those kids, he was like a preacher, talking about setting a good example, having a strong work ethic, not expecting to get things handed to you in life."

"Really, with Brick, all Hoff did was handle the transaction," Kip said, defending him. "Coach Kelly and several boosters and alumni—Brick's own uncle headed the pack—were the masterminds, if you will. Like SMU, the Tillman athletic department had a slush fund. A bunch of rich guys—again, Brick's uncle—kept it going. They wanted a winning team, and they were willing to pay to get it."

"After what happened with SMU, how could Dad or any of those men imagine they'd get away with it?" Caroline felt betrayed all over again.

"College sports is no different than any other business—it's all about the money. You know how that goes. With the kids, the athletes especially, it went to their heads. Even with Hoff, I remember him telling me what the extra cash could do for you and Harris."

Caroline sat back. Was that supposed to excuse him? That he'd had noble intentions? "What changed his mind?"

"Oddly, it was Brick himself."

"Tricia said they bought him a condo."

Kip hooted softly. "Yeah. She would have known. She and Brick had a thing going."

"I figured as much," Caroline said.

"She tell you what she did at the Blue Pearl?"

"She was one of the dancers."

"Did she also tell you she was into whatever guy could show her a good time? Your dad was a smart man about most things, but when it came to women, I think he was a little naive. It never crossed his radar screen when he introduced Brick to Tricia that she'd go for Brick behind his back. I'm pretty sure she was paid for it when she and Brick hooked up the first time. Not by your dad. Hoff told me he never messed with that part of it, getting women for the guys. He said he was no pimp—" Kip broke off. "You sure you want to hear all of this? The things your dad confided in me—the interview process can get pretty intimate. He confided a lot to me."

Caroline had never been good at hiding her emotions. "It's hard," she admitted, "but I need to know."

"All right. It's your call," Kip said, keeping her gaze.

Her nod was clipped.

Kip continued. "So your dad got Brick signed up at Tillman, and a few weeks later, when he was back in Omaha—this was during preseason—he went to see the kid. He wanted to check up on Brick, make sure he was doing okay. Your dad was like that. Once he made contact with an athlete and his family, he kept tabs on them. Your dad was a good guy that way."

Caroline's throat closed, hearing Kip's praise. She picked up the teaspoon she'd used to stir her coffee and set it down again.

"Hoff was blown away when he saw the condo. I never saw it, but he said it was swank, loaded with every kind of amenity. After Brick gave him the tour, they were out on the balcony that had a million-dollar view of the river, and your dad says to him, 'What the hell are you doing here?' And you want to know what Brick's answer was? He goes, 'I'm throwin' fuckin' TDs, bro. What the fuck are you doing?'"

"That's horrible."

"I hope you can forgive the language. But here's the point: your dad was shocked. Brick had always been quiet and respectful, grateful for the opportunity Hoff had arranged. Then within a few weeks, here the kid is, mouthing off, acting like he's the king and everybody should bow down. It hit your dad, like, right between the eyes, how wrong it was, paying these young guys, giving them all the perks. They were living like the rich and famous, getting treated like movie stars. It didn't matter if they made their grades. Hell, it didn't matter if they went to class. They were given a pass anyway." Kip paused, his gaze drifting.

Caroline nudged her coffee mug to one side. She felt faintly ill.

"You dad knew it was wrong, but he went along with it until he saw how it affected Brick. After that he didn't want to be part of it anymore." Kip caught her gaze. "You know it's all about the revenue with these colleges, all about drawing the big crowds. You've got to have a winning team, a coach who can win games, to make that happen. The pressure can be incredible."

Caroline wasn't moved by Kip's rationale, if that's what it was. "Was my dad getting paid too? Was he taking money to bring the best recruits to Tillman?"

"Yeah. But not after that day he went to Brick's condo. Hoff had heard I was nosing around, and he called me up. We met several times over the course of several weeks, off the record, so to speak. Hoff was giving me names, information. Like at SMU, he was the tipster who got the ball rolling on Tillman, or *over*, it would be more accurate to say."

"I was just at Coach Kelly's house." Caroline felt light headed. "He brought out all these photo albums and got all teary, looking at the pictures. He talked about how honored he was to have been a coach and mentor—mentor!"—she repeated it—"to so many great players. You would have thought they were his own kids."

"To be fair, Kelly was under the gun from the alumni. Like I said, Brick's uncle led the pack. They paid Kelly a king's ransom; he drove the newest Mercedes, flew first class, that kind of thing. He got results, too; he was riding high. But certain folks were starting to talk, asking questions among themselves. I know I was curious how the country's hottest football prospects were choosing Tillman over the powerhouse programs. It didn't take a genius to figure it out, and the whole thing was a house of cards, bound to come down. Hoff and I would have nailed them—"

"But Dad disappeared."

"Yeah, but really, the whole plan to expose Tillman fell apart before Hoff disappeared when he had the accident. Prior to that we'd planned for him to get into Coach Kelly's office, see if he could find anything—actual bank records were what we needed—to prove money was changing hands, how much, where, when, and to whom it was being paid. It would have been the nail in the coffin, so to speak, the hard evidence any investigative piece needs."

"But then he fell—"

"He never fully recovered his strength or his desire to do his job after that, much less go undercover for the story. He stopped answering my calls. It was like he didn't care anymore what happened. There wasn't much I could do. We'd gotten our hands on some of the paperwork, a memo or two, but it wasn't enough. I couldn't publish without more evidence . . ." Kip trailed off, some of the old disappointment he must have felt at the time lurking in his eyes. "That head injury did a number on Hoff for sure. I know he was in a lot of pain."

Caroline couldn't answer. Her throat was tight with sorrow, the old regret. Why hadn't she reached out? He was her dad, for God's sake.

Kip said, "There's something else."

Caroline met Kip's gaze.

"The last meeting we had?—I told Hoff I was going to the feds. Even though I didn't have the hard proof I felt was necessary to go to press, I had enough to show them something was going on. Hoff didn't like the idea. He got a bit riled, thought I was putting him in jeopardy even though I swore to him I'd never reveal a source. I'd sit in jail first. Had it come down to that, though, he'd have been granted immunity in exchange for his testimony."

"You told him that?"

"Yes, but he didn't buy it. He was—"

"Scared," Caroline finished, and at Kip's inquiring look, she said, "He wrote that he was in a letter to my mom."

"When was this?"

"August 1989." Even as she offered the date, it was coming together in her mind, the danger her dad had felt he was in and the very real threat that had been behind it. Her blood pooled heavily in her stomach.

"August of that year is the last time I saw him at Tricia's apartment. That's when I told him what I wanted to do." Kip leaned back, and Caroline saw he was putting it together too. "Holy Christ—"

It was out between them now—the chilling possibility that her dad hadn't left of his own free will. The notion had skittered like a rat through her mind before, but she'd run it off. Now that was impossible. "Could one of those guys have found out Dad was working with you, that you intended to expose them, and decided to put a stop to it?"

"I don't know." Kip frowned, considering. "Maybe Brick's uncle. We called him Tex, but he's a Nebraska native, and his name is Farley, Farley Dade."

"Tricia mentioned him."

"He's a Tillman graduate and still a big shot there on campus. He owns Dade Oil, among other companies. Back in the eighties he was probably the biggest source of revenue for the slush fund, but the whole time he was funneling cash into that scam, he was fronting an image of the do-gooding benefactor, claiming Tillman's football program set the standard for young men, encouraging them to become heroes, not only on the football field but in every aspect of their lives."

"What a liar. And he's still involved at Tillman?" Caroline felt a jolt of anger mixed with disgust, and it steadied her.

"He's president of the alumni board, last I knew. Brick is a trustee."

"You're serious."

"I'm afraid so, and now I heard Coach Kelly, old Big Dog, is a Hall of Fame nominee."

Caroline shook her head.

"It flat-out burns me up, thinking how these guys gamed the system, and now Kelly's going to be honored for it?"

"What would happen if the story broke now? Would it have an effect?"

"Hell yes. Maybe not legally or sanctionwise, but the guys involved—they're all like Farley, prominent in the business community. There's even a government official or two who participated. They have wives and families and reputations to protect. They wouldn't want so much as a whiff of this garbage getting out." Kip leaned forward. "Why? You look worried."

"Do you know Coach Kelly's son, Jace?"

"Not personally. We've never met. He's head football coach at Tillman now, right?"

"Yes," Caroline said, and she went on, filling Kip in on her visit with Ryan Kelly. She described Jace's seeming hostility toward her that had built throughout her visit and how he'd practically strong-armed her from the house. She related the details of the accident that had occurred directly following her departure. She said, "The cop told me there wasn't any sign of another driver. The nurse said my head injury could have caused me to imagine someone hit me. But it's still so real in my mind—that there was someone behind me who forced me off the road. They came up to my car afterward, opened the door, said my name. No one in Omaha knows my name but Jace and his dad. I just don't think I could have dreamed all of it, you know?"

"You said you went to the Tillman campus before going over to Kelly's house. Who did you talk to there?" Kip asked.

"A trainer, Alexa somebody."

"Did you mention your dad to her? Did you say you were looking for him?"

"Well, yes. I was trying to get Coach Kelly's address, and I thought she'd be more likely to give it to me if I told her the circumstances—that my aunt was dying and I needed to find my dad."

"You played the sympathy card. Did it work?"

"No. It was sheer luck that ultimately got me to Coach Kelly's house." Caroline kept Kip's gaze. "You aren't thinking—?"

"I doubt Farley would have called the welcome-wagon folks if he heard about your visit and the reason for it. Maybe you should go to the cops."

Caroline's breath shallowed. "What are you saying?"

"Think about it. You show up on campus and say you're looking for your dad—a guy who disappeared right about the time I'm telling him I'm going to the feds, which in itself is pretty suspicious—then after you leave the Kellys' house, someone deliberately runs you off the road? Who else could it be but the son of the coach who was on the take?"

"When Jace came to the hotel the day after my accident, he told me not to stir the pot, that I might not like what floated to the top."

"Bingo."

"So if it was him, if Jace did cause my accident, was he trying to scare me into giving up the search for my dad?" A flare of new panic needled her skin.

"Look"—Kip bent his weight on his elbows—"if Jace knows what his dad was involved in, he's got to be as invested as Farley and Brick and the rest of that gang of liars and cheats in covering it up. You and your search for your dad could be making them a little crazy, a little paranoid." Kip sat back. "You can never tell what men—what a bunch of snakes like that—will do when they're desperate."

"But it was thirty years ago," she said, as if Kip hadn't already indicated the passage of so much time was of little consequence when big egos and bigger reputations were at stake.

"Like I said before, there's as much on the line, personally, for them now as there was back then. Kelly's got a Hall of Fame nomination riding on this thing. And Farley—you know what he used to say?"

Caroline shook her head.

"That he'd walked with great men, that he *was* one of the greats. This story comes out, he's not gonna look so great then, is he?"

"Jace told me his dad was the winningest coach in Tillman history."

"It's true."

"How could Jace brag on his dad like that if he knows what he did to get there? Why would he send me to Tricia? It seems counterintuitive, considering she was involved—maybe not directly, but she knew *something* was going on at Tillman. She knew about you, that you were investigating it."

"Who knows? She had a thing with Brick back in the day. Maybe she and Brick and good old Uncle Farley cooked up some plan."

"One that involved running me off the road? That's so crazy." She suppressed a shiver.

"Yeah, well, that's the thing about fear. You tend to go off half-cocked. You don't think so straight. Maybe Jace was just trying to get you out of Omaha, divert your attention. Who knows?"

Caroline cupped her elbows in her palms.

Kip said, "There's something else you should know."

Caroline looked at him, reluctant to know more, although had Kip invited her to walk away, she wouldn't have.

"Rumors Hoff and I heard back then indicated that certain business owners, including Farley, wire transferred money from their commercial accounts into accounts they set up for players and in some cases the players' families."

She straightened. "Are you serious?" In the world of sports recruiting, even she knew that was about as wrong as it could get.

"I'm afraid so. Hoff managed to get a copy of a memo that Dade wrote to Kelly where he indicated some funds would be placed in a certain numbered account. What we needed was a copy of the actual bank transaction. Had we gotten that, had I been able to incorporate that into the story, once it published, the NCAA would have hopped all over it. Hell, even the FBI might have gotten involved. What those guys were doing—it was bank fraud. That's a federal crime. They could have done time."

"The memo wasn't enough?"

"I wanted something stronger, something irrefutable, if I could get it, and I was willing to wait. Of course, it's been long enough now that the statute of limitations has run out."

"So there wouldn't be any legal consequences if these guys were to be exposed."

"No, only personal. But you know, the contributions you feel you've made over your lifetime, the legacy you feel you've built—to have all that ruined by some nasty old scandal getting exposed all over the place—" Kip broke off, shrugging.

Caroline pushed away the mug of coffee the waitress had brought. She'd barely drunk any of it.

"College sports is a pretty small world," Kip went on. "Everybody knows everybody else, and when someone goes down, the rest of us— the rest of the world—can't get enough. We're like vultures at the feast."

"You're talking about media coverage. It would be all over the news."

"I think so, yes."

"You would know, I guess."

"It is my profession."

"Will you resurrect the story now?"

"You mean if you were to find your dad? Probably not, for the same reason I couldn't publish it at the time: lack of hard evidence."

Caroline got out her car keys. "I've kept you long enough."

Kip brushed off her comment with a small sweep of his hand. He insisted on paying the check and walking her to her car. He said if he could be of further help, she should call him. "Will you keep me posted on your search? I'd love to know if you find him."

"I will," Caroline said.

"You'll be careful? I'm serious about you talking to the cops. It couldn't hurt to go on the record, so to speak."

"I've got someone in mind for that," Caroline said. "An old friend I went to high school with. He's a sheriff's deputy." She refrained from speaking his name. It was business, nothing personal.

"Good," Kip said. He looked relieved.

Watching the reporter cross the parking lot to his car, she had a hunch that regardless of his reservations regarding hard evidence, when she found her dad, Kip would resurrect the story. He'd rewrite it, of course, and it scared her, as she wondered how it would end.

12

He keeps still on waking, holding on for as long as he can to the vain belief that where he is—on his belly, feet hanging off a too-short bed—is a dream and not the bald fact and circumstance of his life now. But he knows—knows this bed is his kid bed. The one his mom has kept all these years in his kid room in her house, the big white farmhouse on 14.9 acres eleven miles outside Wyatt. Eleven miles from the home in town that he shares with his wife and his sons—his family that he loves more than—

If you loved us, you would stop.

That declaration Holly throws in his face on a regular basis whispers through Harris's brain, a truth he doesn't want to hear. *Stop the drug taking; stop the lying about it.* Holly thinks that's the extent of it—his crimes, his sins. She doesn't know the half.

Harris plants his face in his pillow, stifling the sound that wants to come—some god-awful noise—jamming it against his ribs. Holly and Connor and Kyle will be at the breakfast table about now, talking about

Harris. Holly will be doing her best to explain why Dad is gone. Harris needs help, she'll say; he isn't in any shape to be their father right now. *He's not the man I married.* Harris hears her voice in his brain. *Or any sort of man at all.* His mind takes it a step further.

It half kills him, thinking of Kyle and Connor, how they'll react. Kyle's disgust, his sneering dismissal of Harris, is a given. Connor is younger, softer. He'll be bewildered and sad. *Come home, Dad. Why can't you just stop taking that stuff, Dad?* Harris imagines Connor will say—or something like it. How will he face his sons? He doesn't even know how he'll get out of this bed and face his mother.

He rolls onto his back. She let him off the hook last night when he showed up on her porch. He rang the bell like a stranger. He felt like one. He does still. He belongs—fits—nowhere. *I don't know who you are anymore,* Holly said to him last night. He doesn't recognize himself, Harris thinks. He doesn't know how his life got so fouled up.

A soft rapping draws his glance to the closed bedroom door.

"I'm in the kitchen," his mother says. "I've made coffee."

He hears her footsteps retreat, her light tread on the stair.

Time to fess up, pay the piper, face the music.

Harris stares at the ceiling. He can't think what story he can invent, what line he can come up with, that his mother won't see the lie right through. He is so tired anyway of the deceit. But he can't think how to set down the burden, the millstone he is around his own neck. He wishes he had someone to talk to. A friend. A real one and not some shrink who's paid to act the part. There's Zeke, but Harris has clouded the relationship with so much half truth and subterfuge he has no idea how to sort it out. Zeke won't stand for it, anyway, once he knows how he's been used.

It's Hoff Harris wants, whom he wishes he could talk to, and the want is an ache, a gaping hole in the dead center of his heart, one that feels as fresh as if it were new. He can't sort out where it's coming from, why it feels so raw now after all these years. But lately everything hurts.

His heart, his brain. It is pain that feels soul deep. Harris settles his elbow over his eyes, burning now.

He thinks of when he and his mom left Oklahoma, the fear that drove them from there. Something else he has to hide, that he can't talk about. It seems he's been afraid ever since. Afraid and alone. Isolated. Abandoned. What if he were to go back, find his birth father, and look him in the face? What would he see? A man or a monster? Would it settle anything, bring him peace, some of that elusive closure he's heard so much about? But he can't lie here feeling sorry for himself. His mom is downstairs; she wants to talk. He thinks of how the conversation will go, how she'll try to dig it out of him, what's wrong, what's happening. She'll name ways to fix it, fix him. He thinks of the extra fentanyl patch Zeke gave him. The war of his thoughts sets his head on fire.

. . .

Harris meets his mother's glance briefly on entering the kitchen and acknowledges her "good morning" with his own. They are both somber. He pours coffee for himself, holds out the carafe, an offering.

"I'm fine," she says.

He flips a chair around, sits on it backward. It's a habit from his kid days—like the back of the chair puts a barrier between him and his mother, her glances that are too penetrating, too all-seeing. The tile floor under his bare feet is cold. The patch on his upper arm itches. He holds his coffee mug firmly in his hands.

"So," she says.

"I'm sorry," he begins, then stops.

She waits.

Harris drops his gaze. Their shared history crowds the air between them, rife with the old panic, the images that he knows haunt her dreams as well as his own. Sometimes Harris thinks they're more bound by the nightmare they lived through than they are even by love. Her only wish is—has always been—for his happiness. How often has she told him that? He thinks not for the first time how lucky he is to have her for his mother. She's always here for him no matter what, a constant in his life. Except for the brief handful of years when Hoff was here, she has had sole responsibility for Harris, raising him, providing for him, protecting him on her own. When he was growing up, she made a thing of it, saying they were partners, a dynamic duo, their own Batman and Robin. He meets her glance, asking if she remembers, and he's glad for her smile, but it doesn't last. He wishes he could say something, do something, to make it last.

"Holly called me," she says.

"Again?"

"She's upset, Harris. You aren't communicating—"

"I tried the other day. She had an appointment." He's pissed, and he knows he's got no right to be, but it's as if Holly is tattling on him. What does she want his mom to do? Ground him?

"It goes deeper than one attempt on your part, and you know it. I'm sorry, but she's right—if you're not willing to face that you have a drug problem, she's right to send you packing."

"Gee, thanks for the vote of confidence, Mom."

"Harris, look at yourself."

Her stare is fixed on his hands, holding his mug, shaking it badly enough that some slops over the edge. He sets it down.

"You need to get help, Harris. If you can't do it for yourself, do it for Holly and your sons. I know they mean the world to you—"

"Do you ever think about him?"

"Hoff? Why do you keep asking me that?" Her hand goes to her heart. "No. Why are you—?"

"I wish we'd known his daughter. Caroline. Wasn't that her name?"

"Yes, but she didn't want to know us, remember? We tried to make her part of our family. I made over a bedroom for her. We did all we could to make her feel welcome, but she—"

"Was jealous." Harris repeats the explanation he was given. His mom and Hoff said Caroline would come around. She never did.

"Can you tell me what's brought this on?" His mom is wearing her shrink look.

Harris drops his glance. "Do you ever think about what our lives might be like if Hoff were still here? I mean like when you were first married to him? I do," he says quickly before his mom can answer. "I know it's stupid," he adds, looking up at her. Her eyes are wide, startled. He looks away again. "I'd probably have gone pro, don't you think? I'd never have quit football, that's for sure."

"Oh, Harris, I know. I have always been sorry that you lost that too." An underscore of futility threads her voice.

He gets his mug to his mouth, manages to drink.

"Are you buying drugs from Zeke, Harris?" She has her eyes on his hands, the way they shake.

Harris sets down his mug.

She goes on. "It's what Holly suspects—"

"Holly doesn't know everything about me, and neither do you."

A stunned silence follows his declaration. He's hurt her, and he's sorry, but if he tells her, he'll lose it. Everything will come out. He can't do it to her, can't cause her more pain. He just can't. "It's the issue with the kid at school—it's on my mind," he says instead.

"But you won't say what it is."

"I can't."

"Can't or won't?"

He doesn't answer.

"Holly's worried it's something to do with Kyle, and that's why you won't talk about it."

"She needs to trust me."

"Trust in a relationship is a two-way street. It's wrong to keep secrets from her, Harris."

He locks her gaze, and he sees the dark and bitter flash of her comprehension knife through the shadows in her eyes as she takes his meaning.

The moment, burning with the remembrance of their secrets, lingers, elongates.

"I don't know how to help you, how to help your family," she says finally.

Her voice trembles, and any thought Harris had of laying it out for her, the truth he couldn't tell Holly—that Gee is the problem, the ongoing issue, and why—evaporates now as if it never existed. It would be a relief to get it out, and he could damn sure use his mother's advice. But as strong as she is, hearing Gee is behind the robberies, how he's got Harris jammed up in his thievery, that even Kyle may be implicated, will be too much. She's been through enough in her life. "It's all right, Ma. I'll work it out."

He might have said more to reassure her, but the sound of the doorbell, followed by three sharp raps of the knocker, cuts him off. His gaze collides with his mother's. She shrugs in answer to his unasked question. She doesn't know who is there.

Harris stands, pulse tapping. "It's probably Holly." Or Kyle, he thinks, ready to have it out with his old man, give Harris hell. But it isn't a member of his family waiting on the doorstep. It's the police, specifically the police captain, Clint Mackie.

Harris's knees loosen. His head goes light. It's all he can do to return the police captain's greeting. The sergeant, Ken Carter, is nowhere in sight. Mackie's alone.

"Captain Mackie." Harris's mom joins them. She's wearing a cardigan over a long-sleeved tee, and she's holding the sweater's front edges in a tight, white-knuckled grip. But she couldn't be more shaken than Harris.

"Good morning, Julia," the captain says. "I'm sorry to bother you folks on a Saturday morning."

"We just spoke at school yesterday."

Harris's mother sounds totally mystified. A silence ensues, growing long enough to become awkward.

"How can I help you?" Harris's mom finally asks. "Do you want to come in? The coffee's fresh."

"I just need a word with Harris. In private?" Mackie looks meaningfully at Harris.

"No," Harris says. "I'm sure whatever this is about, my mom can hear it." He isn't sure, not at all, but to exclude her would only raise suspicion. He exchanges a glance with her, and her eyes are so anxious he almost reverses his decision. But she's already opening the door, and Mackie is following her down the hall. Harris has no choice but to fall in behind them. Dread weights his steps.

"There was another break-in last night," Mackie says, once they're seated at the kitchen table.

Harris's heart sinks.

His mom sets a steaming mug of coffee in front of Mackie. He waves away her offer of cream and sugar. "Todd Sullivan's house."

Todd plays for the Wyatt Warriors; he's a linebacker. A good kid and so-so player with nice parents. Harris clenches his teeth. Fucking Gee! He's broken his promise, gone off and robbed his own teammate? *What a damn bastard!*

His mother is offering condolences. She knows Penny Sullivan, Todd's mother. Penny works in the office at Wyatt High.

Mackie says, "Yeah, she's pretty shook up. Here's the thing, though. We got a call early this morning, somebody anonymous, claiming they know who did it."

Harris's head comes up.

"Who?" his mom asks.

"They named Gander Drake—Gee." Mackie addresses Harris, his stare unwavering.

Harris can feel his mother looking at him too. Now she'll put it together herself that Gee is the student, the one Harris is having the issue with, the thief he's protecting.

"Gee's been questioned," Mackie says, "prior to this latest break-in along with a lot of other students. Just in general, you know. But then this tip came in, so I went by and questioned him again before coming out here. I talked to both him and his dad."

"What did he say?" Harris asks.

"Swore he had nothing to do with it, robbing the Sullivans or anyone else." Mackie looks at Harris. "He says as far as last night is concerned, you can vouch for him. He claims you saw him in the weight room. He was working out. He'd had an argument with his mom, something about a missed dental appointment. He said he had to blow off some steam."

Harris is dumbfounded. He's known Gee was twisted, but he never knew he'd go so far as to use Harris to alibi himself. He never saw this coming. But now fury punches through his disbelief. Heat builds at his temples, behind his eyes. *Don't let it show*, he warns himself. "When was it—the break-in?" Harris stalls for time. His mind is a train wreck.

"Dinnertime. The Sullivans were out to eat. They left the house around six thirty, and when they got back around eight, they found the back door ajar. Your wife says you were gone around that same time last night. You weren't home for dinner. Is that right?"

"You went to my house?" Harris's mouth is dry. It's all he can do to stay seated, appear calm. He has no idea if his act is working.

"I talked to your son—"

"Kyle?"

"The younger one. Connor. He showed me his cast, said he broke his finger at baseball practice last week. That's tough so early in the season. He said he's lobbying his coach for permission to play anyway."

Harris's mom laughs, but the sound is forced. "He told me the same thing. If anyone could do it, though, it would be Connor."

Harris wonders, When did his mother speak to Connor? After Holly was done complaining her ear off? "Did you talk to my wife, too, this morning?" Harris asks Mackie.

"Yes. She's the one who said I could find you here at your mother's."

Harris can't even imagine how bad it would wind Holly up, finding a cop on her doorstep on a Saturday morning. He wonders how much worse it can get.

"It's not a problem, is it?" The captain's look is intent.

"Of course not."

"So you can vouch for Gee? What time did you see him? He said y'all talked for a while. About what time was it? You remember?"

Harris grabs his mug, taking a swallow, making a show of it, mind clattering over the possibilities—that the captain will know it's a lie if Harris covers for Gee. But what choice has he got? Maybe Mackie's only looking for confirmation of what he wants to believe. Maybe he's like everybody else, and he looks up to Gee, Wyatt's own hometown hero and star, a role model younger kids can idolize. Maybe Mackie even thinks Harris is a good guy.

"You saw him?" the captain prompts. "You saw Gee in the weight room at the high school between six thirty and eight, eight fifteen last night?"

"Yeah, I had some paperwork to catch up on." It kills Harris, covering for Gee. He wants to out the punk, call his bluff, and let him fry. Harris would do it, too, if he were the only one who would be affected by the consequences, if his family wouldn't also suffer. There's barely a snowball's chance in hell now of making it right with them, but even that will disappear if they learn one of his students, his players, is Harris's drug supplier. Harris has got to go along with Gee, play his dirty game. He can't lose his family . . . he's nothing without them. It nearly levels him, thinking this, but he can't allow it. He meets Mackie's gaze. "I was there, in and out of the office during that time, and I did see Gee. We visited a bit. I left the school around nine or so." Harris names the time he left Zeke's. He forces himself to hold Mackie's gaze.

The captain nods. "I figured the tip was bogus, but we've got to check." He sips his coffee and goes on, talking about the improbability of a kid with Gee's talent and prospects being dumb enough to risk his future breaking in to houses. "Unless he's in it for the thrill." Mackie's glance shifts from Harris to his mom. "That's kind of how it's beginning to look, as if it's more than one kid, and they're out for excitement."

"How do they get in?" Harris's mother asks.

"Oh, they've got expertise, the right tools. I'll give them that. The homeowners never suspect a thing until they get inside and find stuff missing. Electronics, jewelry, cash. Just the small stuff they can handle easily."

"Scary," Harris's mother says.

"A lot of folks are loading their guns, sitting up nights. We need to get who's responsible before somebody gets hurt."

No one says anything for a moment. It is everything Harris can do to remain in his chair.

"About Gee," Mackie begins, and he waits for Harris to meet his eyes. "What's he got now—like, five offers on the table? I heard Oklahoma's in the mix. Any clue who he'll sign with?"

"His dad played for Penn State, and they're all over Gee, but his mom and granddad are UT alums. It's a toss-up right now, but if I had to bet, I'd say UT."

"Folks here in Wyatt'll be glad if he stays in state, close by. He'd get a crowd at his home games for sure, his own cheerleading section."

They all three stand, and Harris leads the way from the kitchen, down the hall to the front door. Mackie pauses on the threshold, and turning to Harris, he says, "There's just one other thing."

Harris's heart stalls. *Keep it together, keep it together . . .* A voice rasps advice in his brain. But he's cracking under the stress. He can feel his resolve softening, weakening.

"The caller this morning—"

"Was it a man or a woman?" Harris hadn't realized he would ask, but suddenly he wants to know. A suspicion has grown in his mind that

Zeke is the caller, that the old man has gone back on his word, although Harris knows in his core the sun would burn out first.

"I'd rather not say," the captain answers. "The person claimed Gee was selling drugs too. Opioids, mainly. The caller said we'd find them in his car."

"Did you?" His mom asks the question he doesn't have breath for.

"No, but then I didn't figure I would." Mackie looks from Harris to his mom. "Y'all ever hear a rumor about Gee dealing drugs?"

"No, sir," Harris says. At least this is the truth. He never has heard so much as a whisper about Gee's drug dealing.

"I can't imagine it," his mom says.

"Yeah, me either. Makes me wonder—cop mind, you know—" Mackie points to his head. "What motivated the caller? I figure it's someone who's jealous of the kid or his family. Sometimes it doesn't pay to be rich, does it? Some folks want to cut you down, make you pay out of spite."

Mackie opens the door. He's got one foot over the threshold when he turns back. "I guess y'all wouldn't know of anyone who'd have a reason to set him up?"

Zeke Roman. Even as Harris shakes his head no, the name sits behind his teeth, despite his conviction that the old man wouldn't break his word. It's chilly in the open doorway, but in his panic, Harris is sweating.

His mom answers that she has no idea either.

Mackie addresses her. "What about drug dealing taking place on campus at the high school—you ever hear a rumor about that?"

"Heavens no," she says, offended, appalled—some combination. "Have you?"

"A time or two." Mackie looks off toward his cop cruiser, parked in the drive. "If it's true, it makes me wonder if the robberies are connected. It's probably nothing. A lot of talk. But if it is kids breaking in to folks' homes, drugs might be what they're looking for, or the cash to buy drugs, or items they can pawn for money or trade for drugs—you see where I'm going with this."

Harris doesn't respond. No way can he trust his voice. Inside he's jelly, weak with disbelief.

Beside him, his mother shakes her head. She says she can't imagine it.

Mackie's sympathetic. He says he can understand how it's hard to believe. "Here's the thing, though—we keep hearing the students talk to y'all. They trust you. So I'm thinking if anybody were to get the lowdown, so to speak, it would be one of you." Mackie divides his glance between Harris and his mom, and Harris gets the sense the cop is waiting for one of them to confirm knowledge of the situation he's already in possession of. Mackie will whip out the cuffs next. He'll read Harris his rights. Harris's blood sluices through his veins.

An improbable half smile quirks Mackie's lips. "Remembering my days as a jock at Wyatt High, there's a lot of talk goes on in a locker room."

"Yeah," Harris says. "Most of it BS. You know how full of it young guys are." He laughs, a truncated sound.

Mackie grins, looks again at Harris's mom. "You're obligated to report drug activity on campus, right? Zero tolerance and all that."

"Yes, Captain. I know my legal and professional responsibilities and take them very seriously."

"All right, then." Mackie gives them a short nod. "Y'all have a good day."

"You too, Captain," Harris's mother says.

Harris offers no such felicitations. He watches with his mom as the cop walks to his squad car. Once he's inside it, Harris closes the front door, bending his forehead against it. His relief is short lived.

"*What* is going on?" His mother's voice behind him is as sharp as a razor.

He straightens, and he's in the process of saying, "It's nothing," when she interrupts him, warning him not to say that, not to put her off.

"I know better," she says, and when he turns to her, her eyes are hard on his.

13

Caroline—Saturday, January 13

M artha answered Caroline's knock, looking grim. She held open the door.

"What happened?" Caroline came inside, anxious eyes on Martha's face.

"Lanie fell in the night last night, trying to get herself to the bathroom. I found her when I got here this morning. Heaven only knows how long she was lying on that cold floor. She was shaking all over. She's just now quit it."

"What did the doctor say?"

"She won't let me call him. She says she's tired. She let me check her over, and I didn't feel anything broken, but she needs x-rays, a CAT scan, something beyond what a retired nurse like me can do."

"She is so stubborn."

"I know, but she did agree to move downstairs. I pulled some strings and got a hospital bed moved into the dining room this morning."

"Oh, Martha, you're a wonder." Caroline gave the woman a hug.

Martha was embarrassed, but she seemed pleased. "It was what needed to be done," she said when Caroline released her. "You go on in there now. She'll be glad to see you."

"Well, look what beauty has come through my door this morning." Fatigue shadowed the delight in Lanie's eyes.

Caroline went to her bedside and, taking her hand gently, bent to kiss her aunt's cheek. "Are you all right? Martha said you fell."

"She makes too much of things. What do you think of my new digs?"

Caroline looked over her shoulder through the windows at the patio and the garden beyond it. "You have a lovely view."

"I hope someone will care for the flower beds in the spring," Lanie said.

"Oh, Auntie Lanie, please, please say you'll see your doctor." Caroline's voice broke, and she regretted it, but it was unbearable watching her aunt slip away. She could feel it, how little time was left.

Lanie patted her arm. "I know you're sad, honey, and I'm sorry for it, truly, but don't hold on to that sadness. Promise me. Feel it if you have to, but then let it go, won't you?"

"I don't know how to be here in this world without you, though." Caroline sounded like a child crying for the moon, and it was a terrible thing putting the burden of her grief on Lanie, as if dying weren't burden enough. "I'm sorry," she whispered.

"It's all right, honey. I'm so glad I mean so much to you, grateful for the chance I was given to see you grow into the beautiful woman you are; to have shared that has been such a gift. We have a lot of love between us, don't we?"

"Yes," Caroline said. "I'm so thankful for it, for you. I know I have to let you go—" She clenched her teeth against the sob that rose in her throat.

"You'll be fine, sweet, fine as frog's hair."

Caroline smiled at the well-loved joke. "You can't be finer than that, can you?"

Lanie gave Caroline's arm a final pat. "Tell me what you've been up to. Bring a dining chair over here."

"I've got some news about Dad." Caroline retrieved one of the linen-upholstered chairs to Lanie's bedside. "I don't want to wear you out, though."

"No, don't worry. I want to hear."

"I met with an investigative reporter this morning. He knew Dad back in the late eighties. They were close friends, in fact." At Lanie's prompting, Caroline went on, recounting her conversation with Kip Penny, picking her words carefully to soften the presence of any threat, wanting in the worst way to cast her dad in a kinder light. She might have saved herself the trouble.

By the time she was finished, Lanie's disgust and disappointment were evident in her expression. "So at the very least Hoff knew the athletes were being bribed to play," she said.

"I hate it, too, but at least he was trying to make it right." Caroline gave her aunt the ray of light she clung to.

"What he wrote to your mom, that he was scared, it makes sense now." Lanie raised her hands, brought them down, a futile gesture. "It's my fault—"

"No, Aunt Lanie, don't take it on yourself." Caroline was dismayed.

"If only we'd been on better terms, though, Hoff might have come to me. He must have felt so alone. If I could go back—if I could just know he's all right." Her fingers worried the coverlet.

Caroline set her hand over them, holding them still, feeling Lanie's pain, fighting her own regret. "We'll find him, I promise," she said, and her voice was unsteady even as her brain warned she had no business making such promises. "The private investigator you called—when was it?" she asked after a moment.

"Probably a month or two after the Christmas holiday in 1989. I would have waited longer had it been any other time of year. I was so accustomed to going weeks without a word from him, you know, because he traveled so much. There weren't such things as cell phones then. He'd have to pull off the road, find a phone booth. But he'd do it. Especially at holiday time. You remember."

Caroline did. Holidays and birthdays, hers and Lanie's, were the occasions when her dad would make the effort to get in touch no matter where he was or how far away. She remembered the clinking sound the coins made when he dropped them into the pay phone. She'd been seventeen in 1989, still angry and hurt, and she hadn't cared when there'd been no call and no gift from him that year under Lanie's tree. She hadn't thought twice about it.

"I had a bad feeling," Lanie said. "That's why I called Julia, and when she didn't know anything, I went to the police, for all the good it did. I thought surely an investigator would be able to track Hoff, but he never found a thing."

"Do you still have his contact information?"

"I should, in my address book, in my desk upstairs. His name was Thomas Williams, no, Williamson. I believe Williamson was his last name."

"Be right back," Caroline said.

Lanie's eyes were closed when Caroline returned. She picked up her purse, and her hand was hovering above Lanie's brow when her eyes fluttered open. "I didn't want to wake you."

"I do this, just drop off." Lanie smiled.

"I found Mr. Williamson's number. I'll call him. Who knows? Maybe we'll get lucky."

"You'll let me know."

"Of course. And you rest. Mind Martha, okay? Otherwise you'll have to deal with me, and she's a lot nicer."

"Ha! You are some meanie."

"What is it?" the somber note in her aunt's gaze prompted Caroline to ask.

"Honey, I think we have to accept that your dad's death is a possibility."

Having Lanie put it into words, the outcome they both dreaded, made it sharply real. Caroline closed her eyes, shook her head.

"I know you don't want to consider it, but we have to be prepared. Hoff could have died of any number of things by now. A stroke, a heart attack. Cancer, like me. Even natural causes . . ."

Or unnatural ones. That was Caroline's thought, but not one she would share with Lanie.

· · ·

Caroline was on her way back to her mother's house when her phone chimed. Pulling to the curb, she tugged it from her purse, and her heart shifted on seeing Rob's name in the caller ID window. She hadn't answered his calls since returning from Wichita to Houston. In response, his messages had become increasingly plaintive. Why was she avoiding him? When was she coming home? He needed her. Their business was suffering. That bit was laughable. It wasn't *their* business. Not in the way she had understood it to be.

But she couldn't put off talking to him any longer. Late yesterday when he'd called, he'd said if he didn't hear from her within twenty-four hours, he'd come to Houston. She didn't want that; she wasn't ready.

"Finally," he said when she answered.

"I've been busy," she said.

"Things are falling apart here," he said. "I'm falling apart."

"You're just worried I'm going to turn you in," she said.

"Are you?"

A beat.

"What do you want me to do, Caro?" he demanded when she didn't respond. "Go to jail?"

"I don't know." It was the truth.

"Fucking do it! Turn me in, if that's what you want, and get it over with. I can't live this way."

"*You* can't live this way? You did this, Rob! You told the lies, put us and our employees and their families at risk! You compromised me, my integrity, my word. You and only you! I didn't know—"

"You could have, if you'd wanted to."

Caroline jerked upright as if he'd slapped her. "What?"

"You had access to the forms. Anytime you wanted to see the paperwork, you could have. You're a partner, an *equal* partner—"

"Instead I trusted *you*—my *partner*."

"This isn't productive—"

Caroline cut him off. "In addition to helping with the business, I was raising our daughter, Rob. I was baking cookies for her to take to class; I was going to teacher conferences when you were tied up with work; I made sure we ate healthy and had clothes on our backs. I took Nina to her piano lessons and softball practice."

The silence that fell was heated, blind.

Rob broke it. "Remember our first house, the snowman you, Nina, and I built in the yard after we moved in?"

Caroline didn't answer, although she did remember. Nina had just turned two. New Wheaton, their company, had been struggling but had finally shown a profit big enough to finance the purchase. They'd been happy, celebratory. They'd thought of having another child, a sister or brother for Nina, but it hadn't happened.

"The heat was always going out," Rob said. "We'd have to all three pile in the bed to stay warm."

"You sang lullabies until Nina and I fell asleep." Rob had a beautiful voice, low and soothing. When he and Caroline had danced together, he used to hold her close and whisper sing the words to love songs in her ear.

"When I saw you at Drake the first time—we were at the library. Do you remember that day?" he asked, and Caroline thought he was attempting to woo her, distract her. It made her sad. "I thought you were the most beautiful girl I'd ever seen. You still are."

She stared through the windshield. Rob had sat down across from her at the library on campus; he'd struck up a conversation, which she'd wanted to ignore. She'd been in running-away mode still, having left home a scant week earlier, and desperately trying to convince herself she'd been right to break her connection to her mom and dad, their issues, her past, all the drama. *And Steve* . . .

The appearance of his name in her mind now, coupled with the rest, startled her. *Steve: the road not taken.* It was the way she'd come to think of him and their failed romance. She had not taken that road because she couldn't handle the risk of love that had been too lovely and too huge. Love that was gone now, that she hadn't any right to anyway. And who knew where that road would have led had she had the courage to walk down it? But she didn't want these ideas—these feelings inside her heart, this doubt that confused and shamed her.

"Rob?" she said. "I can't—I'm not coming home. Lanie fell last night, and when I saw her just now—it's really beginning to hit me—I'm going to lose her. She's not going to recover. I need to be here, with her, with Mom."

"I'm sorry about Lanie," Rob said, "but *I* need you, Caro. We're in this together. You have as much to lose as I do."

"It's not enough to blame me; you have to threaten me too?" Fury knotted her brow. She gripped the steering wheel.

"I'm not—"

"How many times do I have to say it? We aren't in this together, and even if we were, *you* have to make it right. You have to do the right thing."

"Are you saying you won't turn me in?"

The hope in his voice on the heels of what had seemed like his warning struck Caroline as bizarre. She bent her head to her knuckled fist. "I can't handle this right now, Rob."

He started to speak, to wheedle or argue, Caroline didn't know. "I have to go," she said, and she ended the call before he could respond.

• • •

Her mother was at the dining table leafing through a photo album when Caroline came home. "You were such a happy little girl," she said. "Look at you in this picture. You were three. We were in Galveston. You loved the beach, dirty as it was. I swear I can almost hear you giggling."

Caroline bent over her mom's shoulder, peering at the image of her child self. She was in her bathing suit, sitting upright on her dad's shoulders. He was holding her ankles. She had her hands knotted under his chin. She'd probably been choking him, but they were both laughing, eyes scrunched, mouths open. It opened an old ache inside her. "I wished for a long time that I'd been born a boy," she said.

Her mother looked up sharply.

"I thought at least then Dad would have had the son he wanted."

The line between her mother's eyebrows deepened. A complication of emotions troubled her expression. "Your dad wanted you—"

"I know. I didn't mean—it's just he would have been so thrilled if he'd had a son, you know. A kid who could compete, be an athlete, a real football player. That's why he took to Harris. Maybe Harris was even the draw with Julia."

"What has brought this on? Lanie? Is she the one feeding you this nonsense?"

"No, Lanie would never—"

"I'm sad that she's dying, but I hate how she's got you mixed up in this wild-goose chase after your dad, and now she's filling your head with these absurd ideas. No one, no other child, could ever replace you in your dad's heart, Caro. Certainly not Harris Fenton."

"Lanie's never said Dad didn't want me or anything close—"

"I've told you before: He left me and our marriage. He didn't leave you. He was there, too, when Lanie took you, as much as he could be."

"I know. I didn't mean to upset you. I'm just saying it's not fair to blame Aunt Lanie for how I feel."

Her mother was trembling when she closed the photo album cover. "No other child could have ever replaced you in my heart either, Caro."

Her mother's eyes when she looked up at Caroline were glazed with tears. The sight took Caroline aback. Her mother seldom allowed herself to appear vulnerable.

"I love you more than I have ever loved anyone, including your dad, and I loved him irrevocably. He broke my heart."

"Oh, Mom, I know. I'm so sorry for what he did, how he was—is." Caroline sat abruptly in the adjacent chair; she took her mother's hand. "I wanted him to be proud of me. I wanted his attention, but I always felt I could never measure up."

"You think he didn't see—that he didn't know what you were doing? The time you tried to pass yourself off as a boy at the football tryouts. Do you remember?" Her mom broke off, half smiling, swiping at her eyes.

Caroline laughed. "It was dumb. He was embarrassed."

"Yes, and also touched to his core. He took you on his scouting trips a lot more often after that."

"I loved that he included me."

"Your dad didn't think women had any place on the football field, but he thought you had an eye for spotting talent."

A beat.

"Harris quit playing football," Caroline said.

"Really?"

"Kip Penny told me. Kip isn't a ghost, Mom. We had coffee this morning at Neilson's. Kip saw Harris play back when he was in middle school or junior high, and he was every bit as talented as Dad said. But he quit and started playing baseball instead."

"Is there a reason you're telling me this? Does Kip know where your dad is?"

"No, but if Kip's right, Dad may not be a ghost, either, except in the sense that, like you have said, he may not want to be found." Caroline wanted her mother to see it.

She waved her hands. "If you're going to start in again with all that business about your dad taking money—some recruiting scheme—"

"It's true. Kip filled me in on all the details."

"What details?" It was a challenge.

Caroline repeated the gist of her conversation with Kip for the second time that day, omitting, as she had in her recounting to Lanie, any mention that Caroline's nosing around in Omaha might have stirred up one or more sleeping dogs. Her mother didn't need the worry of it any more than her aunt Lanie. Caroline wanted badly to believe she and Kip were being overly dramatic to suspect that Jace or Brick's uncle or any one of the boosters from back then would pursue her in an attempt to stop her or silence her.

"Kip doesn't intend to publish the story now, does he?" Her mother sat with her spine flattened to the back of the chair, her arms crossed.

"I don't think so. He feels he doesn't have enough hard evidence to back it up."

"Well, it wouldn't be right. Your father isn't here to defend himself."

"Are you defending him?"

"Maybe it's hard for you to believe I would have any kind feelings toward him, but we did have many good years together. I knew him from the first day we attended the same kindergarten, and one thing I know is that those boys were everything to him. I know he believed in what he was doing. He found kids—and you know this, too—so many of them from the poorest families, families that could never have afforded to send their sons to college—but your dad found a way for it to happen. He always knew a coach, a college, where a particular athlete's skills and personality would fit in—you know as well as I do it isn't all about athleticism. A boy has to have discipline, a work ethic, the grades—integrity, for heaven's sake—" She broke off.

Caroline waited.

"It wasn't about making money off those kids, Caro. What you're saying your dad did—that's not who he is."

"No, but don't you see? The very fact we know that about him makes it even more plausible that if he got himself involved, however briefly, in this particular case with Tillman, and then changed his mind—" Caroline broke off before she could say more and cause her mother the very concern she had moments ago been determined to keep from her.

"You're saying he knows where the bodies are buried."

Caroline held her mom's gaze, jaws solidly clenched.

"Tell me, Caro. I can see you're worried."

She sighed, and pushing her hair behind her ears, she said, "According to Kip, the men who participated were local businessmen and city politicians, in addition to the coaching staff. It's possible money changed hands via illegal wire transfers."

"Bank fraud, essentially." Of course her mom got it right away. Her professional career was in banking; plus she was no one's dummy.

"Yeah. I doubt they wanted publicity about their dirty dealing then any more than they do now."

"Well, it's funny, don't you think, and I don't mean ha-ha funny, that right when a reporter is going to alert the authorities, your dad, the key informer, so to speak, up and disappears. I'm surprised Kip is still around to tell the tale."

"I know, but he didn't indicate he had any concern about himself—"

A sound came.

"I think that's my phone," Caroline said. "I'll make us some lunch," she called over her shoulder on her way to the kitchen. She got her phone from her purse. She recognized the number. It belonged to Jace Kelly. Her hello was wary. Her pulse faltered.

"We need to talk," he said.

"So talk," she said with a boldness she didn't feel.

"Not on the phone. I'm here, in Houston, meeting with the parents of one of the recruits I saw down here a couple of weeks ago. Remember, I told you I'd recently been to Houston when you were in Omaha."

Had he? She guessed it was possible, but she was drawing a blank.

"Can we meet?" he asked.

"I'm not sure that's a good idea." A low hum of warning buzzed in her ears. She thought of Kip's advice that she should involve the police. She thought of her suspicion that despite Jace's denial, despite her watching him get into a cream-colored sedan back in Omaha, he'd somehow been the driver of the big, dark SUV that had run her off the road. Now he was here? Was he setting her up?

"Please? It can be anywhere, anytime." He was openly pleading.

"There's a park down the street from my mom's," she said, and she gave him directions. It was always crowded on Saturday afternoons. What could he do to her in a park in broad daylight that was overrun with parents and their kids? "Can you be there by two o'clock?"

14

Harris—Saturday, January 13

It's Gee, isn't it? He's the student you have the *issue* with."

Harris doesn't answer his mother. They are still at the front door, and Harris has angled his gaze to one of the sidelights that bracket it. Beyond the porch he can see Mackie sitting in his squad car, phone to his ear. Who's he talking to? Why isn't he leaving? *Backup.* He's calling for backup. Help to take Harris down, take him into custody. A cold wash of panic sours Harris's mouth, clouds his brain.

"Answer me." His mother's demand cleaves his skull. "I talked with Gee's girlfriend last week. Amber's concerned about him too."

Harris jerks his gaze to his mom.

"I found her crying in the restroom. She wouldn't tell me what was troubling her other than she was worried about her boyfriend. She and Gee have been going together for a while, haven't they? Several months, anyway. I thought maybe she was pregnant, but now—Captain Mackie was talking about drugs—"

"Did you ask Amber what was wrong?"

"Of course I asked her. I told you she wouldn't say. Harris, what is going on?"

"I'll handle it." He passes his mom, heading for the stairs, taking them two at a time. It might appear that Kyle and Gee are no longer close, but act or not, Kyle's girlfriend, Samantha, and Gee's girlfriend, Amber, are definitely best friends, and best friends tell each other everything. Whatever the hell is breaking Amber's heart about Gee, she's bound to have told Sam, who would then tell Kyle. She's probably already told him. They had plans to go to the basketball game last night. Whatever the problem is, Harris has a bad feeling it's got nothing to do with an accidental pregnancy and everything to do with Gee and his dope dealing—and Harris.

Upstairs, he shoves his feet into his Nikes and then pauses, letting his gaze drift. Is he overreacting, being paranoid? But no. He can't let it go. He's got to see Kyle. One look at his son's face, and Harris will know. He grabs his keys, his cell phone, heads back downstairs.

His mom, having divined his intention, is waiting by the back door. "Where are you going? We need to talk."

"Later." He attempts to brush by her.

She grips his arm. "No, Harris, don't go off like this, in a state. Nothing good can come of it. Tell me what you're planning." She locks his gaze. "We can work it out, whatever this is about—together."

He takes her hand gently from his arm. "You can't help me, Ma. Not this time."

Calling his name, she follows him from the house onto the driveway, halting her steps when she realizes she can't stop him. He backs onto the concrete apron and heads down the narrow lane, watching her small, agitated figure recede in the rearview, and he's sick to be the cause of her distress. He has chafed against it in the past—her single-minded focus on him, on his happiness and safety, even though he knows the logic behind it. He feels the same compulsion toward his own kids. A mama lion has got nothing on him. He knows, knows in his bones, in the sockets of his eyes, the roots of his teeth, he'd kill anyone who threatened his kids' lives. So he gets why his mom is so hell bent, especially given those years spent with his birth father. But in this case, understanding brings him no relief. Only more remorse, more guilt. It has all gone wrong, so wrong he wonders if he'll ever be able to make it right.

Reaching the highway a half mile from the house, he brakes. Heading east would take him to Greeley. From there he could go north, up through Waco to Fort Worth. Farther. He could keep driving, leave the whole goddamn mess, the entire state, behind. Going west will take him into Wyatt, to his house and Kyle and whatever it is Kyle has heard about Harris from Sam. Rather than get blindsided, Harris could find Gee, but what are the odds Gee will tell him what Amber was crying about in the restroom last week? Probably nil.

He tugs his phone from his pocket. There are no calls except from Connor, who has left a message. "Dad, can you come home? Mom's pretty upset, and Kyle won't talk."

The sound of his voice, small and worried, pierces Harris's heart.

He tosses his cell phone into the passenger seat and turns right toward town—Zeke's house is on the way. It's risky, seeing him again. While Harris has told Zeke most everything, the old man doesn't know the worst of it—that Harris has been buying dope off Gee. It'll kill Zeke if he finds out. But Harris has got to know if he's who tipped the cops about Gee. Harris has to let Zeke know he's playing with fire, that Gee is much more than your average hormone-amped, stressed-out teenager. He's twisted up inside, broken in some way.

He's a maniac.

Psycho.

The term stands up in Harris's brain. He thinks of how he's used the label in the past, or heard it used, mostly in reference to serial killers, school shooters, and suicide bombers. He's never thought of Gee in those terms before, but the markers for it are there, aren't they?

One in one hundred children born today are psychopathic.

Harris recalls the statistic his mother quoted a while back when they were talking about a recent school shooting. It shocked him. *That many?* he said to her. She listed the hallmarks: lack of empathy and remorse; emotional detachment; bullying; ignoring rules; blaming others; chronic, long-term lying—

Stealing. Not occasionally, but compulsively.

On the flip side, these people are charmers and manipulators. Despite the popular perception, a psychopath isn't always a killer. They don't always murder or have a history of abusing animals. They can be high functioning and successful. The star football player on your local high school team, for instance. The one who's got everybody fooled.

Except Harris.

But who is he kidding?

Glancing in the rearview mirror, he almost doesn't recognize the guy whose image is reflected there. His eyes are dark circled and sunken. He hasn't shaved, and the silver-flecked black stubble of his beard shadows his cheeks and jaw. He looks like shit, and he's starting to feel pretty rough too. It comes to him with a stomach-churning jolt that he's left the second of the two fentanyl patches Zeke gave him last night under the mattress at his mom's house. *She could find it. No, she'll never look. What if she does?* The dialogue shifts uneasily through his brain. Where's he going to get more—something, fentanyl, anything? That's the question.

Zeke won't give him any, not this soon.

Harris thinks about turning around, going back to his mother's, but looking again at the rearview, his gaze homes in on a car, the plain, dark-colored sedan several car lengths behind him. It's been there awhile, hasn't it? Keeping an even distance. A frisson of unease slips up his spine. Could be a cop—Mackie or some other law officer at the wheel. *Maybe I'm losing it, imagining things.*

The weather has warmed up by the time Harris arrives at Zeke's. It's almost seventy. The old man says he's been out on his deck, repotting some cactus. He offers Harris a Coke when they pass through the kitchen on their way outside.

Harris accepts the drink, although he wants—needs—something stronger.

"Didn't figure I'd see you this morning." Zeke scrapes red-tinged leaves from a nearby towering maple off a padded deck chair. There's an edge in his voice, and Harris knows he's expecting to be hit up for painkillers and that he'll say no. Harris might have to ask, though. What the hell. It's not like he's got any pride left.

He sits down across from Zeke at the round patio table. A corner of the deck is littered with sacks of potting soil, a collection of clay pots, and several wickedly spined plants. Harris recognizes the round shape of a good-size golden barrel cactus. He thinks some of the others with leaves like knife blades are agaves or possibly aloes. He's not into gardening. That's Holly's thing.

"You look like hell." Zeke makes the comment not looking at Harris.

"I got a visit from the cops this morning, the police captain. Clint Mackie. You know him?"

"We've met a few times. What was he doing at your house?"

Harris doesn't correct Zeke's misapprehension. "Did you tip the cops that Gee took your ring?"

"Huh?" Zeke looks totally at sea.

"There was another break-in last night, Todd Sullivan's house. Do you know Todd? Junior at Wyatt High? Nice family. They were out to dinner when it happened. Same MO as all the other robberies. No busted doors or windows. No sign or clue who did it. But this morning, according to Mackie, somebody who wouldn't give their name called the Wyatt police and said Gee was responsible. This caller said Gee's also pedaling dope at Wyatt High. Was it you?"

"No! I told you I'd leave it to you, what should happen." The old man is annoyed, and confused in a way that seems genuine.

"You're pissed Gee was here." Harris is insistent. "In your house—"

"Okay, but it's hearsay. Cops don't give a damn about hearsay. They want proof."

Harris thinks a moment. It's true what Zeke says. Even Harris doesn't have physical proof it was Gee who took Zeke's ring. It's not as if he saw the kid do it. He's going on gut instinct. "You know what's on the line, right? It's not just Gee's life—assuming it's him—that's going to get screwed up. It's mine, too, and Kyle's."

"Gee's pedaling dope?"

Harris doesn't answer.

"You buying it off him?"

The moment waits, but Harris is too long in his denial, and the old man's gaze sharpens with knowing, the taint of disgust. "You are, aren't you? That's why you won't report him for the robberies. He's got you over a barrel, doesn't he?"

Harris turns his Coke can around. It's as if his brain is jammed shut, stuck like a faulty door.

"Answer me," Zeke insists. "Tell me I'm off base, losing it, crazy—something!"

But Harris can't. He can't even look at Zeke. Can't lie to the old man. Not again. But he can't tell him the truth either.

The silence feels haunted by their past, the wealth of good memories they share.

Zeke says, "You're not okay, are you, kid?" and his voice has gone soft now.

Harris's throat closes. His eyes burn, and he pinches the bridge of his nose. He senses Zeke holding back, giving him space. When he's able, Harris says, "That's the first thing you ever said to me. Do you remember?"

"In the locker room. Your first day of Aggie baseball practice. You looked like a young man who'd lost his best pup."

"'You're not okay, are you, kid?' That's what you asked me." Zeke's kindness that day nearly cost Harris his composure then too. It was as if Zeke could sense the secret Harris was protecting, the wound that still festered. How could he have hurt this man? How could he go on hurting him?

"You're in deep shit, buying drugs off a minor, a student at the same damn high school where you're the goddamn athletic director." Zeke is angry now, but the note of compassion is still present, an underscore to his disappointment and alarm. "What the hell are you thinking?"

Harris lets the question hang, his shame so thick in his throat he can't speak.

"Does Holly know? Kyle? My God, you don't really think Kyle's in on this crap with Gee? Dealing dope, busting into houses?"

"No. Not the drugs. I'm sure of that. And I'm nearly positive he doesn't know anything about the break-ins, either, unless—"

"Unless?" Zeke prompts.

Harris flicks a glance at him. "Might be best if we leave it where it is. I don't want you involved."

"Involved? I'm already involved, man. Tell me what you know."

"I think Gee's girlfriend, Amber, might have found out that Gee's dealing. Amber and Kyle's girlfriend, Samantha, are best friends. It's possible Amber has told Sam, and you can bet if that's true, Sam has told Kyle."

"Okay. But what's that got to do with you?"

Harris shifts his feet. He drinks his Coke, sets down the can, keeping his gaze on it. "Sometimes, making a buy, I've texted Gee—we've texted back and forth. What if Amber has seen those texts on Gee's phone? What if she told Sam, and Sam told Kyle his dad is buying drugs off Gee?"

"Jesus—"

"I think Gee might know about us"—Harris gestures between himself and Zeke—"that I'm getting stuff from you too. I think he stole your ring and planted it in Kyle's dresser drawer as a warning to me to keep my mouth shut. But now he's involved Kyle—"

"But if Gee wanted you to find it, why would he put it in Kyle's room?"

"Because he wants Kyle implicated. He wants us all to go down. My gut says Gee's planted other stuff throughout my house. Only God knows where. He told me once there wasn't a house or a building he couldn't get into. He can do whatever he wants, set me and Kyle up—or even Connor and Holly—any way he wants. Then all it'll take is one call to the cops, one anonymous tip. They'll get a warrant, and if they find anything—"

"They've got to have more than a tip, don't they? That's not enough to give them probable cause to come into your home."

Harris shakes his head. He doesn't know the answer.

The silence hovers and seems filled with Harris's panic.

He breaks it. "What am I going to do?"

"What are you going to do? Get help, man." Zeke abandons his chair, and going behind it, he grips it, gnarled fingers digging into the cushion.

The sun is behind him; his face is in shadow, but Harris doesn't need to see his expression to know it is outraged, scathing.

"Tell the cops what you know about Gee," Zeke says, "and check into a rehab. You can beat this, Harris."

He doesn't agree. Doesn't really know how to define the *this* Zeke claims Harris can beat. It's as if he's walked into a swamp, and now he's mired in the muck to his knees.

"I should have seen it coming." Zeke walks to the deck's edge. He turns back to Harris. "I should have known. You've been asking me for meds too often lately. You haven't been back to see Ben Cooper, have you?"

Harris's lack of an answer is answer enough. His monumental failure doesn't need the shape of his words.

"I wonder how much of what you're taking has to do with actual pain." It's as if Zeke is talking to himself. He returns to the table, stands looking down at Harris. His gaze is kind and yet troubled with apprehension. "This is on me."

"No—" Harris begins.

"I'll go with you to the cops." Zeke talks over Harris. "I'll tell them my part, surrender my license, whatever it takes to get you back right."

"No," Harris says again, getting to his feet. "You're not part of this. I'll handle it." He crosses the deck to the back door. He's got to get out of here, can't stand the look of Zeke's heartbreak and disappointment a second longer.

Zeke follows him, arguing, but Harris's brain fills with white noise, shutting out the words, deafening him to even the sound of Zeke's voice.

. . .

The car, the dark sedan, is behind him again. The image hangs in Harris's rearview some five or six car lengths distant, keeping pace. It's been there since shortly after Harris left Zeke's house. He's westbound on a farm-to-market highway, headed toward Greeley, the Madrone County seat. Lots of folks drive this highway. Could be anybody back there. But Harris knows better. Somebody is targeting him. Could be Mackie or some other cop. Or Gee. Or Gee's punk cousin.

Any other time someone tailing him might have scared him, but right now all he feels is his need. It throbs in his veins, hammers his temples. Not a mile away from Zeke's he had to pull over to puke. He spent five minutes with his hands braced on his knees dry heaving into the roadside scrim, but nothing came up other than bile and the Coke he'd drunk.

Dope sick. That's what it's called.

Zeke and Holly are right. Harris has got a problem.

He knows it, but he can't look at it yet. Not head-on. He can't think about his family or the danger he's brought to their door. He's got to get right first, get something to help himself. Now. Pray to God Cal is home. Pray she hasn't moved or OD'd or been arrested. Pray she still has a stash of something she'll be willing to sell him.

Calliope McBride is it: Harris's last hope.

He met her at Dr. Cooper's office after his last back surgery two years ago. Cal was in recovery, too, and they fell into a conversation, vented their mutual angst over the brutality of rehab, lack of sleep, pain that was constant. Typical stuff you'd expect two people in such circumstances to talk about. Cooper was gradually backing them both off their meds, and they were both suffering. Cal was the first to say it: if Cooper insisted on cutting off her supply of oxycodone, she'd find an alternate source. Harris was all ears. Cal had connections, she confided. Selling dope provided her with a living. A woman on her own, of a certain age—sixtysomething, she said, but Harris figured she was closer to seventysomething—handicapped in the way she was, how else was she supposed to make a living? Becoming a Walmart greeter held little appeal. She couldn't sit or stand for long periods anyway.

Harris couldn't either. He'd tried reasoning with Cooper, pointing out that as a high school coach, he was more active than Cooper's average patient. He'd assumed Cooper would cut him some slack, give him more than the usual leeway with the meds. But when he'd brought it up, Cooper had given him the same brusque shoulder he'd given Cal. Cooper had suggested Harris could get a different, less physically demanding job, as if changing jobs, changing professions, were easy to do in your forties. In Cooper's waiting room, seated next to Harris, Cal commiserated.

She patted Harris's hand, and the half dozen or so rings on her fingers glimmered in the pale wash of institutional light. *I've got what you need, sweetie*, she said. But he hasn't seen her in a while. Not since last August, the day Gee caught him puking out behind the field house before football practice. The team had just started two-a-days, and Harris was filling in for one of the assistant coaches, whose wife had just delivered their first child.

Harris was dope sick that day, too, but by his own hand. He'd taken a silent pledge and been off the drugs for going on seventy-two hours. Gee came behind the building to pee. He asked if Harris was all right. He sounded concerned, said he'd go for help. They shared a look, and somehow Harris's whole pathetic situation was laid bare between them. Gee knew in that moment who Harris was and what he needed. He pulled a small plastic sleeve, not much bigger than a postage stamp, from his jeans pocket and held it out to Harris so he could see them, the round, soft-yellow tabs.

Two Oxycontin tabs, forty milligrams each.

Salvation. A godsend, a lifesaver. Harris barely thought twice. *How much?* he asked.

For you? Hey, it's on me, Gee answered, like any good salesman. *This time*, he added.

Because that understanding was present between them, too, that Harris was inherently weak and that Gee was preternaturally gifted in his ability to identify and exploit human weakness. Harris has wondered since if Gee followed him on purpose that day, if the punk somehow knew how bad Harris was hurting. Gee's always around, lurking in some corner, always with a remedy handy in his pocket. Harris can't deal with him anymore. That's over.

Done.

He knows it's like shutting the barn door after the cow has gotten out, but he's sticking to it. Cal will help him out, no strings attached. Assuming she's still in business.

In six months anything could have happened. The woman could have been busted, died of an overdose, been taken down by some other dealer. She's regaled him with enough stories about her line of work that he knows it can be dangerous.

If it doesn't work out with her, he'll have to head north to Fort Worth or Dallas. He's heard of a couple of locations up there. He hopes it doesn't come to that.

He checks the rearview. Before he goes too much farther, he's got to shake whomever's on his tail.

15

Caroline left a note naming the location where she was going but not the person whom she was meeting. At least if she didn't come back, her mother would know where to send the police. She arrived at the park fifteen minutes early and, leaving her car, found a good vantage point from which she could view the entrance. She wanted to see Jace before he saw her.

She'd been right at least about the park being crowded. It had warmed up considerably since this morning, and the air was packed with noise from a small horde of children and their winter-beleaguered parents.

Jace appeared at the park's entrance at 1:55 p.m. Caroline watched him, breath paused, as he played his gaze over his surroundings. Several of the benches were unoccupied, and there were one or two that were half-concealed by playground equipment or shrubbery. She thought if he headed for one of those, she'd leave, and he'd be none the wiser. But he sat down on a bench near the entrance in plain sight of anyone who cared to look. Tipping his head back, he seemed to be reveling in the unseasonable warmth of the winter sun.

His eyes opened when her shadow fell over him. He jerked upright. "God, you scared me," he said.

Good, she thought. Pulling her sweater tightly around her, she sat next to him. Despite her precautions, apprehension jumped in her brain. "So why did you want to see me, Jace?"

"I figure you got an earful from Tricia." He sounded tentative.

"I think you know what I heard." Caroline could be equally cagey, she thought.

"Yeah." He pinched the bridge of his nose. "Pretty sad, huh, what our dads were up to."

"What confuses me is why you sent me to see her. Tricia was surprised too. Did you honestly think Dad was there?"

"He could have been. Last I heard he was with her." Jace raised his palm. "That's the God's honest truth."

"Makes me wonder what isn't." Caroline couldn't keep the edge from her voice any more than she could lower her guard.

"Tillman football doesn't run like that now. Nobody pays our players."

"Did you know when it was going on?"

"Hell no. I was just a kid, not much older than you." He glanced sidelong at her. "Did *you*?" A note of challenge edged his voice.

She shook her head. "It's hard for me to believe even now."

Jace ran his palms over his head and, bending forward, braced his elbows on his knees. "My dad was my hero, you know? He was the guy I looked up to and trusted most. It kills me that he was basically buying players. Not building a team. Not bringing them together to work as a unit or instilling in them a system of values that would serve them throughout their lives like he preached. Just bribing them, paying them to play for him."

It was Jace's obvious disappointment in his dad that got to Caroline. She knew how he felt. She was let down and baffled in the same way. Maybe she had it all wrong and had no reason to be concerned about him. "When did you find out?"

"Dad told me a couple of years ago. I think he just wanted to get it off his chest."

"After he retired?"

"Yeah. I'd been named head coach by then. Believe me, it was one hell of a shock. You know who Brick Coleman is, top football recruit at quarterback back in the day?"

"I know he was given a condo and a car—"

"Pretty much whatever he wanted. Your dad recruited him, but it was his uncle, Farley Dade, who made it happen. Dade and his bankroll."

Caroline could have said she'd heard about Farley from Kip, but she didn't want to stop Jace. She had to hear what he would say. "Your dad went along with Farley?"

"It wasn't like he was given a choice. It was that or lose his job. And you know how it was with him. Coaching at Tillman was Dad's life."

"Was he ever threatened?"

"Not overtly. It was implied."

Caroline's pulse fluttered.

Jace shook his head. "Farley Dade." The way he said the name made it a curse. "That guy is a piece of work."

"In what way?" Caroline asked.

Jace shifted his glance. A child's laughter broke around them, sounding incongruous. A woman called out: "Cory, don't." A horn honked.

"Answer me, Jace. I need to know—the truth, not some story."

"The truth is I'm the one who ran you off the road in Omaha last week."

Jace brought his gaze around, and for a moment all Caroline could do was stare at him.

"I'm sick about it, Caro. Sick and sorry as hell."

"I thought it was you," she said faintly. She saw again the blinding glare of headlights that were too close, felt the jolt when her car was rear-ended, and the remembrance of her fear when the car began to slide was visceral, too real. "You bastard! I could have been killed!" She was on her feet now, backing away from him. People were staring. Caroline didn't care. She turned to go.

Jace took her elbow.

She jerked it from his grasp and kept walking.

"Please hear me out," he said. "Please, I want to apologize—explain. It could help you find your dad. For real this time."

She stopped. Turning to him, she said, "Why should I believe you?"

"Give me five minutes, okay? We'll sit down again in front of all these folks—what can happen?"

Against her better judgment, Caroline followed him back to the bench.

Jace scrubbed a hand down his thigh. "When I came after you that night—"

"What made you do it?"

"Not what—who."

"Who?"

"Farley. Brick's uncle. You remember talking to Alexa—"

"The trainer at TSU."

"Yeah. I guess she ran into Dade right after that and mentioned you were looking for Hoff. The son of a bitch called me and went ballistic. He's scared you're going to find Hoff, and all the shit that went on back in the day with the recruits is going to come out. If that happens, he basically let me know my dad can kiss his Hall of Fame nomination goodbye. Dade's got the influence to do it, Caro, and all I could think was how it would kill Dad, losing that honor—"

"Even though he cheated to get it. And don't tell me you're not worried about your own job and reputation if folks find out you've known all these years." Disgust burned through Caroline's apprehension. Jace seemed pathetic now, and forlorn. "Why did you come to the car afterward and say my name?" Her confusion was genuine. If he'd lingered a moment longer, she would have come to herself enough to recognize him, to be certain of his presence.

"I know it won't make sense," Jace said, "but the second it was done, all I could think was I had to help you. I was—I don't know how to explain it. The whole thing was surreal. It was like I was outside myself."

"Why are you telling me now? You realize there's an accident report, an ongoing investigation—"

"I haven't slept worth shit since it happened, Caro. I'm not the kind of person who resorts to violence. Or I never thought I was." He curled his hands into fists. "Goddammit, I'm a dad and a coach, but I did it. I ran you the fuck off the road!" He wiped his hands down his face. "If you want to, turn me in. I deserve it. And I want to reimburse you. Your medical bills, damage to the car, whatever."

"It's not necessary." Caroline didn't want his money. She didn't want to be beholden to him. "I'm surprised the security guard who was there, the police officer who came—I guess they didn't see you?"

"I beat it when I heard the siren. I know how it makes me sound, but my kids have got no one but me."

"But the next morning, when you came to my hotel—if the whole point was to stop me from finding Dad, why tell me about Tricia?"

"I knew the minute I said it that it was a mistake, the stupidest thing I could have done, but like I said, I'm no criminal. My mind doesn't work that way." Jace wiped his brow, gripped his knees. Still, Caroline could see he was shaky. She almost felt sorry for him.

"Does Farley know?" she asked.

"Yeah, but he thinks you hit a brick wall. He thinks maybe it was a genius move, my sending you there." Jace glanced at her. "Dad's nomination isn't the only thing on the line, Caro. Farley said he'd have my job, too, if I didn't get rid of you."

"Get rid of me?" Caroline repeated. "Like how? Murder? Is that what happened to Dad? Did they kill him?" Shock thinned her voice. She felt unhinged.

"No! Dade just wanted you the hell out of Omaha, away from my dad and the Tillman campus. Those guys, even Dade—they wouldn't go that far. Not now, not back then."

"How do you know? Like you just said, you ran me off the road, for God's sake!"

"I was out of my mind, not thinking straight. I feel awful—"

"Yes. You've said." His reassurances did nothing for the tension coiled tightly in her stomach. "Tricia told me about an investigative reporter, Kip Penny?"

"I know who he is. So?" Jace looked cautious, as if he were uncertain of her motive in bringing up the reporter.

"So I talked at length with him this morning."

"Does he know where Hoff is?"

"No. But he seems to think there's still a lot Dade and his cronies could lose. They could have been involved in bank fraud, Jace. Did you know that?"

He might as well have said yes aloud, given how quickly he averted his gaze.

"Did you know Dad disappeared right after Kip said he was going to alert the FBI?" Her panic at the timing, at its potential meaning, wanted to stand up in her gut. She shoved it down. She couldn't allow it or the conclusion it would lead her to—that this double-dealing bunch of crooks had murdered her dad to shut him up for good. It didn't matter that they hadn't targeted Kip too. He wasn't the one who had gone after the hard evidence, the banking documents Kip had insisted he'd needed. Without those, the reporter was no threat to Farley Dade and his gang of thugs, and they'd logically left him alone. She fisted her hands, feeling her nails bite into the soft flesh of her palms. She would not, could not, lose it.

"It was a long time ago, Caroline." Jace was trying to placate her. "There's no way the feds would come after Dad or any of those guys now."

"But your dad, Farley Dade, and his gang of boosters—they did go after my dad back then, right?" She locked Jace's gaze.

"No," he said, "they didn't."

"How can you be so sure?" Frustration knifed through her voice.

"Because Dad and Farley hired a private investigator at the time to look for Hoff. Even you would have to agree that's not something you do if you killed the guy. And no, before you ask, the PI didn't find him."

"You know that for a fact." Caroline felt the tiniest thrill of relief. Jace was right. You wouldn't pay money to have someone hunt down your murder victim.

"The investigator's name is Bill Devlin. His brother, Joel, is a police detective, and at the time he was working missing persons in Omaha. Joel did some digging off the record. Cops didn't have the tools to hunt down a person back then like they have now, but Joel did what he could. He put out a description of your dad. I think there was even a photo of him. It went all over the US, and a few tips did come in, but none of them panned out."

"What would have happened if they had, if they found Dad?" Caroline asked over the darker thrust of renewed disappointment. It had been the same with the investigator Lanie had hired. It was as if her dad had vanished into thin air.

"I don't know. They would have wanted to be sure he didn't talk— and no, they wouldn't have resorted to violence, I'm telling you." He cut her off before she could speak. "They would have tried to reason with him, tried to pay him off, probably, but I swear to you they wouldn't have killed him. It would have been too risky, and if they got caught—they wouldn't go that far. You've got to trust me on this."

Caroline looked away. Anything might have happened. For all she knew Jace was lying. She wanted to shake him. She wanted to threaten him the way he had her. She could do it too. Call the Omaha police on him for causing her accident. Unlike her situation with her husband, she had no loyalty whatsoever to Jace.

He spoke again before she could. "There's more. Don't freak on me, okay?"

She jerked her gaze to his. "Just tell me." She was angry now and glad for the heat of it, grateful for how it settled her nerves.

"A while back, maybe a year or so ago, when Dad heard about his nomination, he got hold of Bill and asked him if he'd take another look for Hoff."

Caroline's heartbeat slowed. "He found my dad?"

"Not exactly. It's weird. I don't really understand myself what led Bill to this person. Guy lives in Kerrville, drives a semi. When Bill showed the guy Hoff's photo, he said he knew Hoff, that he gave him a ride. They got to be friends after that, I guess."

"Are you serious? Where is he? Here? In Houston?" Caroline's voice seemed separate from her and far away.

"No, he's in Texas, but out in the country, near a little town—" Jace got out his wallet, took out what looked like a business card, and handed it to her. "Turn it over."

She did and read the information written there: *Lone Pine*, and beneath it, *south of Lampasas*. Caroline looked up at Jace. "I've never heard of Lone Pine, but Lampasas is in the Hill Country." She felt light headed, breathless. If she'd had to stand up, she doubted she could have managed. After everything she'd been through, to think he was here in Texas . . . it was almost more than she could take in.

"Is that close?"

"It's northwest, about a four- or five-hour drive." She put her fingertips to her temples. "I can't believe . . ." She found Jace's gaze. "He's been here all these years?"

"If it's really him, I guess so."

"His second wife—Julia—she and her son, Harris, live out there, in Wyatt, not far south of Lampasas." Caroline took a moment, trying to settle her mind, work out the significance of her dad being so close to his second family, if there was a significance. Lanie had said Julia had promised to call if she heard from Hoff, but there was also the chance that he would have requested that Julia not contact his family. "Did Bill talk to the man?" she asked Jace.

"He went there. The location—it's not like a formal address."

"What do you mean?"

"The way Bill talked, the place is pretty far off the road, back in the woods. He said it was run-down, more like a shack. No water or electricity, nothing like that. He knocked on the door, and when no one answered, he walked around on the property, but he never saw anyone."

Caroline didn't know what to make of the images Jace's words painted in her mind. She didn't even know how to think about them. She let her gaze drift. The swing set was empty now. The woman and her children who had been there were gone. In fact, the whole park was deserted. It was colder, Caroline realized. A wind had come up. She huddled in her sweater.

Jace said, "Bill waited in his car, hoping someone would show up, but they never did. He had to leave."

"So he doesn't know if the guy living there was my dad or not."

"Not positively, no, but he stopped at a café north of Lone Pine in Lampasas on his way to catch his flight out of Dallas. He had the guy who identified Hoff in the first place—the truck driver—come and meet him there. Bill showed him the photo again, and he was positive it was Hoff, although that's not the name the man goes by. There was a waitress there, too, and a couple other folks looked at the photo—they all agreed it was Hoff—"

"What name does he go by?" Caroline was almost afraid to ask, afraid to feel the fizz of excitement brewing in her brain. It was hard to breathe.

"Ray Berry."

"Raymond Berry?" She sat upright, disbelieving, unable now to stifle the surge of her hope.

"You know the name?"

"My dad's favorite football player of all time was Raymond Berry."

"Wide receiver for the Baltimore Colts back in the day, right?"

"Yes. He and Johnny Unitas were one of the greatest pass-catch teams in football history. Dad always said Raymond was the epitome of the character and discipline it takes to play the game. My God . . ." She was dumbfounded, nearly paralyzed with the wonder of it.

"You really think this guy could be Hoff?"

Caroline looked at Jace. "Dad used to say we were partners, like Unitas and Berry. *I* was Unitas; *he* was Berry." Her voice caught; her eyes burned with tears. It was so right, so perfect, the exact name her father would have chosen to create a new identity. She stood up. "Where can I reach Bill?"

"That's his business card you're holding. His contact information is on the front." Jace stood up too.

She turned the card over. *Bill Devlin*, it read, along with his Omaha-based address and phone number. She glanced at Jace. "Thank you, I guess."

"I'm really sorry, Caro, for coming after you." Remorse graveled his voice. "I let Dade get to me—"

"You should go to the police in Omaha about him, Jace. This whole thing with the recruits, even if it was twenty-plus years ago, he's obviously still invested in covering it up. Suppose he doesn't stop at threatening your job?"

Jace looked off into the middle distance.

"If the police had their eye on him there, I wouldn't have to look over my shoulder. It's the least you can do. I won't pursue charges in regard to the accident," she added, and she felt it a fair bargain. She didn't know whether the threat of violence from Dade was real or not, but it would be a relief to know he was under scrutiny by law enforcement either way.

"Yeah, okay, I can do that." Jace looked away, brought his gaze back. "It's funny, isn't it? How when you want to do the right thing, the fallout is never contained. There's always some kind of bullshit collateral damage. Innocent folks who're gonna get hurt."

Thinking of Rob, Caroline could have said she knew all about it, that honesty had a price, a dark side. Instead she wished Jace well. What he'd done, she thought on her way to her car, as bad as it was, at least he'd owned it. He'd taken steps to make it right—*if* everything he'd said was the truth, and if she wasn't a fool for wanting to believe him. She thought of Kip's suggestion that she involve the police. She'd said the same thing to Jace. Maybe the time had come to take her own advice, no second thoughts or second-guessing.

Inside her car, she keyed the ignition, turned up the heat, and pulled her phone and Steve Wayman's card from her purse.

16

Harris—Saturday, January 13

You weren't followed, were you, hon?"

Harris turns from the window above the parking lot, where he's left his truck, and looks around at Cal. Her drapes are some god-awful pattern, brown with orange flowers, but they're thick, so although it's afternoon on a bright, sunny day, the light in her apartment is shrouded in darkness; her round face is a puzzle of shadows. Still, he can tell he's upset her, showing up out of the blue. He tries to reassure her. "If I was, I lost them coming into town."

He took the turnoff for the old rail yard on the outskirts of Greeley as he came into town, having remembered the yard from his high school days. It was where kids went to drink and smoke dope. Mess around in the railcars that were abandoned there. He parked between two of them, rusted walls hulking on either side, waited, and saw nothing, heard nothing other than the muted sound of traffic from the highway, the wind blowing through patches of dry waist-high grass.

"I'm surprised to see you," Cal says, backing toward the La-Z-Boy recliner in the corner of the living room and sitting heavily. She parks her cane between her knees. "But I guess this ain't a social visit. You don't look too good."

"Yeah, pretty much feel like shit." Harris wipes his face. "I'm sorry to show up out of nowhere. I tried calling, but your number isn't working."

"I got a new one. In my business it pays to change it up every so often." Cal motions Harris to a seat on the couch. "Switch on that lamp there, if you want." She gestures toward the end table.

He says it's fine.

"Too much light hurts my eyes these days," Cal says.

"How have you been?" Harris asks.

"Fair to middlin'," Cal answers. "Got diagnosed with diabetes. Now along with everything else I got to watch what I put in my mouth. But you didn't come to talk about my health. What can I do for you?"

"I wish I could say nothing," Harris laughs. The sound isn't funny.

"Hon, don't we all. You should see all the pills I got to swallow these days. Everything that's wrong with me has just ruined my life. My daughter won't let me keep the grandkids no more. She says she can't trust me. Like it's my fault." Cal heaves herself from the chair. "Like I asked to be in this world of hurt."

Harris watches her leave the room. Has he asked for this? Does it even matter? He puts his head into his hands.

"I've got Oxy, forties, or morphine tabs," Cal hollers.

From the bedroom, Harris thinks. "Whatever," he calls back.

She brings him the Oxys and a glass of water.

He swallows them dry, chases them with water. Pulls cash from his pocket, handing it to her. Forty bucks he got earlier from the ATM. He was afraid to withdraw more, although given the state of his marriage right now, he has a lot more to answer for than where he spent forty dollars. "Give me whatever this'll buy?" He looks up at Cal.

She nods, disappears, and comes back with a small plastic vial. "There's four in there. I'm doin' you a deal."

Harris thanks her and gets up.

"You need anything else, you call first, okay?" She gives him her new cell number, and he programs it into his phone. "Don't come by here no more. I'll meet you. I don't want to give my daughter any more reasons to keep the grands from coming here."

"I'm sorry," Harris repeats.

"It's all right. But them kids mean the world to me. I just want to get back right so she'll let me keep 'em, you know? I just want to be a regular grandma that bakes cookies with 'em and snuggles with 'em on the couch. Simple stuff like that." Her voice quavers.

"Sure," Harris says without enthusiasm. He goes to the window and cracks the drape, searching the parking lot again for a sign of anything unusual, even though he knows he's making Cal nervous.

"You see anything that shouldn't be there?" she asks.

"No. Probably just paranoia." He tries a smile, and on a whim he goes to her, brushes her cheek with a kiss.

She smiles up at him, pleasure pinking her face. "You be safe now, you hear?" she says. "And don't be such a stranger. Folks like us have to stick together."

He wants to say he's nothing like her, that her comparison sickens him, but the stone-cold truth is that they are alike, both of them afflicted in the same sad way. At the door, he turns to salute her, fingertips to his brow. "Thanks," he tells her, and closing the door, he walks quickly to the stairs, heels ringing on the concrete. Already he feels better, steadier. He feels filled with purpose, as if he might yet get out from under the pile of shit that's buried him.

He's beneath the window of Cal's apartment, his foot resting on the driver's-side running board of his truck, when the dark-colored sedan stops behind the truck bed. Before he can fully register that it's very like the vehicle that followed him earlier, the driver cracks open the car door. Harris sets his foot on the pavement, steeling himself. Maybe, if he's lucky, it's just some stranger looking for directions. He lets the truck door close, prepares to say he can't help them. That's his last coherent thought before he registers it's not some stranger who's blocked him in.

It's Kyle; it's his son.

Harris's knees loosen. "What the hell—?" he begins.

"Yeah, Dad!" Kyle rounds the front of the car. He's red faced, shouting. "What the hell! You tell me, okay?" Pinning Harris to the side of the truck, he thumps Harris's chest. "Tell me, Dad. What the hell, because I'd really like to know."

"Whose car are you driving?" Harris asks like it matters. But even as he speaks, the knowledge is sinking like an ax blade into his brain—that it was Kyle who followed him, who fooled him deliberately by driving someone else's car.

"I know everything, Dad." Kyle grabs a fistful of Harris's windbreaker, jerking him forward, shoving him back. "I know you're on dope, that you're buying it off Gee. Gee! Of all goddamn people! What the fuck, Dad? You're the athletic director, the fucking coach. You're all the time preaching about ethics and morals, making the right choices, being a leader!"

Harris can't answer. He feels sick. Even if there were an answer, he's lost the power to speak. When Kyle slugs Harris in the chest again, Harris doesn't react. He doesn't look at Kyle but beyond him. Something draws his gaze up, and he sees Cal looking down on him from her window. The curtain flicks shut the moment their eyes meet. He's on his own. She can't help him. He thinks of a story she told him once of how she got her name: Calliope. Her mama, she said, loved the circus, everything about it, including the music. His life is a circus, Harris thinks.

"You're on something now, aren't you?" Kyle jerks Harris by his jacket. "Aren't you?"

"What do you want me to say? That you're right, I'm on something? Okay. Yeah. I am." He sounds defiant, like a kid would sound, like he's got a right to a defense. What a joke.

"I looked up to you, you know?"

Kyle's voice cracks, and Harris's heart staggers. He wants to grab his son and hold on to him. He wants to bring Kyle down into his lap and rock him as if he were a baby. But Kyle is grown now, a man, and life isn't so simple anymore.

Kyle gets hold of himself, and when he says, "Growing up, I wanted to be just like you," he's speaking through teeth clenched hard against his hurt, the sense of Harris's betrayal of him. How has it come to this? How is it that Harris has failed so completely to become the father he dreamed of being, the one he never had except briefly in Hoff? His mind flashes on that other father, his birth father. He feels revolted. He feels an oily scrim of fear flood his mouth. He doesn't know why, where it's coming from. Somehow now the light is dazzling—

"You're pathetic." Kyle releases Harris, shoving him back against the truck's door. The handle bites into Harris's back. "I told Mom she should divorce you."

"Does she know where you are? Did she send you after me?" Harris fights to stay present.

"Are you serious? No way. She's sick of you too. Sick of your lies."

"What about Connor?"

"What about Connor?" Kyle mocks. "Like you care. He wants you to come home. Poor kid doesn't know better."

They stand silent, squared off, toe to toe, gazes locked. Nothing in the silence between them but the sound of the wind, the occasional passing car, now an incongruous burst of laughter down the way. Harris is conscious of Kyle's breath, labored, heated. Harris can barely feel the air going into and out of his lungs. They have reached an impasse, a point of no return. They are lost, Harris thinks, in a foreign country without a map. He doesn't know what to do. His mind feels scrambled.

He can't think why he's here. He should get out, get to his mother. She's in danger—

"What the hell is wrong with you, huh, Harris?"

He staggers when Kyle shoves him. He wipes his hands down his face. "Look, I'm sorry—"

"It's too late for that bullshit now, *Harris*."

His name from Kyle's mouth is like acid, burning Harris's face, his heart. Not *Dad*. His teeth clench against the pain.

"It's all over town," Kyle says. "By Monday it'll be all over school. Everyone knows you're a doper. Gee's your dealer. Are you robbing houses with him, too, *Harris*? You part of his posse? You and Gee, BFFs forever? Is that how it is? God! What are you? Like, ten? Connor's got way more going for him than you."

"What do you mean, it's all over town?"

"Amber read the texts on Gee's phone about you buying dope off him and the break-ins—all the shit you and Gee are doing."

"I'm not part of that, robbing the houses," Harris says, but something is happening inside his head. Where is his mother? He can hear her groaning, crying. Jesus God, he's got to get to her. But he is nothing, nothing at all, against the madman who has her—

"She told Sam." Kyle talks over the noise in Harris's brain. "Sam told me last night."

"Your mother—?" Harris can't articulate more. Panic has thickened his tongue. A sound comes, the whoop of a siren—a cop's siren, giving notice. Over Kyle's shoulder, Harris catches a glimpse of it on the other side of the parking lot. He looks back at Kyle, eyes wild, questioning, doubting, despite the gut punch of his feeling, his understanding that Kyle is responsible.

Kyle has summoned the law.

"Yeah. I did it. I called the cops. I told Mom somebody's got to stop you and Gee."

"Jesus Christ! Do you know what you've done?" Harris turns, jerking open the truck door, intent on escape. He's off balance when Kyle's arm circles his neck. The pressure of Kyle's biceps swells against his throat, crushing bone and sinew, pinching off his carotid artery. The sound of his heartbeat thunders in his ears. But now his mind reels, and the old dream that has haunted his nights is alive around him. The images that jab his brain fuel a terror inside him that is old, nearly as old as he is. His mother's screams grow louder; they are primal, horrified. A figure lurches into the scene. Harris looks through splayed fingers, a child's fingers. The monster he sees, with its round marble eyes, is real; he's here.

The darkness deepens, eating away at Harris's peripheral vision. He's a boy, fighting the monster, fighting for his and his mother's lives. In some warped pocket of his mind, though, he recognizes there's a difference this time. He's no kid anymore. He's bigger, stronger, than his opponent. Acting on practiced instinct, he squats, kicks his foot behind his faceless attacker, and in the same moment that he unbalances him, Harris takes the monster down. He feels the impact of the concrete jar the length of his body; he hears the attacker's grunts of pain. Now Harris has him pinned between his knees. He smashes his fist into the monster's face once, again, feeling the flesh give way, feeling the attacker's blood slick his knuckles. He is only subliminally aware of the voice that calls out, pleading, "Dad! Dad, stop! Please stop!"

Harris doesn't stop, not until someone comes up behind him and grabs his wrist, wrenching it down and behind him. His other arm is caught, too, in an iron grip. He's pulled to his feet.

The man holding him, speaking near Harris's ear, says, "That's enough."

Seconds pass before the haze begins to clear from his brain, and it hits him, what's happening, that the man, a sheriff's deputy from his uniform, has handcuffed him, that he's been informed he's under arrest for assault—of his own son. Harris can't take it in. His shock makes him light headed, weak in his knees.

The officer sets him against the side of his truck bed, telling him, "Wait here," and, "Don't move," before turning to Kyle and offering him a hand. Kyle's face is blood smeared; one eye is closed, already darkening. He swipes at a cut on his mouth.

The sight sickens Harris. "Kyle, are you all right?" Does he ask out loud? Harris can't hear his own voice above the noise of panicked horror in his brain. "Jesus," he says, and he repeats it, "Jesus." Prayer or curse? He doesn't know. "Is he all right?" Harris appeals to the law officer, who, like Kyle, ignores him.

The deputy wants to call an ambulance, but Kyle refuses. He's eighteen now, as of last month. An adult. The law can't make him do anything, and neither can Harris.

"I just want to go home," Kyle says, and his voice trembles.

Harris's throat closes. "Son, I'm sorry. I lost it. I didn't know—I thought—" He stops. *Never tell . . .* The admonition falls across his brain, severing whatever words, whatever explanation, he could offer. After so many years the habit of secrecy is ironclad; it's part of him, flesh and bone. He blinks up at the sky, fighting tears. When he levels his gaze, Kyle meets his eyes but only briefly. "I'm so sorry." Harris says it again. His knees are weak at the sight of his son's battered face, the idea that his fists—his hands—have caused the damage. The same hands that cradled Kyle as a baby.

Harris felt an urge to cry on the day of Kyle's birth too. Looking down into Kyle's tiny face, scrunched and red, frowning mightily, Harris's heart swelled, and his head went light with a frothy glow of sensations he couldn't name, some combination of love and joy and wonder. He caught Holly's glance, and her jubilant, smiling image blurred in the prism of his tears. He remembers thinking he had never understood the nature of love before, how in the space of moments he was seized with devotion, the commitment to protect this little being, this tiny bit of life, with all he had in him. Whatever it took. If he were called on to give his own life for Kyle, he would. Instead look what he's done. What would have happened if the cop hadn't come? How far would Harris have gone? Would he have come to himself, stopped himself?

Kyle walks past him to the car he drove here in.

The deputy takes his elbow, escorting Harris to the patrol car.

"Is he okay to drive, do you think?" Harris asks as the lawman guides him down into the back seat. Wayman is the deputy's name, according to the name tag over his uniform shirt pocket: **S. WAYMAN**. Harris has heard the name before, he thinks. But where? From whom? He can't remember.

"Yeah, if you can call driving with one good eye okay." A mix of pity and disgust is evident in Wayman's tone, his demeanor. He slams the squad car door, goes back to Harris's truck.

Harris stares at the seat back. He knows Wayman'll find it, the packet with the four tabs of Oxy. He should have taken them all. He should have bought all Cal had and downed it. Maybe it would have been enough to kill him.

• • •

At the Greeley County Jail, a booking officer, not Wayman, hounds Harris for information: his name, where he lives, his age. He's frisked again; they take his stuff, wallet, car keys, cell phone, the change in his pocket. He's asked for his shoes and socks. An officer reads him his rights and asks if he understands them. He's told that he's charged with assault and possession of a controlled substance. Again he's asked if he understands. Even as he answers, "Yes," he wants to tell them, "Hell no," though in his heart he knows he's put himself here, in this god-awful place. The observer in his brain wonders how he could have let it happen, allowed himself to sink so low.

He's taken to a phone hanging on the wall at the end of a short concrete hallway and told he can call someone, an attorney, a member of his family. It's Saturday, but if a judge can be found, if Harris can lay hands on the cash, it's possible he could be bonded out. Harris lifts the receiver. Who to contact? Who wants to hear what he's got to say? Who would want to help? Not Holly. Not after the damage he's inflicted on their son. She'll have seen the evidence by now. She'll know about the drugs, how he's enabled Gee. She'll want nothing more to do with him, and he can't blame her. He imagines his mother will feel the same way. He returns the receiver to its resting place.

"I've got no one to call," he tells the officer.

He's given an orange jumpsuit, a stack of bedding, and rudimentary hygiene supplies: a comb, a toothbrush, a paper-wrapped bar of soap. After he's strip-searched and showered, he's led to a cell, roughly six by eight feet. There are two metal beds topped with thin mattresses bolted to one wall, one above the other. A sink/toilet combo stands in one corner. He's the only occupant. He sits on the edge of the bottom bunk, skin crawling with shame.

Time passes, enough that it loses meaning.

Nausea comes over him in waves. He loses count of how many times he's sick. He feels on fire; sweat soaks his jumpsuit, turning the rough fabric to ice, making him shiver, making his teeth clack together. His brain and his very bones ache with need. It's tearing him open from the inside. Sometimes he cries aloud; at least he thinks the noise comes from him. The sound is harsh, like sandpaper against his throat.

Lights go off and come back on.

Metal doors are racked open and shut.

Someone calls his name. Lifting his gaze, he sees a shadowy figure outside his cell door, grinning in at him, mocking him. It looks like Gee, morphs into Zeke's likeness. Now Hoff's image. Now Holly's, Kyle's, his mother's, in quick succession. He rolls onto his side, knifing his hands between his drawn-up knees, putting his back to their leers, their fingers raised in accusation.

17

Caroline flinched at the sound when her cell phone went off on the nightstand next to her bed. Up on one elbow, she fumbled for it, thinking: *Steve.* But when she answered, it wasn't his voice she heard; it was Martha's. She was at the hospital, Martha said, St. Joseph's, in the emergency room, where an ambulance had brought Lanie shortly after three in the morning.

Dread gripped Caroline's stomach. "I'm on my way," she said, shoving the covers aside. She was dressed and on the road within minutes. The streets were mostly empty at this early hour, and she drove well above the speed limit, heart racing. *Please, please.* But even as the prayer repeated in her brain, she knew the futility of it, that one day, no matter how hard she begged, she was going to lose Lanie. *Just not now, not today. Please . . .*

Caroline parked, and entering the hospital, she found Martha in the waiting room outside the ER.

The women embraced.

"The doctor hasn't been out yet," Martha said when they sat down.

"What happened?" Caroline asked.

"I stayed with her last night. Something told me I needed to. Of course she argued, and she flat-out refused to let me sleep in a chair in the dining room with her. She wanted me to go upstairs, get in a regular bed."

"But you didn't."

"No. If I was going to do that, I might just as well have gone home. I bedded down on the living room sofa next door and kind of catnapped. I checked on her a couple of times before midnight, and she seemed okay, but when I looked in on her a little before three this morning, her breathing was labored. I didn't wake her, didn't bother to ask her permission; I just called 911. I'm pretty sure she's furious at me."

"It's my fault," Caroline said, stricken with remorse. "I should never have told her yesterday about the man in Lone Pine, that he might be Dad. I thought it would give her a boost."

"Well, I think it did. She was so hopeful after you left."

"But maybe it was too much excitement." It hadn't occurred to Caroline such news might have the opposite effect, sinking her aunt instead of buoying her. "I should have kept my mouth shut until I had a chance to check it out."

"She did say she wanted you to call that private detective—"

"Thomas Williamson, I know, and I tried. The number's no longer in service."

"What about another detective? You shouldn't go to see the man alone."

"I've left a message with someone, an old friend who's in law enforcement."

"Lanie will be relieved," Martha said.

Caroline thought of how Lanie would tease her. *Steve Wayman?* she'd say, and she'd have that knowing twinkle in her eye. Caroline imagined it; she prayed Lanie would be well enough again for such a moment.

Martha said, "How about coffee? I'll see if I can find some that's decent."

Caroline thanked her, and leaning her head against the wall, she thought of her mother. She'd been appalled that Caroline intended to pursue the lead Jace had given her.

He ran you off the road. You could have been killed. What if the information he gave you is some kind of trap? You should go to the police, Caroline.

Her mother had been so insistent that Caroline had been forced out of defense to say she'd contacted Steve. "He's a cop, Mom, a sheriff's deputy. He'll know how I should handle it."

They were in the kitchen, doing the dinner dishes. Her mom was washing, Caroline drying. Her mother didn't respond at first, but after several moments she shut off the water and asked, "Is there something going on between you?"

"Steve and I?" Caroline was dumbfounded. "No! Why would you think—?"

"Last October, when you saw him—something about the way you talked about him, it was—"

"Nothing," Caroline said, but it hadn't been nothing, had it? Her feelings for him now weren't nothing . . . she dropped her glance, feeling dismayed.

"The summer you dated before you went off to college, I worried you were too serious."

"Yes, well, I went to Iowa, didn't I, and met Rob." *And got pregnant.* Those words were there, but it was unnecessary to say them. Her mother knew. Caroline set a plate on the stack in the cabinet, making a clatter. She had never for an instant regretted having Nina, but if she wasn't careful, especially lately, she could get angry all over again at her decision to have casual sex with a guy she hadn't been sure she'd loved, and she could deplore her negligence when it came to swallowing her nightly birth control pill—for all the good it did.

"Caro?" her mom said tentatively.

She twisted the dish towel in her hands. "I guess the marriage, it's not—it's not turning out too well."

"I'm so sorry, Caro." Her mother's expression softened. "Have you decided what you're going to do? Is there any way to work it out?"

"I don't think so. Maybe if Rob would step up, if he'd take responsibility, but I don't see that happening." Even as she spoke, Caroline wondered, Was she being honest with herself? Was it only Rob's failure behind her lack of hope, or was her discontent deeper? It felt as if her unhappiness was of longer duration than her discovery last fall of Rob's dishonesty. But she'd soldiered on in service to some long-ago vow not to end up divorced like her parents.

"You can't trust him."

Caroline glanced at her mom. "No," she answered, and she felt certain about this one thing at least. Maybe her principles were more inflexible than she'd like them to be, but Rob had crossed a line as far as she was concerned. He'd pulled this same stunt twice—years apart. But all of that aside, she knew she'd question anything he said from now on.

"Well," her mom said, "if anyone knows there's no love where there's no trust, it would be me."

"I'm sorry, Mom. I mean if my looking for Dad—if it's hurting you."

"No, I understand. He's your dad, after all. It's not as if I haven't wondered myself where he is, how he is. We had some good—some wonderful years. And," she had said, taking Caroline's face in her hands, "we had you."

They'd both been fighting tears by that point.

Even now, recalling the conversation, Caroline was still surprised at her mother's candor. *I'm glad you're getting help from Steve.* That had been her final comment.

Caroline could only hope she would hear from him, but she wasn't confident. Her message to him had scarcely been cogent. She'd stammered out an apology for her behavior last October, saying something to the effect that she usually didn't drink so much. She'd made reference to Rob, his legal troubles; then, backtracking, she'd said it wasn't Rob she needed advice about. *It's my dad*, she'd said. *He's missing*. Who knew what Steve would make of that? In any case, when she'd been in the midst of leaving her number, her phone had cut off. She wasn't certain now if he'd have a way of returning her call if he wanted to.

Caroline looked up when Martha returned, a steaming Styrofoam cup in either hand. "It's out of the machine," she said. "All I could find."

Taking a cup, Caroline thanked her.

Sitting down, Martha said, "I would feel like you."

Brows raised, Caroline met her glance.

"If it were me, I'd want to go to Lone Pine, too, and see for myself if the man was my dad."

"I thought I would leave today."

"Well, you know I'm not going anywhere. If you do, Lanie won't be alone."

The rush of Caroline's gratitude brought tears to her eyes. Martha patted her arm. "I should call Mom," Caroline said.

"You go on, honey. I'll find you if the doctor comes."

When she answered Caroline's call, her mother didn't bother with a greeting. "Where are you?"

"At the hospital with Lanie. She was having difficulty breathing, and Martha called an ambulance. She's so frail now, Mom." Caroline had found an exit door into an atrium and come outside, but the fresh air and sunshine were having little effect on the weight of her sorrow. "She'll be gone soon. I just know it."

"I should come," her mother said.

"Yes. If you want—" *Closure.* That was the right word, natural to say, but somehow Caroline couldn't.

"I've known Lanie longer than your dad. Did you know? We lived in the same neighborhood, on the same street. We jumped rope together, played jacks, giggled about boys. We were sisters before we ever became sisters-in-law." Her mother's voice quavered. "Once she tried teaching me to sew. I was terrible at it. No patience. But she was gifted. She created her own designs, made her own patterns. Do you remember the dress she made for you one Easter? It was before your dad left us. You must have been four or five. It was of white organdy—"

"With tiny lavender flowers." Caroline knew because her mom had saved it. She'd found it swaddled in layers of tissue while going through the boxes in the linen closet.

"Yes, and a wide lavender ribbon sash. Oh, you were so adorable in it. Hoff bought you a pair of white patent-leather shoes and little socks with lace trim."

"There was a hat, wasn't there? It had lavender flowers—"

"Lanie decorated a straw hat to match."

"Where is it? Did it get thrown out?" Caroline could see it in her mind's eye.

"Packed," her mother said. "It's in one of the boxes you're having shipped home."

Home. The word sounded somehow foreign. Caroline couldn't imagine it for a moment, the house in Des Moines where she lived with Rob.

"Lanie always wanted to be a mother; did you know that, Caro? But the closest she ever came was caring for you."

"She hardly ever talked about it, Mom, and I never really asked her. It seemed as if it made her sad. I know she was engaged once—"

"Yes, to the love of her life. But he died just weeks before their wedding, had a massive coronary. He was only twenty-seven. It was horrible for her. There's never been anyone since that I know of."

The door into the atrium opened, and a woman came out. Her eyes were scoured looking, red with grief, or possibly it was only allergies. Caroline left the bench in the atrium's center and walked to a gate in the far corner.

"I'll get myself together now and come there. You're at St. Joe's?"

"Yes," Caroline said. "I'm so glad you're coming," she added.

"I don't want Lanie to leave this world without her knowing I love her in spite of everything."

. . .

It was late morning before the doctor came to say Lanie had pneumonia and they were admitting her to the ICU. By then Caroline's mother had arrived. Nearly two more hours passed before she, Martha, and Caroline were allowed on the ICU floor to visit Lanie, one at a time. Martha went first, and when she returned from her ten-minute visit, Caroline knew her stoicism was contrived, more an act of will for Caroline's sake. She gave Caroline and her mother a brief hug and, dividing her glance between them, said there were machines making all kinds of noise, and they should be prepared for that and for how pale Lanie was. *Faded* was the word Martha used. "Try not to be alarmed. They're doing all they can—within limits," Martha added.

Caroline blinked away the ready threat of tears. She knew Lanie had a DNR—a Do Not Resuscitate order. She'd made it clear that she wanted no heroic measures taken once her body began to fail. Caroline and her mom had them too. It made sense; of course it did. But standing at Lanie's bedside a few minutes later, barely able to detect the rise and fall of Lanie's chest, Caroline felt an unreasoning urge to shout for a doctor, a nurse, anyone who could stop the terrible thing that was happening. She took Lanie's hand, her heart heavy in her chest, and she knew if Lanie were able, she would ask to be allowed to slip away. *Let me go*, she would say.

Caroline bent her lips to her aunt's ear. "Let me find Daddy first," she whispered. "Let me bring your brother home."

. . .

It was the habit of years and a desperate need for reassurance that drove Caroline to call Rob later. She'd left the hospital and come to her car, still parked outside the ER, needing fresh air, a break from the awful waiting.

At first Rob was gentle. "I know this must be so hard for you, Caro."

"I'm scared I won't find my dad in time." She named her gravest fear.

"Well," he said, "you've done your best."

Caroline stared through the car windshield. *Done my best?* "No," she said. "I've got this lead now. The man in Lone Pine could be Dad. I've got to check it out."

"What? I thought you would come home now. I mean after Lanie—"

"No, Rob. I can't." Did he truly not see?

"What about our situation?"

"It isn't *our* situation, Rob. It's yours. *You* faked the documents."

"What if I were to throw myself on their mercy, plead ignorance, say I didn't understand? You'd back me, right?"

Caroline stared through the windshield. Would she?

"It would be better, though, don't you think, if we made an appointment to see them together?" he went on. "If we explained—"

"There's no *we*," she insisted, angry now and unable to conceal it. "You keep trying to make me a part of this. Now you're asking me to lie—?"

"Like they say—" Rob continued as if she hadn't spoken. "It's better to ask forgiveness than permission. I mean, what can the IRS or the insurers do? Ah, well, I don't really know what they can do." He barked a short syllable of anxious laughter. "That's what's got me spooked."

"I can't believe the way you're talking, Rob. Do you hear yourself? I don't think I even know you anymore—" It scared her, and at the same time it hurt, saying it aloud. The spoken words brought into sharpened focus the differences between them that until now had only lurked in the shadowy recesses of her mind. The gap was there and real in a way she hadn't anticipated. There would be no going back from this, she thought, and her heart faltered.

"I don't know what you mean, Caro."

"Then I can't help you, Rob. We're in two different places. You must see it—" She was pleading with him.

"But I need you."

"I'm sorry, but my aunt is dying. My mother is uprooting her life, and I've just found out it's possible my dad didn't simply walk out on me and Lanie; he may have disappeared under suspicious circumstances. I can't just leave—"

"So what you're telling me is all that is more important than me—than us."

He waited, but she didn't break the taut silence.

"Caroline?"

"I don't know what to say." She didn't. It was as if Rob, the business, the life they'd built in Iowa, belonged to some other woman, one who had been sleeping and was now waking as if from a long dream. It was the oddest sensation. Caroline had no idea how to interpret it. She felt sad, frightened, and somehow grimly determined all at once.

"If you decide to turn me in, will you at least have the decency to tell me beforehand?"

"What about your decency toward me, Rob?" Caroline asked, her voice cracking, breaking.

A heavy sigh was his only response.

She could picture his gesture, the impatient sweep of his hand over his head. "I have to go," she said, and she severed their connection.

18

He has no idea how much time has passed or what day it is when an officer appears outside his cell door, and his head is finally clear enough that he feels certain it *is* an officer and not his mind raving.

"Steve Wayman," the man says. "You remember me?"

Harris struggles to sit upright. "Yeah," he says. "You're the cop who pulled me off my son. I owe you, man."

Wayman nods to someone down the corridor out of Harris's sight. The cell door starts to slide open. "You mind if I come in?"

"Does it matter?"

Wayman doesn't answer. The cell door closes as soon as he's stepped inside.

"What day is it?" Harris asks.

"Monday. You been in here since Saturday."

"God! Are you serious?" Harris stares at the deputy.

Wayman nods. He leans against the wall opposite where Harris is sitting on the bunk. "Looks like you're having a rough time."

"Kyle! How is my son Kyle? Do you know?"

"You banged him up pretty good, but lucky for you, none of what you did was life threatening."

Harris keeps Wayman's gaze. Is that supposed to comfort him?

They share a beat.

Wayman says, "You're the athletic director at the high school in Wyatt, head coach of the baseball team, right?"

"I was. I doubt I've got a job anymore." *Everyone knows you're a doper. Gee's your dealer.* Kyle's declaration burns in Harris's ears.

"You know a kid, a senior by the name of Gander Drake, goes by Gee." The deputy isn't asking.

In the moment before Harris answers, he remembers where he heard the deputy's name before—that it was from Gee. Wayman and the Wyatt cop, Ken Carter, had gone to Gee's house and questioned him in connection with the robberies. "I know Gee," Harris admits. No way to deny it.

"He's your supplier. You buy drugs from him, is that right?"

Harris looks down, but he knows—knows in his gut—he's done with it. The lying and covering up. Done with the dope. He doesn't know how, whether he can pull it off. Maybe it won't make a difference. He's likely got no chance in hell of making it up to his family, but he's got to try. He looks at Wayman. "Yeah. I buy from him." *Sometimes.* The word hovers on his tongue, but he keeps it there. It's possible Gee has already nailed Zeke, and there's nothing Harris can do about that. But he won't give up Cal. Let her downfall come at someone else's hands.

"Well, here's the thing." Wayman comes off the wall. "I've been working with the Wyatt police trying to resolve a case, a string of robberies in Wyatt and a couple outside city limits in Madrone County—you know what I'm talking about, right? We've got reason to believe you know Gee's involved. There's another guy working with Gee, his cousin, Darren Causey."

"You've talked to Gee's girlfriend, Amber, right? Have you arrested Gee?"

"Not yet, but we will soon, and when we do, if you were to help us get these two, help us make the charges stick, it could help you out of this jam you're in."

"Testify against them, you mean." Harris can't sort out how the prospect makes him feel.

Wayman leans back against the wall, crosses his arms over his chest, waits.

"You guys realize I'm not involved in the robberies, don't you? This isn't some kind of cop game?"

"It's no game. There are text messages between you and Gee, most of them regarding drug buys, but there's one where he says something to the effect that if you talk to law enforcement about what you saw, he'll come after you. So we know you witnessed something—direct activity by Gee and Darren—related to the robberies. We want to know what it was, and yeah, we'd need your testimony at trial. In exchange, it's possible the DA would be open to making some kind of deal, let you plead to a lesser charge. Maybe your sentence could be deferred, especially if you were to agree to enter a rehab facility. Specifics would be up to a judge and the DA to work out."

He doesn't deserve any deals—that's what Harris wants to say. But Wayman goes on before he can.

"Gee's young. He's got a chance here to turn his life around, but he's the kind of kid that's got to hit a wall hard enough it'll wake him up. You can help with that, help this kid get back on track."

Never forget that as a player, you're a role model. You're somebody's hero. Maybe you'll inspire a kid to turn his life around . . . Hoff said that to Harris once. Words to that effect. He expected great things from Harris. Not this, nothing like what Harris has done. Hoff would be sick to see Harris here. He looks at Wayman. "You still have your dad?"

"No. He died a couple years ago."

"Yeah, I—my dad's gone too." Harris's voice hooks on the words. They're like stones in his mouth. He feels the salt burn of tears and pinches the bridge of his nose. "It was longer ago than that. I was thirteen, barely. Well, he wasn't my real dad, but he was the closest thing to a dad I ever had. I've been thinking about him a lot in here. Seeing him. Maybe it's coming off the dope."

His visions of Hoff have taken him back to the earliest days, when his mom and Hoff first got together. Those sunlit, treasured days when Harris had no reason to believe they wouldn't last forever. With Hoff to protect them, they finally felt truly safe. Oklahoma, that long, nightmarish highway journey away from there—all of that was behind them.

"I know when I see him it's not real," Harris tells Wayman, "but it's like I can hear him talking to me, about how bad I've screwed up. God, he'd be so damn disappointed in the mess I've made."

"You've got the same chance here as Gee. You can turn this around. I've seen families broken by worse come back together when they can see the commitment to do the right thing is real."

Harris wipes his hands down his face. He looks at Wayman. "You get a chance to tell your dad goodbye?"

A look crosses Wayman's face when he says, "No," some conflicted mix of guilt, regret, and love that Harris recognizes.

"Me either," Harris says, and it's the elements of humanity and kindness in Wayman's expression and demeanor that lead him to add, "Things between him and me and my mom got kind of rough at the end. He wasn't perfect; no one is—" He breaks off. Sorrow and regret are bitter in his throat. He swallows them down, pushes himself to say it, the rest of what's in his heart, the truth he wants to keep. "He was a better man, a better role model, most of the time, than I've been in all eighteen years I've been a dad to my sons. I wish I'd told him . . ."

"There's still time to get straight with them."

"I doubt they'll want anything to do with me after this."

"What about your testimony? You can stop Gee before he moves on to committing worse crimes."

"That's not going to make me a hero, not to my, or Gee's, family."

Wayman allows the silence. He even seems comfortable with it, as if he knows Harris will see it—that taking the stand and telling the truth, about himself, about Gee, is the only choice he's got.

"All right. What the hell. I'll do it," Harris says, and he thinks it's probably stupid, working with the cops. But everyone already hates him. He's got nothing and no one left to lose.

• • •

"You've got a visitor." The officer—a deputy Harris doesn't know—opens the cell.

He sits up, working his tongue over his teeth, around the dry corners of his mouth. It's been hours—he thinks over a day may have passed since Wayman was here—but Harris feels only marginally better. At least he's done puking, but everything aches. He runs a shaky hand across his scalp, his matted hair. He needs a shower. "What day is it?" he asks.

"Wednesday. You been in here four days." The lawman answers as if he gets the question all the time, as if supplying such information is part of his job description. "Stand up," he says. "You gotta be cuffed before I can take you down to the visiting room."

Harris squints at the guard. "I don't want to see anyone."

"Well," the cop says, "they're here, came all this way to see your sorry ass, so get up."

Harris does as he's told, letting himself be handcuffed and led out of the cell and down the corridor like a dog. At the door to the visiting area, he catches the guard's eyes. "You know who it is?"

"Your mama," the cop says. "If it was anyone else, I wouldn't give two hoots in hell if you saw her, but I had her in the ninth grade for algebra back in the nineties when she was still teaching at Wyatt Junior High. She cut me a lot of slack then. I'm returning the favor now, because for some reason she thinks a loser like you is worth saving." The cop thrusts open the door, pushing Harris through it, making him stagger.

Righting himself, he sees her, his mother, sitting small and erect at a table in the left-hand corner of a room that's furnished with a collection of Formica-topped tables and hard plastic chairs. Except for Harris's escort, they're alone. Their eyes lock, and hers are shadowed with pain and consternation that borders on fear. His gut lurches. He drops his glance, hating that she has to see him here like this.

The guard shoves him again toward the table.

When he sits opposite her, she bends toward him. "I've come every day since I heard from Holly, and every day Jason"—she indicates the deputy, who's retreated and is leaning now against the wall near the entrance door, with a terse nod—"told me you were sick, not able to talk. The drugs—" Breaking off, she looks away.

"You didn't have to, Ma." Harris regrets how he sounds, as if he's blaming her.

"Of course I did," she says, and her voice, although barely above a whisper, is harsh. "You're my son, no matter what you've done." She stops again, fighting for composure.

His own throat jams. "Have you seen them, Holly or Kyle or Connor?" he asks when he can speak again.

"I went to your house. I couldn't believe—didn't want to believe it when Holly called Saturday to say you'd been arrested, that you had— but then I saw Kyle, his face, with my own eyes. My God, Harris, what were you thinking? Your own son? How could you do that to him? Was it the drugs?"

His eyes feel scalded with an unwanted threat of tears, and he raises his cuffed wrists, pinching the bridge of his nose to stop them.

"Oh, Harris." His mother's sorrow breathes through the words.

He can't look at her.

When he lowers his hands, she slides her palm over them, leaving it there. He feels her warmth seep into his knuckles. "I've spoken to an attorney," she says. "He says if you'll agree to go into rehab, you might get off with probation. You can say it was the drugs, that you were hallucinating and didn't realize—"

Harris locks her gaze. "It wasn't the drugs, Mom. You and I both know—the drugs are—"

"You take them because you're in pain with your back." She's insistent, pleading with him to go along. It's the party line, the rote excuse, and it's bullshit. She's got to know they can't keep it up.

"C'mon, Mom—" He holds her gaze, willing her to see it, how it's eating him alive from the inside.

Her eyes are sheened with tears, and yet she broadens her smile, which is more a terrible grimace, wrung with anguish. "I know you can get off them, Harris. Look at you now. Three days, and it's okay, isn't it? I know you don't feel great, but if you can keep going, if you can stay away from them, in time, you'll feel better, stronger. Rehab will help—"

"No!" Harris raises his wrists and brings them down with a clatter on the table.

The officer—Jason—comes off the wall.

"It's fine," Harris tells him. He faces his mother. "I'm losing it, Mom. When Kyle came at me, I didn't even know who he was. It scares the shit out of me when I think about it. He's got every right to be pissed at me for doing drugs, every right to come at me, but what if the cop hadn't shown up? Huh? What if I keep on losing it? Am I going to end up in a padded cell somewhere?"

"Harris—"

"Mom, please, I'm trying to tell you—" His voice breaks, and he stops, fighting to keep his cool, keep his voice down, keep it steady. "We both know what the drugs are about. I try so hard—but I can't fight it. Look what I did to my kid—"

"He's hurt by all of this, Harris. Connor and Holly are too. They don't know what's happening to you."

"You aren't listening to me—"

"Of course I am. You need to get help."

"How, Mom? What kind of help?"

"This is my fault."

"What?" He looks at her, nonplussed.

"All of this." Her arm encompasses the room. "I'm a counselor"—she thumps her chest with a closed fist—"trained to help kids in trouble, but I didn't help you. My own son is suffering, in jeopardy, because of my mistakes. I'm afraid for you, Harris, afraid of what's happening to you." Tears slick her eyes; her head wobbles on her neck. "I should have known—should have realized—"

"Don't do this, Mom. Don't beat yourself up." Harris darts a glance at the guard and looks back at his mother, bending toward her, keeping her gaze. "It'll be fine. I talked to a deputy yesterday. It's possible I can make a deal with the DA and get off with probation."

"What kind of deal?"

"Let's wait to talk about it until I get out of here, okay? It'll be a good thing, maybe."

She pulls in a chest full of air, swiping at her eyes, the hair at her temples, settling herself. "I hope so," she says.

Harris looks off into the middle distance, thinking hope is what you hang on to when you've got nothing else.

19

A bit over five hours after leaving her mother's house, Caroline had reached the Hill Country and managed to get herself lost. She was parked on the darkening shoulder of some numberless, caliche-topped nowhere road, studying a road map on the screen of her cell phone when it went off, and she flinched, almost dropping it. Looking at the tiny screen, her heart almost stopped. *Steve.* Making the connection, she said his name out loud and then went silent, heart tapping hard against her ribs.

"Caroline?"

She bit her lip, stifling an urge to laugh and repeat his name, making a joke. She thought of severing the connection. Instead she said, "I think I'm lost."

"Are you here in the Hill Country? You said in your message—"

"How did you get my phone number?"

"My caller ID. You gave me your number in October. I added it to my contact list."

"Oh."

"You don't remember."

Her face warmed. "Well, to be honest, that whole evening is something of a blur. I—I don't usually drink like that, you know, one after the other. I was—I was kind of a wreck." Why was she repeating this? "I'm really sorry to have been so much trouble."

"You weren't any trouble. It's fine. In fact, I've thought about calling you a time or two to see whether things worked out with your husband, the business."

"Thank you. I mean for your concern that night and, well, everything. Nothing has really changed, though." She looked through the windshield. She was parked up against a rock outcropping, but across the road the land was flat. It might have been a meadow or a farmer's field. There wasn't enough light to tell.

"I truly wish I could be of some help, but as I said before, the kind of trouble you mentioned, it's not my field of expertise. Did you contact an attorney? I still think that's your best bet."

"I remember you said that, and no, I haven't. Actually, I was calling about another matter."

"You mentioned—it has to do with your dad?"

"Yes. I could probably star with my family on reality TV." Caroline's laugh was short, inappropriate. She didn't know how to interpret Steve's silence. Fresh humiliation burned in her throat. "Never mind." Her gaze drifted, unseeing.

"A minute ago you said you were lost? Where are you trying to go?"

"A little town called Lone Pine. Do you know it?"

"Yeah, but I wouldn't call it a town. There's not much there other than a gas station, a liquor store, and a graveyard."

"No hotel?"

"No. There are hotels here in Greeley. You would have gone through it a while back."

"I turned off 73 just north of there. I remember passing a restaurant, where a lot of eighteen-wheelers were parked."

"Bo Dean's. It's a combo truck stop / café. Terrible coffee and worse food. Lampasas might be a better option for a hotel, though. It's not as far, maybe five or so miles on up 73, if you can get back there."

Lampasas. Just south of there was where Bill Devlin, the private investigator Ryan Kelly had hired, had met the truck driver and found the waitress who had both identified her dad as having been there.

Steve spoke into her silence. "I can probably figure out where you are, try and come to you—"

"No, that's okay. I should go to Lampasas. I have a lead—"

"Why don't you tell me what this is about, Caroline? What are you looking for?"

Not what, who. Her thought came and went. "I might have told you, I mean years ago, that summer after high school—"

"When we dated?"

"Yes." She was relieved the fact was acknowledged at last. She couldn't figure out why they hadn't mentioned their prior relationship when they'd run into each other last October. Looking back at the kids they'd been, reminiscing about old times—after so many years it should have been easy. Instead she'd felt—she *still* felt—a kind of tension between them, even a certain wariness. But maybe her feelings were the lingering effect of her embarrassment over her behavior then.

"When we dated," she repeated. "I think you knew this—that I wasn't in touch with my dad?"

"I remember."

"I've never heard from him, no one has, not in years." She looked through the windshield, and there, in the farthest glow from her headlights, she glimpsed a doe as it leaped across the road, and the sight caught her up in an undercurrent of subliminal joy. Closer by, dozens of moths swirled in the same light, glittering like tiny stars.

"Have you found him?" Steve prompted.

"Maybe. There's a man in Lone Pine who could be him." She rubbed her eyes and sighed. "I shouldn't bother you with this."

"Can you get back to the truck stop?" Steve asked. "Bo Dean's? I could meet you there. We could drive somewhere else for coffee. Or dinner. Have you eaten? I was about to go out for a hamburger. There are other places—"

"Just how bad is the coffee at Bo Dean's?"

He laughed, and she joined him, but inside she was shaking.

. . .

She stood inside the door of the truck stop, and when her eyes connected with Steve's, she suffered a fresh outbreak of anxiety mixed with regret at having involved him. He was little more than a stranger, a boy she used to know, grown now into a man. Although they were looking directly at each other, he lifted his hand, indicating his location in a booth near the back, or perhaps he was waving away her hesitation, which must have been obvious.

He stood up as she approached, seemingly glad to see her. His smile, the way it quirked one side of his mouth and crinkled the corners of his eyes, was as endearing as her memory of it. But the blue of his eyes seemed more weathered, his look more rugged, as if he spent a lot of his time outdoors. His hair was still dark but cut short now, military style. She remembered running her fingertips through it where it had curled over his shirt collar in high school. She recalled the sense of his breath warm on her face when he'd turned toward her and smiled. He had told her once—the last time they'd been together before she had left for Iowa—that he loved her.

You shouldn't, she had advised him.

It was a mistake walking back into his life now. The thought rose and was replaced by another, an admonishment not to flatter herself. They'd been eighteen when they'd had feelings for one another. It was ancient history. She made herself walk toward him. He was likely as married as she was. If he'd said last fall, she didn't remember. Hopefully his marriage had aged better.

He looked uncertain, a bit abashed, as if he couldn't decide now that she was close enough whether to shake her hand or hug her. They did neither.

She slid into the booth, and he sat across from her. The red vinyl felt lumpy and cold beneath her jeans-clad legs. She made a production out of setting her purse to one side, tugging at the sleeves of her black wool blazer. She was wearing it over a cream-colored cashmere sweater, but still, she was chilled and wished she'd brought her coat.

His gaze was congenial but seemed guarded.

"I'm sober, I promise."

"I can see that," he said. His gaze on hers was steady, penetrating.

"I'm truly sorry about last time, that night—"

"It's fine. You were upset. I understand."

"I don't remember much about it, what all I said."

"You were worried your husband might have committed some illegalities with your business. You didn't know your liability if that was the case."

"Well, that was definitely the case, and I still don't know my liability."

"As I explained—"

"I know. Business fraud isn't your area of expertise."

He kept her gaze.

She felt her face warm. The waitress came. They ordered coffee. Steve asked for extra cream.

"I'm embarrassed to say this, but I don't know anything about your life now," Caroline said when the waitress left. "If you told me before—"

"You don't remember."

"No. I'm sorry. You're married? Children?"

"No to both. I was married once for a short time. It didn't work out."

"I'm sorry." She offered the customary bromide, while inside she fought regrettable fillips of amazement and delight. A stern voice in her brain warned she wasn't here to hook up with him.

"No reason to be." He shifted his weight on his elbows. "You have a daughter, you said."

She smiled. "Yes. Nina. She's in college at Denver University, in her sophomore year." How much longer would she be able to stay there if Rob's actions cost them the business, put them into bankruptcy? Caroline pushed the questions away.

"You've lived in Des Moines since you graduated college, built a transportation business, and in your spare time you like to garden—so much that you've wondered lately if you wouldn't like to take a few landscape architecture classes. I'm pretty sure that's what you said."

"I told you all of that?" She was delighted again in spite of herself.

"Uh-huh." He grinned. "You also said you hated winters up there worse than you ever hated the long, hot, sticky summers down here."

She smiled. "It's nice to know I don't lie when I drink."

"No. Drinking or sober, you're one of the most honest, down-to-earth people I've ever met—always were."

His words—as deeply touched as she was by them, she could have argued she didn't deserve them. Instead she thanked him. "It means so much to me, hearing that from you."

He shrugged. "Honesty is rare these days. Trust me, I'm a cop. I know."

"It surprises me, you being in law enforcement. Did I say that before? You were going to veterinary school."

He shifted a bit, dropping his gaze.

"What happened?" Something in his demeanor made her ask.

"My roommate at U of H—his sister was held hostage for the better part of a day by her husband."

"Oh no!"

"Actually, she'd filed for divorce, and he was angry enough about it that he came back to their house with a gun and threatened to shoot her unless she agreed to stay married to him. Ha! Yeah, like that was going to happen."

"He didn't—?"

"No. The cops were able to talk him down. She got away from him, unharmed, and he went to jail for a while. She was damn lucky, though, and so was he."

"Her ex."

"He got a year or thereabouts. Had he gone through with his threat and killed her, he could have gotten life, possibly a death sentence. She could be six feet under, but because of the police, the way they handled the situation, both of them are still alive, still breathing. It made an impression on me."

She was intrigued. "So . . . what? Did you decide then and there to go into law enforcement?"

"Pretty much, yeah. I thought what if I could do that, save lives like that? I was a kid. What did I know?" He laughed. It wasn't humorous. At her look he said, "The cops don't always get it right, or they don't get there fast enough. People die. The wrong people, the right people." He shrugged.

"The switch you made, becoming a cop, it's not so very different, really, from becoming a veterinarian."

Steve angled his head, perplexed.

"You always said whatever you did, you wanted to be a force for good on the planet, and here you are, but instead of helping four-legged animals, you're helping the two-legged variety." She smiled.

He grinned, looking self-conscious. "What about you? You think you've found your dad?"

"I don't know for sure." Caroline paused when the waitress reappeared.

She set down the mugs of coffee and four small pitchers of cream. When she left, Steve said, "You still drink your coffee black?"

"You remember that?" She was surprised, somehow touched.

His gaze on hers was underscored with humor. "You said sugar and cream wouldn't help the taste. I think the only reason you drank coffee at all was to look grown up."

"Probably."

"We didn't have a Starbucks on every corner back then."

"It's a good thing. I'd probably have been enticed to drink all those concoctions they make with whipped cream and gotten as big as a house." She picked up her mug, sipped, grimaced. "That's too bitter even for me."

"Add both creams. Even a spoonful of sugar helps."

She did as he suggested and tried it again. "Tolerable," she said.

"About your dad," he said.

"There's a man—not in the town of Lone Pine itself but outside it—who could be him. He's kind of a hermit, I guess."

"What makes you think he could be your father?"

"It's a long story."

"I've got no plans." His smile was one sided, easy in the way Caroline remembered, that way that made her heart turn over.

"I've been in Houston, helping my mom pack up her house—she's moving into a condo community for seniors—anyway, I found an old letter my dad wrote to her when I was sixteen. I didn't even know they were in touch. Mom never said—she always made me feel I shouldn't talk about him to her." Caroline stopped, hearing how she sounded: resentful, self-pitying—still sixteen. She couldn't look at Steve.

"Maybe she avoided the subject for your sake," he said. "You were pretty angry at your dad back then."

Caroline looked up. "You said then I should give him a chance."

"Anger cuts both ways." Steve kept her gaze. "I'm sorry for the circumstances that brought you, but I'm not sorry you're here."

Caroline warmed beneath his regard, the confusion of her emotions. He'd been the first boy she'd loved, and she could still see that boy, still feel him, in this man sitting across from her. But the man was a stranger. Yet she couldn't deny she was drawn to him. She felt at ease with him, as if all the years between then and now had lasted only a moment. "Dad had a terrible accident a few weeks before he wrote Mom the letter."

"When he fell at the stadium."

"You know—?"

"You told me."

"I did? Oh . . . when I saw you last October." She covered her face briefly with her hands. "Is there anything I didn't talk about?"

"Not then. You told me about it the summer we dated, before you went to Iowa. The actual accident happened when we were high school freshmen, I think, or sophomores? Anyway, you were still beating yourself up that you didn't go see him. And you were also still pretty pissed off at your dad for remarrying."

Caroline sat back, flustered and somehow buoyed by his reminder of how close they'd been. They'd told each other everything. They'd imagined they would spend their lives together. Once they had gone to a state park, where guests were asked to register. Steve had picked up the pen and written *Mr. and Mrs. Steven Wayman*. It had thrilled her.

She had an urge to ask if he remembered doing that, but it felt wrong—even that she had the desire bothered her. Suppose he said yes? Suppose he said no? She loosened her gaze from his, watched as her fingertips traced the table's edge, saying she regretted it, that she'd been so angry with her dad.

He knew about regret, Steve said, and when she looked up, he caught her glance and kept it, and the moment hung, waiting, prescient, alight with their history of what-ifs and if-onlys.

Caroline looked away first. "What time is it? I'm sure I've kept you long enough."

"It's after seven. Are you hungry? We could go for a burger."

"Do they make a grilled cheese here? I don't think you can mess up a grilled cheese, can you?"

"Let's ask." Steve got the waitress's attention.

She shouldn't keep him, Caroline thought, but she didn't want him to go. Neither did she want to go with him somewhere else and lose the moment, the warmth of their connection. Bad coffee aside, they were fine here. The noise level was comfortable, the occasional louder clatter of dishes and cutlery underscored by a lower, more constant hum of conversation from other patrons. Outside it was cold and dark. Night wrapped the building like a cloak.

The waitress came over and agreed she could have the sandwiches right out, along with bowls of tomato soup, if they wanted.

Nodding, Caroline thanked her.

"That would be great," Steve said, and once the waitress was gone, he found Caroline's gaze. "When did you last see your dad? I know you told me, but I've forgotten the details."

"Umm, I was maybe fifteen or sixteen? He drove down to Houston from Wyatt, where he lived with his second wife."

"Wyatt's south of here, not too far—thirty miles."

"I saw the exit for it, driving up."

"His wife had a son, didn't she?"

"Yes." Caroline didn't want to go into it, her petty jealousy of Harris. "When Dad came to Houston, he stayed with Aunt Lanie. The last time, when I was fifteen, Mom drove me over there. I didn't want to go; Mom made me. The second I got there, Dad started in, pressuring me to go to Wyatt with him for the weekend. I told him I would never go. Ever. I said horrible things." Caroline brought her knuckled fist to her mouth, seeing it in her mind, hearing herself. "I told him I hated him, Julia, and Harris, and if he loved them so much, why didn't he just go be with them and leave me alone. I told him—" Caroline paused and glanced at Steve, but on seeing his compassion, she jerked her eyes away. "I told him I hoped they all rotted in hell."

"You were just a kid, Caro, a hurt kid—"

"I was evil, saying those horrible things." Steve started to protest. Caroline put up her hand. "Please don't defend me."

"All right," he said softly. "What happened after that?"

"He left. I never saw him again. Oh, he called a handful of times, and we talked. I should say he talked. I kept it up, giving him an attitude, until pretty soon he stopped calling. I've always figured it was my fault." Caroline held her hands in her lap, one thumbnail picking the other. She was mortified by her confession. Until now only Lanie had known how awful she was.

"Well, I never met him, but there was always something in the way you talked about him—I know you were mad, but underneath I could tell you really loved and missed him. I bet he knew it too."

Caroline glanced up at Steve, grateful and somehow also shamed by his kindness. It was a moment longer before her throat loosened enough that she could speak normally. "When I was growing up, until he remarried, he took me everywhere with him. He used to dance me around on his feet—" She paused now, afraid she would cry in spite of herself.

She saw it when Steve's hand moved, when it stopped short of touching hers. She wanted that, his touch, and her desire for it disconcerted her. She was glad for the interruption when the waitress returned with their soup and sandwiches. They busied themselves with their meal.

"Mom thinks he was scared because some woman's husband was after him."

Steve looked up from his soup, brows raised. "I remember he cheated on her, didn't he?"

"Yes. Mom's convinced he had a woman in every town. She's probably right. He cheated on his second wife too."

"Men have disappeared for less," Steve said. "Hell, men have been killed for less." He sat back. "Wow. I'm sorry. I shouldn't have said that. It's the cop coming out."

"It's a possibility." Caroline shrugged. "One of them, anyway, although I haven't found any evidence of his being caught. From everything I've heard so far, it's more likely his disappearance is related to his job."

"How so?"

"He was involved with some men, the head coach at Tillman State and some of the boosters and alumni—they were paying athletes—" She stopped. "It's such a wild story."

"It might go well with dessert. We could take a chance, try the chocolate pie. What do you think?"

She smiled. They ordered a slice of coconut pie to go with the chocolate, and while they ate them, Caroline recounted the details of her meeting with Coach Kelly and her subsequent literal run-in with Jace that had first landed her in the hospital and then led to her flying to Wichita to talk to Tricia, who had mentioned Kip, the investigative reporter. "He's the one who put the pieces of the puzzle together for me, the trouble Dad was in, the threat that was hanging over him. Kip, too, I guess, if he went ahead and exposed what those guys were doing." Caroline set her fork on the opposite side of her dessert plate. "Kip suggested I might need to watch *my* back."

"Because of Jace. That guy should be arrested—"

"Not Jace. Kip was talking about the men involved in the recruiting scam. They still have a lot to lose even thirty years after the fact, if the story should come out. Kip and Jace both warned me about this guy Farley Dade. His nephew, Brick, played for Tillman."

"Brick Coleman, who played for Chicago? He was a powerhouse for the Bears back in the late eighties, early nineties."

"That's him. He won a lot of games for the Tillman Tigers too. Of course he, and who knows how many other football players, was paid to do it."

"By his uncle."

"By a whole bunch of boosters and alums. There were rumors of a slush fund, according to Kip, and wire transferring of funds between all these bogus accounts, and Jace's dad and mine knew about it and went along."

"Now you're talking bank fraud." Steve was grim. "That's serious business."

"They could have gone to prison if it could have been proven, but in the end, according to Kip, my dad vanished before he could get his hands on much hard evidence."

"Well, I've got to say I don't like the sound of it. And what's the deal with this guy Jace coming around, acting like he's sorry?"

Clearly Steve wasn't buying that Jace's apology was sincere. She shrugged. He might be right. What did she know? She'd never have believed Jace would try to harm her under any circumstances, and yet he had.

"So the man in Lone Pine," Steve said. "How did you find out about him?"

"From Jace. His dad hired a private investigator, who found a trucker who identified my dad from a photo. The man told the trucker his name was Raymond Berry."

"Played for the Colts back in the day. Wide receiver, wasn't he? Partnered with John Unitas?"

"I forgot you played football. You used to grill me on stats."

"You're the only girl—definitely the only cheerleader—I ever met who knew the game as well or better than me." He grinned, then sobered. "It could be a coincidence."

Caroline felt a prick of annoyance. "Raymond Berry was a hero of my dad's. He even called himself that." She went on, explaining it to

Steve the way she had to Jace. "When I was a kid, he'd say we were a team like Berry and Unitas. *I* was Unitas."

"Huh."

"I have to check it out."

"You always were stubborn." Steve's fresh grin teased her.

She had to work not to smile back. "I don't know what you mean."

"Remember the time you ran out of gas? I was at work, two blocks away, but rather than call me or walk the two blocks to get my help, you walked a mile to a gas station, bought a can and a gallon of gas, and walked back."

"You were working."

"I would have come."

She didn't answer.

"I would have come to Iowa when you went away to school. I would have driven there to see you anytime you wanted."

"I admit I was stubborn . . ." She trailed off, keeping his gaze, feeling the regret she saw mirrored there. The moment elongated, and her heart shifted, impatient, restless in her chest. Memories of how she'd left him, refusing to explain, to acknowledge his pain, slipped through some crack in her mind.

"You admit it, but—?" he was asking her, his gaze intent, searching.

"We were kids," she began. "It was another—" *Life.* The word hung there, unsaid. *I couldn't do it.* More words poured into her brain. She pressed her fingertips to her eyes, helpless to stop the careening train of her thoughts. It was as if sitting in such close proximity to Steve had opened a long-closed door in her mind. How could she tell him now, she wondered, after so many years, how frightened she'd been, that his love for her, and hers for him, had been too huge?

Suppose she had trusted it and given Steve everything she was in return, and he had left her, abandoned her, the way her dad had? She couldn't have survived it.

So she'd done it first—

Before Steve could.

The revelation bolted through her brain. It took her breath. It had never come to her in such concrete terms before or with such force.

She felt Steve's grasp gentle on her wrists, and she let him pull her hands away. She wiped her face, under her nose, and lowered her trembling hands to her lap.

"Caro?" he said. "Talk to me."

She shook her head. She needed time to think it through. Her flash of insight felt crazy and scary. It dismayed and yet somehow exhilarated her. But there were too many feelings, a simmering brew of emotions jetting through her mind. It was too much to articulate. "I'm sorry. I shouldn't have called you, started this. I'm sorry, too, for before, that summer, I mean—the way I left—"

"It's all right."

"It's really hard to talk about—the way we were then, what I did—"

"Then we won't." His eyes and his voice were so kind.

"It's just, right now, the most important thing—" She struggled for composure, the breath to speak logically. "I've got to find my dad. I'm running out of time."

Steve's brows rose, a question.

Caroline explained about Lanie.

"Oh God, that's awful." Steve's eyes were dark with concern. "I know how close you are to her. She was a second mother to you."

"Yes." Caroline's throat was too tight to say more.

Steve seemed to understand. He wadded his napkin, tossed it onto his empty plate. "Well, I can't let you go alone to Lone Pine." He brought them back to the business at hand, the life they lived now, and she was both relieved and saddened. She didn't know what to do with her feelings; there were so many, too many.

She said, "You would go with me?"

"Yes. What time is good for you tomorrow? I'm off, so I'm free anytime."

"Is eight o'clock too early?"

"No. I'll pick you up. You can get a room at the Ramada here. It's just a mile or so down the highway."

She agreed it was a plan, and when the waitress came with their check, she snatched it, insisting she would pay it.

"See?" He slid out of the booth. "Stubborn, just like I said."

She punched him lightly on the shoulder, and for a moment none of the years that had passed since that long-ago summer mattered.

She followed him to the Ramada in her car, and he walked her into the lobby and waited while she checked in.

"Thank you for everything," she said, taking her tote from him.

"You're welcome. Thank you for dinner."

They shared a beat.

"Eight o'clock?"

"Yes," she answered, "if that works for you."

He said it did, turned to go, and then turned back. "What about your dad's second wife? Have you talked to her? Is it possible she or her son would know where your dad is?"

Caroline admitted that she hadn't. "Aunt Lanie called her when she didn't hear from Dad over the holidays that first year. Julia said she didn't know where he was, that he'd left her too."

"Maybe you should try her again? Might be worth another shot."

"It's my plan B, I guess, if I need one. I kind of hate the idea, though. Kid or not, I was pretty rude to Julia, to say the least, and my dad left her for someone else. I doubt she needs or wants to hear from anyone named Hoffman, and who can blame her? I really have to wonder if she or Harris would even speak to me, much less help me, and who could blame them?"

"Harris—that's an unusual first name. His last name wouldn't be Fenton, would it? I arrested a guy by that name a few days ago here in Greeley. He was released this morning on bail. His home address is Wyatt."

• • •

Steve produced a thermos of coffee when Caroline climbed into the cab of his truck on Thursday morning.

"It's not Starbucks," he said, "but it's good and strong. You look like you could use a shot."

"That bad, huh?" She knew it was. She hadn't slept.

"No. I didn't mean—" He looked away, looked back. "You know better."

Now it was her turn to drop her gaze. He had always told her that he'd have loved her no matter how she looked. The fact that she was so pretty was a bonus, he'd said. *Like dessert*, he'd told her. "Did everything work out okay last night?" she asked. He'd been called in to work just as they were parting.

"Yeah, it was fine. They needed help serving a warrant; turned out to be nothing much, though. I'm sorry I had to duck out on you." He glanced at her. "I mean it."

Face warming, Caroline sipped her coffee. "You were going to tell me about Harris Fenton. You said you arrested him?"

"Yeah. It's a pretty sad situation." Steve turned onto the highway. "When I drove up to the scene, he had a kid—what turned out to be his own kid—on the ground, just whaling on him. He did a pretty good number on the kid's face."

"Are you serious?" Caroline was appalled. "Was the kid acting out, involved in some kind of delinquency?"

"The kid—his name is Kyle—was trying to stop his dad from taking drugs. If you can believe that."

"No. I—wow, that's terrible." It was the last thing she'd expected to hear, that Harris was on drugs. Never mind that he'd assaulted his own son.

"Yeah, I know. Usually it's the other way around."

"How old is Kyle?"

"Seventeen. He was pretty shaken up. Pissed big-time, but scared, too, you know? I could tell he really loves his dad, but Fenton was messed up, not rational. It was like he didn't really know it was his son he was slugging."

"Was it the drugs, do you think?"

"Maybe. But I have a feeling there's more to it. I've seen my share of fights, bar fights, street fights, where it's a personal thing. You know, somebody goes off over something the other guy said or did. This was different. Fenton wasn't there." Steve glanced again, briefly, at Caroline. "The way he looked at me—I don't know. There was just something crazy going on. Kind of made me think of this other situation I had recently—" He paused.

"Situation?" Caroline prodded, intrigued in spite of herself.

"A domestic thing. Guy pulled a gun on his wife. I could tell there was a lot of turmoil going on back there." Steve took his hand off the wheel, raising it to the level of his eyes as if to indicate the space behind them. "Turned out he was a war vet, saw a lot of action in Afghanistan. He came home with a whopping case of PTSD. What set him off that night was a car that backfired. I felt bad for him and for his wife. You could see they didn't know how to handle it; they were both sick it had happened. Fenton had that same look."

They rode a mile or so in silence. They'd turned off the main highway some miles back and were driving now on a narrow, twisty ribbon of black asphalt, barely two lanes wide. A ragged mix of winter-brown grass and underbrush crowded the pavement's edge closely enough that had she wanted to, Caroline could have reached out the truck's window and run her hand over it. She wouldn't have wanted to drive this road alone. She wouldn't have wanted to make this trip by herself at all. She thought again of Harris, of how Steve had described the small details of his appearance, noting even the shades of emotion.

But Steve had always been perceptive and sensitive and kind. He'd had a tender heart. Clearly he still did. How hard must it be to be a cop with a nature like his? She wondered how he managed it. She could have asked, but it seemed too personal. She finished her coffee and set the thermal mug in the cup holder on the wide console between them. "It's got to be hell, watching your parent do that to himself. Take drugs, I mean."

"A parent with any kind of addiction has got to be hell on a kid."

"You were close with your dad, I remember. Close to both your parents. I envied you that. Do you remember those weekends we went to your folks' house on Lake Livingston? I loved spending time up there," Caroline said wistfully. "Your parents were always so much fun and so comfortable to be around."

"They liked you too." Steve found her gaze. "I hate having to tell you this, Caro, but they were killed a few years back."

"Oh, Steve, no! I'm so sorry."

"Thank you," he said.

"How? I don't mean to be nosy—"

"No, it's okay. It was a boating accident, two years ago. Drunk driver T-boned them. Hit them full on, doing eighty, eighty-five. He never knew he hit them."

"That's horrible."

"Well, it may sound horrible, too, when I say it was a good thing. Going that fast, hitting them that hard, my folks probably didn't know what happened either."

It was reflex when Caroline reached out to him, putting her hand on his arm, dropping it for the briefest moment to his thigh. He met her gaze when she withdrew her hand as abruptly. She couldn't read his expression. If he'd asked, she couldn't have defined her own feelings in the moment any more than she could have last night. The idea that she might have abandoned Steve out of fear was appalling to her. She'd grieved over his loss for weeks, had been grieving when Rob had initiated a conversation with her that day in the library at Drake. Rob had pursued her, and she'd let him. Even now he didn't know about Steve;

she'd never talked about him. It would have been too painful—that was what she'd told herself. Steve was the past; she'd told herself that too. It bothered her now. What kind of girl did that?

Steve broke into her thoughts. "Is this the place, do you think? Cactus Café? Does that name ring a bell?" He was slowing the truck as they approached a building on the left-hand side of the highway. "We're about four or five miles north of Lone Pine."

Caroline looked in the direction he indicated. "It must be it."

The café was old, ramshackle; the red gingham curtains in the windows were faded. Steve pulled in alongside a semi. The parking lot was littered with them.

"You good?" Steve looked at her as he came around the front of his truck.

"A bit nervous," Caroline admitted.

An old-fashioned bell jingled when they opened the door.

"Sit anywhere you want, folks," a waitress said in passing. "I'll be right with ya."

Instead of taking a seat, Caroline followed her to the counter, digging her dad's photo, one she'd pulled out of an album at Lanie's, from her purse. "I'm looking for information." She edged her way onto a stool. Steve came up behind her.

The waitress set the coffee carafe she'd been carrying on a burner and, wiping her hands on her apron, turned to look at Caroline. Her glance dropped to the photo.

"Do you recognize this man?" Caroline asked. "He would be a lot older now."

"Yeah, that's Raymond Berry," the waitress said. "Don't ever call him Ray either. He won't answer."

Caroline's heart rose. "He said that?"

"Oh yeah. He's a stickler. Full name or nothing."

"Is that significant?" Steve asked.

"Raymond Berry, the football player, wouldn't answer to anything but his full name either," Caroline answered Steve. "Dad told me about it, how his dad was called Ray and he wanted to distinguish himself and insisted that everyone call him Raymond." Caroline turned back to the waitress, feeling almost breathless with anticipation. "He lives around here, doesn't he? Can you tell me how to get to his place?"

"What's your interest in him? He's not much for company."

"I think he's my dad." Caroline kept the waitress's gaze. She wasn't going to back down now.

"Really?" The waitress looked at the photo and back at Caroline. "I can see a resemblance. You got the same eyes, that high forehead. Come look at this, Pat." She—her name tag read **MAUREEN**—waved over another waitress.

Pat listened to Maureen explain Caroline's errand. She examined the photo Maureen held, and looking between it and Caroline, she said, "Well, I'll be. Y'all do look alike. He never said nothin' about a daughter, though." Pat looked from Caroline back to Maureen. "You ever hear him talk about having a daughter?"

"No," Maureen said. "But that don't mean he didn't have one. Lotta men want to disown their kids. Buncha deadbeat dads trying to get out of child support." She shot Caroline a sympathetic look.

Caroline didn't want to take the time to correct her impression. Her dad didn't fall into that category, or at least he hadn't neglected paying child support until around the time he'd disappeared.

Beside her, Steve must have sensed her impatience. He said, "Can you give us directions?"

"His place isn't easy to find." Maureen reached for a napkin. "Not like you can program it into your GPS."

Pat handed Maureen a ballpoint pen. By the time she'd sketched it, the map ran the length and width of the white rectangle. She handed it over. "Good luck," she said.

Back in the cab of Steve's truck, Caroline looked down at the napkin. "Turn right when you see the windmill? Take the left at the old falling-down barn?" She looked over at Steve. "What happened to street signs?"

He smiled. "You left those back in the city."

• • •

Twenty minutes and a few wrong turns later, coming down an unpaved road, they saw the battered mailbox Maureen had noted on her drawing. Steve slowed as they approached the small, run-down house it fronted. Maureen had indicated there was a live oak near the building, but she hadn't said the house, which was little better than a shack, would appear to be leaning into the tree's embrace.

"Want me to turn in?" Steve's nod indicated a driveway that bore only remnants of the crushed granite that had once, perhaps in better times, provided its surface.

"I guess." Caroline wasn't at all sure. Her heart seemed to have stalled in her chest. She didn't want to think of her father living here in this small, dark, sad place. The windows that flanked the front door were covered in cardboard; the door itself hung aslant in its frame. It made her shiver to imagine the winter wind blowing under it.

"Do you want me to go with you, or do you want to go alone?"

Caroline looked at Steve. "You are so kind," she began, but then a noise pulled her gaze and Steve's forward. A man had come out of the house onto the sagging front stoop. Cold sunshine illuminated the planes of his cheeks, highlighted the shape of his brow, the set of his ears and jaw. His longish hair was silver and reached the collar of his flannel shirt in back. He raised his hand as if in greeting, or maybe he was going to touch his temple. Her gaze was riveted by the movement, studying that long-fingered hand, the heavier but narrow bone of his wrist. She knew that hand. Lifting her gaze, she knew that face, the shape of the man's head. His eyes were in shadow, but she knew him, and in that moment of knowing, she drew in her breath.

"Dad?" she said, and the word came on a sigh.

20

Harris—Thursday, January 18

It's his first morning back at his mom's, and they're in the kitchen when his cell phone rings. He sees it's Zeke. Glancing at his mom, he says, "I've got to take this," and he's relieved when she doesn't stop him from leaving the room, when she doesn't demand to know who is calling him.

"I'm in town," Zeke says without preamble.

Harris walks out the front door onto the porch. In the distance, a plume of dust rising into the air draws his eye. A vehicle is heading slowly up the drive. His breath freezes in his chest. Almost unconsciously he steps back. The porch is wide, L-shaped, and he sidesteps toward the deep, shadowed corner.

"I heard the cops are headed your way," Zeke says.

"Do you know what they want?" He was released just hours after his mom had left the jail yesterday, following his bail hearing. His trial is set for March, unless he makes the deal Wayman talked about. His mom is pushing hard for it, but Harris wonders if it'll happen now. His mom heard when she was arranging for Harris's bail that Gee has dropped from sight. Talk is his folks have packed him off to Europe or Mexico.

Zeke says, "It depends who you talk to. People are upset, Harris. There's a bunch of folks who're convinced you were in on the robberies with Gee, that it's how you supported your habit, selling off stolen electronics. Maybe the cops think there's something to it."

"It's bullshit, Zeke, and you know it."

"What I know is you just spent the last three days detoxing in a jail cell." Zeke is pissed and torn up over what Harris has done and the consequences. *You're worse off than you know, Harris, going after your own kid*, he said when the two made contact yesterday. *Jesus Christ, what were you thinking?* Then: *I know you had no choice, but you can't go cold turkey off opioids. There's a process to it.*

Evidently going cold turkey is dangerous. Not that law enforcement gives a crap about that.

"You make an appointment to see your doctor like I told you?" Zeke asks.

"Not yet."

"Let him help you, Harris. Let him get you into a rehab facility. If you can do the deal the DA is offering, get out with only probation—and it's possible, it really is, since this is your first offense—the judge is bound to recommend a program of some kind in any case."

It amazes Harris that these people—Zeke, his mother, Wayman—imagine they know how best Harris can recover his life, make amends, be forgiven.

As if any of that were possible, as if he were even worthy of another chance.

"Yeah." Harris is watching the car's approach. It's still too far away to see what kind it is or who's driving. But he knows—in the back of his mind he has no doubt—Zeke is right. It's the police. From either Wyatt or Madrone County.

"Harris?" Zeke prompts. "There's no shame in asking for help."

"Honestly? I think the best thing for my family, Holly and the boys and Mom, is for me to get out of here." Harris is retreating farther now, backing toward the stairs that lead off the side of the porch. His truck is on the drive behind the house. He's left the keys in it. He thinks maybe he knew it might come to this. His gut is in a knot; his ears are ringing. He's about to descend the steps when his head swims bad enough that he's got to stop, grip the stair rail to keep himself upright. Lack of sleep, he thinks. Or maybe it's the dope sickness, the wasting and persistent effects of withdrawal. But more likely he's just plain scared out of his mind. He stands still, waiting for the black dots that are eating his peripheral vision to clear.

"What do you mean, get out of here?"

Zeke's voice needles Harris's ear. "I mean leave Texas, maybe go to Mexico. It's easy enough to get there, easy enough to disappear. Gee's done it."

"Son, you aren't thinking straight."

"Look, Zeke, I appreciate you, man—"

"You understand how it's going to look if you run?"

"I don't care how it looks—"

"There was another break-in last night."

"Yeah. I heard. Gee's gone, so it's got to be the cousin or some copycat. It was the same MO."

"No, it wasn't," Zeke says. "The robbers—and there were two of them—had a gun."

Harris's heart drops.

"Joe Moncrief, the homeowner, got shot. You know Joe, don't you, Harris? He's got a kid, a daughter, at the high school. Lucky for him it was only a flesh wound, but you see where I'm going with this, right? It's not just a simple break and enter now. Whoever it was, they're on the string for *armed* robbery and assault with a deadly weapon and who the hell knows what all. It's a damn sight more serious when you bring a gun to a crime. That's significant prison time, Harris. And your name is messed up in it."

"I didn't do it, Zeke. Ask Mom. I was home with her all night."

"That's fine, son, just fine. You got your mom to cover for you. Moms lie for their kids all the time. I don't care how old the kid is. Family members lie for each other. You think the cops are going to believe her?"

Believeherbelieveherbelieveher . . .

Zeke's words echo away in Harris's brain. He touches his temple, frowning. *It's not the lies you tell everybody else that matter so much, but the lies you tell yourself can kill you.*

Hoff's voice comes from nowhere, bringing with it a sense of the man so strong it weakens Harris's knees. He sits down hard on the stair, gripping the rail. He is dry mouthed, blind. Shaking. It is all coming apart, and he's powerless to stop it.

"Harris, you still there?"

"Whatever happens, however I can fix this, it's not for me. I don't really care what happens to me." Harris struggles to keep a hold on what is solid and real, the wooden step under his butt, the stair rail rough against his palm, his concern for those whom he loves . . . Holly, his children, his mother. But his vision has gone watery; his eyes burn.

"Then who, son? Who are you willing to throw away your life for?"

Harris ignores Zeke's question. "She had no choice. You get that, don't you?"

"No, I don't understand—who're you talking about?"

"She only wanted to protect me." Harris is aware on some level as he speaks of the sound of car doors slamming nearby, one, then two, but he feels separate from the noise. He might be in another country or at the back of the moon.

He feels the vibration when whoever was in the car walks up onto the porch. The knocks on the front door are official sounding and loud, and he hears those too. He knows it's the police, and now, despite what logic tells him, that it's not possible, he's certain they've come for his mother. He's brought the cops to her doorstep when he swore he never would.

21

I'm *scared, Maggie. Scared of myself—for myself.* The line from her dad's letter to her mother was present in Caroline's mind as she approached the man on the stoop. Her dad had clearly felt threatened when he'd written it, and he looked ready to bolt now.

She felt Steve come abreast of her, and she was grateful when he cupped her elbow. His presence steadied her. Her father squinted at them. He wasn't wearing a jacket and had his arms tightly crossed against the morning chill. A fitful breeze ruffled the feathery wisps of his white hair. She waited for a sign that he knew her. She pictured how it would happen, the way he would step down from the crooked little porch and come toward her, recognition lighting his face. She imagined their embrace.

But he remained where he stood, watching, intent. His expression didn't lighten with the joy of recognition or any recognition. It weighed on her, his lack of a reaction. Still, when he said, "Can I help you folks?" she took a hopeful step toward him.

"Are you Raymond Berry?" she asked.

He came down to their level, into the light. "Yeah. Who're you?"

Caroline kept his gaze. The resemblance was so strong . . . the high brow, the shape of his head, the set of his jaw . . . but she saw now it wasn't him.

Her brain shut down. Her breath left her in a gust. Raymond—this Raymond Berry—wasn't her dad. Had it not been for Steve's grip, she might have fallen to her knees. She had counted on this man being her father, and he wasn't. Where would she go now?

"It's not him?" Steve asked, quietly, gently.

"No," she whispered.

"Who are you?" Raymond Berry asked again. "Are you the cops? The repo guy already got my car."

"We're not here to cause you any trouble," Steve said. "My friend thought you were someone else."

"Well, if you don't got no business here, I suggest you git off the property. I don't much like strangers comin' around."

Steve apologized. His grasp tightened on her elbow, signaling they should go, but somehow Caroline's feet were rooted where she stood. Her gaze was still hooked on Raymond Berry's face, as if by some miracle looking could make him be her father.

"Go on now. Git." Berry shooed them with his hands.

Steve brought Caroline around. Putting his arm across her shoulders, he propelled her toward his truck, opened the door, assisted her into the passenger seat. Caroline stared sightlessly through the windshield. She didn't look at Steve when he joined her in the truck's cab. They didn't speak. The porch was deserted when they backed out of the drive, but Caroline saw Raymond Berry's face at the window, the face that was so like her dad's. *Stop*, she wanted to say. *Maybe if I saw him again . . . Maybe he just doesn't remember who he is . . . Maybe if I were to sit with him and talk . . .*

"Is there any chance it could be him? Any doubt in your mind about it?" Steve seemed to read the direction of her thoughts. "I can turn around—"

Caroline met his eyes. "No. My head knew it wasn't Dad probably from the first glance. The resemblance is uncanny, but that's all it is."

"You wanted it to be him."

"I so wanted to bring him to Lanie." She clamped her teeth, locking hot tears of disappointment behind them. What use were they?

"I know. I'm so sorry, Caro . . ."

"No, I'm sorry for wasting your time," she said once she could trust her voice.

"I was glad to do it, glad to be there, if it helped." They reached the highway, and Steve made a left turn, heading south, back toward Greeley.

"It did," she said. She was afraid to say how much, afraid her emotions would overrun her.

"I guess you've had someone run his banking and social security information. He'd be over sixty-five, wouldn't he, collecting a check by now? Would he have had retirement? Investments? Anything traceable like that?"

"There's nothing—not that either of the private investigators could find, anyway."

"So what's left? Plan B?"

"Contacting Julia. Yes, I guess so." Dread pooled in Caroline's stomach at the thought. She picked at her thumbnail. "What information can she have, though, that isn't nearly as old as what I already know—and that's assuming she doesn't hang up on me?"

Steve changed lanes.

"And now, there's Harris's arrest . . . his issues with drugs . . ." Caroline trailed off, picked up again. "It's not great timing, is it? Not that any time would be easy. You said earlier he was released?"

"Yesterday morning. I believe his mother, Julia, got him out on bail."

"What a horrible thing for a mother to have to do. Has Harris been arrested before? Do you know? Can you say?"

"His record's clean. Not a speeding ticket on it. The story I've gotten is that he was prescribed Oxycontin from a doctor when he had back surgery a few years ago. He was probably hooked before he knew it. It happens to a lot of folks."

"It's all over the news," Caroline said, and it was wrong of her, but she was relieved that their conversation had turned away from her troubles. She thought it was deliberate, that Steve understood how shattered she was, and he was creating a distance, giving her a safe space to breathe. "It's terrible how people—ordinary people—start taking prescription drugs and end up addicted and losing everything. Jobs, families, homes—their lives."

"What I hear, Harris is one of the good guys. Really well thought of in Wyatt. He's the athletic director at Wyatt High School. Head coach of the baseball team, too—or he was."

"I heard that. It seems strange to me, though. Dad raved about Harris's football skills, how devoted he was to the game."

"You couldn't compete. I remember you telling me that once."

She held his glance for a moment before he turned his eyes back to the road. She was touched by how much he remembered of what she'd told him so many years ago. She said, "I thought Dad finally had the son I could never be."

"How old was Harris when your dad disappeared? Do you know?"

Caroline thought for a moment. "Twelve, maybe thirteen? We're something like four years apart, I think."

"Must have been as tough for him as it was for you."

Something in Steve's voice made her look at him.

"Harris mentioned his dad when we spoke. I could tell the guy meant a lot to him. It seemed as if it really bothered him that he never got to say goodbye. I know how he feels. I didn't get to tell my folks goodbye either."

Caroline touched Steve's arm, although she knew she shouldn't.

"Do you remember I told you about that domestic I had, the war vet with PTSD?"

She did, Caroline said.

"Paranoia and delusions are symptoms of posttraumatic stress. Do you know much about PTSD?"

She shook her head. She'd never known anyone who was afflicted.

"When the car backfired, the husband went for his gun the way he would, the way he'd been trained to do, in a combat situation. His wife was the only one home, so he thought she was responsible. She was the enemy, out to kill him. In his mind, he was only taking steps to defend himself. It could have been the same for Harris. Sometimes opioid use can lead to the same type of paranoia and hallucinations."

"He thought his son was someone else, a stranger out to get him?"

"He could have. When I questioned him at the scene, he told me he'd taken Oxy. When he was strip-searched, they found a fentanyl patch. He said he'd been taking more drugs, more steadily, lately. And his kid did admit to trying to restrain his dad by grabbing him in a choke hold. I'm no doctor, but it's possible lack of oxygen played a role. It would be instinct to fight back in any case when you're under attack."

"Kill or get killed."

"PTSD can operate like that."

Caroline suppressed a shudder.

"Just a possibility. I'm not trying to excuse the guy."

Steve turned in to the Ramada and pulled up alongside Caroline's rental car.

She turned to him. "I don't see how I can call Harris or Julia now, given what they're dealing with."

"It's a bad time, but what if your dad's disappearance—what if it's something they know about and can explain, or what if it's impacted

Harris in a way that affects him even now?" Steve's look was intent. "Sometimes when folks fall into this kind of situation, it's got its roots in the past. Stuff that happened back when."

"Do you know of something—specific, I mean?" It was Steve's demeanor that made Caroline ask.

"Just a feeling I got from talking to him. His situation, what happened with his son—I don't know. People like Harris don't belong in the system."

Caroline didn't know what to say. What had gone wrong? That was the question in her mind.

"It's possible he can help us with another case, a series of residential break-ins in Wyatt." Steve broke the silence.

Caroline looked at him.

"There've been a couple of robberies up this way, too, between Wyatt and Greeley. Turns out Harris saw one robbery going down last November, on Thanksgiving Day. He can ID the two guys who are responsible. One's a senior at Wyatt High, the quarterback for the football team. All-state, all-American—had his pick of colleges."

"That's awful. He's blown his whole future."

"Pretty much."

"A house was broken in to in Wyatt last night, wasn't it?" Caroline said. "I heard about it on the news this morning. The homeowner was shot. Was it the same kid? The football player?"

"Yeah. He and his cousin are in custody now. The Wyatt police chief called before I picked you up and said they were caught in a stolen car west of San Antonio. They were probably headed to Del Rio or somewhere where they could cross the border into Mexico."

"If Harris saw them breaking in to a house back in November, why weren't they caught then?"

"He didn't report it. Long story," Steve said in answer to Caroline's questioning look. He turned toward her, keeping her gaze, and the moment lingered, long enough that she grew warm beneath his regard;

she felt physically embraced by it. It seemed to her the world had shrunk to enclose her with Steve in the cab of his truck.

He said, "You have no idea how many times since last fall I've wanted to call you."

Her yielding to him, to the desire that seemed implicit in his voice, was almost imperceptible, no more than the smallest shift of her shoulders, the forward tilt of her head. "I wish—wish you had." How often in the months since she'd seen him had she imagined it, whole conversations with Steve, and then, feeling guilty, had shoved such notions away? But now he was so close, and his feelings for her were so clear in his eyes, and her longing to know this man, to have him in her life again, was wild inside her, sweeping caution away.

"I don't want to be the guy on the side or the one who breaks up a marriage," Steve said.

"No," she said. "I would never want it that way. I couldn't put you in that position . . ." She respected him way too much. Neither did she want to hurt Rob.

He touched her cheek, and pulling loosened strands of her hair away, he tucked them behind her ear. Her heart paused. She eased her hand over his, feeling the shapes of his knuckles, even the thrum of his pulse. Or was it her own pulse she felt? She had no answers for the questions in his eyes.

"I should go," she said.

"Back to Houston?"

"For now, until I get Mom settled."

"And after that, will you go home to Des Moines? Are you—are you working things out there?"

Caroline lowered her hand and her gaze to the broad console that divided them. "I don't think so."

"I'm so sorry, Caro. I know what you're going through is painful. I would help you if I could. You know that, don't you?"

He meant it; she could hear the genuine caring in his voice, and it closed her throat. Her gaze rose when he took her hand, and she watched, mesmerized, as he kissed her palm, the inside of her wrist. His gesture, the intimate sensation of it, opened an ache deep inside her and enlivened a memory from their past, and she saw them in her mind's eye, lying together in the bed in Steve's apartment. Their legs were entwined, and he was tracing the path from her breast to the curve of her hip.

She knew, looking at Steve, he was remembering such a moment too. He returned her hand gently to the console, and facing front, he said gruffly, "You aren't free," and it was true. She wasn't.

"I wish I were," she said, and she knew her desire for Steve was a betrayal of her marriage vows, vows she probably should never have made. But she couldn't go back, couldn't correct her past mistakes. She could only go forward, being as honest with herself and everyone else from now on as possible. She got her purse, opened the truck door, and got out, wincing at the cold. Looking at Steve across the seat, she thanked him for going with her.

"It was nothing," he said.

They couldn't seem to break their locked gaze or the silence that was packed with words, all of them impossible.

Steve flashed an abrupt grin. "If you're ever back this way, call me. I'll let you buy me dinner again."

She smiled. "Only if we can go back to Bo Dean's."

"Was it the food or the ambience?"

"The company," she said. "Maybe I'll be back sooner than you know," she added, and she felt her face warm with dismay, a kind of vexation. As Steve had said, she wasn't free.

"I hope so," Steve said. He gave her a small salute and a one-cornered smile. "Be safe," he told her.

She nodded and, shutting the truck door, went to her rental car and got in, and within moments the rearview mirror captured his image at the wheel of his pickup as he passed behind her on his way out of the parking lot. She thought of going after him, but it would be wrong of her on too many levels. She got out her phone instead and called her mother to tell her the man in Lone Pine wasn't anyone they knew.

"It was a wild-goose chase after all," Caroline said to her mom.

"I was against it only because of how hurt and disappointed you would be."

"I know, and I am, but I'll get over it. I'm worried about Lanie, though. She so wanted to see him. How is she?"

"In and out," her mom said. "I think there's not much time left."

Caroline said she was on her way, that she would come to St. Joe's on her arrival. She glanced at the time on the dashboard panel. "I should be there by six or so," she said, and hanging up, she called Nina.

"Oh, Mommy, I'm so sorry," she said when Caroline explained once again that Raymond Berry wasn't any relation. "I'm coming down there," Nina said. "Daddy's coming too. Gramma says we should if we want to see Lanie before—while she can still know—"

"No."

"No, I shouldn't come?"

"Of course you should, but your dad and Lanie aren't close."

"I don't think it's Lanie he wants to see."

Caroline didn't answer.

"He thinks you're going to file for divorce."

"He said that?"

"Are you?"

Divorce. The word hung in the space behind Caroline's eyes. Her mind walked around it, viewing it as if it were a foreign object. *Divorce?* a voice asked.

"Mom?"

"I don't know what's going to happen."

"I don't want to choose sides, not that I like what he's done—"

"We would never expect that, Nina. Whatever happens, we both love you. None of this is your fault."

"Yours either."

"I'm not so sure of that, but I am sure it's nothing to do with you."

"He said I'll probably have to leave school. He doesn't think he'll be able to afford it if he has to pay back taxes and fines and I don't know what."

"He said that?" Caroline's disbelief was tinged with annoyance, even pity. Was Rob trying to scare Nina? Did he want her to feel sorry for him?

"I didn't understand half of what he was talking about."

"Listen to me, Nins"—Caroline spoke strongly, with a confidence she was only beginning to feel—"I'm going to do everything I can to see to it you can continue going to school. I'll ask Gramma to help us if I have to. It'll be fine, I promise. Try not to worry."

"You too, Mommy. Okay?" Nina's voice caught.

"Text me your arrival time when you've made your reservation," Caroline said. "I'll pick you up."

"What about Dad?"

"Are you okay to come on your own?"

"Yes, of course."

"I'll speak to him, then. There's no point in his making the trip. It doesn't sound as if he can afford it anyway." Her remark might have been funny, she thought, if it had not been so painfully true.

Her call to him, moments later, rolled to voice mail. "Please don't come down here, Rob," she said and paused, trying to think of what else to say. But there was nothing else. "Please," she repeated.

· · ·

She was some thirty or so miles south of Greeley when she saw the exit sign for Wyatt, and she wasn't entirely conscious of it when her foot backed off the accelerator. The sign loomed at her, growing larger on her approach, and when at the last minute she veered into the right-hand lane and onto the exit ramp, no one could have been more surprised.

But how could she go back to Houston, back to Lanie, walk into the hospital room and tell her beloved aunt, who was dying, that she'd failed? She had to see Julia and Harris first and find out what they knew, and damn the timing. Caroline would never forgive herself if she were to learn after Lanie was gone that they knew her dad's whereabouts, and if only she'd asked them she could have found him and brought him to Lanie, granting her last wish.

Of course, once she reached the center of town, she had no idea how to find the Fentons. It was past midday, after two, according to the clock mounted high on the face of the turreted courthouse. She circled the town square once, then again. The impulse that had led her here seemed foolish now. She spotted a café. CRICKET'S, the sign read. Her stomach rumbled, and it occurred to her she hadn't eaten all day. She would stop and have a sandwich, she decided, and then be on her way.

A woman behind the counter looked up when Caroline tried the door. A man seated near her on a stool shouted, "We're closed."

The woman laughed, waving him off, and coming to the door, she unlocked and opened it. "We are closed, but if you're desperate, I can figure out something."

"I'm light headed," Caroline said. "If that qualifies me."

"It does. I can't have you fainting on the sidewalk."

Caroline followed the woman inside.

"Have a seat." She indicated the row of stools. "I'm Gilly, and this is my friend Jake. He's not usually so rude."

"I'm trying to talk her into helping me bake cookies for my daughter's kindergarten class."

"He's the homeroom mom," Gilly said.

Caroline smiled. She noticed Jake's fingernails were painted a shade of blue as true and unblemished as a fresh summer sky. "I wouldn't want to get between a man and his baking," she said.

"Sit down," Gilly said. "We have plenty of time."

"She makes great cookies," Jake said. "Great everything. Try the chicken salad. Trust me, it's the best in Texas."

The glance Jake and Gilly exchanged was somehow intimate and teasing at the same time. Caroline thought of Steve and wished she wouldn't. She said, "Chicken salad would be wonderful."

"Here or to go?" Gilly asked.

"You should have a slice of her peach pie too." Jake was grinning now.

"Is it the best in Texas like the chicken salad?" Caroline joined in their fun.

"World famous," Jake said.

Gilly's face flushed with some mix of embarrassment and delight. "Lord, will you hush?"

"If y'all don't mind, I'd like to have it here. It's hard to eat and drive."

"Don't mind at all," Gilly said. "Back in a jiff." She disappeared into the kitchen.

Jake asked, "What brings you to Wyatt?"

A wild-goose chase. Her mother's answer came glibly to her tongue. Caroline was at a loss, though. "I—it's complicated."

When she thought about it later, she would guess it was Jake's lack of a response that caused her to go on, the fact that he didn't comment, didn't press. And there was the silence. Although it was broken by the small domestic sounds coming from the kitchen as Gilly made Caroline's lunch, it seemed to wait, a cup that needed filling. "I drove up from Houston yesterday. I'm looking for my dad. We lost touch years ago, but I know he lived here in Wyatt once, back in the eighties. He'd remarried by then to a woman here. She had a son . . ."

"What's your dad's name? I know pretty much everyone in Wyatt." Jake's grin was wry. "Small town."

"Garrett Hoffman. He goes by Hoff. He isn't here now. I'm sorry. It's confusing."

Gilly came with Caroline's sandwich. Setting the plate in front of her, she asked, "What can I get you to drink? I've got some peach tea left, or maybe you'd rather have coffee. It's chilly today."

"Peach tea is fine," Caroline answered.

"She's looking for her dad," Jake said.

"Oh?" Gilly filled a glass with ice and tea and brought it to Caroline. "He lives here in Wyatt?"

"Not anymore. Or at least I don't think he's here, but his second wife and her son—they still live here."

"Garrett Hoffman," Jake said, speaking to Gilly. "Have you ever heard that name around here?"

She thought about it and after a moment shook her head. She didn't think so, she said.

Caroline took a bite of her sandwich and set it down.

"His second wife—do you know her name?" Jake asked.

"Julia. Hoffman, I guess, although I don't know that she kept my dad's name. She has a son, Harris—"

"Harris Fenton?" Jake and Gilly shared a glance, one that was loaded with caution.

It was a moment before Caroline got it—that they knew about Harris's arrest and were concerned for him. Concerned about his privacy. They would feel an obligation to protect that, and rightfully so. Ordinarily Caroline would have respected that, but time was short and growing shorter. "My aunt, my dad's sister, is dying," she said. "She and my dad haven't seen each other in nearly thirty years. I want to bring him to her before she passes. I'd like for her to have that peace."

"You think the Fentons know where your dad is."

"Yes," Caroline answered Jake.

He unfolded his arm across the counter, nudging the sugar shaker an inch to one side, contemplating it.

"It's not as if it's a state secret," Gilly said. "It was on the news."

Jake shot Caroline a glance from under his brow. "Harris was arrested recently," he said.

"I know," Caroline answered. "The deputy who arrested him is a friend of mine. He's trying to help me locate my dad too. It's the reason I came out this way. We had a lead, but it turned out to be nothing."

"I can't see the harm in your calling Julia," Gilly said. "Can you, Jake? If she doesn't want to talk, she can say so."

"I don't have her phone number," Caroline said.

"I've got it." Jake pulled his phone from his jacket pocket. "We worked together on a community fund-raiser a few months ago."

Once he'd texted the contact information to her, Caroline thanked him. She asked for the check, but Gilly wouldn't let her pay for lunch. She and Jake walked her to the café door; they wished her luck. It was odd, given the short time they'd been acquainted, but Caroline felt a connection with them.

Back in her car, she sat holding her phone, but when she couldn't stop the erratic thump of her heart or work out in her mind the right thing to say, she tapped Julia's number and pressed the phone to her ear. After a series of rings, when Julia's voice mail answered, Caroline didn't leave a message. Instead, she dialed the number for Julia's landline, which had come with the contact information Jake had shared.

22

H arris? Are you all right?"
Phone to his ear, he looks up at his mom. "I'm talking to Zeke," he tells her, or at least he thinks he's speaking out loud, but his voice sounds distant.

She sets her hand on his shoulder, and her touch anchors him. "The police are here," she says. "They want to ask you some questions."

"What's going on?" Zeke asks.

"I've got to go," Harris tells him.

"Are the cops there? Harris, don't do anything stupid. Okay? Don't go on the run. Call me—I'll come there if you need me. All right? Harris?"

"Sure. Yeah," Harris says. Zeke is still talking when he ends the call. Getting to his feet, he says, "They want to talk to me?"

"Yes, honey. About Gee. They've arrested him." Her gaze is steady, but he sees the anxiety fishing through her eyes. "Are you okay?" she asks.

"Yes," he says, although he feels unsteady, somehow light headed.

"All right, then. It's Captain Mackie and Sergeant Carter who're here, the same officers who came to interview all of us at school."

"Yeah, I remember." Harris follows her through the back door and into the kitchen.

The lawmen are standing near the table. Greetings are exchanged. Harris's mom invites the officers to sit.

"I have coffee, a fresh pot," she says, looking from the captain to the sergeant.

"That would be mighty good if it's no trouble," Mackie says. "It's turning colder out. I have a feeling Old Man Winter isn't done with us yet."

Harris sits down opposite the officers. "Mom says you arrested Gee."

"The police in Del Rio got him," Mackie says. "What a shocker. I can't believe—but that's the way it happens sometimes. The kid with the most going for him—but you know."

Mackie locks Harris's gaze. Harris shoves his hand over his head.

"Gee and his cousin are being transported back here now."

"Yeah. Well, I gave a statement to Deputy Wayman about what I saw them doing last fall."

"I heard."

It's only two words, but they hold a world's worth of pity. The police captain couldn't have stated it out loud more clearly, how sorry he is for how low Harris has sunk.

Harris's gut clenches.

"We need to clarify a few things," Mackie says.

"Wayman indicated if I cooperate, the DA might be willing to cut me some slack."

"It's a possibility. Greeley County is working with us, but we still need to hear everything you know, not just about the robbery you witnessed but also about the drug operation. I'd like to tape your statement, if it's okay?" He sets his phone on the table.

Harris says it's fine with him. Get it over with—that's all he wants.

His mom brings mugs of coffee, cream, and sugar to the table and sits down. She and Harris exchange a look. He doesn't want her to stay, to hear his recounting of his activities, which will only distress her further, but he knows she won't leave him. And in a way maybe she needs to hear, to know the truth, just how low he's fallen. He talks for nearly an hour. Mackie asks about the night Harris claimed to have seen Gee at the school working out. "Was that true, or were you covering for him?"

"Covering. He had me over a barrel."

His mother's heartbreak, hearing how Harris allowed Gee to use him, is tangible. Harris wishes he were a better son, a better man, worthy of the sacrifice she has made for him. There's no way he can make it right; the damage done is as irrefutable as it is irreparable. It is like a badly mended bone, Harris thinks, one that would need rebreaking in order to be set straight, and even then he's doubtful that healing would take place. People can talk all they want to about closure and forgiveness, but there are certain situations, certain crimes, where the only way for the human heart to survive is by forgetting—as much and for as long as that's possible.

Finally the lawmen are done. They thank Harris's mother for the coffee and Harris for his cooperation. They say they'll be in touch. Once they're gone, his mother makes lunch, grilled cheese sandwiches accompanied by cups of chicken soup, which neither of them can finish.

They spend a couple of hours cleaning up the vegetable garden, raking aside the dead vegetation, fall-planted tomato vines and cole crops—broccoli, cauliflower, cabbages, and spinach—that didn't survive a late December spell of days when the temperature never got above freezing. The air is cold enough now that Harris can see his breath, and yet leaning on his rake, he swears he can feel a hint of spring in the fitful breeze. His mom scoffs when he mentions it. She repeats what Mackie said, that Old Man Winter isn't done.

"I'm going for a drive," Harris says later, when they're putting the garden tools away in the barn.

"Where to?" His mother is alarmed.

"Nowhere. I just need to get out." He sets the rakes into their slots.

"Holly and the boys aren't going to talk to you no matter how many times or for how long you sit parked in front of your house, Harris."

He looks at his mom. It doesn't surprise him that she knows about his frequent trips. But he does wonder if she feels it, the sense of something building. It's as if the very air is waiting, electric.

"I talk to them daily, as you've asked me to, and they're fine. As fine as they can be under the circumstances. Even Kyle is doing okay. I told you Holly said yesterday his bruises are fading."

It's not enough. Harris would say it if it wouldn't hurt her.

"You're only making it worse driving over there so often. Holly could complain that you're stalking them."

"I have to do this, Mom."

She walks to the open barn door, stands with her back to him. He doubts she's taking in the view.

"I'm not going to hook up to buy drugs. That's over. I know it'll take a while before you trust me again, but that's all right. Every day, you'll see."

She doesn't answer.

He wants to tell her it'll be okay, but he's got no idea if that's true. He thinks—hopes—he's done with lying too. "I'll be back in time for dinner," he tells her. "I've got my phone. If you need anything, if anything happens."

He's nearly to his truck when he hears her call out to him.

"I love you, Harris," she shouts. "You know that, don't you?"

He pauses. "I love you, too, Mom." He says it softly, though, and doubts she has heard, but then before he can change his mind, he walks swiftly back to her, embracing her tightly for a moment before releasing her. Retracing his steps, he's inside his truck before she can respond. He's startled her, no doubt. While they have always been close, showing affection toward one another isn't their custom. It happens only when times are fearsome and hard, like now.

• • •

A half hour later, he's turning in to his subdivision in town, driving down his street. The neighborhood is quiet. It's after four o'clock. School has ended for the day, but there aren't any kids playing outside. The wind has picked up, and the sky is a featureless gray sheet. No doubt Connor is at baseball practice. Even with his broken finger he would insist on going. Harris should be at ball practice, too, running his team through their drills, but it's unlikely he'll ever work in school sports at any level again. In addition to the fact that he's an addict, that he's bought dope off a student, he's also assaulted someone. Not just any someone but his own kid. What administrator, what parent, would trust him on hearing that? He's sickened by what he did to Kyle, that it was Kyle's chest he planted his knee on, Kyle's face he battered.

Harris's chest tightens with panic at the memory. He pulls to the curb in front of his house, bends his head to the steering wheel. After several moments, hearing a sound, he lifts his head and looks toward the house. Connor is there on the front porch. His appearance is ritual, as if they've made a silent pact. He's wearing shorts and a Dallas Cowboys T-shirt, and he's barefoot. In January, when the temperature can't be more than forty degrees. He lifts his hand, the one with the splint, in a small wave. Harris waves back. As it does each time he sees his son, it takes every ounce of his strength to keep himself from bailing out of the truck. He wants so badly to grab Connor into a bear hug. He knows Connor will smell a bit like mint and boy sweat. He'll cut loose with a laugh that rides up from his belly. Harris wants to hear that; he wants to hold his son, but now—for the first time since he began this routine—Holly appears. She stands behind Connor, staring at Harris. He can't read her expression. Unhappy—she's unhappy and miserable, angry and hurt. Because of him. He's hurt her and Kyle and Connor so much.

Kyle has come outside now, and even from where Harris sits, he can see the warning in Kyle's eyes, which are still so bruised Harris can't stand the sight of them. There's a cut on his cheek, and his upper lip is cracked and swollen. It vacuums the breath out of Harris's lungs, seeing Kyle's injuries. Holly crosses her arms over Connor's chest and pulls him to her, as if to show Harris ownership. Or is she only being protective? Either way, there's no room for Harris up there on that porch. His mother is right: if he pushes Holly, he'll only make matters worse. He touches his brow, a small salute, shifts the truck into drive, and heads down the street, watching in his rearview until his family's image disappears.

· · ·

After leaving his neighborhood, he drives west on FM 1643, determined to skip town. He'll go to California, or possibly he'll turn south toward El Paso and cross the bridge into Mexico. He puts his foot down on the accelerator. His head is a war zone, hotly debating the question of whether or not his family will be better off if he disappears. After a while, approaching Interstate 10, the major east/west artery that bisects the state, he slows, and it's almost without conscious thought that he pulls over onto the road's shoulder. Turning off the ignition, he sits looking into the distance as far as he can see, throat tight, heart hurting.

He could keep going, lose himself somewhere. It would be cowardly, the action of a weak man, a rat, but so what? His kids have no respect for him anyway. But no matter where he goes or how far, he'll never outrun his head or the nightmare that jolts him from sleep. He'll never escape the truth of who he is and what he's done to his family. It'll stay with him, chewing him up from the inside. He thinks of Kyle and Connor, the fine men they're growing up to be. Maybe it's selfish, and maybe he's got no right to hang around and watch them from a distance, but he's got to. He can't leave them. Can't rob himself of the chance that he might someday get the opportunity to make it up to them, make it right. He's got to stick it out, no matter how slim his chances are—for his sons. It's for them that he makes the U-turn and heads back to his mother's house.

He finds her on the deck, tending the grill. When she looks up, her face on seeing him is bright with her relief. He has the sense that she knew he'd entertained the idea of escape. Or maybe she thought he'd gone to get high. She takes the meat from the grill, setting it on a small platter.

"It's your favorite," she says. "Pork chops."

"You shouldn't—Mom, it's too cold to be out here."

Her expression deflates a bit.

"But thank you." He takes the platter from her, and he's surprised when his mouth waters.

"I did scalloped potatoes, too, and the little snow peas you like."

She smiles at him, and in her eyes there's a memory from when he was younger, before Hoff, the days when he missed having a dad but wasn't yet aware of how much. Whenever she made scalloped potatoes then, they flipped a coin to determine who would have to scour the dish. Harris almost expects her to produce a coin now and ask him to call heads or tails. But she doesn't. She dishes the plates. He sets the table with silverware and napkins and pours a cup of coffee for her and a glass of iced tea for himself.

Harris tries to eat but can't do more than pick at the meal. His mom doesn't do any better.

"I saw Holly and the boys," he says.

"Holly called. She was upset."

"I didn't even get out of the truck."

"She didn't know what you wanted."

Harris wipes his mouth.

"She said Kyle's better. The swelling and bruising is better."

"He'll never get over it, Mom. Neither will I."

"I know I sound like a broken record, Harris, but you need help—"

A telephone—the landline—rings. His mother jumps. "No one calls that number anymore," she says.

"I'll get it," Harris says, leaving the table. The landline is in the study, adjacent to the living room.

"Probably someone selling something," his mother says.

She's at the kitchen sink scrubbing the scalloped-potato dish when he comes back. She glances at him over her shoulder, and he knows he must look as sick as he feels when he sees the color drain from her face. "Who was it? What's happened?" She shuts off the water.

"It was Caroline, Caroline Corbett. Caroline *Hoffman* Corbett."

"What—what did she want?"

Harris recognizes the question is rhetorical. They both know the answer. She wants the truth, the one only he and his mother know.

"What did you tell her?"

"She wants to come here and talk to us. She apologized if this is a bad time. I think she knows I was arrested."

"She's coming now?"

"She wanted to. She said she was just down the road. She agreed to wait until morning. It will give me a chance to speak to Steve Wayman and ask him to be here too."

"The deputy?"

"Yes. He's a good guy. He'll be fair if it comes down to—to legal action." Harris keeps his mother's gaze. Delaying overnight will give her time to adjust to the reality of what they're confronting. She needs that. For himself, he's ready. He wants it out in the open before it kills him.

It isn't as if they haven't both known this day would come. That Caroline would contact them at some point was inevitable.

They planned for the eventuality almost thirty years ago.

23

Caroline—Friday, January 19

She followed the directions Harris had given her, turning off the farm-to-market road onto the private drive at the mailbox labeled with the Fenton name. She drove slowly, reluctantly. If only she could have gotten this over with yesterday. She resented it, the delay of hours Harris had imposed on her. Everyone in her family was upset with her, and for a second night in a row, she hadn't slept. Her self-control was shot, and she was afraid she would cry. She was afraid of what she was going to hear. The one thought that stood out in the heaving sea of thoughts in her head was that nothing after today would be the same.

The house, an old, steep-gabled, two-story farmhouse, faced in native limestone, came into view, and Caroline stopped, letting her gaze drift over the length of the porch, higher to the metal roof, glinting dully in the chilly January sunlight. A tired voice in her brain said she didn't have to go through with it, talking to the Fentons. But a deeper knowing said she'd come too far; there was no way to leave now, not without the answers she'd come for.

On the porch, Caroline rang the bell and listened to it echo. Footsteps approached, light and quick. The woman who opened the door introduced herself. "I'm Julia," she said.

Caroline was speechless. She'd expected Julia to be blonde and curvy like Tricia, but this woman was tall and slender, a near wraith, with dark, silver-streaked hair and dark eyes that were finely drawn. She stood very straight and wore a loose caftan-type sweater over a knit turtleneck top. Her regard of Caroline was steady, even kind. The only hint of agitation came when she touched her throat. Caroline noticed she was trembling. That made two of them.

"You must be Caroline," she said, breaking the strained silence. She held open the screen door. "Won't you come in?"

Caroline followed her from the foyer into an expansive living area. A wall of windows overlooked a series of landscaped gardens, terraced beds that were bordered by less constrained plantings of spiny prickly pear and assorted agaves interspersed with native grasses now gone to seed. A man standing at the windows—obviously Harris—turned from the view and approached her. He was four years younger, forty-one, but he looked so haggard and drawn he might have been ten years older. He looked to Caroline as if he'd just come up from hell. Her heart dipped with something like compassion, but truthfully, her mind had been overtaken by a storm of mixed emotions. She and Harris exchanged names, and as if by mutual agreement, they didn't shake hands.

"Would you like something to drink?" Julia asked. "I've made coffee, or there are soft drinks, water . . ."

"I'm fine," Caroline said. "Thank you."

Julia and Harris sat down on the sofa opposite Caroline.

Moments of silence built one upon another, a precarious tower.

Caroline knotted her hands in her lap to hide their shaking. Across from her, Julia seemed diminished, bruised in a way that suggested long-term suffering. Maybe it was the result of Harris's recent arrest, but Caroline was afraid her visit was responsible, that exactly as she'd feared, it had opened old wounds. "I'm not sure where to begin," she finally said.

Julia uncrossed and recrossed her legs. Harris set his elbows on his knees.

They weren't going to help her, Caroline thought. "I'm sorry to have waited so long to meet you. I regret it now."

"It's all right," Julia said.

"You decorated a bedroom for me." Caroline looked up, suddenly aware that bedroom was here, possibly right over her head. It occurred to her that had she been more amenable, she might have grown up tending the gardens, exploring the woods beyond them. She might have known this quiet, elegant woman.

"Your father and I were always hopeful of enticing you to visit."

Caroline looked at Harris. "You didn't mind that your mom remarried?" *You weren't jealous of me the way I was of you?* That was what she meant.

"No," he said.

"Harris has few memories of his birth father," Julia cut in quickly. "It was such a blessing when Hoff came into our lives. He and Harris bonded right away. They were great together. I used to tease Hoff that he fell in love with Harris before he did with me." Julia's smile was warm and genuine.

Caroline's felt pasted on. Looking at Harris, she said, "Dad talked a lot about your talent on the football field, how much you loved the game, but I heard you coach baseball, right? At the high school in Wyatt?"

"I did, yes." Harris glanced at Julia, and after a moment, bringing his gaze back to Caroline's, he said, "To be honest with you I've been in some legal trouble recently. The result of—well, I could say it was drugs—"

"He's not taking anything now—" Julia interrupted again.

"I heard about it." Caroline spoke over her, and maybe it was rude, being so direct, but Harris had introduced the subject, and she didn't see the point in further small talk. "Steve Wayman is a friend of mine. He's helping me with the search for my dad. That's why I wanted to talk to you both. The fact is I should have come years ago, but I was afraid, and more recently—well, I didn't—I didn't want to rake up the past. It can be so painful—"

Caroline stopped and waited for a response, but none was forthcoming. The Fentons regarded her, blank faced, stoic. She went on. "You know Lanie—my dad's sister—she's in the hospital, in the ICU right now, dying. She—she wants to see her brother, Hoff, you know, before—before it's too late. We all lost touch, and I've been trying to find him with no luck. I wouldn't have bothered you about it, but I literally have no place else to go, no one left to ask. So here I am." She divided her gaze between Julia and Harris. "Do you know where Dad is?"

"No," Julia said.

"Yes," her son answered.

"Harris!" Julia's utterance of his name was a protest, a command.

"We had a plan, Mom." Harris kept Caroline's gaze. "I'm so sorry to tell you—"

"I shot him." Julia spoke over Harris.

Caroline looked at her, breath gone, head vacant. "You shot him?" The words seemed to echo in her brain.

"I'm so sorry."

"I don't understand." Caroline jerked her gaze to Harris. "What is she saying?"

"Hoff is dead," Julia said, and her voice was eerily flat. "I killed him."

"Mom!" Harris was warning her. "You don't have to—"

"This is how it will be!" She addressed him sharply.

He slumped forward, elbows on knees, head hanging.

Caroline watched them; she heard them, but they might as well have been speaking in a foreign language. She couldn't grasp the import of their words. Her breath was shallow, and her heart was beating too fast. She put her hand over it, moved it to her throat. She'd never fainted in her life, and she refused to do it now.

Julia said, "You were estranged from him."

Caroline looked at her. Was that an accusation?

"He missed you horribly. It was awful to see, his heartbreak over— oh—" Julia pushed herself to stand. She paced to the window. "I sound as if I'm blaming you, and it's not that at all. You know he fell at the stadium in Omaha. You were what? Sixteen?"

"What does it matter how old I was?" Caroline demanded. "My God! You killed him? Are you insane?"

"Please, if you could just hear me out." Julia spoke quickly. "He was never the same after that fall, but you couldn't have known because you weren't here. I'm not accusing you. It's just a fact, okay?"

Caroline fought to keep her composure, her wits. She made herself breathe.

"I wanted to go to him, but he forbade me. I found out later he had a girlfriend, Tricia. Maybe you know that he was cheating on me?"

Caroline nodded curtly. "I met her."

"Then you know Tricia was younger, and possibly that's why Hoff trusted her with his care. His excuse to me at the time was that he didn't want me *burdened* with his disabilities." Remembered anger sharpened Julia's tone. "It wasn't until January, a month after his discharge from the rehab facility, that he came back here. But he wasn't the same man. He smoked. He'd always liked a beer, but he switched to hard liquor— a lot of it. But the worst thing was his temper. Every little thing set him off. He wouldn't see a doctor, so I went myself to a neurologist." Julia paused, voice cracking. She flattened her fingers over her mouth. "I described the man Hoff had been, gentle, fun loving, and caring, the best husband, a wonderful father to Harris—" She stopped again, anguish thick in her voice.

Liar! The word burned on Caroline's tongue, but some element in Julia's demeanor prevented her from speaking it. Her grief over the telling was dark in her eyes. It was etched into the grooves that bracketed her cheeks. There was her frailty. Her bones were nearly as visible as Lanie's. Her skin was translucent. Caroline crossed her arms over her middle, holding herself tightly.

Julia went on. "The neurologist couldn't be specific without seeing Hoff, but he said a head injury as severe as the one Hoff sustained could alter areas in his brain that controlled his impulses and emotional balance, the parts that essentially made Hoff who he was. The doctor advised that the changes might be temporary, but it was just as possible they were permanent. He recommended Hoff find a psychiatrist." She paused as if she were steeling herself for whatever she would say next. "When I came home and suggested it, Hoff shoved me up against the wall, hard enough to rattle my teeth, and told me to mind my own business."

Caroline stared at the floor. *Shut up!* She would have screamed it, but her tongue was useless, thick and dry in her mouth.

"He once dislocated her shoulder," Harris said.

"He fixed it, though," Julia said. "He knew exactly what to do."

Was she defending him? Proud of him? A man who had assaulted her? Caroline was appalled. Were Harris and Julia really talking about her dad?

"Sometimes he was sorry too." Harris's tone, his expression, was some mix of anger, defense, and remorse. "But never sorry enough to stop. Mom asked him—we both wanted him to leave. I don't understand why he didn't, why he stayed—he was so pissed all the time. No one could do anything right."

"I've always thought he was scared," Julia said.

Scared of myself, for myself . . . The line from her dad's letter fell through Caroline's mind, a brick through water. Had she been wrong to suspect his fear was related to his involvement in Tillman's athletic scheming? Had he instead been frightened of the man he'd become after his head injury? Had he been aware of the monstrous changes within himself and powerless against them? It would be terrifying, she thought. Even hearing about it was terrifying. Her brain kept trying to rebel. She wanted to wake up, wanted to run.

"I knew I had to do something when he went after Harris," Julia said, and she was speaking now in a kind of robotic monotone. But her eyes were jumpy, and she was continuously rubbing her left thumb over her right palm. "I knew we couldn't live that way any longer. Hoff was bound to kill one or both of us."

"You didn't call the police?"

"Are you kidding?" Harris asked. "Once I spilled my glass of milk at the dinner table, and he ordered me to clean it up, but then he didn't like how I was doing it, and he grabbed the mop I was using and broke it across my back. What the hell do you think he'd have done if we'd called the cops on him?"

"I don't know! I just want the truth!" Caroline was on her feet now. She switched her attention to Julia. "Tell me"—Caroline hurled the demand at her—"when you shot my dad, did you do it to keep him from killing Harris?"

"Hoff attacked him. He had Harris in a headlock. I—"

"When?" Caroline flung her hand in the air. "How long ago did it happen? Harris was young, wasn't he? Just a kid—? Were you ever going to tell me?"

Julia looked away.

"It happened in November," Harris said in a flat voice. "The day before Thanksgiving in 1989."

"In 1989." Caroline repeated it softly. "That long ago, and in all these years, you never once thought about what Lanie and I were going through?" Her voice rose again, becoming shrill. She was shaking and gripped her upper arms. "Do you have any idea how difficult it's been, the sheer hell it's been, not knowing where in this world he was?" Caroline locked Julia's eyes. "My God! Lanie called you. It was early in 1990. She told you she'd filed a missing person report, asked you if you'd seen him, heard from him, and you lied—"

"You have to understand—"

"Understand what, Julia? That you killed my dad and never told us?" Caroline grabbed her purse. Her head swam when she straightened, and she locked her knees.

"He had his hands around her neck," Harris shouted, coming to his feet. "He was going to kill her."

Caroline stared at him. "What did you say?"

"Harris! Stop." Julia came away from the window. "If we could sit down, if you could give me a chance to explain."

But Caroline was done. She didn't care what more they had to say. She'd heard enough. She walked swiftly from the room, bent on leaving, but flinging open the front door, she was astonished to find a man standing there. It was a moment before she recognized him. "Steve?" Her heart faltered.

"Harris called me." He looked past Caroline, and following his gaze over her shoulder, she saw Harris standing, white faced and quiet, in the arched living room doorway. Julia stood behind him. Her agitation and grave alarm were palpable.

Caroline turned back to Steve, knees weak in her relief at his presence. "Julia shot my dad."

"Why don't I come in." He spoke gently, but it was the note of authority in his tone that calmed her.

She stepped away from the door, and she allowed it when Steve slipped his hand beneath her elbow. They followed Harris and Julia back into the living room, and when Steve said they should sit, they obeyed him. Caroline resumed her place on the sofa she'd deserted minutes ago. Steve sat beside her, a cushion away. Harris and Julia sat on the opposite sofa.

Caroline addressed Steve, her confusion apparent. "Why did Harris call you? What is happening? I don't understand any of this."

Reaching over, he put his hand on her arm. "I know this is really hard for you, Caro, but I think if you can let me handle it, we might get your questions answered more quickly." He held her gaze, waiting for her to acquiesce, and when she didn't, he said, "There are legal considerations here, statutes that may still apply. Do you understand what I'm saying? I think that's why Harris called me."

"You know Julia shot my dad? He told you?"

"Harris explained a bit about what was involved when he phoned me earlier this morning. I called you, but you didn't answer."

Caroline pulled her phone from her purse and saw it had been silenced. By accident, she thought. Maybe when she'd stowed it in her purse earlier. Turning it on, she saw there was a call from Steve and a voice mail too. Returning the phone to her purse, she met his gaze. "Did Harris tell you his mother shot my dad?"

"He only said your dad had been killed here and that there were extenuating circumstances. He asked if I could be here—"

"I asked him to come because I trust him," Harris said.

Caroline looked at him. Her heart pounded in her ears. "I don't understand any of this."

"I think Deputy Wayman's concern is that, depending on the facts, a murder charge could be made," Julia said in her monotone voice. "It doesn't matter how long ago it happened; there's no statute of limitations on murder, is there, Deputy Wayman?"

"You shot Dad on purpose?" Caroline was horrified.

"No," Julia said.

"Julia, Harris"—Steve looked between them—"you understand you can have an attorney present, that it might be best in this situation if you did."

The two exchanged a glance. More than that, some kind of private dialogue took place, one only they could understand.

They're protecting each other. The thought surfaced in Caroline's mind.

"There'll be time for that later," Harris said.

"Julia?" Steve asked.

"I just want to explain." She seemed resigned.

"All right," Steve said.

"When it happened"—Julia found Caroline's gaze—"Harris was so young, not yet thirteen. I was afraid of what would become of him if I was arrested. His birth father was abusive. I left him when Harris was six. My parents were dead, killed in a motorcycle accident when I was four. I was raised in the foster care system, bounced from one home to the next. It was a nightmare. I couldn't bear the thought that my child would be forced into it too."

"It wasn't a matter of her getting yelled at or hit once in a while." Harris sat forward, ignoring his mother's whispered protest. "She was made to do things—sexually."

The word sat among them, tainting the air.

Caroline's heart broke a little.

"It was only in two of the homes." Julia spoke to her knees.

"In one of them, the wife watched." Harris's gaze remained fixed on Caroline. Did she get it? he seemed to ask. Did she understand the magnitude of the cruelty his mother had endured?

"I couldn't let it happen to Harris," Julia said. "I did think of telling the police what I'd done when he turned eighteen, but he was still struggling with Hoff's . . . loss, and I was afraid—I've always been afraid to—to not be . . . nearby, in case he needed . . ." She didn't finish.

Steve interrupted. "Let me stop you here, Julia, and ask you once again: Are you sure you don't want to call an attorney? I can pretty well guarantee from what I've heard already that I'm going to have to take you both in for further questioning. No doubt there'll be an investigation."

"I understand," Julia said. "I don't want an attorney."

"Mom—" A low note of warning lay deep in Harris's voice.

"No, Harris. Let me tell it. It's the only reason I've agreed to this, to speak at all." Julia was adamant. "You promised."

What had he promised? Caroline wondered.

He shot her a glance, one that was at once infuriated and bleak.

He would lose his mother after this. Julia could well end up in prison. But Caroline had little sympathy. At least Harris would know where his mother was; at least he could visit her.

"You know I work at the high school in Wyatt?" Julia addressed Caroline.

"Yes," she answered. "You're a guidance counselor."

Julia nodded. "So that day school let out early because of the holiday. I remembered I'd forgotten cranberries and stopped at the grocery store. It was mobbed, and I was late getting home. Ordinarily, Hoff wouldn't have been there that time of year. With the football season in full swing, he'd have been on the road, scouting. But since his head injury, he hadn't resumed his schedule. He'd actually talked about changing careers, maybe going into coaching. He had a teaching certificate."

Caroline had forgotten that.

"He also had a lot of connections. I thought maybe things would work out. I think even you were feeling better about him, weren't you, Harris?"

"Yeah. If he'd been himself, if he could have gotten back to that person, he would have made a great coach. He was so good to me and Mom, the best dad a kid could ever ask for." Harris's voice was furred with emotion.

"What happened?" Steve sat forward, elbows on his knees. He wasn't in uniform, but he was every inch a lawman, even dressed in civilian clothes.

"I came in through the kitchen door," Julia answered. "It was dark in the house, which seemed odd. There were strange noises, thumps, what sounded like scuffling. It flashed through my mind someone had broken in, but Hoff's car was in the driveway, and I knew Harris was home. I'd spoken to both of them when I called from school to tell them I was going to the store. Hoff asked if I'd pick up a can of shaving cream for him. He didn't sound upset at all. Harris seemed fine too. It was barely an hour later when I came in here, right into this room, and found them. I thought at first they were playing some kind of game—"

"Mom—" Harris said.

He wanted Julia to stop. Caroline could almost understand his impulse. She would want to protect her mother as far as she could too.

"Hoff had his hands around Harris's neck, choking him. It was horrible. I shouted at Hoff to let Harris go." Julia's voice rose, and her own breath was shallow as if from recalled panic. "I don't think he heard me. I don't think he knew where he was. His eyes—they were empty, as if he was gone. I knew if I didn't stop him, he'd kill Harris."

"No . . ." Caroline's protest was little more than a moan. Her eyes on Julia's were hot with pleading.

Julia's eyes were dark with sorrow. "I'm so sorry—"

"What did you do?" Steve brought her back to her accounting.

"I grabbed Hoff's arm and dug my nails into his flesh. He let Harris go—"

"And grabbed her." Harris glanced at his mom.

"I got away, though, and went for the phone," Julia said. "The landline, over there." She indicated the table against a far wall, where a phone receiver sat up on a base.

"Hoff jerked the cord out of the wall," Harris said. He looked at Caroline. "The son of a bitch was a maniac. His face was twisted like nothing you ever saw. You wouldn't have recognized him."

She crossed her arms tightly over her middle. She had never known her dad to so much as raise his hand in anger.

"When did the gun come into play?" Steve asked. "Whose gun was it?"

"Hoff's," Julia said.

"He had a gun?" Caroline asked. It was news to her. But then, she hadn't really known her dad, had she? Not since she was a very little girl.

"He kept it in the glove compartment of his car," Julia said. "He was on the road so often in remote areas he felt he needed it for protection."

"How did it get inside the house?"

Caroline thought with the way Steve addressed Julia, the way he was looking at her, she might have been the only other person in the room.

"I—somehow I got Hoff off balance," she said. "When he fell, it gave me enough time to get outside to his car."

"Mom, no." Harris sat forward, putting a hand on her arm, wanting her to stop.

Julia went on as if he hadn't spoken, wasn't present. "Hoff's car was parked near the back door."

"I can't do this!" Harris was on his feet now, staring down at his mother. "I can't keep the promise anymore."

Still she ignored him. "It was unlocked, and it took only a moment to grab the gun from the glove box. I knew if I didn't stop Hoff, he'd kill Harris, kill us both."

"You didn't stop him!" Harris turned to Caroline, locking her gaze. "Mom didn't shoot Hoff. I did."

24

Harris hears his mother groan in protest, and it hurts his heart. It's the last thing she wants, for the truth to come out, and the last thing he wants is to cause her more pain. In 1989 when it happened, the story she invented to protect him was that Hoff left them for another woman. Now she's told the story they agreed to tell if the original story of Hoff's disappearance were ever exposed as a lie, and Harris has let her do it, let her take the blame, even though since Caroline's phone call last night he has been on fire to come clean. He didn't anticipate, though, how hard it would be to break this promise so long kept. But it is the right thing, the only way out of this hell for him and his mother.

He feels her grip his wrist, hears her say his name, but he doesn't—can't—acknowledge her, and keeping Caroline's gaze, he says, "There was no way Mom could get away from Hoff. He was too strong."

Caroline looks anguished, confused.

What would she have done in his shoes that night? Harris would like to ask her. He's glad for Wayman's presence, glad the deputy and

Caroline are friends, that along with Harris and his mom, Caroline, too, has Wayman for support.

His mom releases his wrist, and he turns to her, and the sight of her tears falling, how they speckle her hands clutched in her lap, shakes his resolve. But he can't let her take on the burden of his guilt. He doesn't care that he was only a twelve-year-old boy at the time. He's a man now, and he's killed someone. And his shame and remorse, the aching remnants of his love for the man, Hoff, who was his victim, are eating him alive.

"I set him off that day," Harris says. "When I came home from school, I saw his car and knew he was home, probably drunk or getting there. It pissed me off. I was so sick of taking his bullshit. When I came in the house, I slammed the back door on purpose. I was looking to get a rise out of him. It was stupid, but I was a kid."

"*Was* he drinking?" Steve asks.

"Yeah. He came busting into the kitchen, yelling he had a damn headache and I should show him a little consideration, a little respect."

Respect? Harris hears his kid self shout in his mind. *Like the kind you show my mom when you're punching her?* The memory dances behind his eyes. *A real man would never hit a woman*, he said. Hoff lunged at him then, but Harris sidestepped him, and when Hoff fell, Harris laughed.

Laughed like a hyena.

Goddamn, I'll show you, you little bastard, Hoff screamed.

C'mon with it, then, Harris taunted. He was so confident he could take Hoff. Too confident.

"He got me in a choke hold," Harris says now. "I couldn't breathe." Harris looks at Deputy Wayman. "He would have killed me if Mom hadn't come home right then."

"She distracted him? You got free?"

"Yeah, but then he tackled her. He got her down, put his hands around her neck, and he was strangling her. Her eyes rolled back. All I could see were the whites. Her lips turned blue. It's like Mom said—if we—if I didn't stop him—"

Caroline's whimper interrupts Harris. He sees that she's white faced, shaking all over, and he's sorry for her, but he's desperate, too, for her to understand. "If you could have seen him—" He locks her gaze. "If you'd been there—" Harris stops; tears scald the backs of his eyes, pack his throat. "I loved him, you know?" His voice thins, breaks. He swallows, goes on. "He was the only dad I ever had, but after his head injury he turned into a monster. He was twisted up inside, like when he cracked his skull, nothing went back together right."

"Hoff had your mother pinned to the floor?" Deputy Wayman's is the cooling voice of reason.

"Yes." Harris turns to the windows; the floor beneath them is where Hoff took his mom down. She's looking there, too, and he knows she sees it, Hoff sitting on her. She will feel his weight again, crushing her ribs, the grip of his hard, calloused hands squeezing her throat.

She'll hear the same thing Harris does: Hoff's groaning. The sound is unearthly.

Crazed.

Harris stands as if mesmerized, and then he wheels, running out of the living room, down the short hallway to the kitchen, and out the back door. Reaching the car, he yanks open the passenger-side door and fumbles in the glove box for the gun, a Ruger, a .22 caliber standard with wood grips, that Hoff got from a buddy of his who'd served in the Marines back in the seventies in Vietnam. Hoff keeps the gun loaded. It's heavy, and Harris grips it with both hands.

Heart banging the walls of his chest, he rushes back to the living room. Hoff is still sitting on his mother with his hands fastened around her neck. In his rage, his jaw is clenched. His knuckles and face are white. His mother's face by contrast is an unearthly shade of blue. Her eyes bulge from their sockets. "Get off her!" Harris shouts, but Hoff doesn't. It's as if Harris isn't even there, begging for his mother's life. He thinks from her look he's too late, that she's already gone, and a wail of protest, of sorrow, bursts from his chest. He is barely aware of it when he pulls the gun's trigger. The recoil makes him stagger; the blast rattles his teeth, deafens his ears. Hoff turns to him, disbelief crowding the mania from his expression, and his gaze softens as if in that instant he remembers the man he was and the love he and Harris shared.

"He fell over," Harris says now, addressing Deputy Wayman. "He didn't move again."

25

Caroline—Friday, January 19

"You want me to believe it was you and not your mom who shot my dad."

"It's the truth," Harris said. He looked drained. Sweat beaded his hairline, ringed the neck of his shirt.

"You were twelve," Caroline said, as if, like drinking alcohol or getting married, a person had to be a certain legal age to commit a murder. She didn't want it to be possible, didn't want to believe Harris. But what she wanted didn't matter. No one could make up the story Harris had told. The horror of it ached in her mind. She wished she'd never come here, never heard—she locked Harris's gaze. "For all I know you're protecting your mother." Caroline didn't know why she continued to challenge him. "Dad cheated on her, and she shot him. Men have been killed for less." She repeated Steve's line. Was it preferable, believing in that scenario? What difference did it make how it had happened? It was sickening, and her dad was just as dead all the same.

"If I hadn't shot him, my mother wouldn't be here. It's that simple, no matter how sorry we are."

Caroline switched her glance to Julia. "You lied just now to protect Harris."

"You're a mother. What would you do? Turn your child in?" Julia didn't wait for Caroline's answer. She appealed to Steve. "Harris would have gone on trial. Even at twelve, he might have been charged as an adult. I couldn't have afforded to hire any legal dream team either." She looked back at Caroline. "All it would have taken to convict him is one juror like you who doubted Harris's story. I wasn't about to have my son spend the rest of his life behind bars for saving my life."

"Did you ever report the previous incidents of abuse to the police?" Steve asked. "Ever go to the hospital? Do you have photos?"

"No." Julia looked down and away. "I didn't want people to think ill of Hoff. I kept hoping he'd come back to himself, to the way he was before. We were happy, so happy, until he—until he fell—" Voice breaking, she paused, then said, "Your dad was a good man, and I know you felt you had lost him to us, but he loved you so much, and he grieved for you, for the breach between you."

"It can never be healed now," Caroline said, not with malice, not even with anger. But her mind was in such turmoil that she truly had no idea what her feelings were.

"What did you do with Hoff's body?" Steve asked.

Julia pressed her fingertips to her eyes.

"We had a tractor," Harris said in a wooden voice, and he went on, describing the hole he had dug with the machine near the back property line some four or five hundred yards distant, out of sight of the house, beyond a wooded area. They had maneuvered Hoff's body there.

Caroline felt sickened. Crossing her arms, she bent over. Where was the end of all this horror?

Steve laid his palm on her back for a moment; then, addressing Harris and Julia, he said, "I need you to show me."

"Now?" Julia asked.

"Yes. I'll need to loop in local law enforcement. Clint Mackie, the Wyatt police chief—do you know him? The county coroner too—"

Caroline stopped listening. It was too hard. But her own thoughts were no easier. How was she going to tell Lanie that her brother had been murdered? There would be no final conversation, no mending of past hurt.

"A forensic team will be called in," Steve was saying. He found Caroline's gaze. "Your dad's body will be exhumed."

She nodded as if that made sense, but nothing did.

"If you want to be there, I'll see if I can arrange it."

"No," she said. Drawing her purse into her lap, she wondered if she could stand, if her legs would hold her.

Steve continued. "His remains will be transported to the coroner's office, and an autopsy will be performed. Once the results are in, they'll release his body back to you for burial."

Caroline nodded. What would be left of him? she wondered. How long was it after death before a body's bones turned to powder? Her aunt Lanie had asked to be cremated. She had asked that her ashes be scattered in the wind. *Somewhere pretty*, she had said. *Somewhere that brings you peace.* She didn't want mourners at a grave site. She didn't believe she would be there. *I'll be the wind in your hair*, she had said to Caroline. *I'll be the sunshine warming you on a cold day.*

"Are you good to drive?" Steve asked. They were in the front hall-way now, waiting while Harris and Julia got their coats from the closet.

"I think so," Caroline said.

"I didn't know details. When Harris called me, he only said there had been a death some years ago and that criminal charges might be involved. I suspected it might have to do with you and your dad—God, Caro, I would have spared you if I could."

"It's so horrible, Steve. All these years, I thought—then I had so much hope for finding him—" Her voice broke.

He cupped the side of her face, and she leaned into his touch, feeling her tears dampen his palm. His eyes on hers were tender. If they were alone, he would have embraced her, and she longed for it. Even standing inches from her, he was a shelter, a source of comfort. "I'm so sorry for all this," he said softly, thumbing her wet cheek.

She nodded and stepped back, knowing if she didn't, his kindness would undo the last of her composure. She wiped her eyes, wanting to thank him, to say she was so grateful for his involvement, that it was only his presence that had made it at all bearable, but before she could articulate a word, he left her to usher Harris and Julia out the front door.

Harris was a half step beyond Caroline when she reached out and touched his elbow.

He jerked around, eyes wide. Caroline was surprised by her gesture, too, but she thought she might never have another chance or the will to speak to him again. She said, "When your mom said a while ago that you made a promise to her, what was it?"

"That if Hoff—if somehow what happened was ever discovered, I'd let her take the blame."

"She must love you very much."

Pointing that out hurt Harris. Caroline could tell by the way his jaw trembled. She could see the fight he waged for control of his emotions in his expression.

"I would take it back if I could," he said when he could speak. "There hasn't been a day that I haven't regretted—" His voice broke, and he stopped and looked away. When he looked back, if it was possible, his eyes were even more raw and grief filled. "I ended my life, too, in a way, when I shot him. I've carried it, you know? I always will."

"I wish he'd gotten help," Caroline said.

"Yeah," Harris said, and giving her a brief nod, he left her to get into the truck with his mother and Steve.

Watching him go, Caroline encountered Julia's gaze. *You're a mother. What would you do? Turn your child in?* Would she? Caroline wondered. If she knew Nina had killed someone, would she alert the authorities? She'd known for months that Rob had broken laws, but she hadn't reported him—for Nina's sake, she realized. Her instinct, like Julia's, was to protect her child. The circumstances were vastly different and yet similar in a way that allowed Caroline a glimmer of understanding, even compassion for the Fentons' actions.

She waited until they were out of sight before opening her car door. The wind was blustery, lifting her hair, sighing through the leafless trees. She pulled her black blazer more tightly around her. Somewhere in the distance she heard the shrill cry of a bird.

Hawk, she thought. It sounded lonely.

EPILOGUE: SIX MONTHS LATER

Harris—July 4

Holly sets the platter holding the hamburger patties she's made for the backyard cookout in the refrigerator alongside a package of hot dogs. All the meat is organic. She's a fanatic. Standing at the counter, slicing onions and tomatoes, Harris remembers how he used to tease her about her penchant for reading labels. He called her the food police. One day, he hopes he'll be able to tease her again. For now he's grateful to be here with her and the boys, grateful for her willingness to include him in their plans.

Getting sober and making amends has been slow going, but he doesn't care if it takes the rest of his life. He's not going to screw it up, this gift of a second chance. He knows it every time he visits and sees Connor's face light up. Kyle is still watchful—waiting for Harris to fall off the wagon is Harris's guess. He doesn't blame Kyle. Harris's past, all that happened—it's a hell of a lot for a kid to process about his dad. The publicity was brutal in the initial days after Harris and his mom were taken in for questioning. Telling Holly and the kids the truth about Hoff and all that had happened had to be one of the hardest things he's ever done. But it's a relief, too, now that his family—now that everyone—knows. And while there are some who go out of their way to avoid him, a good many don't. Coming out of drug rehab, knowing he's got nothing to hide, no secrets to keep, has given him confidence it's going to stick this time. He'll likely never coach again, but he's working toward getting certified as a drug-rehab counselor. He's no do-gooder; he's got no grand illusions he can save anybody, but like his shrink says, while he can't undo the past, he can try to make things right from now on.

"I hope there's enough food," Holly says. "It looks like we'll be feeding a couple of Kyle's friends." She's looking through the french doors into the backyard, where four boys, Kyle and Connor among them, are slugging a birdie over a badminton net. It's a game for sissies, one of them shouts, and they laugh. Holly's parents and Harris's mom are sitting on the deck, watching the boys, and they laugh too.

"It'll be fine," Harris says. "If we run out, I'll go to the store."

"I always overdo it, don't I?" She meets his glance, and he imagines touching her mouth, tracing the curve of her slight smile with his fingertip. A timer goes off, and she pulls a fresh-baked cherry pie out of the oven.

"Should I start the grill?" Harris asks.

"In a bit." She's back at the french doors. "Your mom seems more like herself finally."

"Yeah. At least we know neither of us is going to prison." He laughs, a rough syllable.

Holly doesn't. "Thank God," she says, "and Roger Yellott."

Roger is the local attorney Harris's mother contacted last January, the day following Caroline's visit. While they were free on bond after their arraignment, Harris and his mom were advised not to leave the area, that the investigation into the circumstances surrounding Hoff's death was ongoing. Steve Wayman suggested they'd be smart to hire an attorney. He gave Harris's mom Roger Yellott's name. Harris didn't want legal representation. He didn't give a damn what happened to him. But once Roger heard the story and was familiar with the extenuating circumstances, he asked Harris to let him do his job for both Harris and his mother. By that point lab techs had exhumed Hoff's body. They'd come into the house one day and conducted a thorough examination of the living room where Hoff had died, too, taking scrapings of the base and floorboards and clipping fibers from the carpet. That same afternoon, after the police left, Roger stopped by and found Harris and his mom sitting in the kitchen. Harris felt numb. His mother was mute. Even her tears were silent. Harris watched them slide off her chin. That was the moment he turned to Roger and told him to do whatever it took. "If you have to represent me, too, to get my mom off, do it," he said.

Roger didn't waste any time. Through what remained of January and most of February, he interviewed everyone he could find who had known the Fentons during the time Hoff was a part of their family. Harris's mother's coworkers spoke of days when Harris's mom had come to school heavily made up or wearing a scarf to disguise her injuries. She was astonished and horrified to learn Hoff's abuse of her was common knowledge. Harris was sickened learning the extent of it. One of Harris's mother's closest friends in those days told Roger she'd been afraid Hoff would kill Julia.

"If she were to have x-rays taken," the friend said to Roger, "I'm sure they would show the damage. I know Hoff broke her collarbone. He fractured two of her ribs. One of her front teeth is an implant. Hoff knocked out the real one."

At Roger's insistence, Harris's mother had x-rays made, and they mapped in graphic black-and-white detail the badly healed history of Hoff's abuse. When word got out, a lot of folks were distraught. Many of those who'd been aware were regretful of their silence, which had left a twelve-year-old boy and his mother vulnerable to a man they declared had become a monster.

Five weeks after their arrests, in a move that caught Harris but not Roger off guard, the charge of involuntary manslaughter against him was dismissed, and in a further act of legal leniency, his mom was given deferred adjudication, a term of five years, for her failure to report Hoff's death and for concealing his body. Harris felt light headed on leaving the courthouse. His mom clung tightly to his arm. A handful of folks who knew his mother either as a teacher or guidance counselor came up to them and, hugging them, thanked Harris for saving her life. He was precariously near tears when he spotted Caroline on the fringes of the small crowd. He got the sense she wanted to speak to him, but by the time he had a chance to break away, she was at the bottom of the courthouse steps. He'd never know where the impulse came from that sent him after her.

He called her name just as she turned the corner.

She paused and turned slowly to face him. A cold March wind whipped her hair around her face, stirred the grit on the sidewalk under her feet. Other than the two of them the street was deserted.

Despite his misgivings at having followed her, Harris closed the distance between them, and she watched him, her eyes intent. The directness of her gaze was disconcerting. He shouldn't have approached her. "I just wanted to tell you again how sorry I am," he said when he got within speaking distance. He shoved his hands into his jacket pockets.

"I don't hate you," Caroline said after a moment. "I used to when I was a kid and thought you'd taken my place with my dad. I don't hate you now, knowing how Dad died. I'm sorry for what he did to you and your mom, sorry for his circumstances, that he didn't get help."

Harris couldn't answer. His eyes burned. Maybe it was the wind. He shifted his gaze.

"The way you described him when you first knew him," Caroline said, "that's who he was. When you said he was the best dad a kid could ask for—that's how I remember him, how I want to remember him."

Harris met Caroline's gaze. "You're—you seem so—so okay," he said, and it was difficult, getting the words out around the sorrow packed in his throat.

"I'm getting there. I can't claim to have forgiven you and your mother, not all the way, but it's what I want to do. I want to let it go. I want that for you too. I'm relieved you didn't have to go to jail."

"How? How can you be so—?" He couldn't finish.

"My aunt, Lanie—she was so wise." Caroline paused, jaw trembling. "She died not long after I was here in January, but before—before she slipped away, I was able to tell her—everything. I didn't want to, but she always had a way of getting to the truth, you know? She asked me not to hold on to the anger. She made me see how pointless it is. She said it would kill my joy."

"That's—I just—I don't know what to say."

"There's something else." Caroline paused, as if to consider, but then looking back at Harris, she locked his gaze. "You may or may not believe this, but she said she saw Dad, and he was all right. He was waiting for her."

Harris held Caroline's glance a long moment. He didn't know how to respond or whether he believed in such occurrences. He thought from her demeanor Caroline did believe, and she derived comfort from it.

Harris thanked her for sharing the experience. He said, "You remind me of Hoff, the best of him," and she seemed pleased.

She smiled, touched his hand. He thought, watching her walk away, that it was unlikely he would ever see her again.

Not everyone has been so kind, though. Gee has yet to go to trial, and his family and the team of lawyers Gee's dad has hired to defend him are doing all they can to discredit Harris. Last week during an interview on local television, Gee's lead attorney wanted to know who in their right mind would take the word of a murderer and a drug addict over that of a gifted and disciplined athlete? Harris wishes he could talk to Gee, but Roger has warned him against it. Harris doesn't know what he'd say anyway. That he's sorry he was such a piss-poor role model? Maybe he'd just like to tell the kid not to give up, that he can come back from this. But it's laughable to assume Gee would care what Harris has to say.

"It isn't that I'm angry at you, at least not so much anymore." Holly turns from the french doors. Her face is in shadow. Harris can't read her expression.

Her glance lights briefly on his face and flits away. He waits, wanting to hear what more she might say even as he's afraid of it.

"What I can't get over is that you didn't trust me," she says. "This terrible thing happened to you . . . What did you think? That I couldn't handle it? Am I that—what? Self-absorbed, overly sensitive, too emotional?"

"You're none of those—"

"I could have helped you, been here for you."

Zeke said the same thing. He was pissed that he hadn't known the history. He felt he'd been used by Harris, betrayed by him. And as far as Zeke is concerned, Harris's mother had no damn business asking a twelve-year-old to keep such a terrible secret. Zeke also said if Hoff were still alive, he'd kill the bastard himself.

"I try to imagine what it must have been like," Holly says. "Connor's the same age. Just thinking of him—that he would have to—be driven to get a gun and shoot—"

"Honey, don't." Harris takes a step toward her.

She waves him off. Tears stand in her eyes.

He opens his mouth to argue or possibly to plead with her.

She cuts him off. "I know the man you wanted me to see, the boy—the childhood you invented, where for a while you had a dad named Hoff whom you adored, who abandoned you and your mom. Now that I know the truth, how much more horrific it was, I have to, like, reshape every assumption, every perception, because the two boys, the one with the sort of normal childhood you told me you had, and the real boy who dealt with abuse and ultimately got a gun and shot his stepdad—that boy would grow up to be a very different man from the one I thought I knew."

"No, I don't feel—"

"I fell in love with the man I thought you were, Harris, but for our marriage to work, I need to know—I need to fall in love with—the man you are, the one who is not on drugs, who's working through the nightmares from his past, not running from them."

Hope. Harris's head feels light with it.

"I need time," she says, and she takes a step toward him as if he's asked. "I don't know what the future holds for us."

"That's all right," he answers. "Today is good. Today is enough."

There is a sound now of the french doors opening. Within moments Connor clatters into the kitchen, and as if he can sense a softening of the air between his parents, his face cracks into a grin. He's across the room in an instant, taking their hands, drawing them to him, now gripping their waists. They have no choice but to make a circle. Harris puts his arm around Connor's shoulders, and on encountering Holly's arm, he lifts his gaze to hers, and her smile lights him up from the inside. His throat closes, and he prays the moment will last, that, while fragile, it is the beginning of a new life for him and the beginning of healing for his family.

He looks around for Kyle and finds him standing at the table, mouth downturned, eyes wary. Harris thinks he may not live long enough to regain Kyle's trust, but he'll never stop trying.

Letting his gaze drift now, he wonders what Caroline is doing on this holiday. Barely a day goes by that he doesn't think of her. They've spoken twice since January, and both conversations have been difficult, but each time he has felt they are reaching for a resolution, some sort of mutual understanding. Not long ago he realized that if she had not been persistent in searching for her truth, he would never have begun the search for his own.

He hopes one day he can thank her.

Connor tugs his hand. "Dad, when are you gonna light the grill? I'm starving."

Harris ruffles his youngest son's hair. "Guess we'd better do it right now."

Caroline—July 4

They were on the road early, hoping to avoid the worst of the holiday traffic. Caroline was driving. Her mom rode in front beside her, and Nina sat in back with the small wooden chest that held Lanie's ashes and those of Caroline's father. They were finally going to scatter them, having agreed the farm outside Nacogdoches that Lanie and Hoff's grandparents had once owned was the right location. Caroline's mother had suggested the farm. In particular she recalled a pond there from long-ago visits. Hoff had called it the old swimming hole. He and Lanie and later Caroline's mom had picnicked there. It had always been a good time, she said, a happy place. The farm had since passed to a distant cousin, but when Caroline's mom had called him and explained why she wanted to visit, he'd been warm in giving his consent to the plan. He'd assured her the stock pond shaded by live oaks that she remembered and the old tire swing were still there.

"I doubt it will look the same," she said now.

"When was the last time you visited?" Caroline glanced at her mom.

"Before you were born. I probably won't recognize the place."

Caroline met Nina's eyes in the rearview mirror when she looked up briefly from her phone. She was obviously texting someone. Probably Oliver. A fellow student at the University of Houston, Ollie was the new guy in her life. Nina had finished out the semester at DU and then enrolled in summer classes at the University of Houston, where she'd met Ollie. Caroline was half in love with Oliver herself. Out of gratitude, she thought. There was nothing like a new love to ease the pain of a forced relocation.

The decision that she and Nina had made last spring to pack up life in Iowa and begin anew in Texas had been as difficult as it was inevitable. The timing had made it especially hard. First there'd been the shock of learning of her father's death; then within hours, Lanie was gone too.

That awful and bleak January afternoon, coming back from Wyatt, Caroline had vowed Lanie would never know what had happened to her brother. The drive itself would always be a blur, except for the moments when, from nowhere, a detail, a word—*monster*, they'd called her dad a *monster*—or an image, Julia rubbing her thumb again and again over her palm, would rise in Caroline's brain, and she'd be choking, crying. She pulled over a few times. She was exhausted and pretty much cried out by the time she made it to St. Joe's. She sat in her car outside the hospital, gulping air, trying to settle herself, steel herself, to face her mother, to see her aunt—who according to her mom was hanging on to her life by the barest thread.

"I think she's waiting for you," her mother had said when Caroline had called her a final time from the outskirts of Houston. "I told her you were on your way, that you would be here soon. Hurry, darling," her mother had said.

In the waiting room outside the ICU, Caroline's mom and Martha greeted her with warm hugs. Her mom held her more tightly than Caroline could ever remember. "Don't be so kind to me," she whispered against her mother's cheek. "I'll lose it."

"Just from the little you've told me, I can't imagine what you've been through." Grasping Caroline's upper arms, her mother set Caroline out of her embrace, searching her eyes.

"Lanie mustn't know," Caroline said, and her mom agreed.

Because of the circumstances, the understanding that Lanie would in all likelihood not last the night, Caroline, her mother, and Martha were allowed into Lanie's cubicle together. Caroline went to Lanie's bedside, which was remarkably free of equipment. There was a machine to monitor her vital signs and an IV drip, but everything else that might have been in place to sustain her life had been removed, per the DNR. Caroline took Lanie's hand very gently, not expecting a response. She'd been warned that Lanie's comalike state was deepening. But at Caroline's touch, and at the sound of her voice when she bent to Lanie's ear and whispered, "I'm here," Lanie's eyelids fluttered open.

She lifted her hand from Caroline's grasp and cupped her cheek. "My darling girl," she said, and while she was hoarse, her eyes were clear and bright. "You've had such a horrible time, haven't you."

Lanie seemed to know. How could she know? Caroline couldn't answer her. Lanie's image shimmered in the prism created by her tears.

"He's all right now, you know—Hoff. I've seen him. He's waiting for me."

"Oh, Auntie Lanie." Caroline smoothed wisps of her aunt's fine white hair back from her brow.

"No, no, none of that. I want you to tell me. Can you?" she asked. "How did it happen? How did Hoff die?"

Caroline looked from Lanie to her mother for guidance, but her mother, looking visibly shaken, could only shrug. Who would know what to do?

Caroline looked back at her aunt. "I don't want to burden you with it." She said what she was thinking.

"I don't have all the time left in the world, sweet, and you need to tell it to be rid of it."

So Caroline began, speaking in fits and starts. Lanie's eyes never moved from her face. She kept a hold on Caroline's hand. She was lucid, quiet, and completely present, and when Caroline finished, she said, "Well, it relieves me now that I didn't take you there."

She meant in 1989, when Caroline's dad had wanted Lanie to bring Caroline to Wyatt, forcing her to meet the Fentons. Caroline had thought about that, too, driving back from Wyatt. Possibly by refusing,

Lanie had saved her. But wasn't it equally possible that had Caroline gone, had she seen the shape her dad was in, she could have saved him? She would never know; nor would she burden her aunt with her doubt. Lanie found her gaze.

"You know, honey, that you have to forgive Harris and Julia. Not for them, but for yourself."

"I'm not sure I can." Every fiber of Caroline's being resisted the idea. "I understand why it happened. If Dad was that way, if he did those things, if he was the monster they claim—"

"But you see, none of that really matters. Even if they murdered Hoff in cold blood, you would have to forgive them or else spend your life being bitter. That's a death sentence. Can you understand? That's as confining, as limiting, as a prison cell, only you made it yourself." Lanie's eyes were steady on Caroline's.

"But how—it's as if you're saying what they did is all right, and it isn't."

"No, and that isn't what forgiveness means. It isn't for Harris's or Julia's sake. It's for your own."

Moments passed, and then Lanie squeezed Caroline's hand with more strength than seemed reasonable. "Promise me you'll work on it. Don't hold the anger and hatred. Don't sacrifice your joy in life to that. Okay? Don't hate them. I don't." Her eyes on Caroline's were burning, intense. "Promise me."

She had insisted. Those had been her final words. And Caroline had promised, and remembering that, remembering her aunt's kindness, her sweet, gentle spirit, was like a balm she applied to a wound on an as-needed basis. In March, when she'd gone to Wyatt for the Fentons' hearing, it had been because she'd known it was what Lanie would have done. But it was seeing actual proof of Julia Fenton's injuries and hearing the sworn statements from people who had witnessed how badly and how often she'd been hurt that had brought home to Caroline the hellish nightmare the Fentons had endured at her father's hands. Her anguish had bent her over her knees. A woman sitting next to her had offered water. Caroline didn't know how she had kept it together. Outside the afternoon had been sunny, cold, and windswept, and she had stood on the fringe of the small crowd gathered around the Fentons, praying for the nerve to speak to them. But in the end she'd had no idea what to say, and she'd left.

She would always be grateful that Harris had followed her, grateful for the chance to have shared that Lanie had professed to see her brother. Whether it was true or not, Caroline hoped that like her, Harris would derive comfort from it. But mostly she was glad she'd had the opportunity to say she was working on the issue of forgiveness. He'd seemed to appreciate it. More than that, he'd seemed astonished. Caroline had felt something in her heart loosen; she'd felt as if her dad's ghost had been laid to rest.

She'd touched Harris's hand, offering her own silent gratitude. Maybe no one else would understand. Maybe it was weird. Some might say it was too soon or fake, but what did it matter what anyone else thought? Caroline knew Lanie would be pleased.

It hadn't been long after the Fentons' court hearing that she'd heard from Jace that Coach Kelly had died of a massive stroke. By April, Caroline had added her house, which had gone into foreclosure, her marriage, which had ended in divorce, and the closing of the company she and Rob had started to the list of losses. Prior to filing bankruptcy for both himself and New Wheaton Transit, Rob had had the attorney he'd finally hired dissolve the partnership. He had shielded Caroline in every way he could.

Still, the whole thing was heartbreaking. While Rob's attorney had managed to work his legal magic to keep Rob out of jail, his wages from a job as a driver for a local trucking company were being heavily garnished by the IRS. He was renting a room in someone's house, subsisting on canned tuna and peanut butter, barely making it, he said. In a fit of self-pity, he had accused her and Nina of abandoning him. He'd imagined that once he took action to save her, she would come home; they would rebuild their marriage, the business. Instead she'd filed for divorce and been granted innocent spouse status by the IRS.

Caroline hadn't explained it. It would have been pointless.

Neither had she mentioned that she was Lanie's sole heir. No one could have been as surprised as Caroline when her aunt's attorney had called her into his office and handed her a copy of Lanie's will. Her estate wasn't vast by any means, but it was substantial enough that Caroline didn't have to worry immediately about how she was going to support herself or find a way to ensure Nina could finish college. Lanie's house provided Caroline with shelter, too, and tending Lanie's beautiful garden as it came to life through the spring had given Caroline hope even as she'd grieved for everything that was gone—not only people she had loved but her illusions, the fairy tale she had imagined was her life.

"Maybe your dad would rather have his ashes spread at the Astrodome," her mother said now.

Caroline looked at her, brows raised. While her dad's will had contained instructions that he be cremated, unlike Lanie, he hadn't mentioned a preference as to his final resting place.

"They were some of the happiest times of his life, when he played for the Oilers."

"Yes, but he was happy when you visited the farm, too, right? Besides, who knows what kind of red tape is involved in spreading someone's ashes in a stadium, even if it is pretty much abandoned."

"You said Jace spread his father's ashes at the Tillman stadium."

"Maybe permission was granted because Coach Kelly was so well loved."

Her mother's huff was derisive. She didn't buy that Coach Kelly had been victimized by Farley Dade and his old boy cronies. Neither did Kip Penny.

The reporter had been shocked to learn the truth of her dad's disappearance. But once he'd voiced that and offered Caroline his sympathy, he'd said in a way it was a relief. "I had a hunch Hoff was the victim of foul play, but I was afraid it would be connected to the story I was doing, that I'd put him in jeopardy. You never know how far someone will go when they're desperate."

"No," Caroline agreed, and she went on to tell him about Jace and all that his desperation had led him to do.

"I suspected he was the one who hit you, but honestly, it surprises me that he took it that far," Kip said when she finished.

"Well, even with Dad gone, I'm kind of worried Farley Dade might think I'll try to smear his precious reputation."

"Well, I don't think he's in any condition to make trouble nowadays. I heard he had major bypass surgery a couple of weeks ago and may not make it."

Caroline's heart eased; she couldn't help it. "I guess none of that old business will ever see the light of day, and that's fine with me." She just wanted it over.

"There's no more real evidence to back it now than there was then. There are other, newer recruiting scandals, possibly not on the scale of SMU or Tillman State—wait a minute—" He interrupted himself. "Did you tell Jace about your dad?"

"I did," Caroline said. "He was, like you, like all of us, shocked. He's glad it was nothing to do with his dad. You know Coach Kelly died."

"I heard. Stroke, wasn't it?"

"Yes. He's being inducted into the Hall of Fame, though, posthumously."

"Well," Kip answered. "I kind of hate that, given he was probably as big a snake as the rest of that crew."

But nothing they did had any bearing on your father's death. Caroline had waited for Kip to repeat it, but he hadn't.

"I think this is it," Caroline's mom said now. She pointed through the windshield where a single-lane, caliche-topped road met the highway. "This is the turnoff for the farm."

· · ·

They crossed a cattle guard and found the pond a little farther on at the foot of a gentle slope. Caroline parked off the road on the weedy verge, and they walked single file down a narrow path, their footsteps unsettling tiny explosions of dust and dislodging the occasional slumbering grasshopper. Nina led the way, carrying the crematory box. She stopped a few feet from the water's edge, and when Caroline drew alongside her, she said, "What do we do now?"

She seemed relieved when Caroline took the box from her. It was heavier than she'd thought it would be.

"Hoff pushed me in that old tire swing." Her mom walked to where it hung from the thick branch of a towering live oak and nudged it with her fingers.

"Do you think it's the same one?" Caroline asked. She set the box on the ground, took out the heavy plastic bag, and opened it. She'd had her aunt's and her father's remains comingled. If they couldn't meet one final time in life, at least they would be together now. She felt the weight of what remained of them in her hands.

She was plagued by what-ifs: What if she'd gone to her dad after his head injury and somehow gotten him back to Houston, where she and Lanie, not Tricia, could have taken care of him? What if she'd kept a relationship with him despite her bitterness over his love of Harris? Plenty of kids got angry with their parents, but they didn't sever ties.

"Look at Nina," she had said to Steve one day last week when he'd called. He'd taken to calling her regularly, and Caroline was never sorry to see his name flash on the caller ID screen. "She hasn't cut Rob out of her life," Caroline had said to him. "If only I'd been as tolerant of my father. If I'd been more forgiving of him and Julia and Harris, I would have known Dad wasn't acting right. Maybe *I* could have talked him into getting help."

"You were seventeen when all that was going down, Caro," Steve had reminded her. "Besides, in those days we didn't have as many tools as we do now to deal with folks in your dad's situation."

"What about Harris? When I think of how lost he became, the secret he felt compelled to keep, no wonder he took drugs. I can't imagine the pain he was in. It breaks my heart."

"I'm amazed you aren't mad as hell. I'm not sure I could be so magnanimous."

"You know the promise I made Aunt Lanie. Anyway, how can I be angry at a twelve-year-old boy who was terrified out of his mind? Julia asked me what I would have done had it been me and Nina in similar circumstances, and when I try to imagine it, whatever grudge I have just evaporates."

"You think you would have covered it up the way Julia did?"

"I would have done whatever was necessary to protect Nina, to keep us together."

"It was an awful lot to put on a kid, though, asking him not to tell."

"You're in law enforcement. What do you think would have happened to Harris if she'd reported it? Would the police have believed her story and let her and Harris go on their way?"

"Maybe not. It could have gone very wrong for them."

"Julia did the right thing, then, the only thing," Caroline had said.

"That doesn't look like ashes," Nina said now, peering into the bag Caroline was holding.

She was right. The contents were coarse, more like concrete mix. Caroline scooped some into her palm and, walking to the pond's edge, where the grass was short and the wind was at her back, flung it out over the water. The lighter dust was carried away, but the heavier particles dropped near her feet.

Nina and Caroline's mother joined her, dipping out handfuls of the grit and scattering it. After a bit Caroline upended the bag, spilling the last of its contents into the water, where they were carried for a time on its silvery and immutable surface.

"Should we say something?" Nina broke their silence.

"I loved you both," Caroline's mother said.

"Rest in peace," Nina murmured.

"I'm sorry," Caroline said, and she wasn't prepared for the tears that flooded her eyes.

"Oh, now," said her mother, brushing at Caroline's cheek with her thumb.

Nina pulled her into an embrace. "Mom, even if you'd gone to Omaha after your dad fell, what could you have done? You were sixteen. I wouldn't have known what to do when I was sixteen."

Caroline pinched the bridge of her nose, willing the return of her composure.

"From the research I did," Nina went on, "explosive anger isn't uncommon after a head injury. Nowadays doctors know more; they can help. But thirty years ago? I doubt it."

Caroline wiped her face. Nina sounded like Steve.

"Hoff wasn't the sort to accept help, anyway," her mother said.

"What happened is sad and awful," Nina said. "But it's not your fault."

"No one is to blame." Caroline's mother tucked strands of hair behind her ear. "Hoff's fall was an accident, and that's what brought on all the rest."

"But it's so horribly ironic, isn't it?" Caroline said. "That all these years I thought he didn't care about me because I didn't care about him, and instead he was—dead." She said the word, one syllable, composed of four letters that contained forever.

"You just need time, Caro," her mother said.

Nina tipped her head to Caroline's shoulder. "We're here for you, Mommy, me and Gramma."

Caroline circled her mother and Nina in her embrace, and the three stood, arms around one another, and there was only the sound of their breath and the wind through the grass. Out over the center of the pond, a dragonfly hovered, his wings gleaming in the sunlight like precious jewels.

• • •

Later, having dropped her mother off at her new home in time to play bridge and have dinner with her friends, Caroline wandered through the rooms of Lanie's house, feeling a bit sorry for herself. Nina and Ollie had packed a picnic and gone to Hermann Park to watch the fireworks. They'd invited Caroline, but she'd claimed she was tired. If she'd told the truth—that she couldn't think of anything more awkward than tagging along on her daughter's date—Nina would have hooted and likely dragged Caroline out the door.

She went into Lanie's dining room. The hospital bed was long gone, the table and chairs back in place. Her mother said she should redecorate, make the house more her own, but Caroline thought it was too soon. Running her fingertips along the tops of the dining chairs, she thought how she hadn't been prepared for how lonely holidays might be. Now her throat closed, and she was fighting a renewed and unwarranted press of tears.

What was her problem? She didn't even like the Fourth of July.

It took a moment to shake it off, the sadness, a lingering sense of loss, the old feeling of blame, but once she did, she drove to the grocery store and bought ice cream, her and Lanie's favorite flavor, Blue Bell chocolate chip cookie dough. A gallon. On the way home she decided she would find an old movie to watch from when she was a kid, *Stand by Me* or *Big* or *The Breakfast Club*, and eat the whole gallon by herself.

Maybe before the ice cream she'd have waffles for dinner. Because, by God, she would make a new life here for herself, one tablespoon of sugar at a time, no matter how many it took.

Coming down Lanie's street—now her street, Caroline corrected herself—she saw him from three houses away, a man sitting on her front steps. Narrowing her gaze, she realized it was Steve, and her heart dipped.

He'd parked at the curb. Passing his truck, she pulled into the driveway and made herself take a deep breath. She was so glad to see him. *Too glad*, a voice warned as she got out of the car.

He stood up. "You might not believe this, but I was in the neighborhood," he said, and his grin was abashed, as if he knew how lame it sounded.

"It's fine," she said, her pulse tapping lightly in her ears.

"You don't have plans?"

She opened her grocery sack, revealing the ice cream.

"Huh," he said. "I don't suppose you could use some help with that."

She smiled. "I was hoping you'd ask."

ACKNOWLEDGMENTS

My gratitude first, last, and ever is to my agent, Barbara Poelle. Without her none of the rest of this dream job would be possible. I can't ever say enough good about having her in my corner.

Heartfelt thanks, too, to my fantastic editor Alicia Clancy. I'm so grateful for her support, her enthusiasm, and her expertise and for how she paired me with Tiffany Martin, developmental editor extraordinaire. Tiffany had her finger on this book's pulse from the beginning, and it was through her direction that I was able to put my finger there too. She's the ultimate book whisperer, and I loved working with her.

Untold thanks to Nicole Pomeroy and to my copy editors Riam Griswold, Sylvia McCluskey, and Angela Elson for their sharp eyes and their skill at fine-tuning a book.

When I saw the cover for this book the first time, I just went, "Wow!" The image so perfectly captures the mood of the story. Thank you to Lindy Martin of Faceout for making it so compelling.

Thank you, too, to Gabe Dumpitt and Gabriella Trull and the whole APub team, including the marketing team, all of whom work so hard to ensure the publishing journey is as smooth as possible. Thank you to Donna Postel, who has in her pitch-perfect voice narrated the audiobook versions of my last four novels. Thank you to all the folks at Audible who make audiobooks possible.

My appreciation to the wonderful moderators and members of Facebook reading groups is just endless. There are so many, and I know I'm going to miss some, but to name a few: Athena Kaye and Andrea Preskind Katz of Great Thoughts Great Readers; Kristy Barrett and Tonni Callan of A Novel Bee; Reader's Coffeehouse; Susan Peterson of Sue's Booking Agency; the many admins and members of Bloom with Tall Poppy Writers; and Linda Zagon of Linda's Book Obsession. All the lovely readers/members/moderators/founders are, of course, in the habit of reading books, but they go that extra mile to review them and to talk them up among other members and anyone else who might be interested. They, and all the other groups that I know I've missed, are a tireless and wonderful support for books, and there is such contagious joy in sharing the love of writing and reading with them. I feel so fortunate to have been included in their membership as both a reader and an author. Thanks very much to my assistant, Kate Rock, an active and lovely supporter of books and authors and also the creative and artistic genius behind many of my giveaway graphics and book trailers.

And again, huge thanks to my law enforcement neighbor, Constable Chip Leake, for his patience in finding the answers to my questions about legal and police procedures with regard to the situations depicted in the plot of this novel. Any mistakes or misstatements along legal lines are entirely my own.

A big hug and thanks to my big sister, Susan Harper. I knew the story I wanted to tell but couldn't get it moving, and it was during a conversation with her that she suggested what turned out to be the perfect trigger.

Thank you also to my sons, former college athletes Michael and David Sissel, who both have firsthand experience of the college-level recruiting process. Mike went on to play pro basketball overseas, which only enhanced my research. It was fun and interesting to revisit that time in their lives. I'm particularly grateful to have had the benefit of their knowledge and expertise for this story in regard to college athletics. Any misstatements are my own.

BOOK CLUB QUESTIONS

1. In the opening chapter, Caroline is reestablishing contact with someone whom she hasn't seen since her childhood but who may hold the key to a mystery from her past. Have you ever lost touch with someone still living and had the yen to talk to them again? Perhaps an old childhood friend or roommate from college or your early singlehood days? What keeps you from picking up the phone or dropping them a note via email? Or if you have reestablished contact after a period of years with an old friend or an estranged family member, how did the circumstances come about?

2. In many ways Caroline feels more closely attached to her aunt Lanie than to her mother. Why do you think this happened? Were the circumstances avoidable? Could Caroline's mother have handled the situation differently? Were her actions deliberate or accidental?

3. Are you the adult child of divorced parents? What is the effect of divorce on children? What are some ways to help very young children understand what's happening when a marriage breaks up? What are some ways to make them feel more secure?

4. While writing this book, I thought about someone, my father's brother, who disappeared from my life when I was in my early teens. I recently discovered through Ancestry.com that he has since died. It laid an old family mystery partly to rest for me. Have you ever experienced the unexplained disappearance of someone close to you? Had you been in Caroline's circumstances, would you have waited so long to look for a parent? Would you pursue someone who might simply want to disappear? Do they have a right to go without a word, do you think? Can you envision circumstances that might lead you to wish to leave your known and familiar life?

5. Early on in the story, Caroline regrets making a fool of herself in front of a man with whom she had a relationship in high school. Do you think she would have cared so much how she appeared to him if she hadn't still had feelings for him? Did she make the right decision when she married? Have you ever committed to something of importance because you felt you could make it work? How did your situation turn out?

6. Soon after you meet Harris in the story, you realize he's addicted to pain meds. Do you feel compassion for his dependence, given that it began as the result of chronic

pain? Opioid addiction has been in the news a lot in recent history. Do you have any thoughts about how this situation occurred?

7. When it's doctor-prescribed medication a person becomes addicted to, do you feel the doctor bears any responsibility? The drug companies? What other choices does a person in chronic pain have other than to take the medication?

8. Is Holly right to insist Harris move out of their house and away from their children until he can get help? How would you respond if a member of your family were to become addicted to the very drug that relieved their pain, giving them back some quality of life?

9. If your child were in danger, how far would you go to protect them? If you knew your child was engaging in criminal activity, what would you do? Suppose it was your spouse you discovered was involved in some kind of illegal behavior. Would you inform the police? Can you think of any circumstances that would cause you to cover up a crime a loved one had committed? What do you think about the actions of the characters throughout the story? Were they justified? Were there other options, choices they could have made? Was justice served in the end?

10. Is there too much emphasis placed on sports, particularly football, at the college level? Do you feel that in some cases the boosters and alumni have too much authority

and influence with regard to how young athletes are brought into the college athletic arena? In your opinion is the competition more a matter of dollars and cents than it is athletic ability? When it comes to recruiting young athletes, is the system too aggressive? How level is the playing field among colleges when it comes to procuring the top athletes?

ABOUT THE AUTHOR

Barbara Taylor Sissel writes issue-oriented, upmarket women's fiction threaded with elements of suspense and defined by an emphasis on how crime affects family. She is the author of ten novels: *The Last Innocent Hour*, *The Ninth Step*, *The Volunteer*, *Evidence of Life*, *Safe Keeping*, *Crooked Little Lies*, *Faultlines*, *The Truth We Bury*, *What Lies Below*, and *Tell No One*.

Born in Honolulu, Hawaii, Sissel was raised in various locations across the Midwest. She once lived on the grounds of a first offender prison facility, where her husband was a deputy warden. Interacting with the inmates, their families, and the people who worked with them made a profound impression on her. The experience gave her unique insight into the circumstances of the crimes and the often-surprising ways the justice system moved to deal with them.

An avid gardener, Sissel has two sons and lives on a farm outside Austin in the Texas Hill Country.